Oddly ★ Normal

WRITTEN & ILLUSTRATED
by OTIS FRAMPTON

ODDLY NORMAL, BOOK 2. FIRST PRINTING. OCTOBER 2015. PUBLISHED BY IMAGE COMICS, INC. OFFICE OF PUBLICATION: 2001 CENTER STREET, 6TH FLOOR, BERKELEY, CA 94704. PRINTED IN THE U.S.A. FOR INFORMATION REGARDING THE CPSIA ON THIS PRINTED MATERIAL CALL: 203-595-3636 AND PROVIDE REFERENCE # RICH - 648438. FOR INTERNATIONAL RIGHTS, CONTACT: FOREIGNLICENSING@IMAGECOMICS.COM ISBN: 978-1-63215-484-2

Oddly ★ Normal
CHAPTER #10
OTIS FRAMPTON & TRACY BAILEY
72
OUT of ORDER

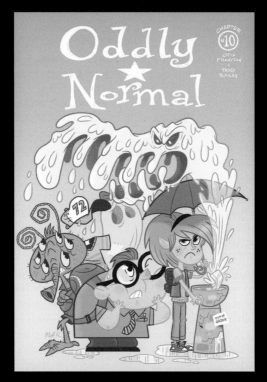

ISSUE #10 VARIANT COVER BY
MATT KAUFENBERG

ACKNOWLEDGMENTS

Thank you to everyone who helped make "Oddly Normal" a reality!

To Mom and Dad... your support for me and my work has been invaluable.

To Branwyn Bigglestone, Jonathan Chan, Monica Garcia, Jennifer de Guzman, Sasha Head, Vincent Kukua, Sarah Mello, Emily Miller, Corey Murphy, Randy Okamura, Tricia Ramos, Ron Richards, Kat Salazar, Jenna Savage, Eric Stephenson, Meredith Wallace and everyone else at Image Comics for their amazing behind-the-scenes work.

To my awesome colorist team: Tracy Bailey, Daniel Mead and Thomas Boatwright.

To the amazing and generous artists who contributed variant covers to issues 6-10: Sara Richard, Maryn Roos, Dan Schoening, Grant Gould and Matt Kaufenberg.

To the many friends and colleagues who have been there for me over the years, including... Leigh Boone, Pat Bussey, John Copeland, Ronn Dech, Tracy Edmunds, Adam Fellows, Brian Fies, Scott Gagain, Jessie Garza, Grant Gould, Judy Hansen, Gisela Hernandez-Rosa, Josh Howard, Doug Netter, John J. Walsh IV and Kate Youngdahl.

And last but not least... many thanks to my "Oddly Normal 2.0" Kickstarter supporters: Janel A, Regi Aaron, Kathryn Alice, Charles Alvis, John Anthony, Matthew Ashcraft, Ray B., David Barnett, Hudson On Bass, Bchan84, Jessie Beck, Alison Benowitz, Jennifer Berk, Daniel Blackburn, Daniel J. Blomberg IV, Leigh Boone, Brian Braatz, Sacha Brady, Michael Branham, Dominic Brennan, Mark Brenner, John Brown, Darren Calvert, Jeffrey Chandler, Michael Chapman, Chris, Chooi, Chouck, Cody Christopher, Justin Chung, Coffinail, Christopher Cole, CoolB, Cathy Cooper, Corrodias, Aaron Cullers, Julian Damy, Brad Dancer, Lara Dann, Joséantonio W. Danner, Daniel & Kanako, Ted Dastick Jr., DebraS, Ronn Dech, James DeMarco, Harald Demler, Arik Devens, Vic DiGital, Brandon Eaker, Tracy Edmunds, Jamas Enright, Susan Eisner, Leandro Garcia Estevam, Evilgeniuslady, Harry Ewasiuk, Dan Eyer, Adam Fellows, Brian Fies, Fletcher, Phil Flickinger, Thomas Forsythe, Mary Frampton, Tracey Frampton, Corey Funt, Andrea Futrelle, Gdm_online, George, Tim Goldenburg, Sara Gordon, Stuart Gorman, Ingrid K. V. Hardy, Michael Hawk, Helena S. M., Jessica Hightower, Stephen Hill, David Hopkins, Michael Hunter, Chris Inoue, Arul Isai Imran, Jayvs1, Delores Jeffrey, Jimi, JMShelledy, Wendy Johnson-Diedrich, Dani Jones, Anne K, Peter Karmanos III, Kathryn, Kelso, Thanun Khowdee, Kirsten, André Kishimoto, Veronika Knurenko, Matthew Koelbl, Laura Kokaisel, Axel 'dervideospieler' Kothe, Karen Krajenbrink, Zeus & Hera Kramer, Manuel Kroeber, Tom Kurzanski, Amber Lanagan, Patrick Larcada, Jeremie Lariviere, Linda LeClair, Matt Leitzen, Yoni Limor, Lulu Lin, Tim Lindvall, Rick Long, Lisa M. Lorelli, MageAkyla, Dan Manson, Marina, Miles Matton, Fergus Maximus, Jamie McIntyre, Tim McKnight, Jeff McRorie, Daniel Mead, Jeff Metzner, Michael and Liz, Mika, Miroatme, Riaz Skrenes Missaghi, Casey Moeller, Björn Morén, Rich Moulton, Movet, Matthew Munk, Molly Murphy, Jussi Myllyluoma, John Nacinovich, Cynthia Narcisi, Bruce Nelson, Sian Nelson, Niels, Michael "Waffles" Nguyen, Rhonda Parker, James Parris, Merrisa Patel, Shane & Marjan Patrick, C. Raymond Pechonick, Tawnly Pranger, David Recor, Rhel, Ben Rosenthal, Harrison Sayre, Ryan Schrodt, Patrick Scullin, Nick Seal, Jenny Seay, Senatorhung, Sgllama, Shervyn, Todd Shipman, Andy Shuping, Ashtara Silunar, Skraldesovs, Chazen Smith, Stephen Smoogen, Ryan Snow, Daniel Snyder, Stormy, Stu, Stephen Stutesman, Erik Taylor, Bruce Thompson, Tialessa, Kevin Tian, Tom Tinneny, Rachel Tougas, PJ Trauger, TriOmegaZero, Mai Tzimaka, Tim The Unlucky, Frankie Vanity, Martha Wald, James P. Walker, John J. Walsh IV, Shannon Wendlick, Paul Westover, A. M. White, Heath White, Kiwi Wiltshire, Daniel Winterhalter, Stephen "Swiit!" Wittmaak, Christoph Wolf, Emiko Wong, Ryan Worrell, Samuel Young, Zabuni, and Matt Zollmann.

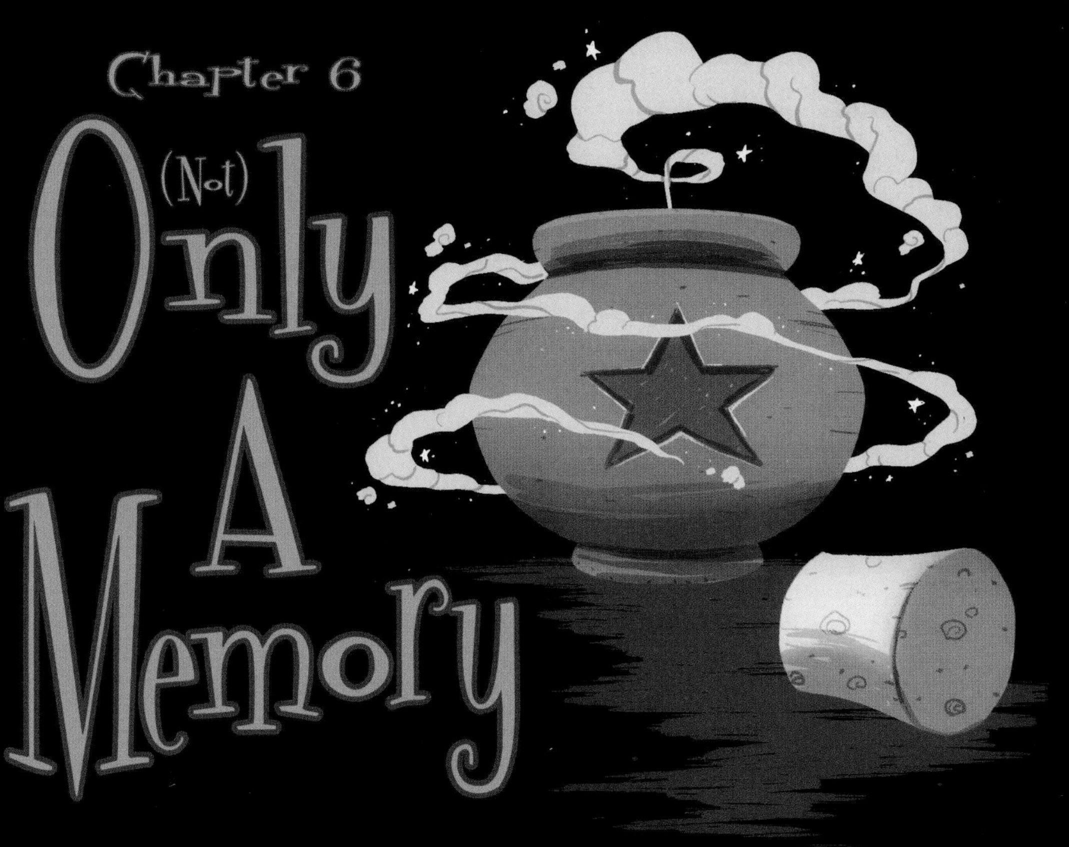
Chapter 6
Only (Not) A Memory

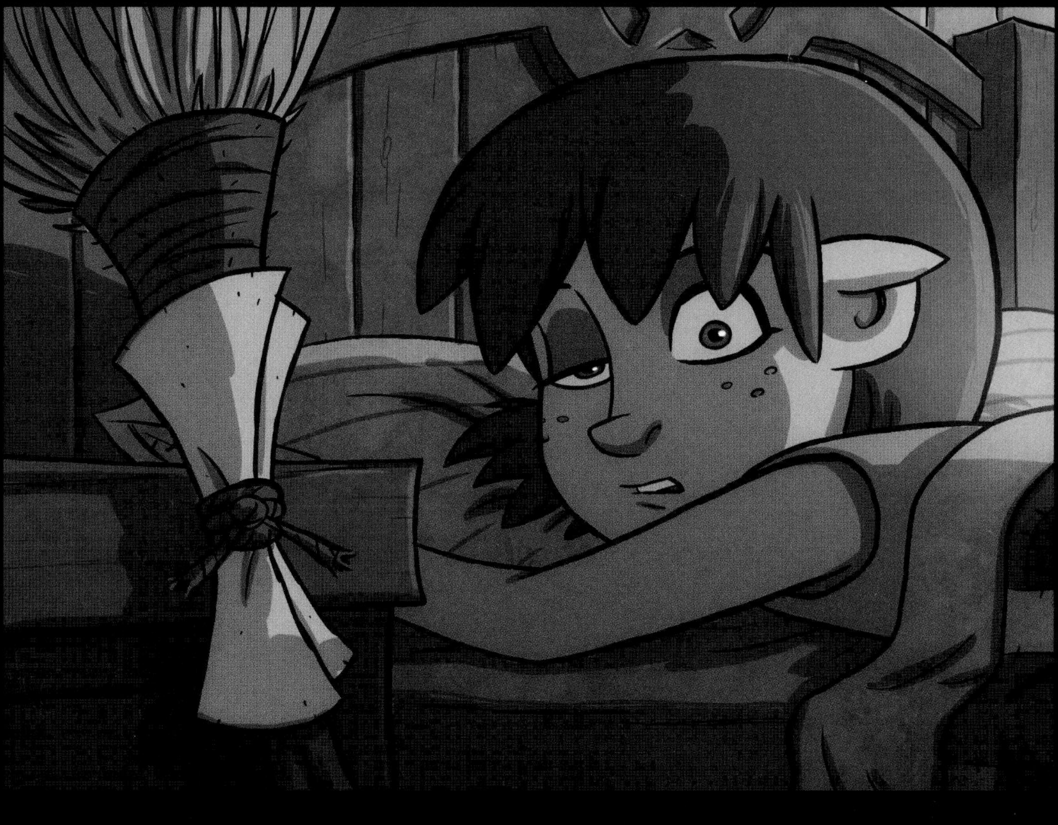

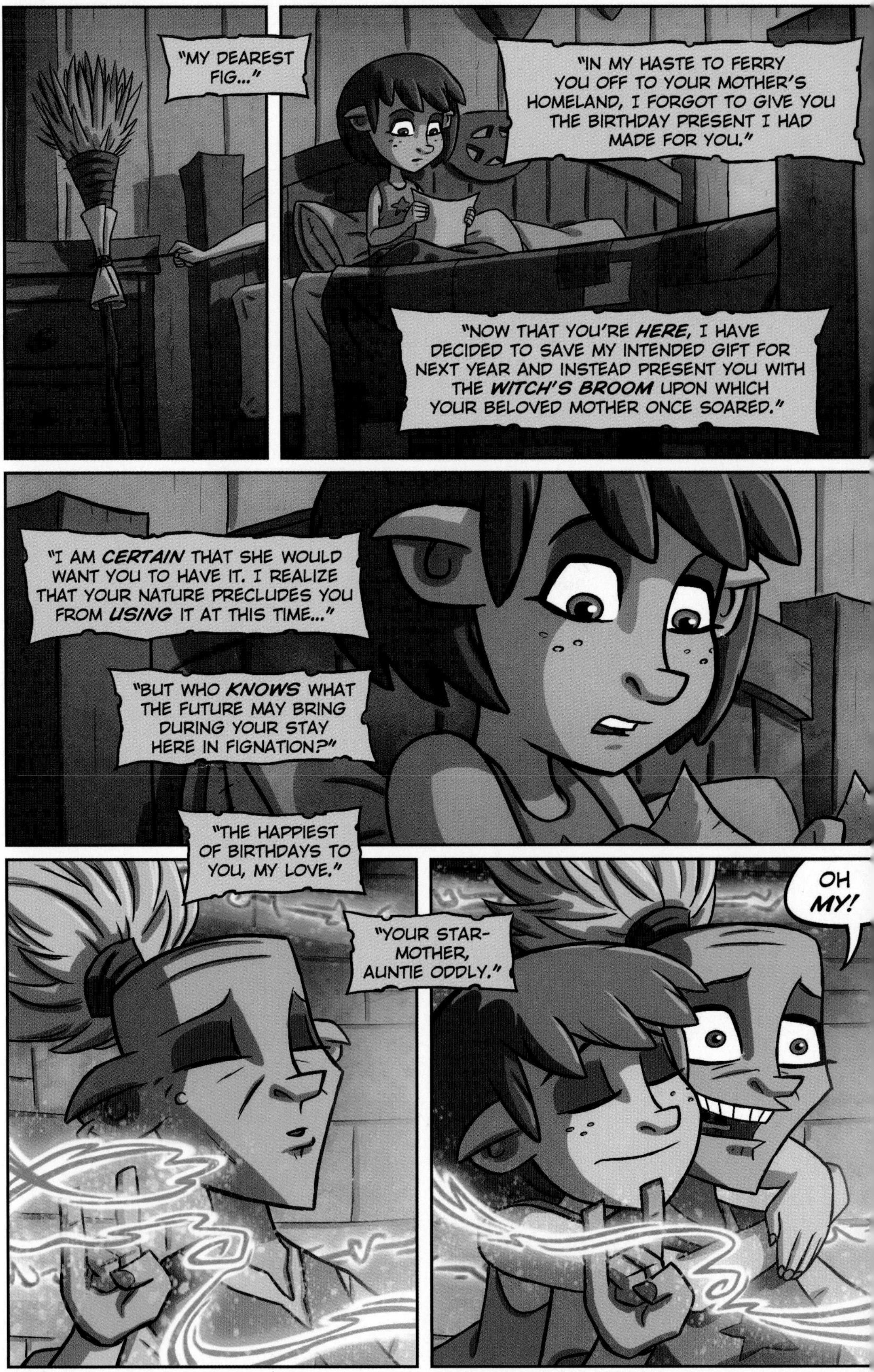
"MY DEAREST FIG..."
"IN MY HASTE TO FERRY YOU OFF TO YOUR MOTHER'S HOMELAND, I FORGOT TO GIVE YOU THE BIRTHDAY PRESENT I HAD MADE FOR YOU."
"NOW THAT YOU'RE *HERE*, I HAVE DECIDED TO SAVE MY INTENDED GIFT FOR NEXT YEAR AND INSTEAD PRESENT YOU WITH THE *WITCH'S BROOM* UPON WHICH YOUR BELOVED MOTHER ONCE SOARED."
"I AM *CERTAIN* THAT SHE WOULD WANT YOU TO HAVE IT. I REALIZE THAT YOUR NATURE PRECLUDES YOU FROM *USING* IT AT THIS TIME..."
"BUT WHO *KNOWS* WHAT THE FUTURE MAY BRING DURING YOUR STAY HERE IN FIGNATION?"
"THE HAPPIEST OF BIRTHDAYS TO YOU, MY LOVE."
"YOUR STAR-MOTHER, AUNTIE ODDLY."
OH *MY!*

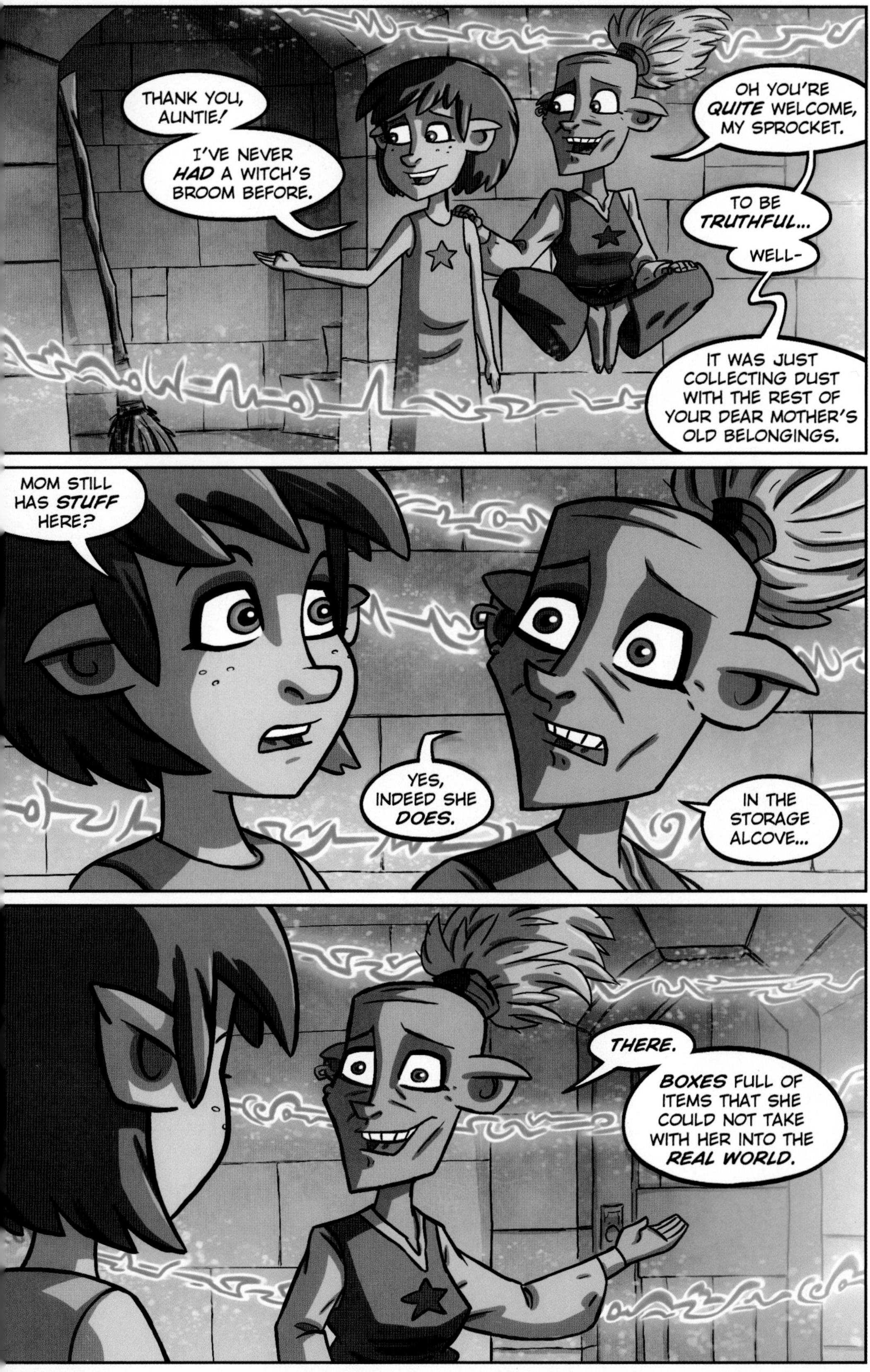
THANK YOU, AUNTIE!
I'VE NEVER HAD A WITCH'S BROOM BEFORE.
OH YOU'RE QUITE WELCOME, MY SPROCKET.
TO BE TRUTHFUL...
WELL-
IT WAS JUST COLLECTING DUST WITH THE REST OF YOUR DEAR MOTHER'S OLD BELONGINGS.
MOM STILL HAS STUFF HERE?
YES, INDEED SHE DOES.
IN THE STORAGE ALCOVE...
THERE.
BOXES FULL OF ITEMS THAT SHE COULD NOT TAKE WITH HER INTO THE REAL WORLD.

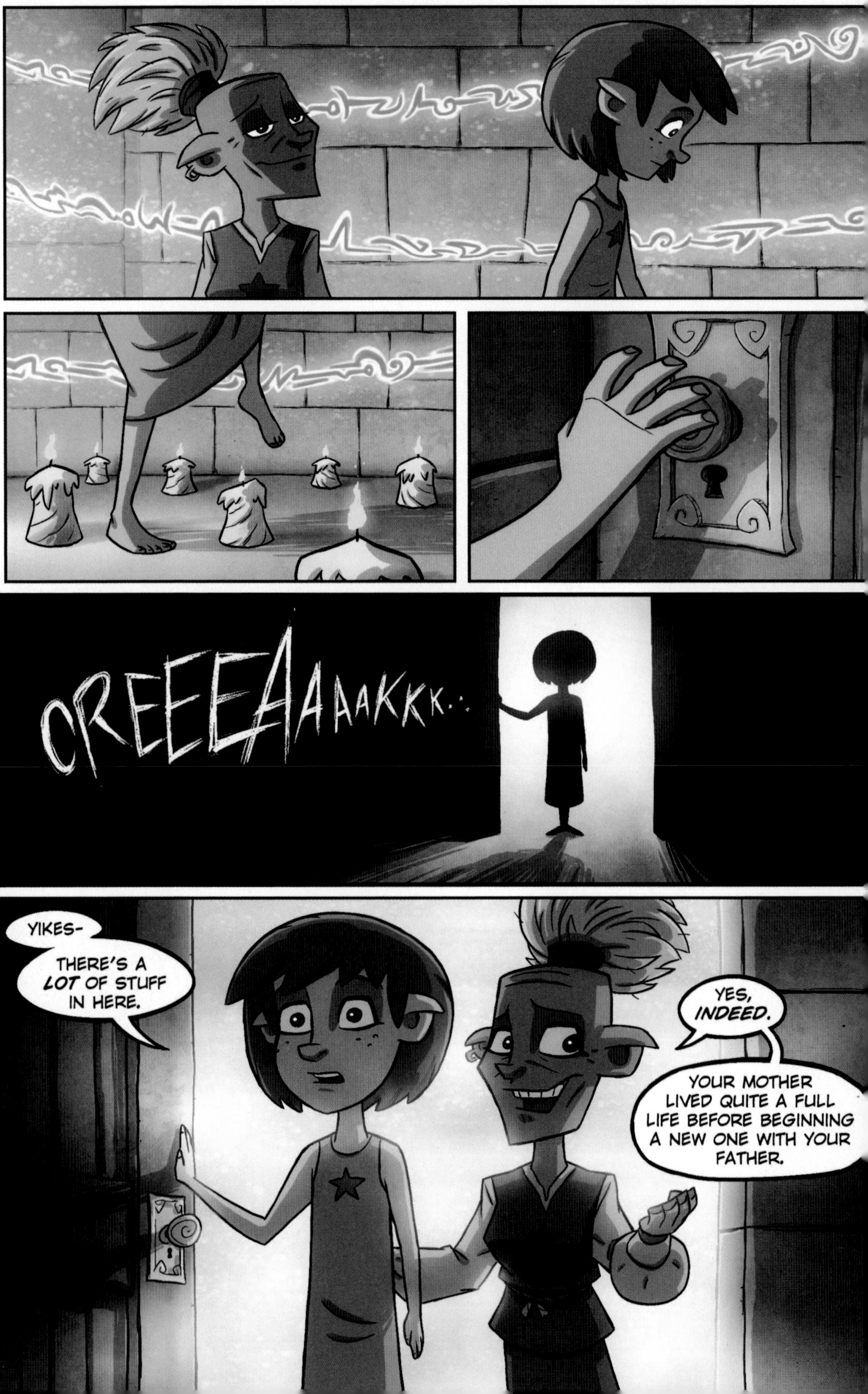
CREEEAAAKKK..
YIKES-
THERE'S A *LOT* OF STUFF IN HERE.
YES, *INDEED.*
YOUR MOTHER LIVED QUITE A FULL LIFE BEFORE BEGINNING A NEW ONE WITH YOUR FATHER.

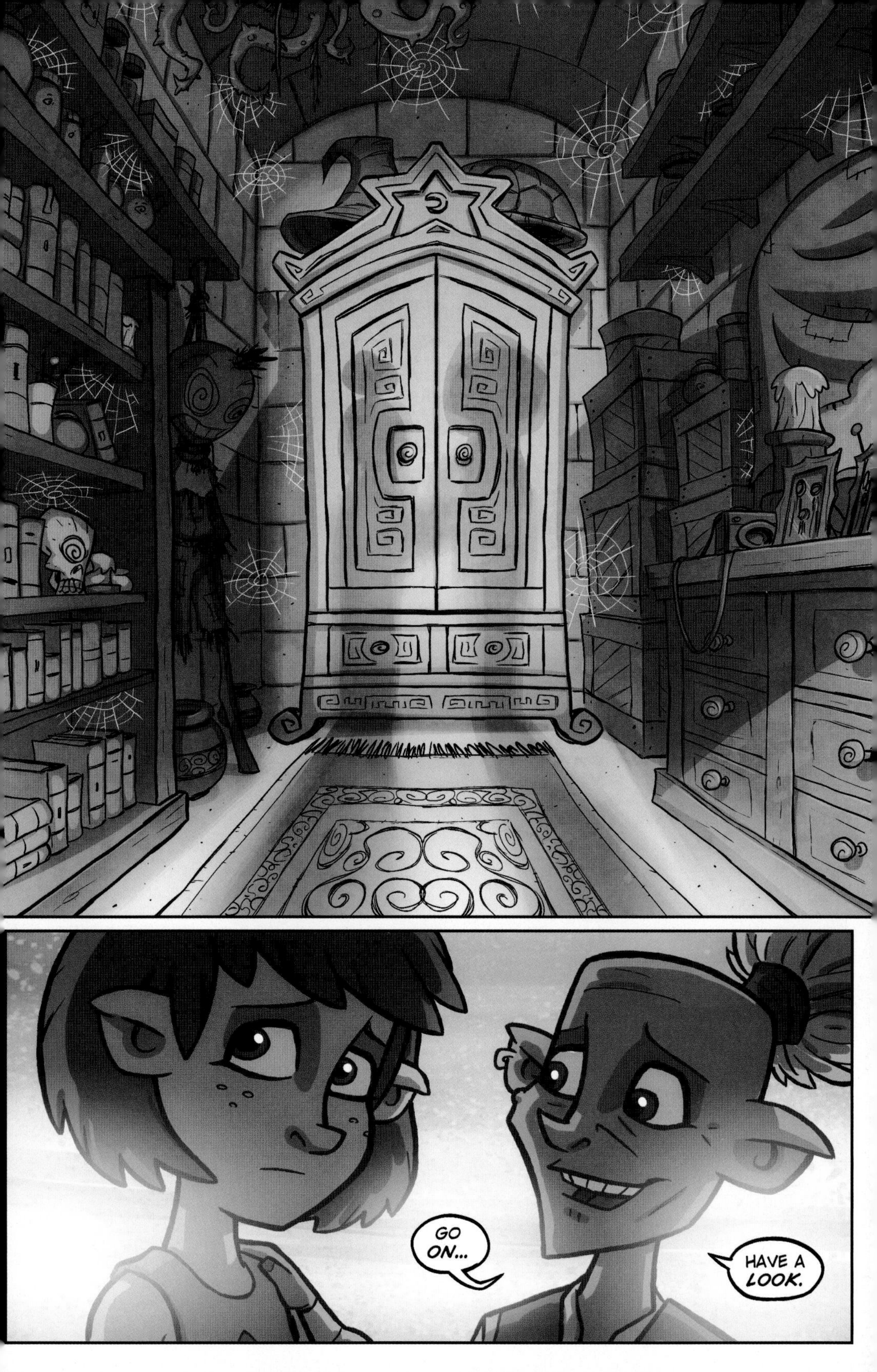
GO ON...
HAVE A LOOK.

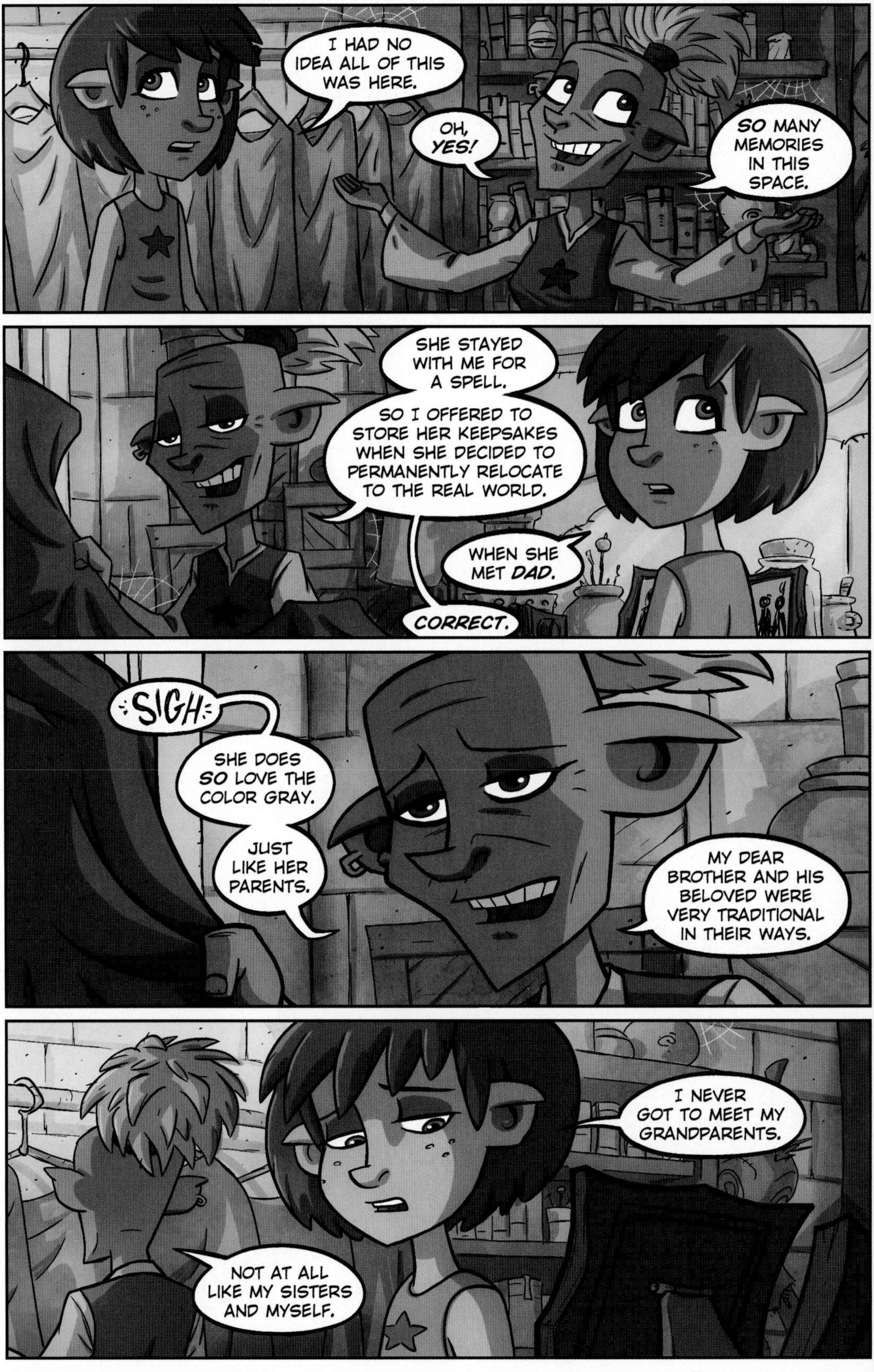
I HAD NO IDEA ALL OF THIS WAS HERE.
OH, *YES!*
SO MANY MEMORIES IN THIS SPACE.
SHE STAYED WITH ME FOR A SPELL.
SO I OFFERED TO STORE HER KEEPSAKES WHEN SHE DECIDED TO PERMANENTLY RELOCATE TO THE REAL WORLD.
WHEN SHE MET *DAD*.
CORRECT.
SIGH
SHE DOES *SO* LOVE THE COLOR GRAY.
JUST LIKE HER PARENTS.
MY DEAR BROTHER AND HIS BELOVED WERE VERY TRADITIONAL IN THEIR WAYS.
I NEVER GOT TO MEET MY GRANDPARENTS.
NOT AT ALL LIKE MY SISTERS AND MYSELF.

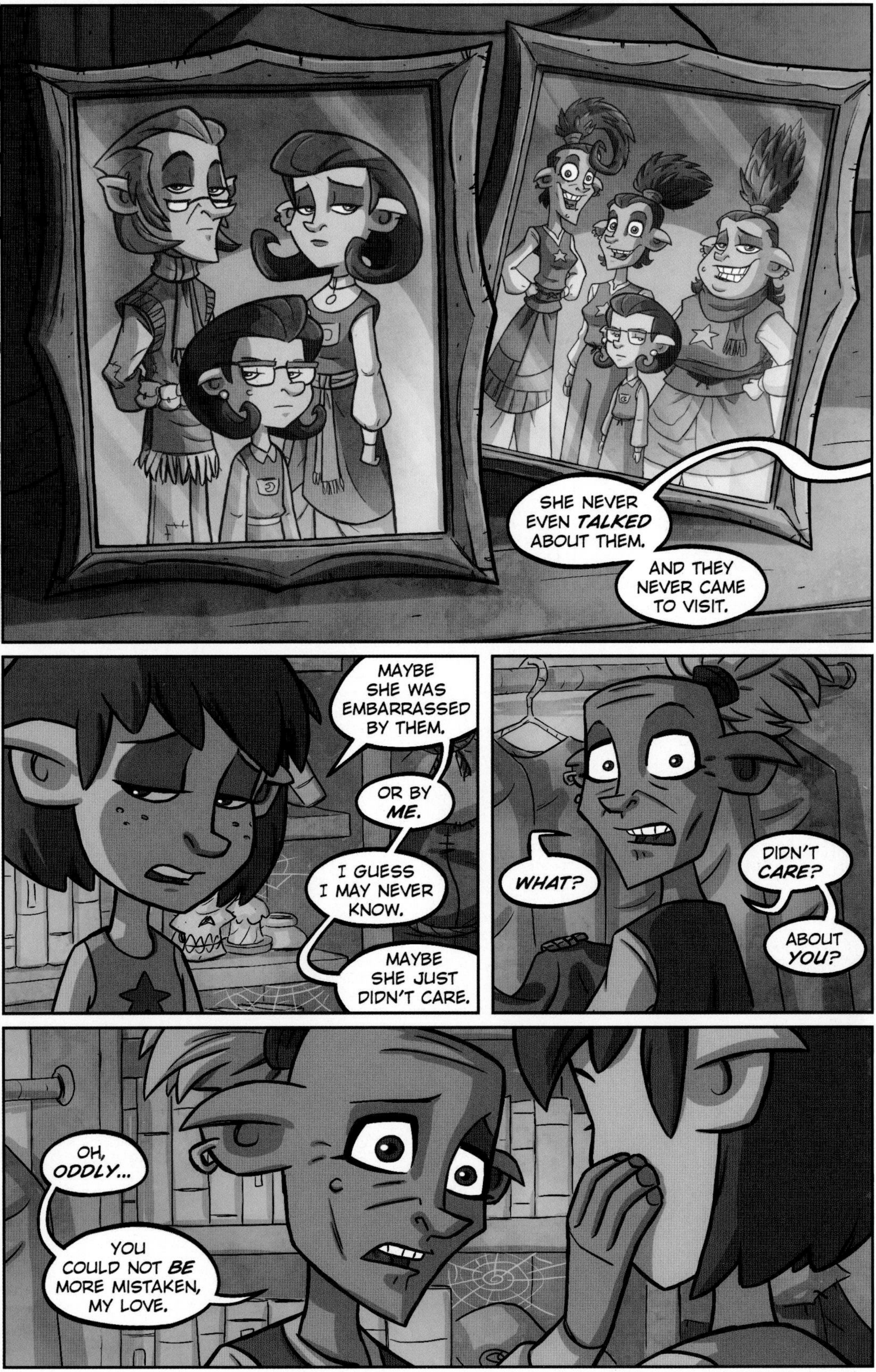

SHE NEVER EVEN *TALKED* ABOUT THEM.
AND THEY NEVER CAME TO VISIT.
MAYBE SHE WAS EMBARRASSED BY THEM.
OR BY *ME*.
I GUESS I MAY NEVER KNOW.
MAYBE SHE JUST DIDN'T CARE.
WHAT?
DIDN'T *CARE?*
ABOUT *YOU?*
OH, *ODDLY*...
YOU COULD NOT *BE* MORE MISTAKEN, MY LOVE.

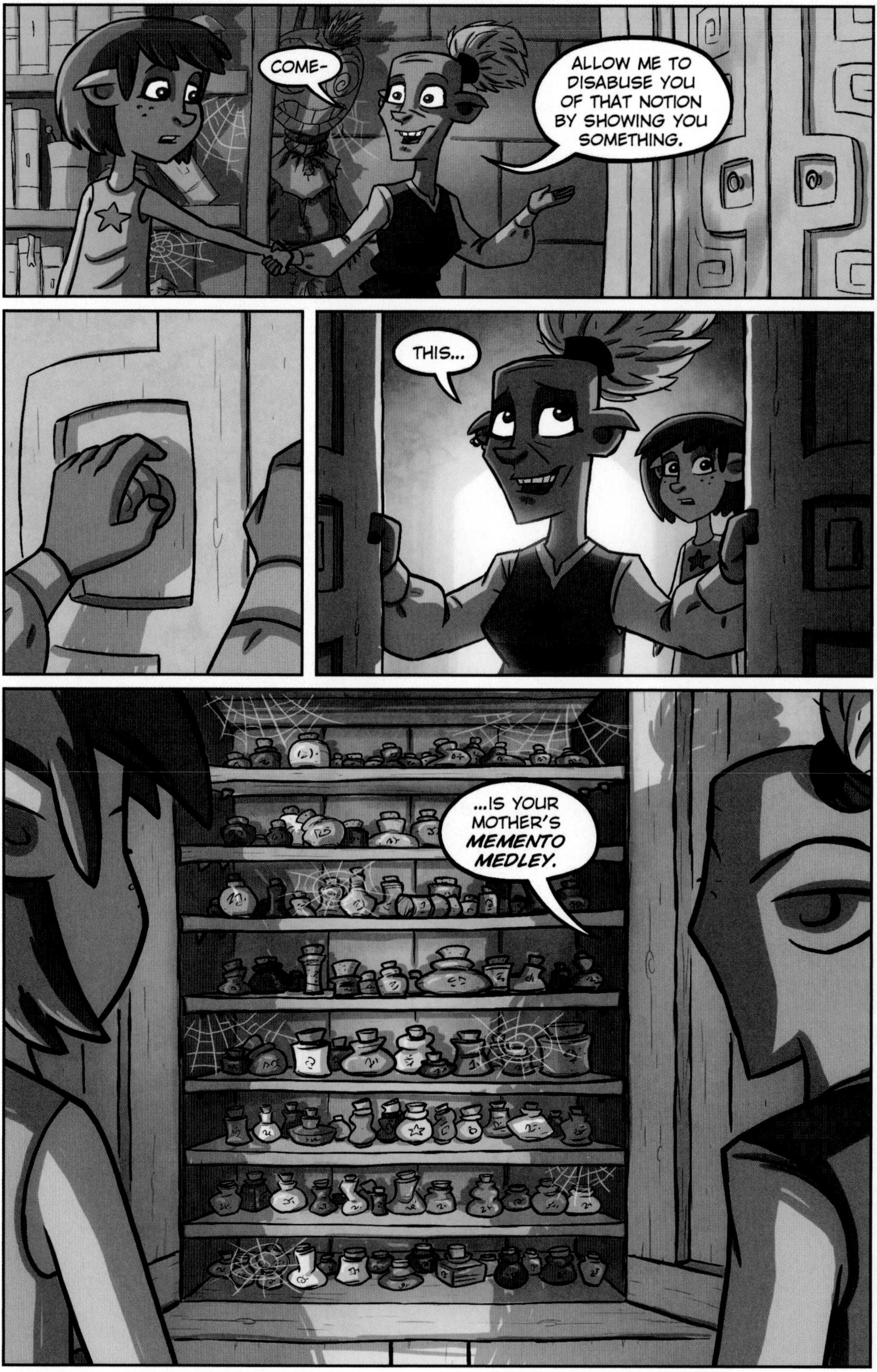
COME-
ALLOW ME TO DISABUSE YOU OF THAT NOTION BY SHOWING YOU SOMETHING.
THIS...
...IS YOUR MOTHER'S *MEMENTO MEDLEY.*

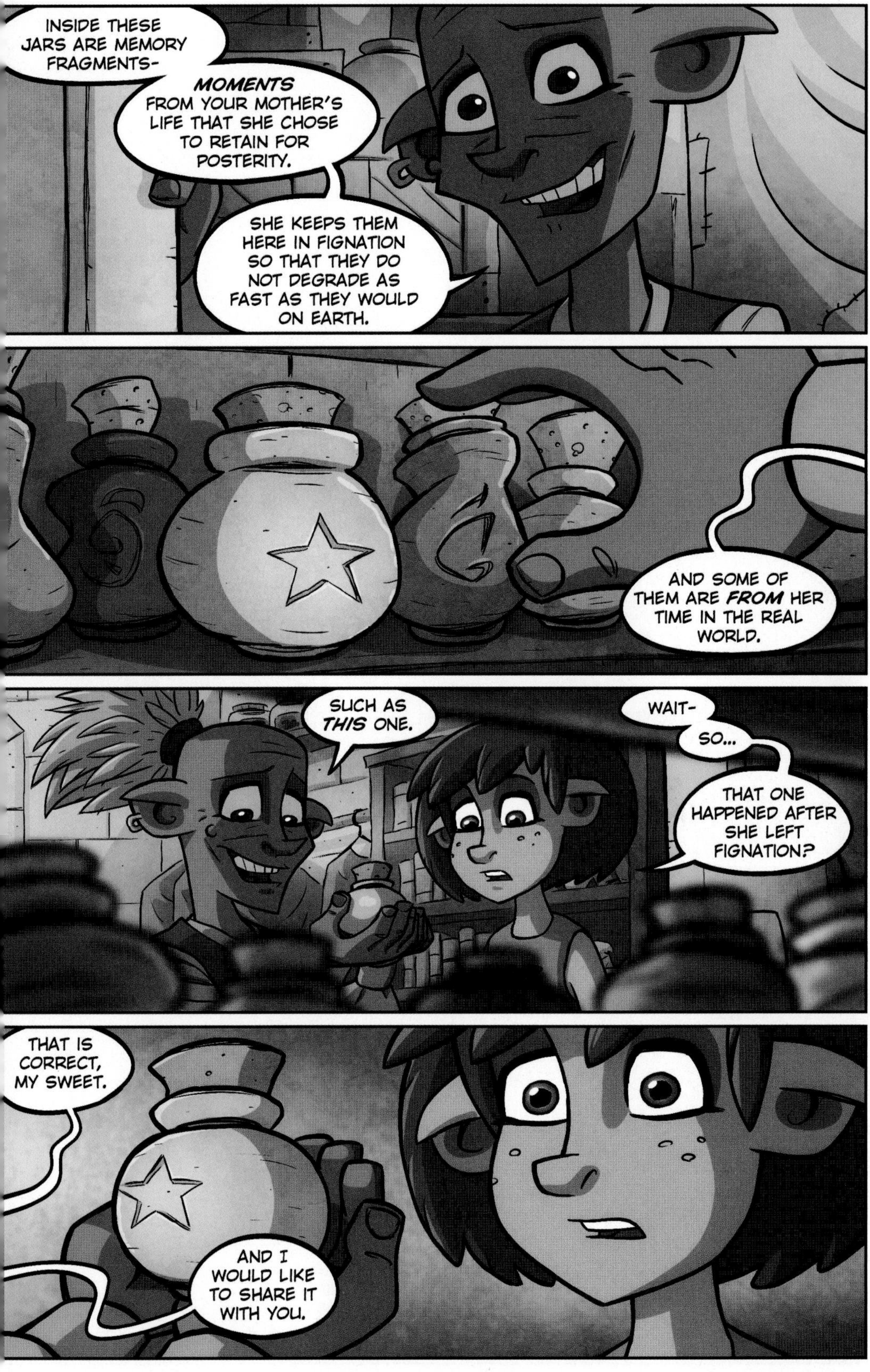
INSIDE THESE JARS ARE MEMORY FRAGMENTS-
MOMENTS FROM YOUR MOTHER'S LIFE THAT SHE CHOSE TO RETAIN FOR POSTERITY.
SHE KEEPS THEM HERE IN FIGNATION SO THAT THEY DO NOT DEGRADE AS FAST AS THEY WOULD ON EARTH.
AND SOME OF THEM ARE *FROM* HER TIME IN THE REAL WORLD.
SUCH AS *THIS* ONE.
WAIT-
SO...
THAT ONE HAPPENED AFTER SHE LEFT FIGNATION?
THAT IS CORRECT, MY SWEET.
AND I WOULD LIKE TO SHARE IT WITH YOU.

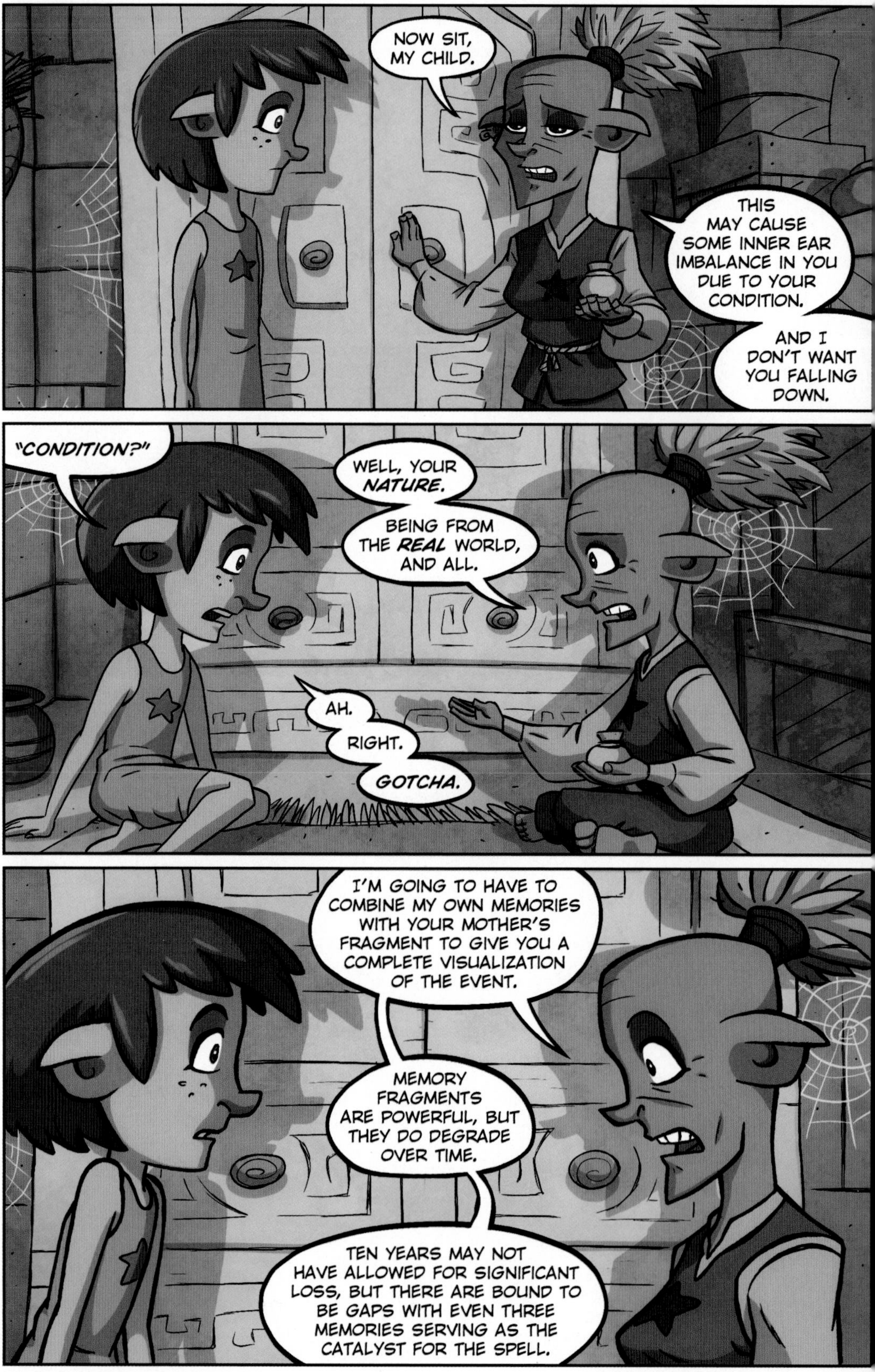
NOW SIT, MY CHILD.
THIS MAY CAUSE SOME INNER EAR IMBALANCE IN YOU DUE TO YOUR CONDITION.
AND I DON'T WANT YOU FALLING DOWN.
"CONDITION?"
WELL, YOUR *NATURE.*
BEING FROM THE *REAL* WORLD, AND ALL.
AH.
RIGHT.
GOTCHA.
I'M GOING TO HAVE TO COMBINE MY OWN MEMORIES WITH YOUR MOTHER'S FRAGMENT TO GIVE YOU A COMPLETE VISUALIZATION OF THE EVENT.
MEMORY FRAGMENTS ARE POWERFUL, BUT THEY DO DEGRADE OVER TIME.
TEN YEARS MAY NOT HAVE ALLOWED FOR SIGNIFICANT LOSS, BUT THERE ARE BOUND TO BE GAPS WITH EVEN THREE MEMORIES SERVING AS THE CATALYST FOR THE SPELL.

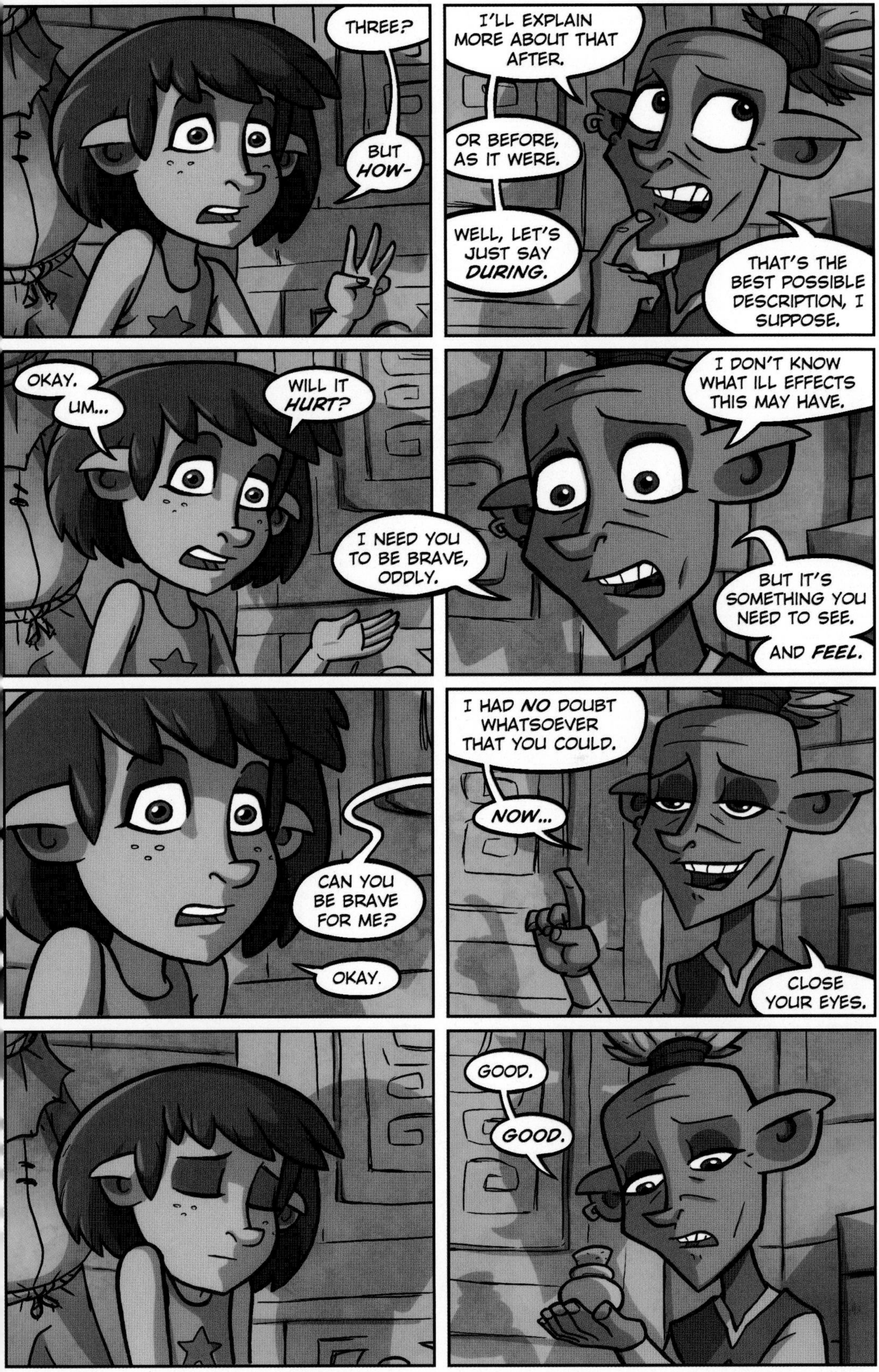
THREE?
BUT HOW-
I'LL EXPLAIN MORE ABOUT THAT AFTER.
OR BEFORE, AS IT WERE.
WELL, LET'S JUST SAY DURING.
THAT'S THE BEST POSSIBLE DESCRIPTION, I SUPPOSE.
OKAY.
UM...
WILL IT HURT?
I DON'T KNOW WHAT ILL EFFECTS THIS MAY HAVE.
I NEED YOU TO BE BRAVE, ODDLY.
BUT IT'S SOMETHING YOU NEED TO SEE.
AND FEEL.
CAN YOU BE BRAVE FOR ME?
OKAY.
I HAD NO DOUBT WHATSOEVER THAT YOU COULD.
NOW...
CLOSE YOUR EYES.
GOOD.
GOOD.

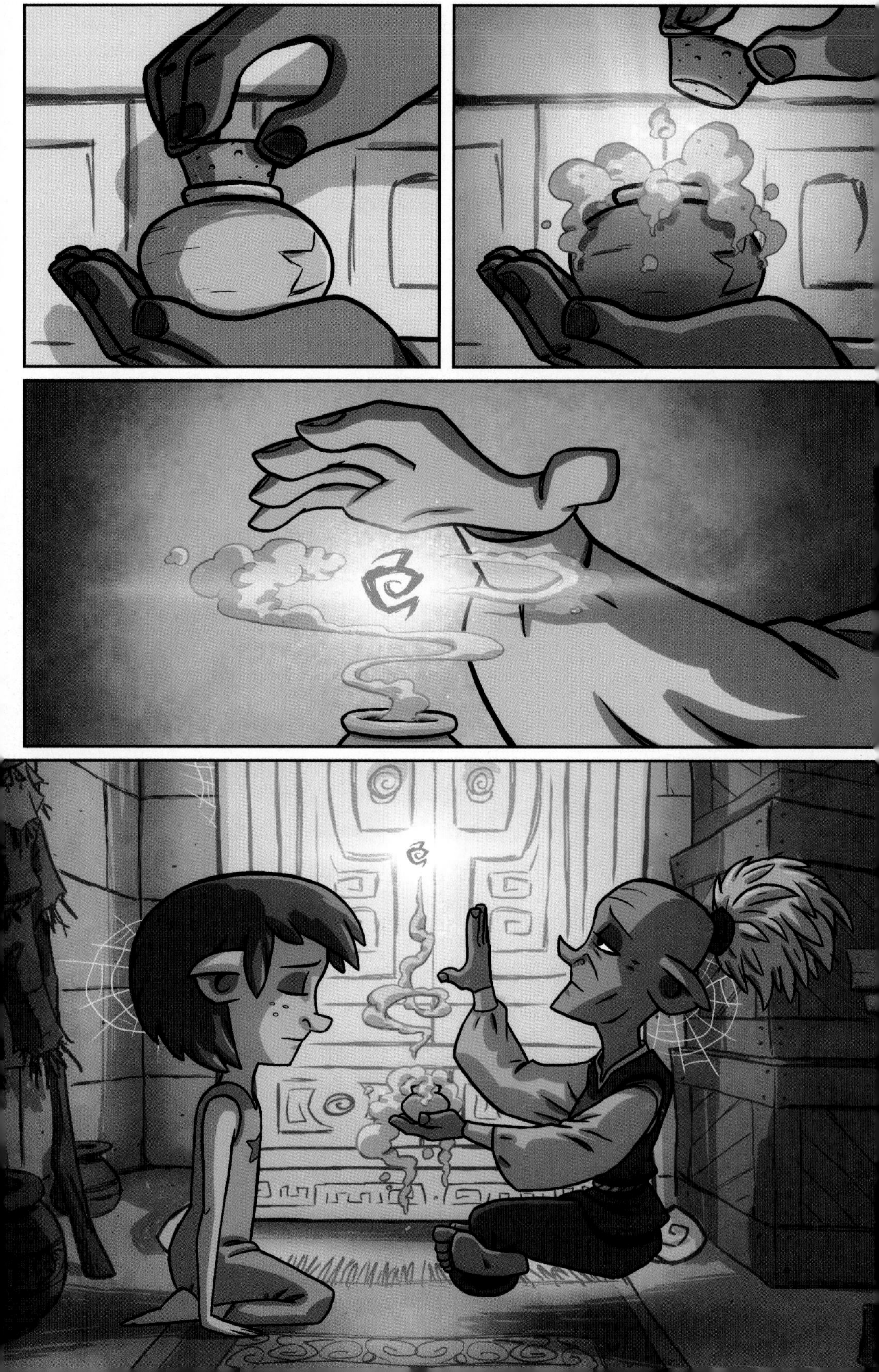

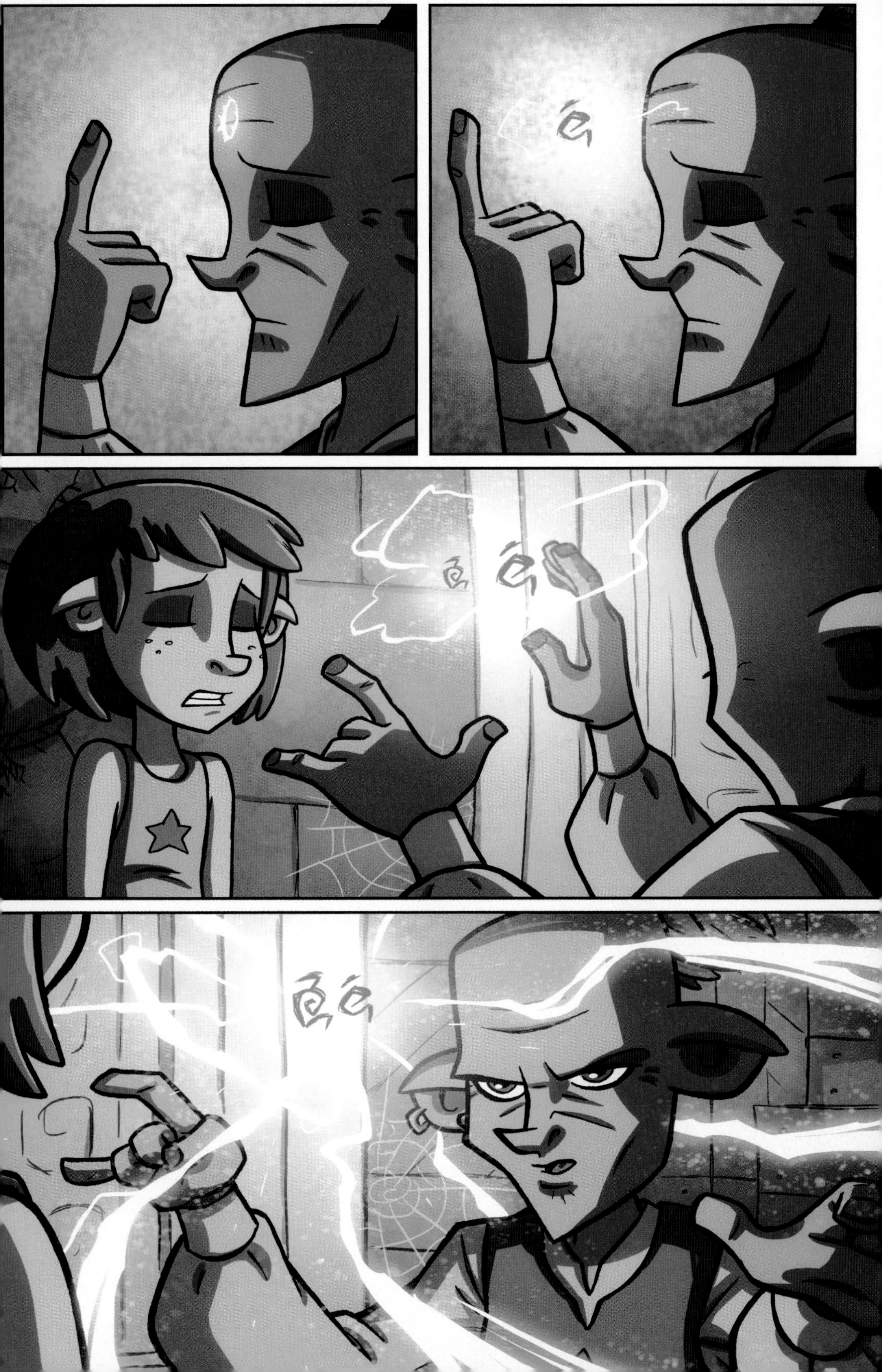

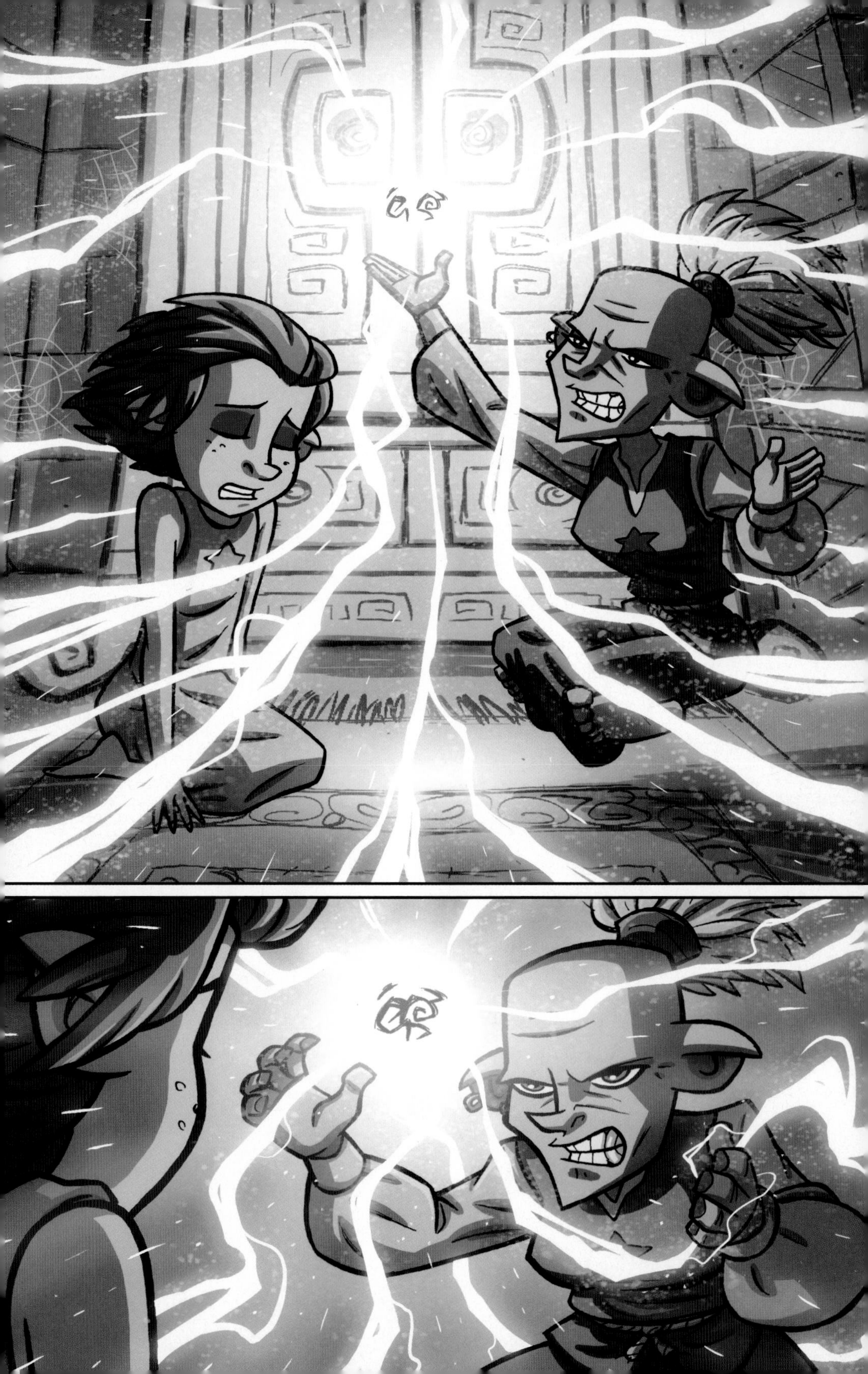

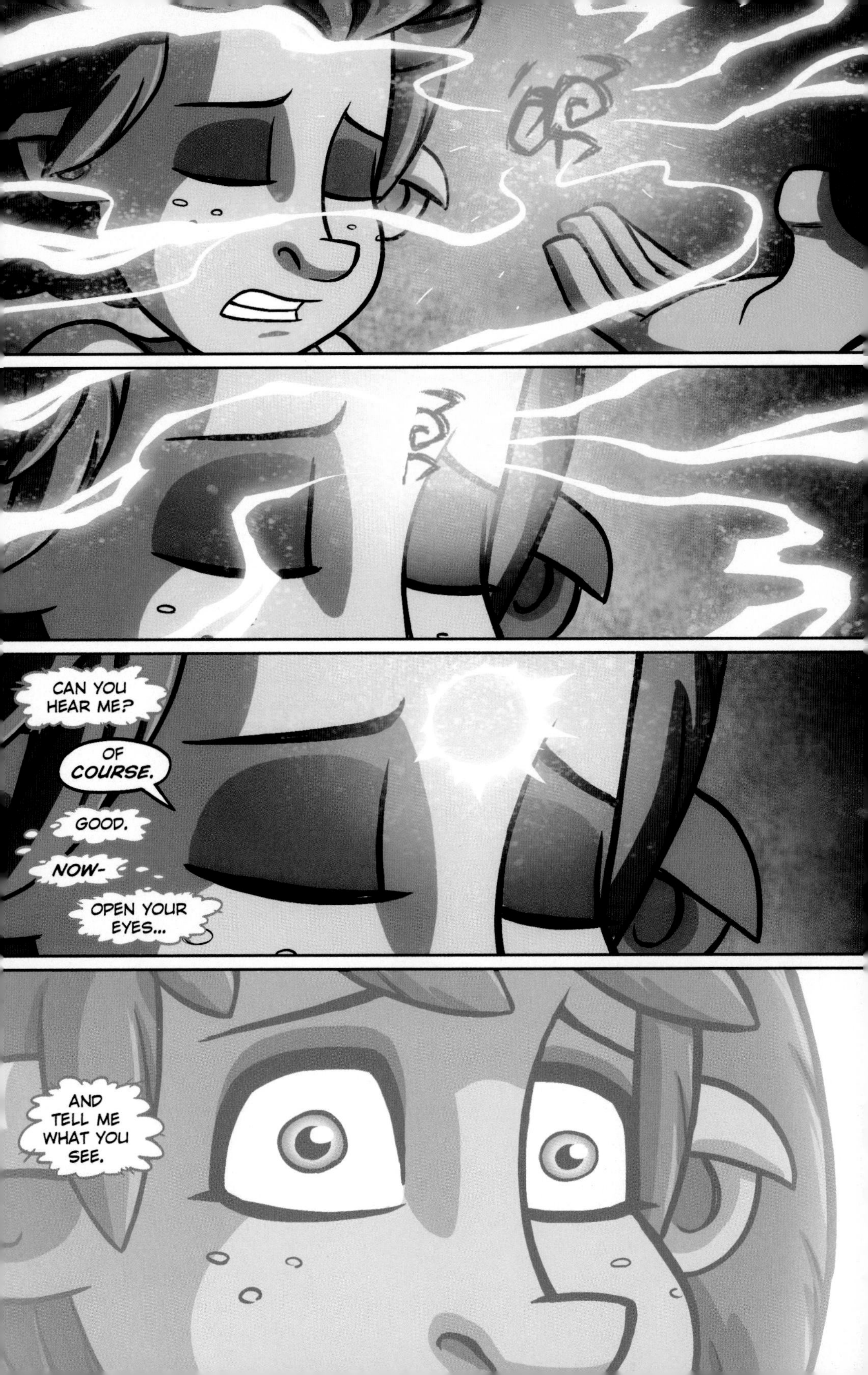
CAN YOU HEAR ME?
OF COURSE.
GOOD.
NOW-
OPEN YOUR EYES...
AND TELL ME WHAT YOU SEE.

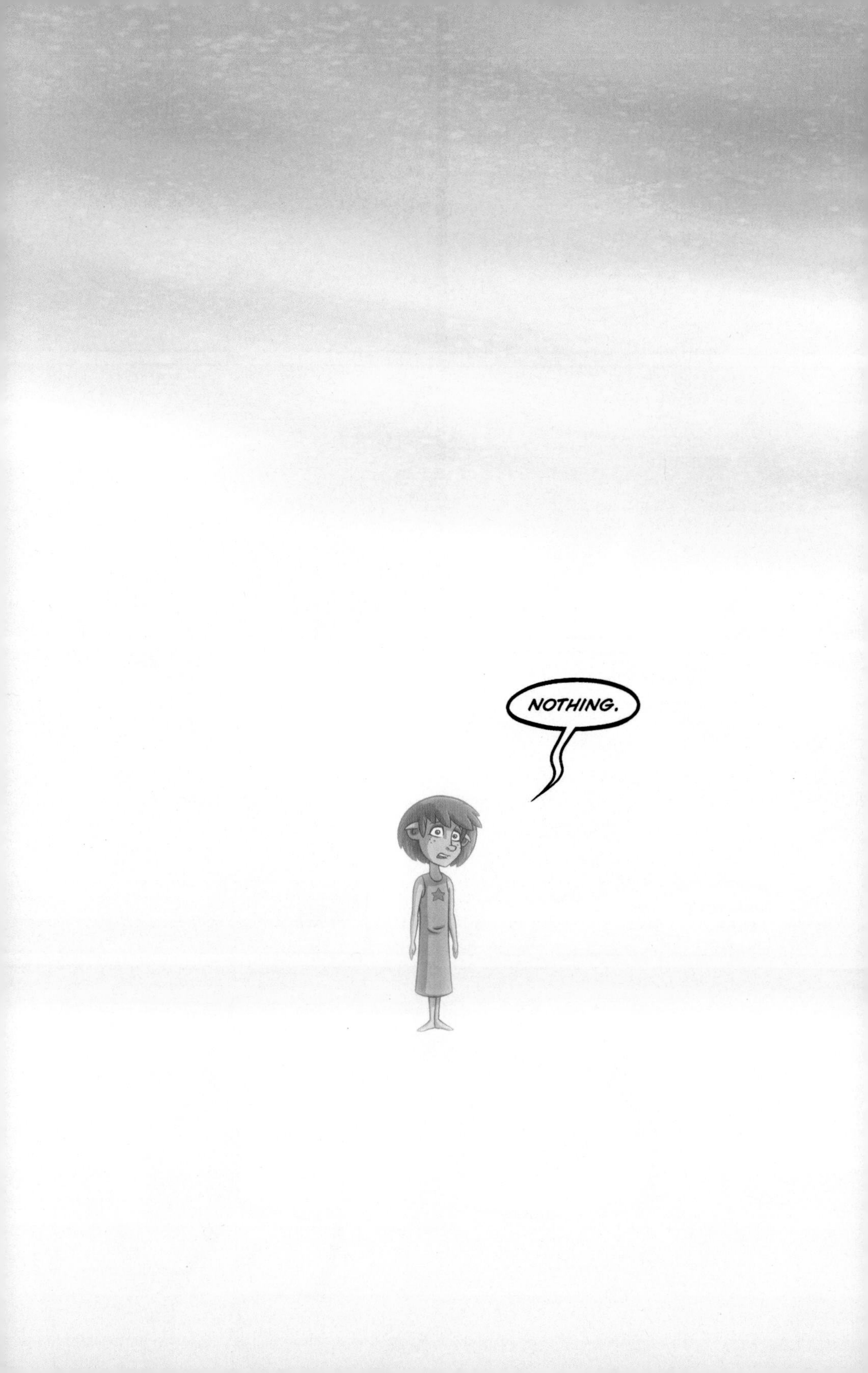
NOTHING.

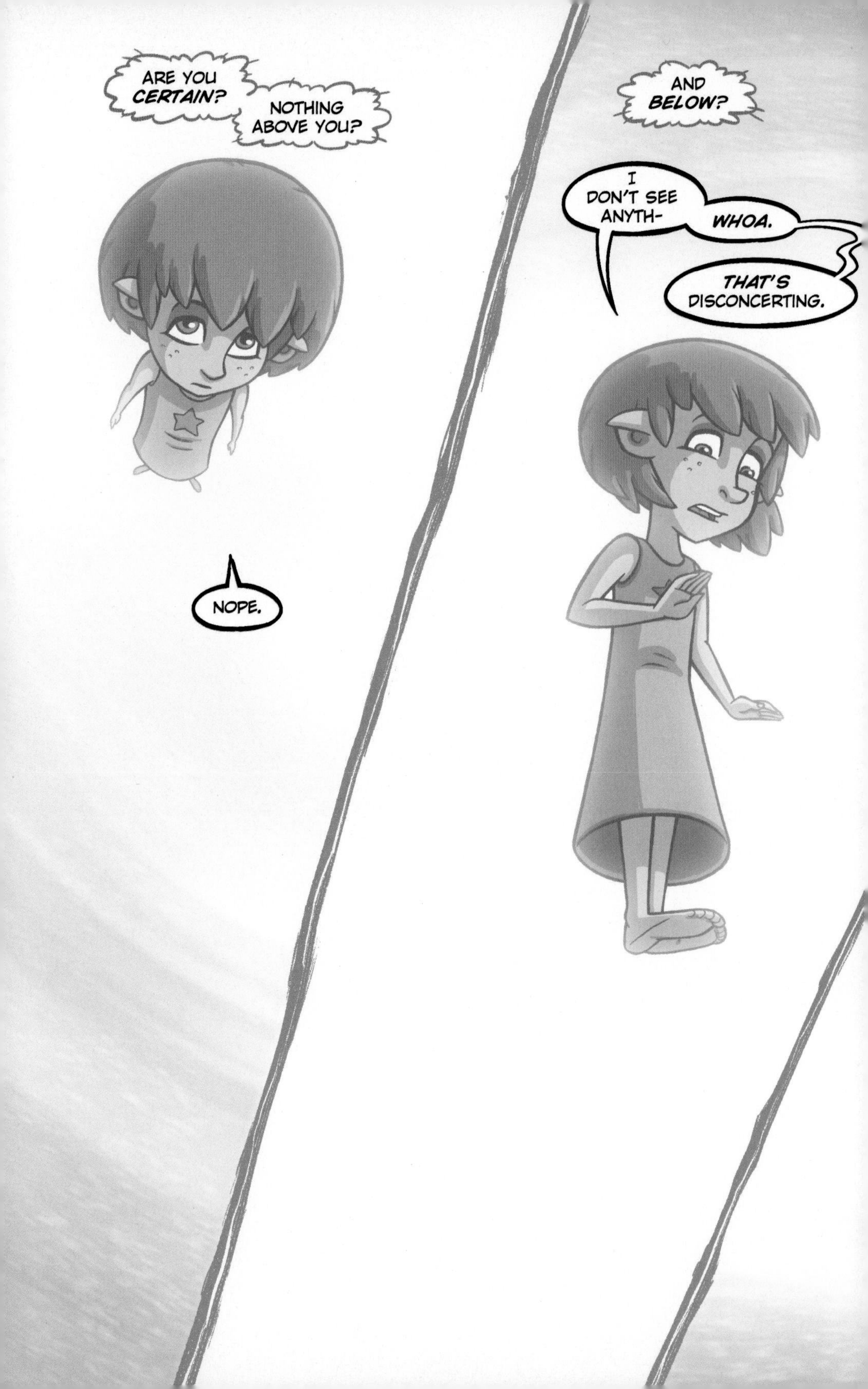
ARE YOU CERTAIN?
NOTHING ABOVE YOU?
NOPE.
AND BELOW?
I DON'T SEE ANYTH-
WHOA.
THAT'S DISCONCERTING.

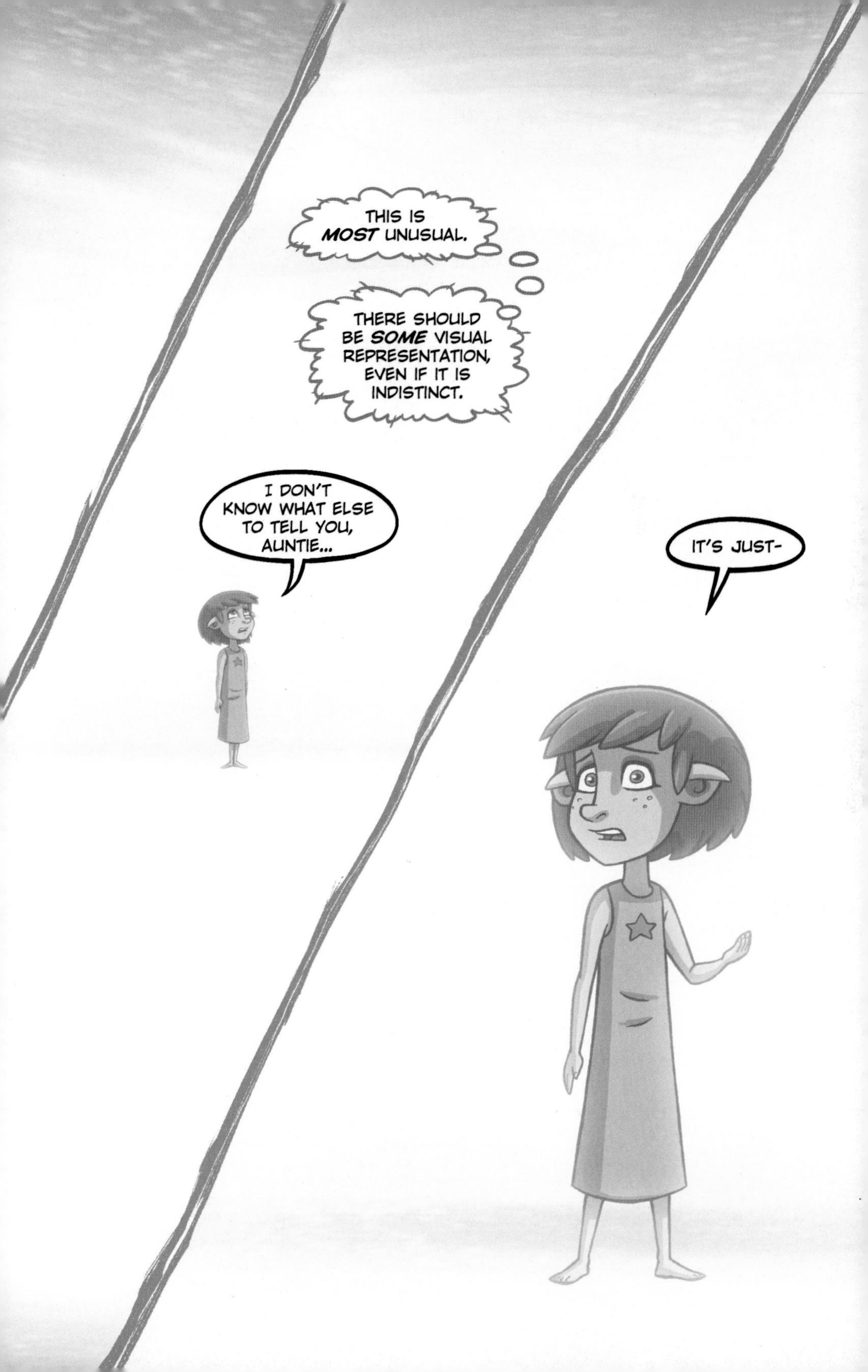
THIS IS *MOST* UNUSUAL.
THERE SHOULD BE *SOME* VISUAL REPRESENTATION, EVEN IF IT IS INDISTINCT.
I DON'T KNOW WHAT ELSE TO TELL YOU, AUNTIE...
IT'S JUST-

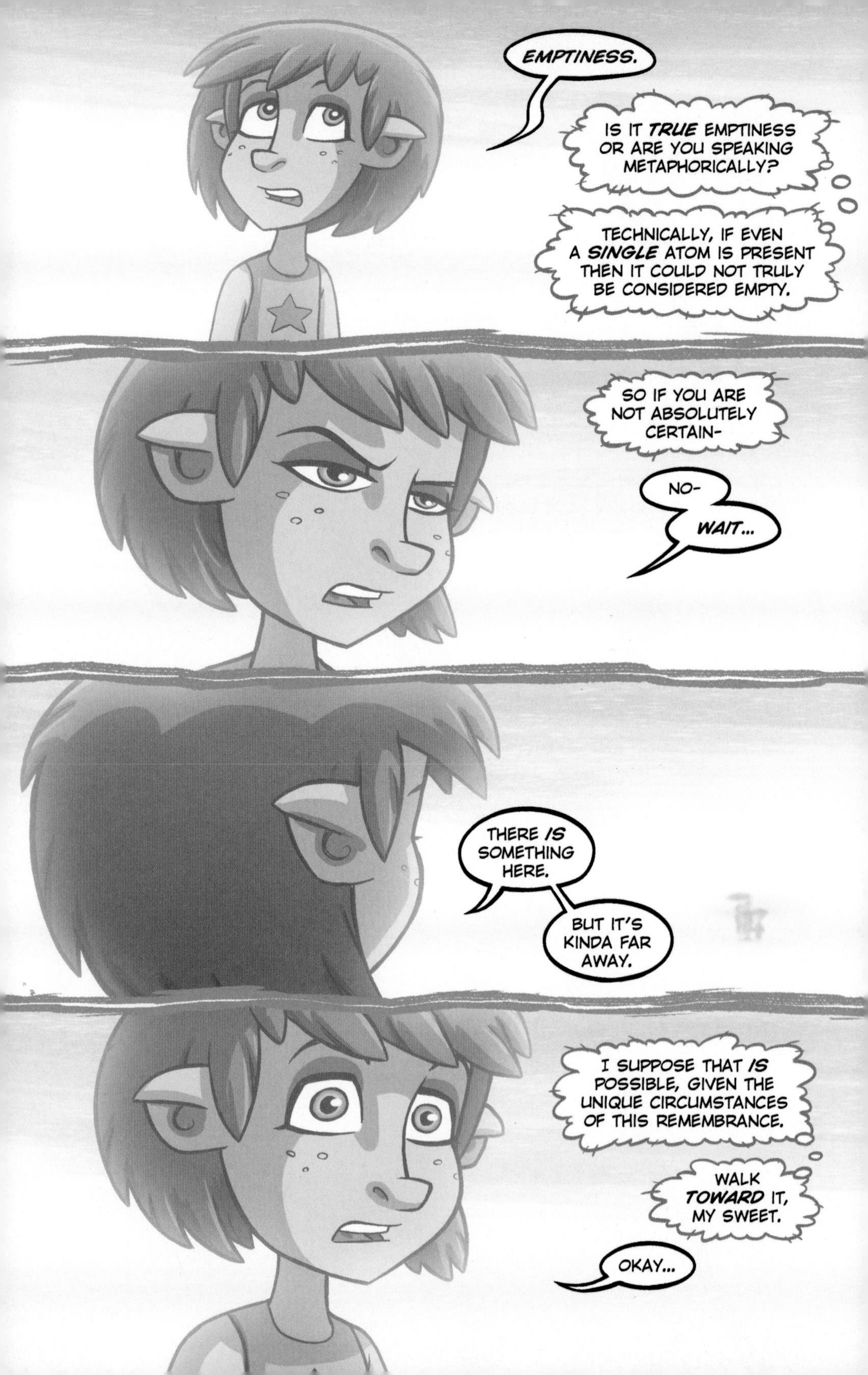
EMPTINESS.
IS IT TRUE EMPTINESS OR ARE YOU SPEAKING METAPHORICALLY?
TECHNICALLY, IF EVEN A SINGLE ATOM IS PRESENT THEN IT COULD NOT TRULY BE CONSIDERED EMPTY.
SO IF YOU ARE NOT ABSOLUTELY CERTAIN-
NO-
WAIT...
THERE IS SOMETHING HERE.
BUT IT'S KINDA FAR AWAY.
I SUPPOSE THAT IS POSSIBLE, GIVEN THE UNIQUE CIRCUMSTANCES OF THIS REMEMBRANCE.
WALK TOWARD IT, MY SWEET.
OKAY...

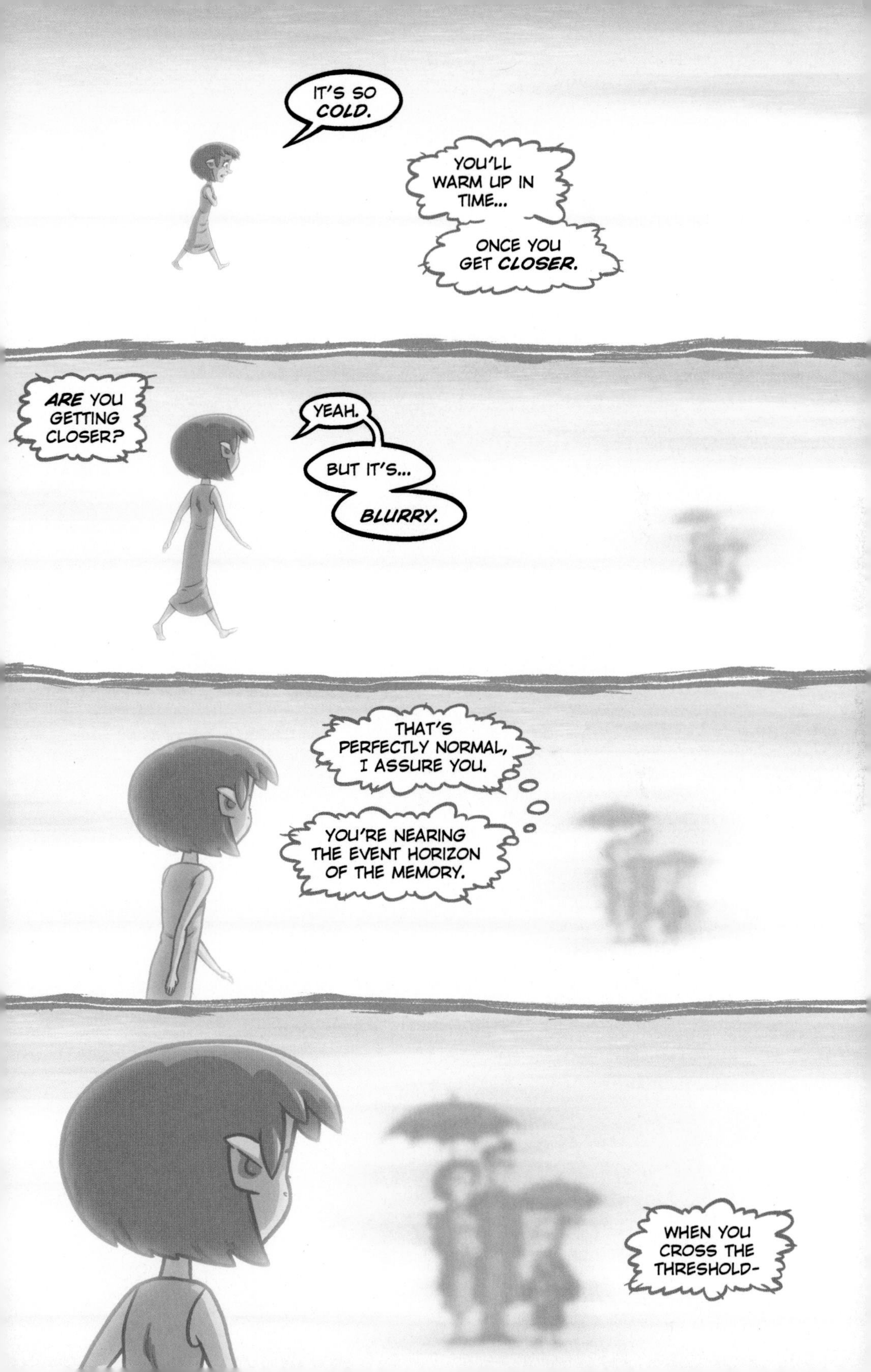
IT'S SO *COLD.*
YOU'LL WARM UP IN TIME...
ONCE YOU GET *CLOSER.*
ARE YOU GETTING CLOSER?
YEAH.
BUT IT'S...
BLURRY.
THAT'S PERFECTLY NORMAL, I ASSURE YOU.
YOU'RE NEARING THE EVENT HORIZON OF THE MEMORY.
WHEN YOU CROSS THE THRESHOLD-

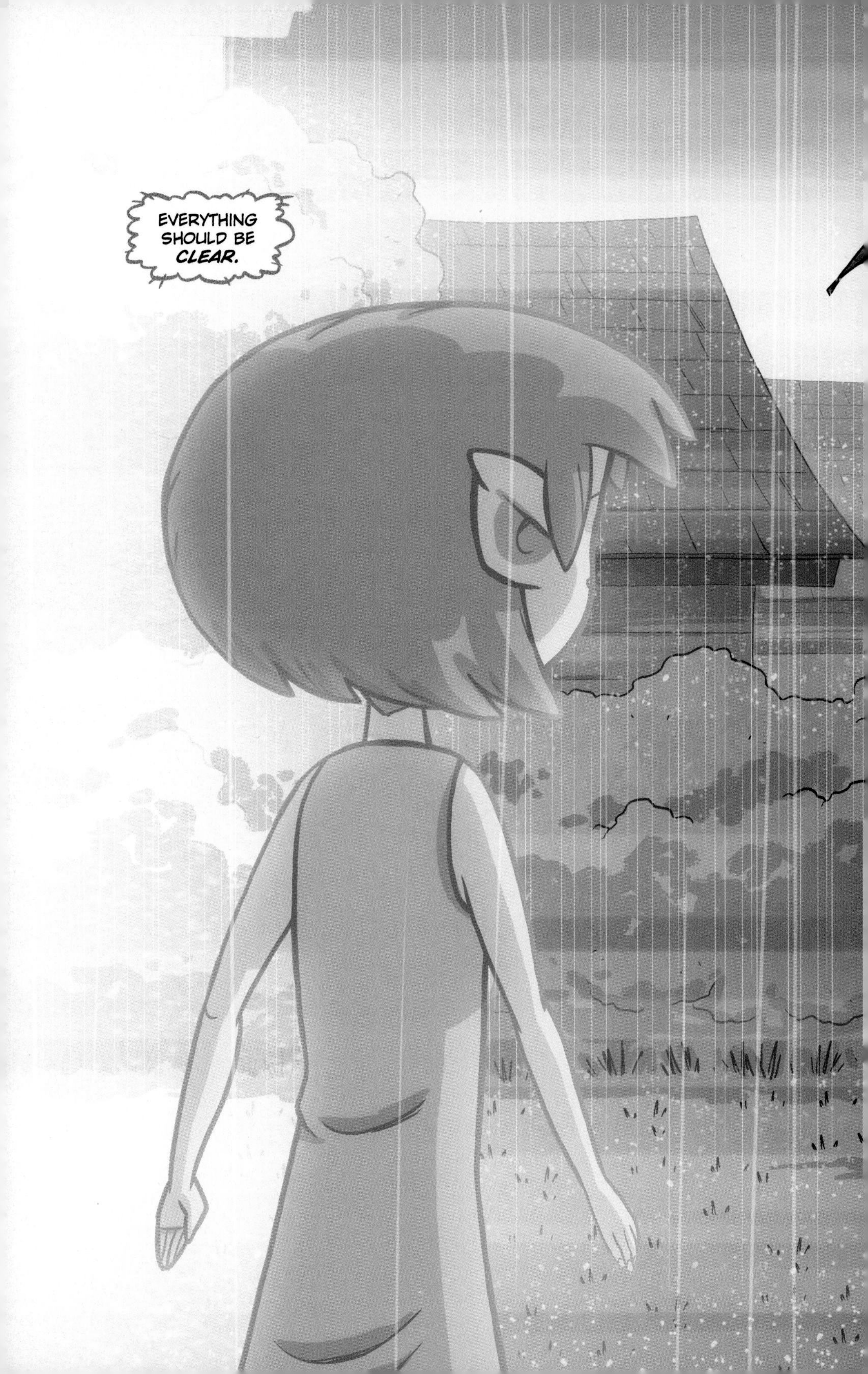
EVERYTHING SHOULD BE CLEAR.

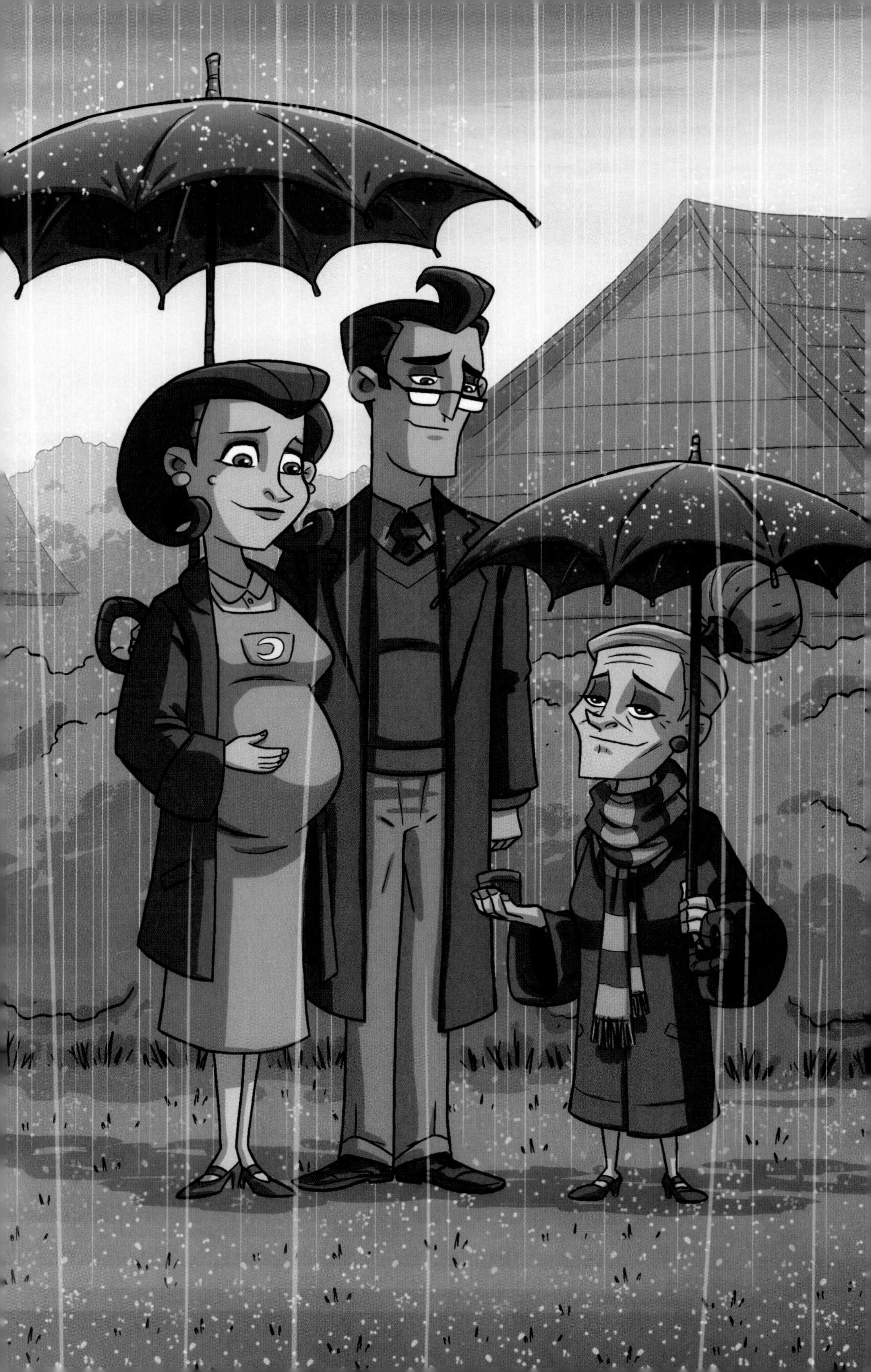

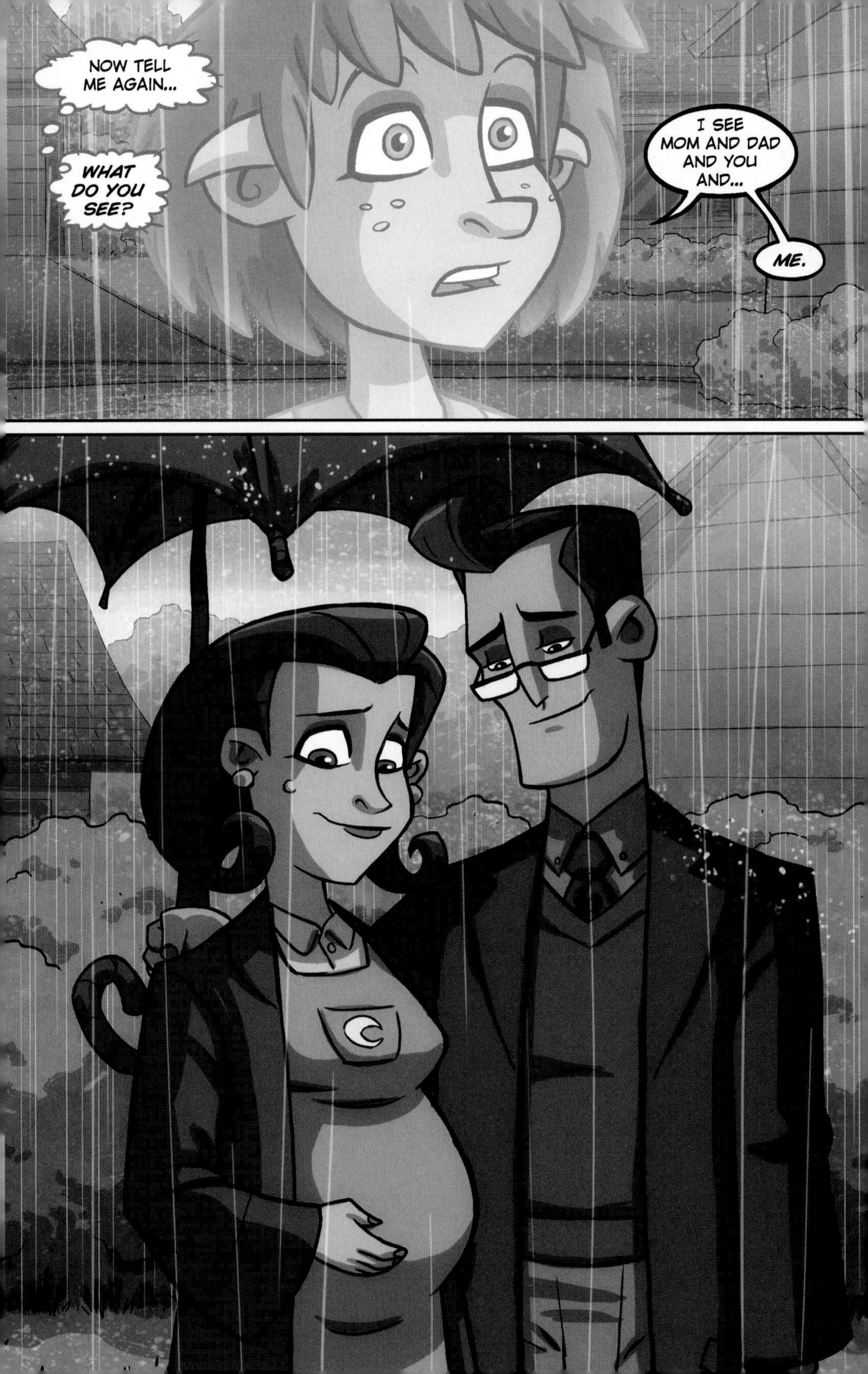
NOW TELL ME AGAIN...
WHAT DO YOU SEE?
I SEE MOM AND DAD AND YOU AND...
ME.

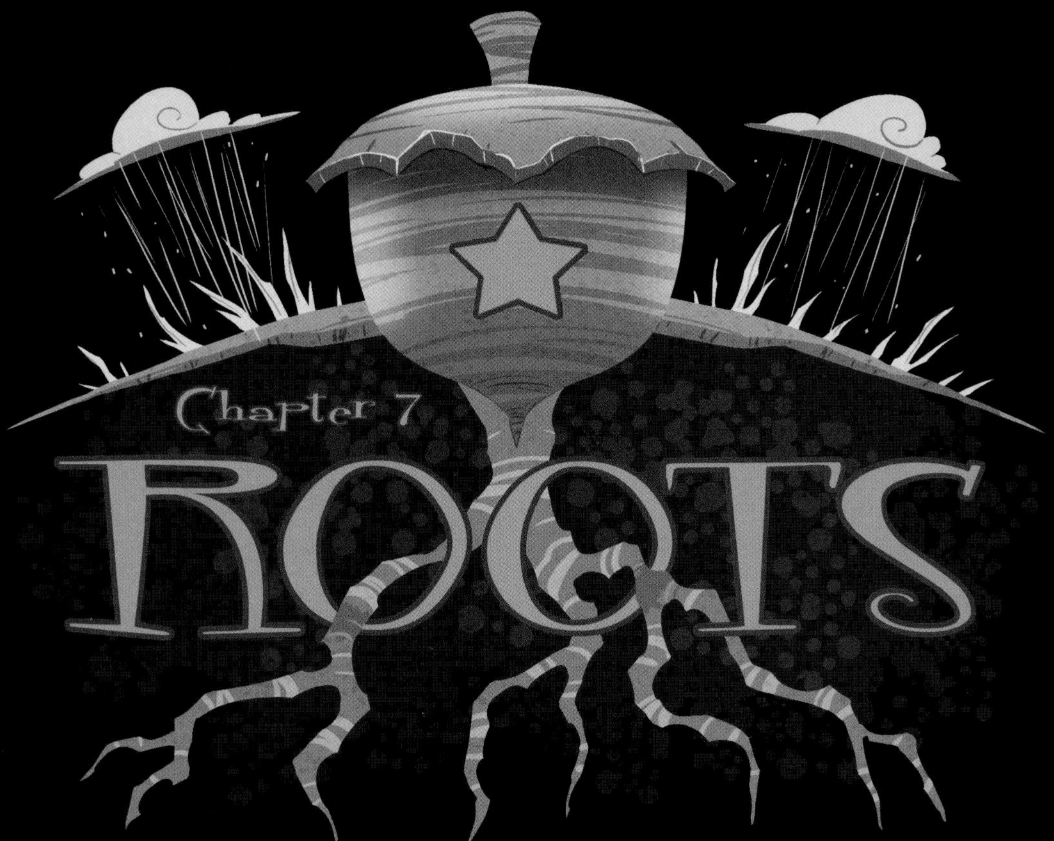
Chapter 7
ROOTS

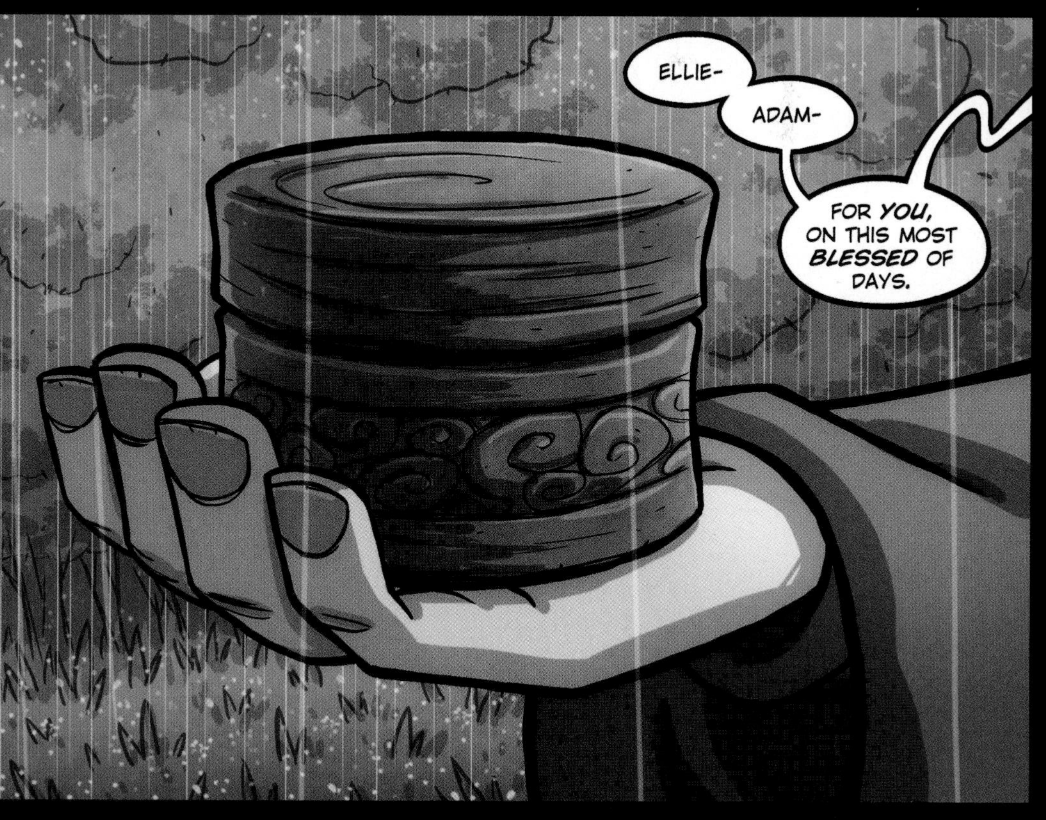
ELLIE-
ADAM-
FOR *YOU*, ON THIS MOST *BLESSED* OF DAYS.

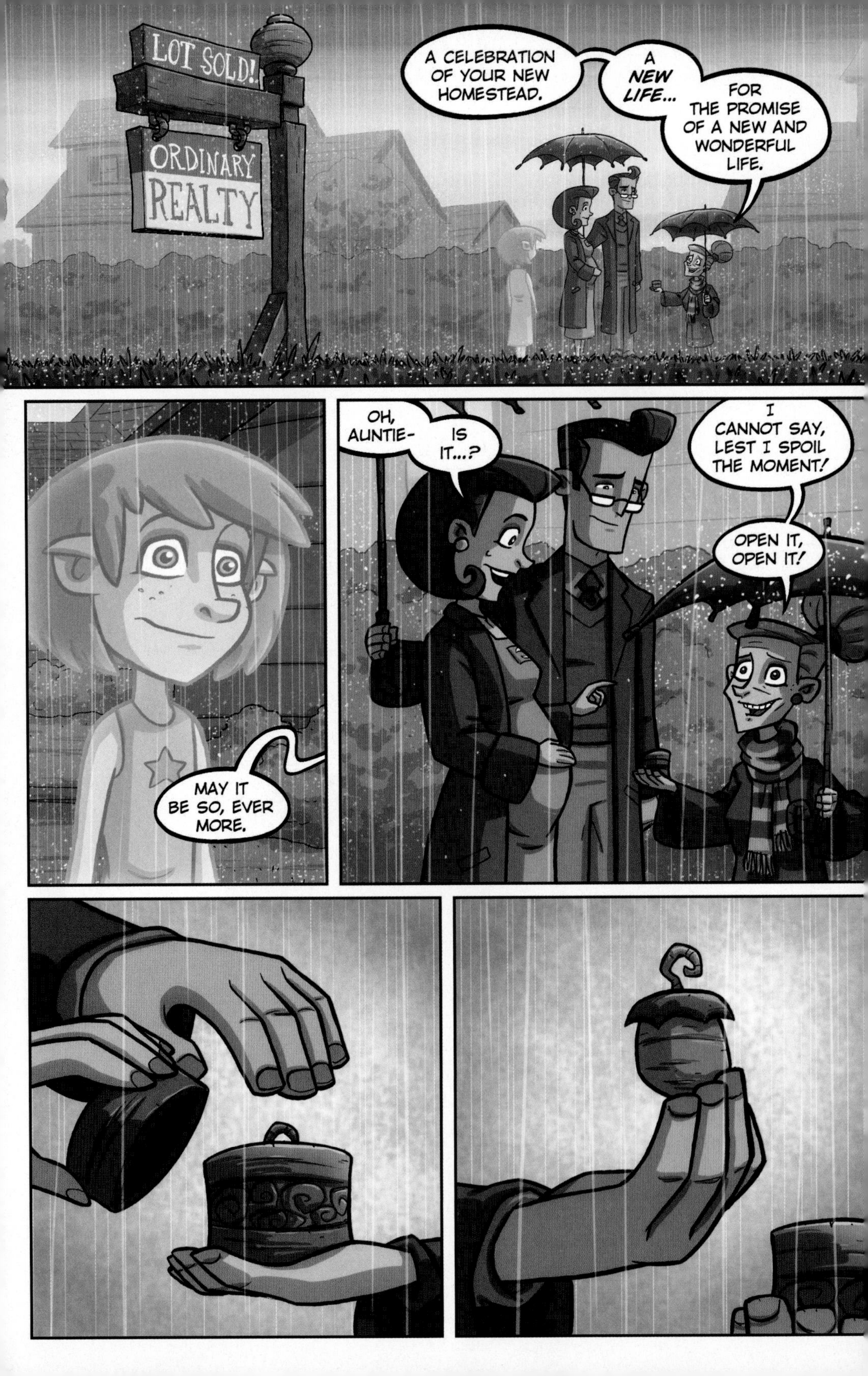
LOT SOLD!
ORDINARY REALTY
A CELEBRATION OF YOUR NEW HOMESTEAD.
A *NEW LIFE*...
FOR THE PROMISE OF A NEW AND WONDERFUL LIFE.
MAY IT BE SO, EVER MORE.
OH, AUNTIE-
IS IT...?
I CANNOT SAY, LEST I SPOIL THE MOMENT!
OPEN IT, OPEN IT!

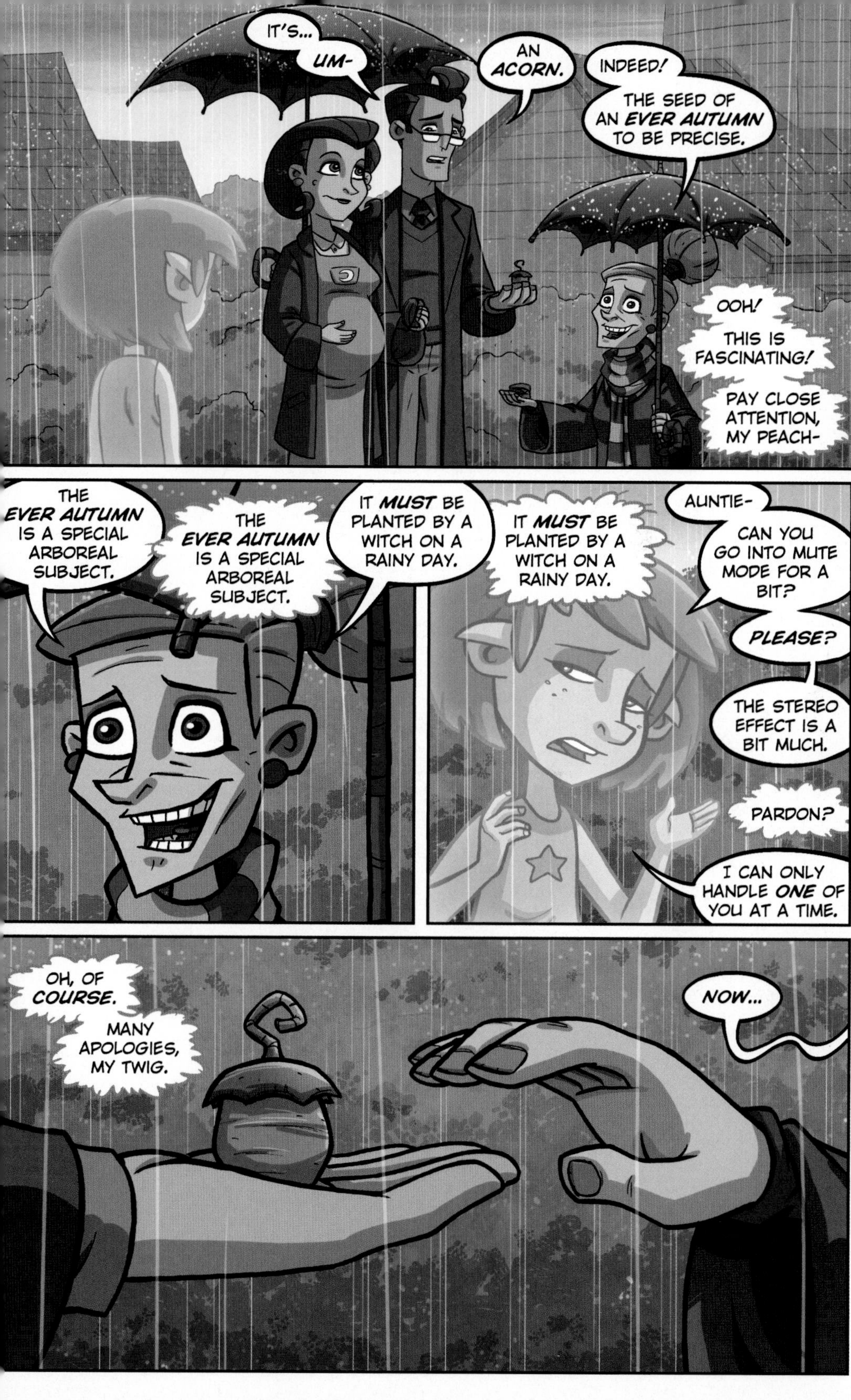
IT'S... UM-
AN ACORN.
INDEED!
THE SEED OF AN EVER AUTUMN TO BE PRECISE.
OOH!
THIS IS FASCINATING!
PAY CLOSE ATTENTION, MY PEACH-
THE EVER AUTUMN IS A SPECIAL ARBOREAL SUBJECT.
THE EVER AUTUMN IS A SPECIAL ARBOREAL SUBJECT.
IT MUST BE PLANTED BY A WITCH ON A RAINY DAY.
IT MUST BE PLANTED BY A WITCH ON A RAINY DAY.
AUNTIE-
CAN YOU GO INTO MUTE MODE FOR A BIT?
PLEASE?
THE STEREO EFFECT IS A BIT MUCH.
PARDON?
I CAN ONLY HANDLE ONE OF YOU AT A TIME.
OH, OF COURSE.
MANY APOLOGIES, MY TWIG.
NOW...

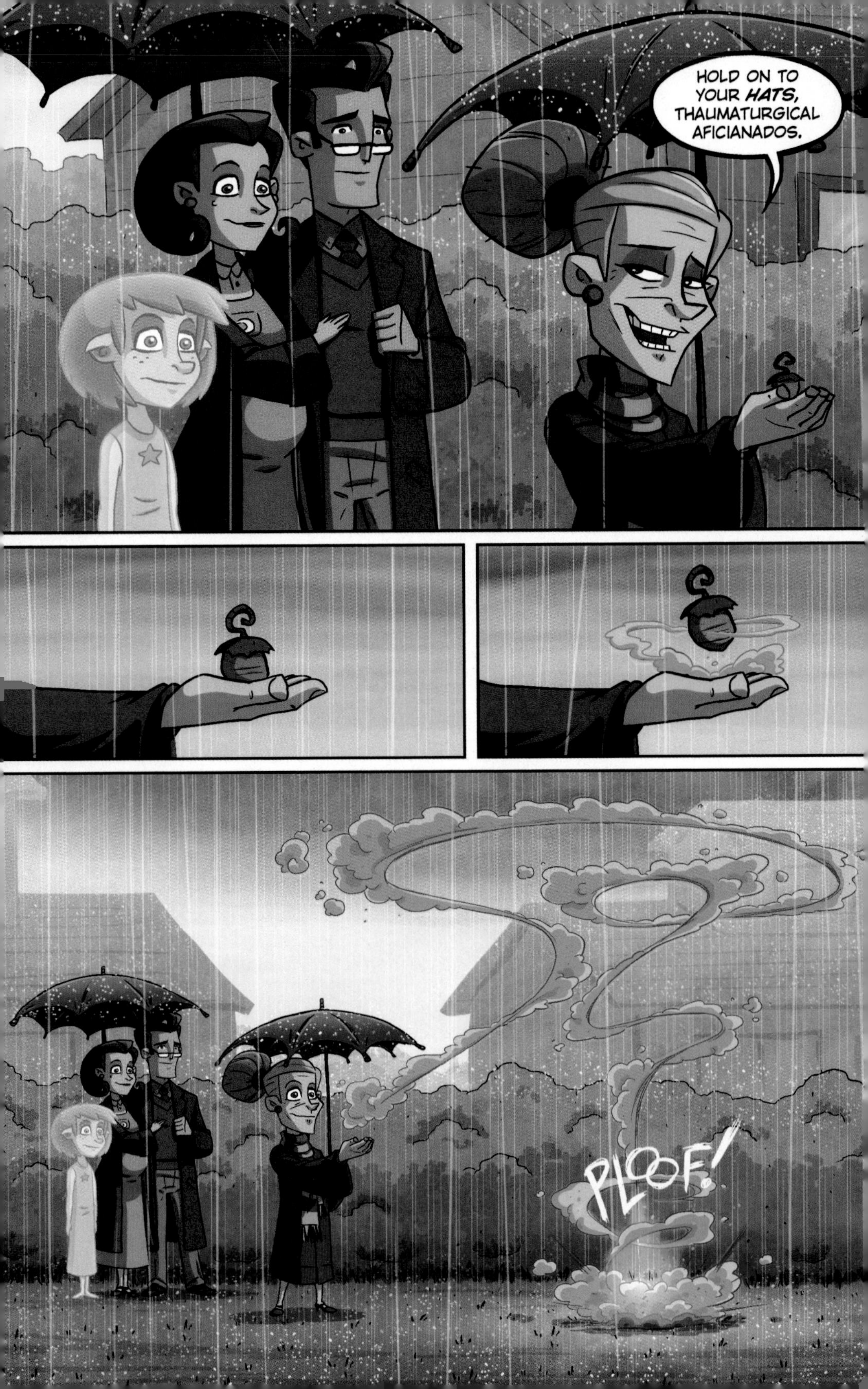
HOLD ON TO YOUR *HATS*, THAUMATURGICAL AFICIANADOS.
PLOOF!

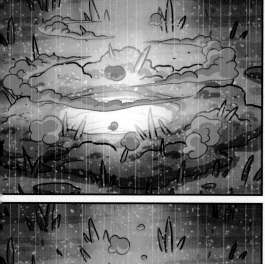

ANY SECOND NOW...

ANY MOMENT...

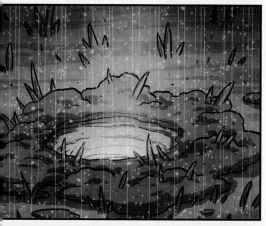

A MOMENT OF PURE DELIGHT IS IMMINENT...

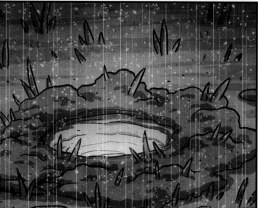

OR...

PERHAPS I'VE BROUGHT YOU OUT HERE TO STARE AT NOTHING-

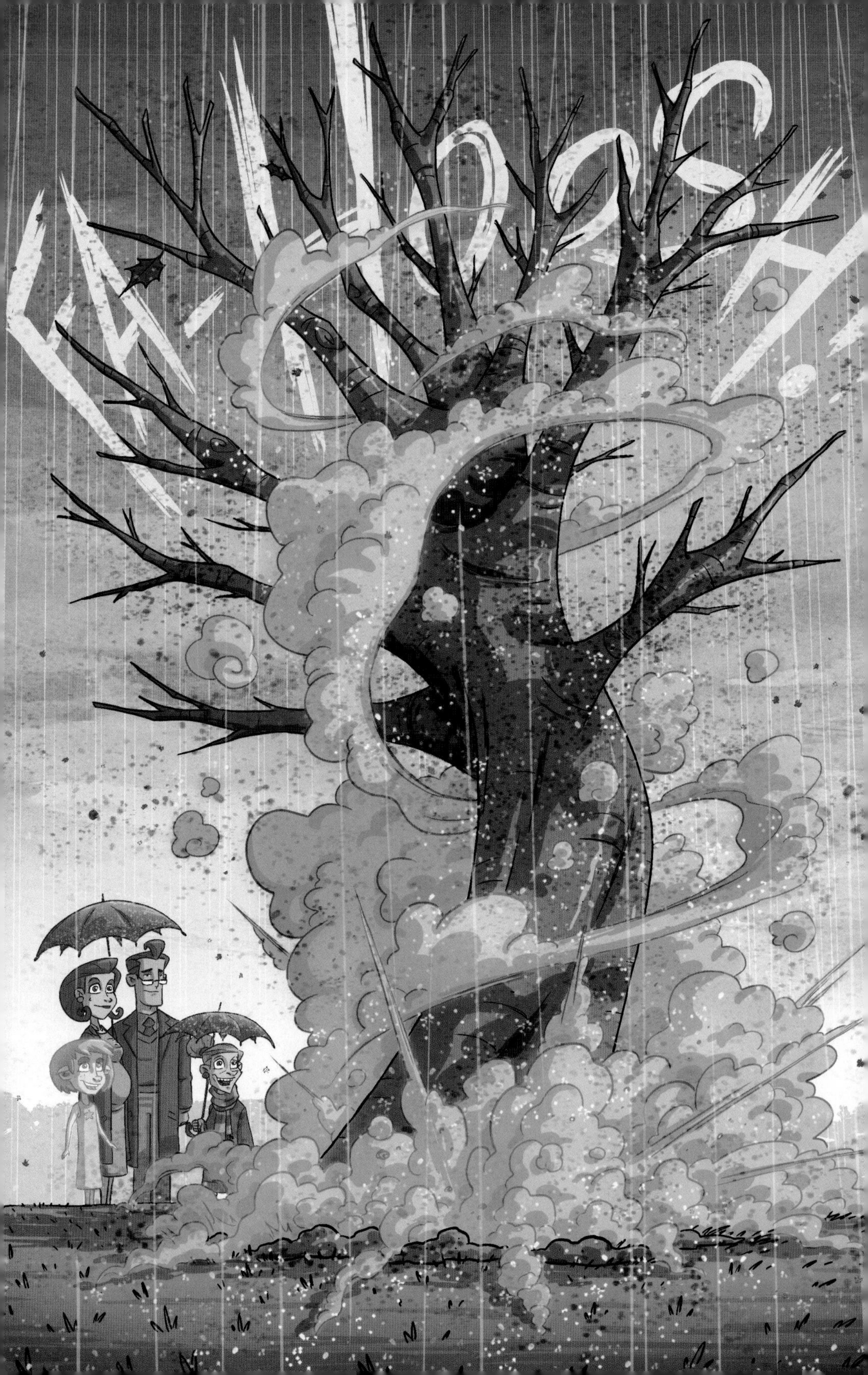
WHOOSH!

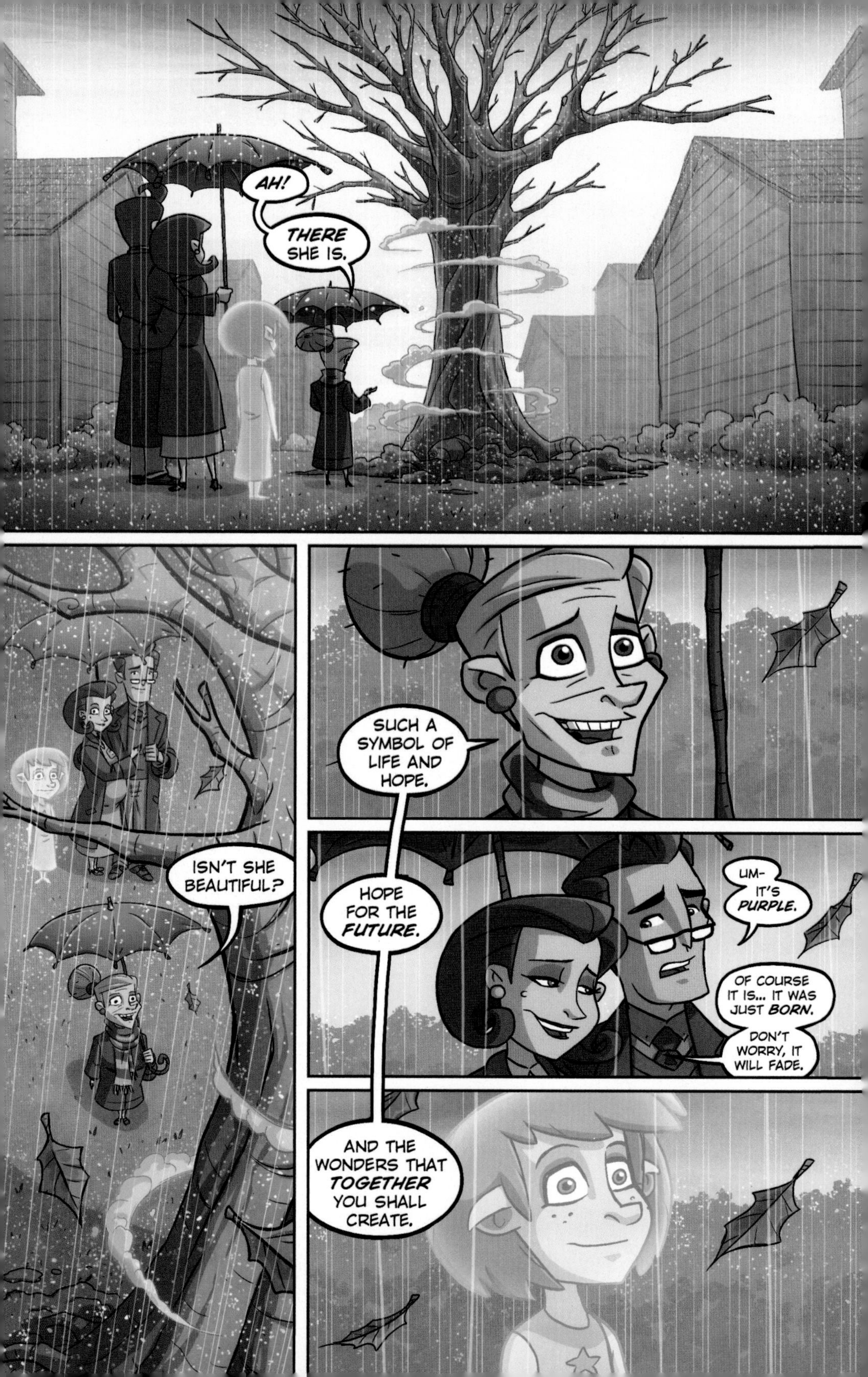
AH!
THERE SHE IS.
ISN'T SHE BEAUTIFUL?
SUCH A SYMBOL OF LIFE AND HOPE.
HOPE FOR THE FUTURE.
UM- IT'S PURPLE.
OF COURSE IT IS... IT WAS JUST BORN.
DON'T WORRY, IT WILL FADE.
AND THE WONDERS THAT TOGETHER YOU SHALL CREATE.

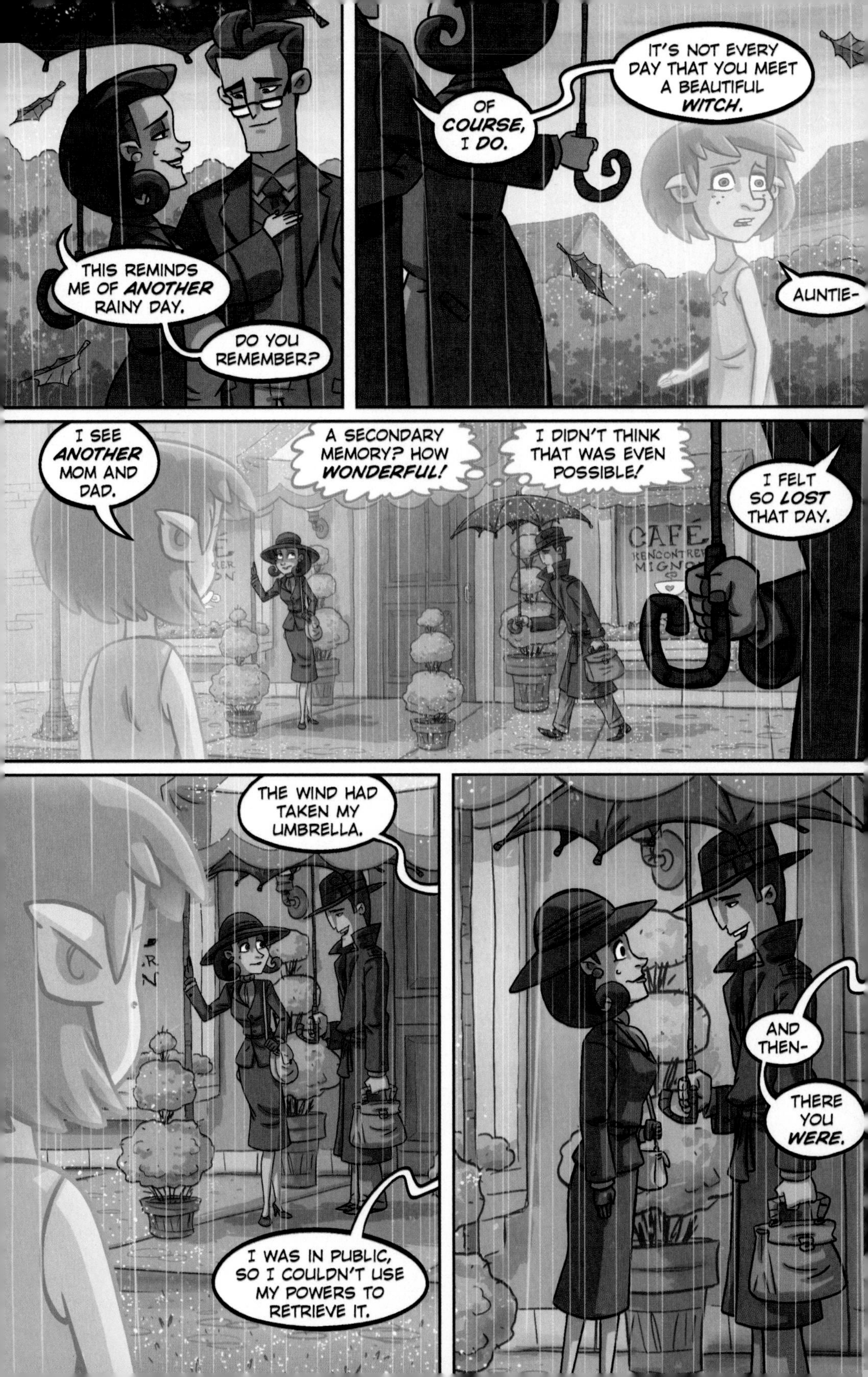
THIS REMINDS ME OF ANOTHER RAINY DAY.
DO YOU REMEMBER?
OF COURSE, I DO.
IT'S NOT EVERY DAY THAT YOU MEET A BEAUTIFUL WITCH.
AUNTIE-
I SEE ANOTHER MOM AND DAD.
A SECONDARY MEMORY? HOW WONDERFUL!
I DIDN'T THINK THAT WAS EVEN POSSIBLE!
I FELT SO LOST THAT DAY.
CAFÉ
THE WIND HAD TAKEN MY UMBRELLA.
I WAS IN PUBLIC, SO I COULDN'T USE MY POWERS TO RETRIEVE IT.
AND THEN-
THERE YOU WERE.

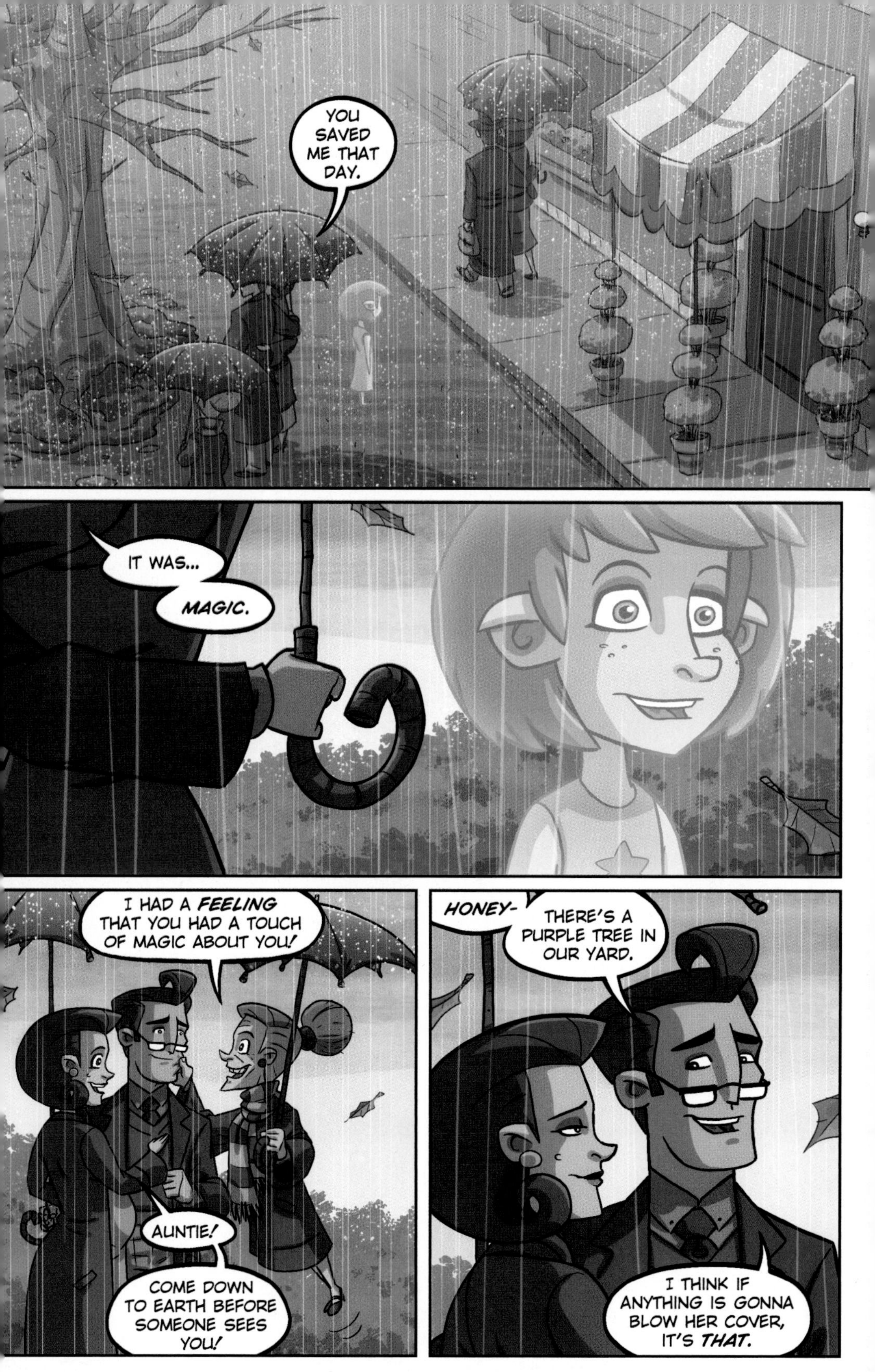
YOU SAVED ME THAT DAY.
IT WAS...
MAGIC.
I HAD A *FEELING* THAT YOU HAD A TOUCH OF MAGIC ABOUT YOU!
AUNTIE!
COME DOWN TO EARTH BEFORE SOMEONE SEES YOU!
HONEY-
THERE'S A PURPLE TREE IN OUR YARD.
I THINK IF ANYTHING IS GONNA BLOW HER COVER, IT'S *THAT.*

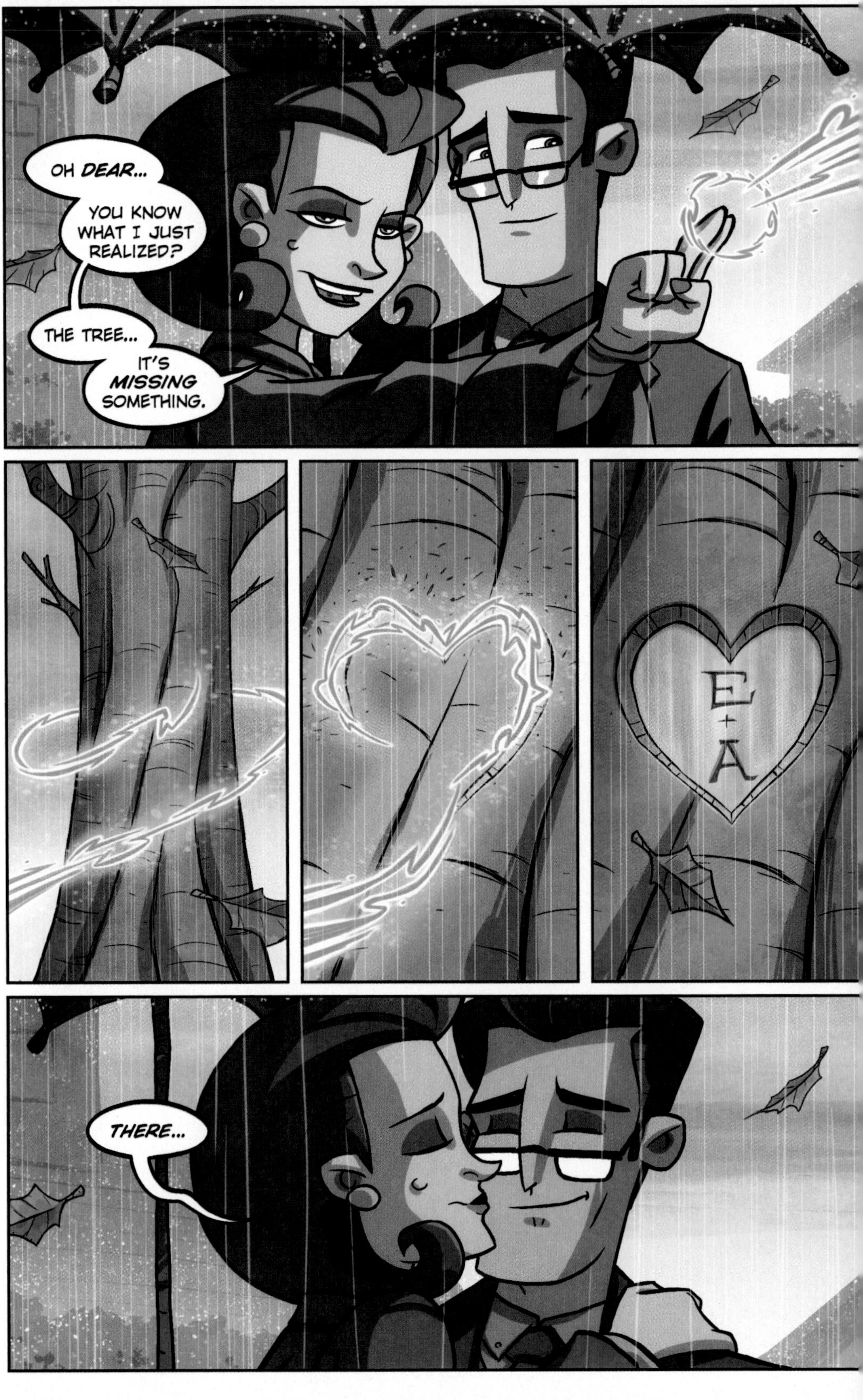
OH *DEAR*...
YOU KNOW WHAT I JUST REALIZED?
THE TREE...
IT'S *MISSING* SOMETHING.
E + A
THERE...

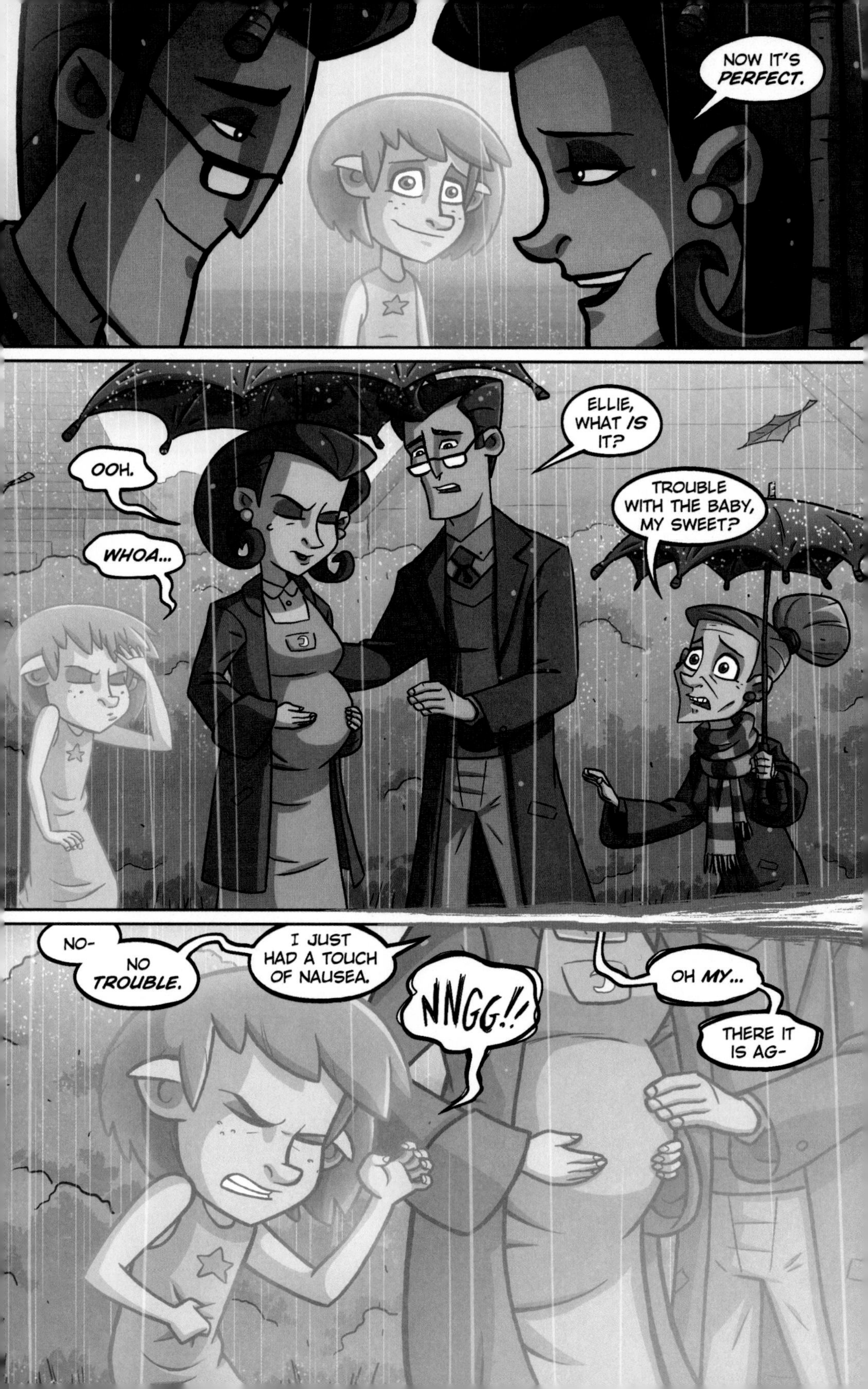
NOW IT'S *PERFECT.*
OOH.
WHOA...
ELLIE, WHAT *IS* IT?
TROUBLE WITH THE BABY, MY SWEET?
NO-
NO *TROUBLE.*
I JUST HAD A TOUCH OF NAUSEA.
NNGG!!
OH *MY...*
THERE IT IS AG-

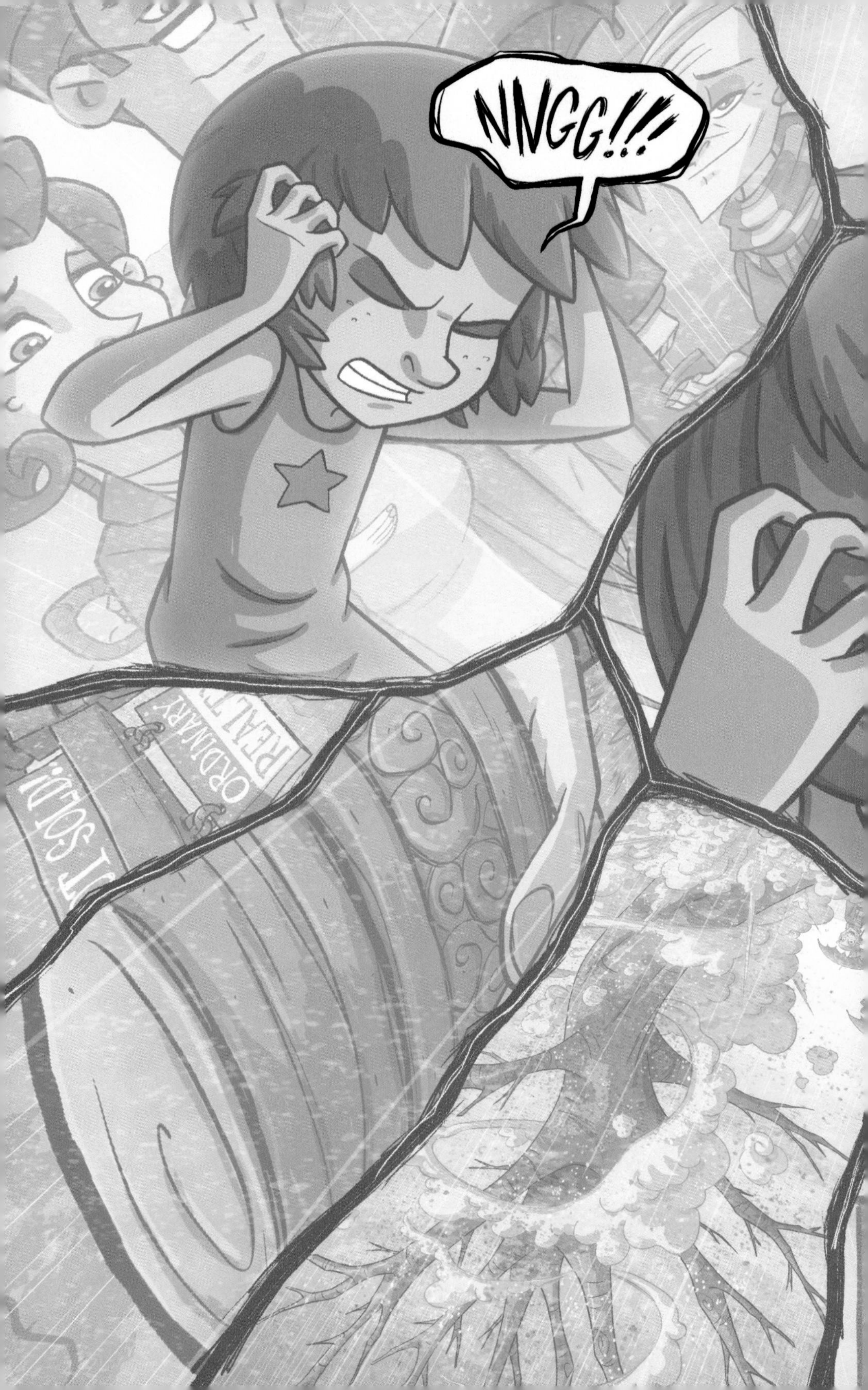
NNGG!!!
ORDINARY
SOLD!

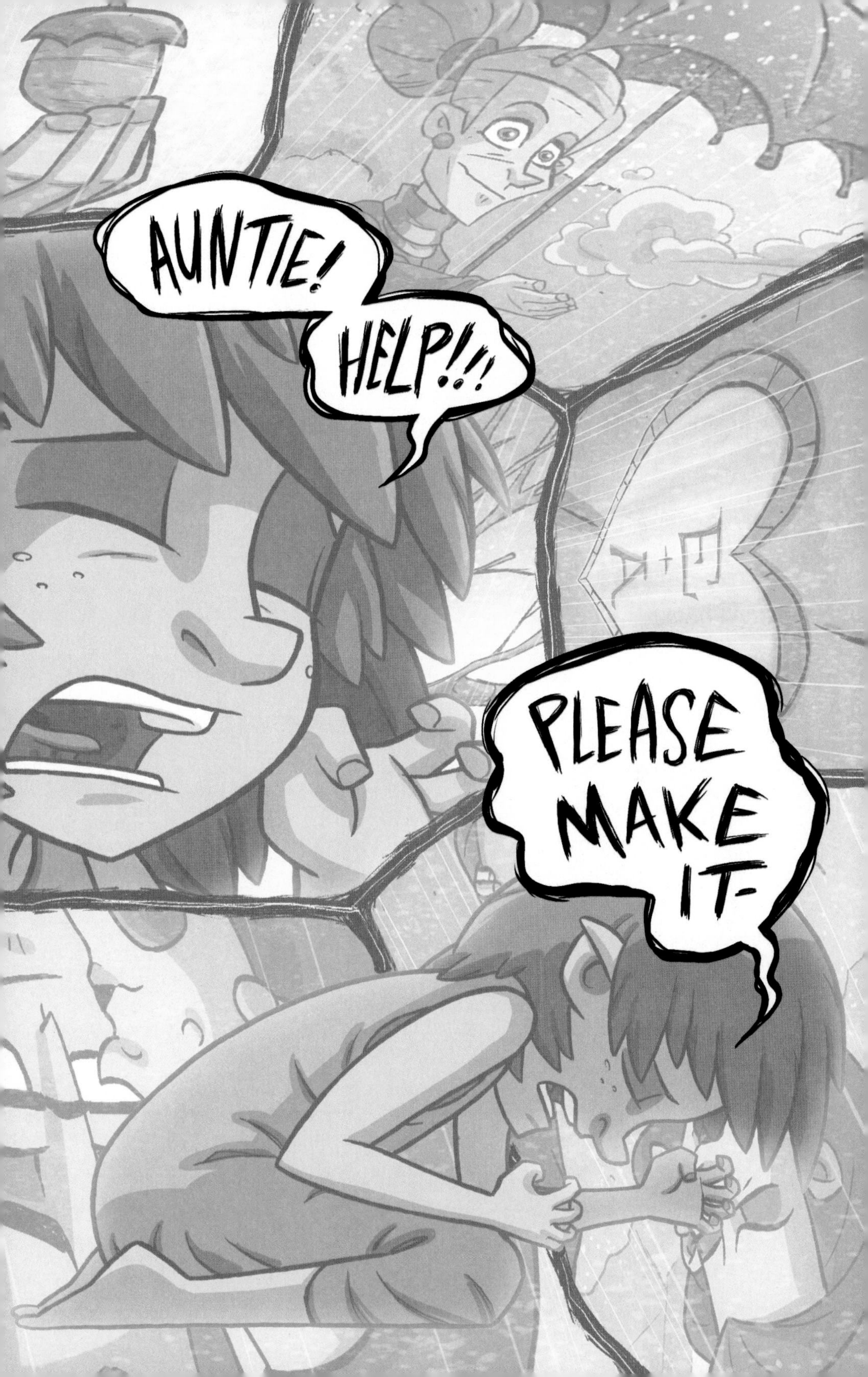
AUNTIE!
HELP!!!
PLEASE MAKE IT-

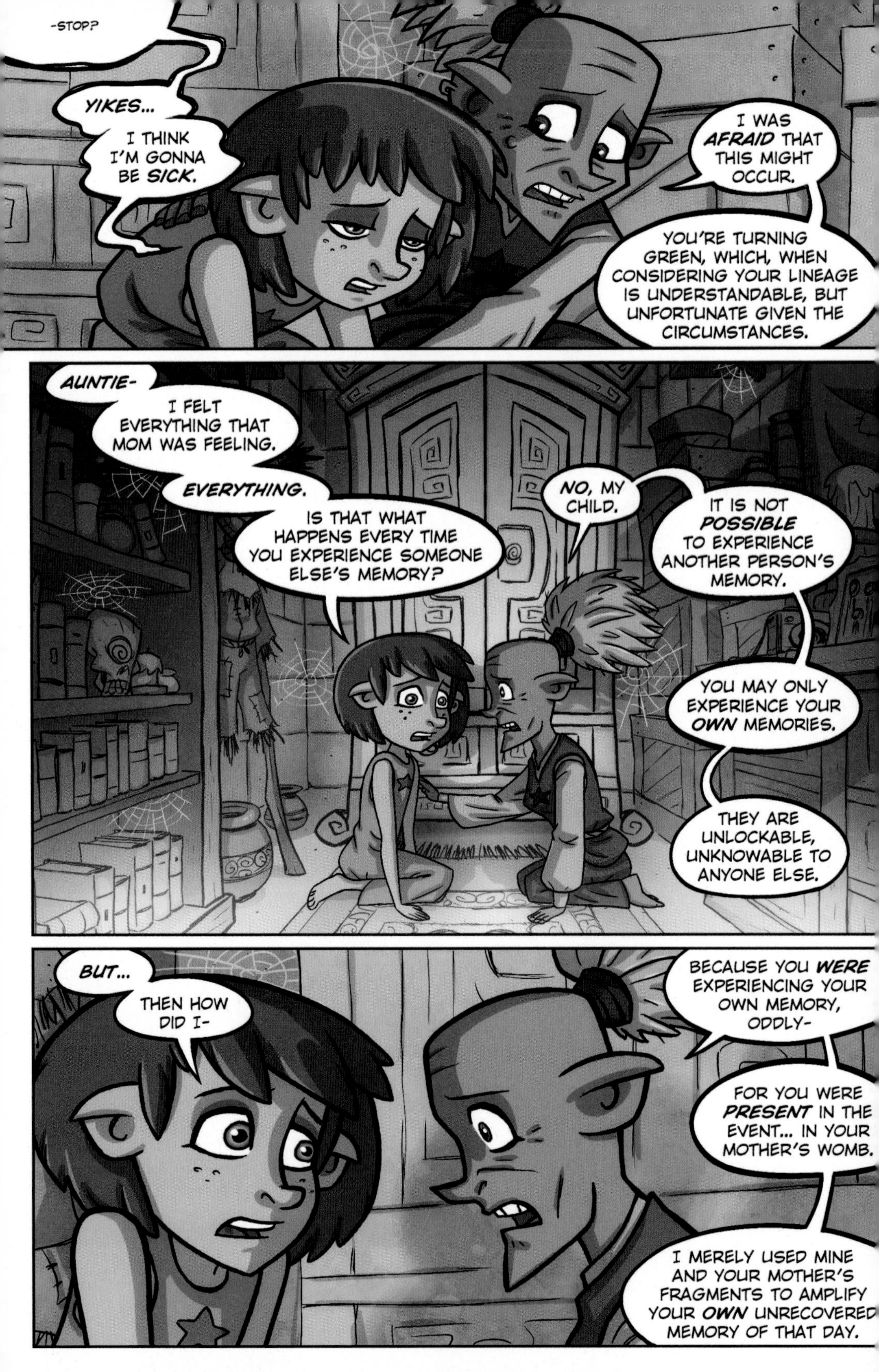
-STOP?
YIKES...
I THINK I'M GONNA BE SICK.
I WAS AFRAID THAT THIS MIGHT OCCUR.
YOU'RE TURNING GREEN, WHICH, WHEN CONSIDERING YOUR LINEAGE IS UNDERSTANDABLE, BUT UNFORTUNATE GIVEN THE CIRCUMSTANCES.
AUNTIE-
I FELT EVERYTHING THAT MOM WAS FEELING.
EVERYTHING.
IS THAT WHAT HAPPENS EVERY TIME YOU EXPERIENCE SOMEONE ELSE'S MEMORY?
NO, MY CHILD.
IT IS NOT POSSIBLE TO EXPERIENCE ANOTHER PERSON'S MEMORY.
YOU MAY ONLY EXPERIENCE YOUR OWN MEMORIES.
THEY ARE UNLOCKABLE, UNKNOWABLE TO ANYONE ELSE.
BUT...
THEN HOW DID I-
BECAUSE YOU WERE EXPERIENCING YOUR OWN MEMORY, ODDLY-
FOR YOU WERE PRESENT IN THE EVENT... IN YOUR MOTHER'S WOMB.
I MERELY USED MINE AND YOUR MOTHER'S FRAGMENTS TO AMPLIFY YOUR OWN UNRECOVERED MEMORY OF THAT DAY.

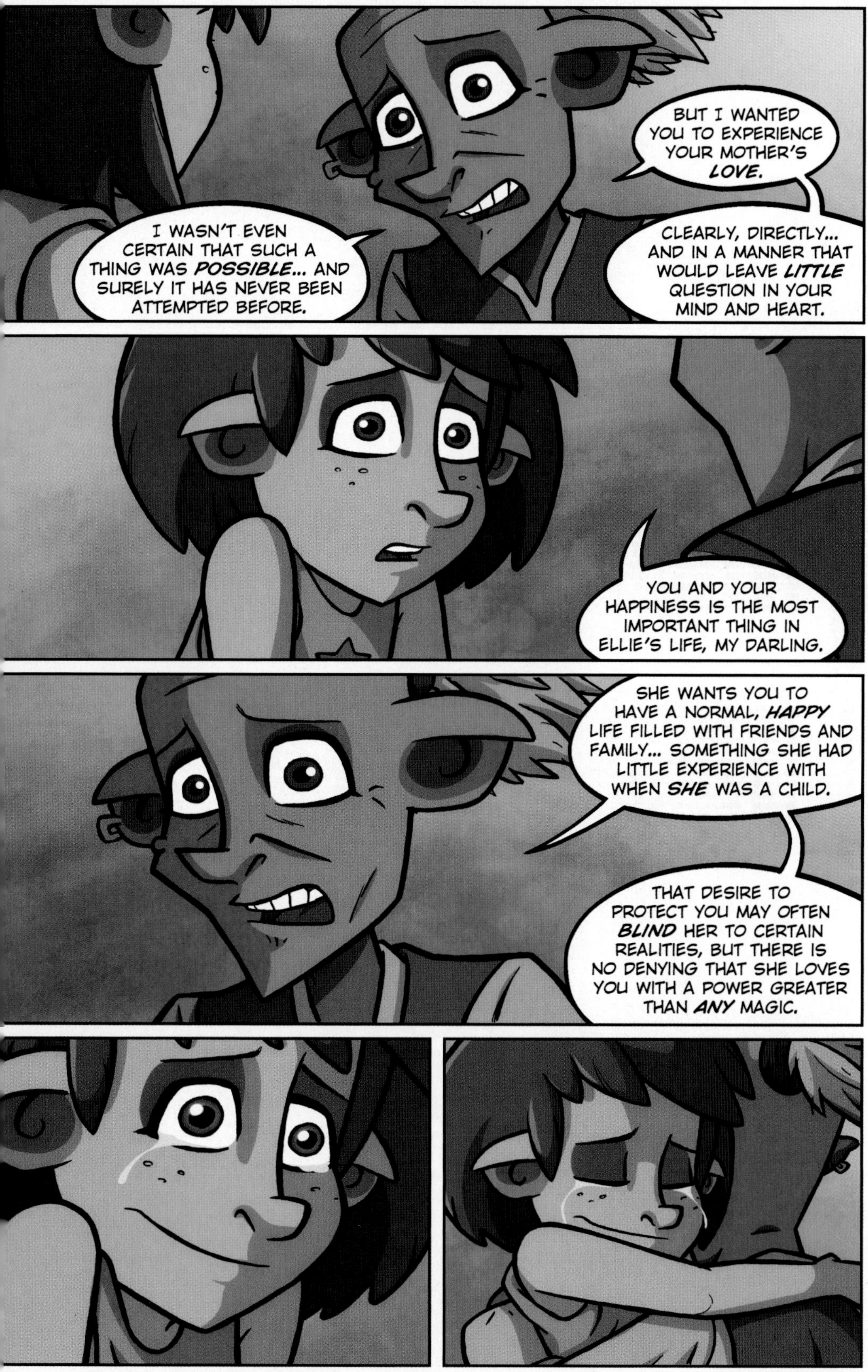
I WASN'T EVEN CERTAIN THAT SUCH A THING WAS POSSIBLE... AND SURELY IT HAS NEVER BEEN ATTEMPTED BEFORE.
BUT I WANTED YOU TO EXPERIENCE YOUR MOTHER'S LOVE.
CLEARLY, DIRECTLY... AND IN A MANNER THAT WOULD LEAVE LITTLE QUESTION IN YOUR MIND AND HEART.
YOU AND YOUR HAPPINESS IS THE MOST IMPORTANT THING IN ELLIE'S LIFE, MY DARLING.
SHE WANTS YOU TO HAVE A NORMAL, HAPPY LIFE FILLED WITH FRIENDS AND FAMILY... SOMETHING SHE HAD LITTLE EXPERIENCE WITH WHEN SHE WAS A CHILD.
THAT DESIRE TO PROTECT YOU MAY OFTEN BLIND HER TO CERTAIN REALITIES, BUT THERE IS NO DENYING THAT SHE LOVES YOU WITH A POWER GREATER THAN ANY MAGIC.

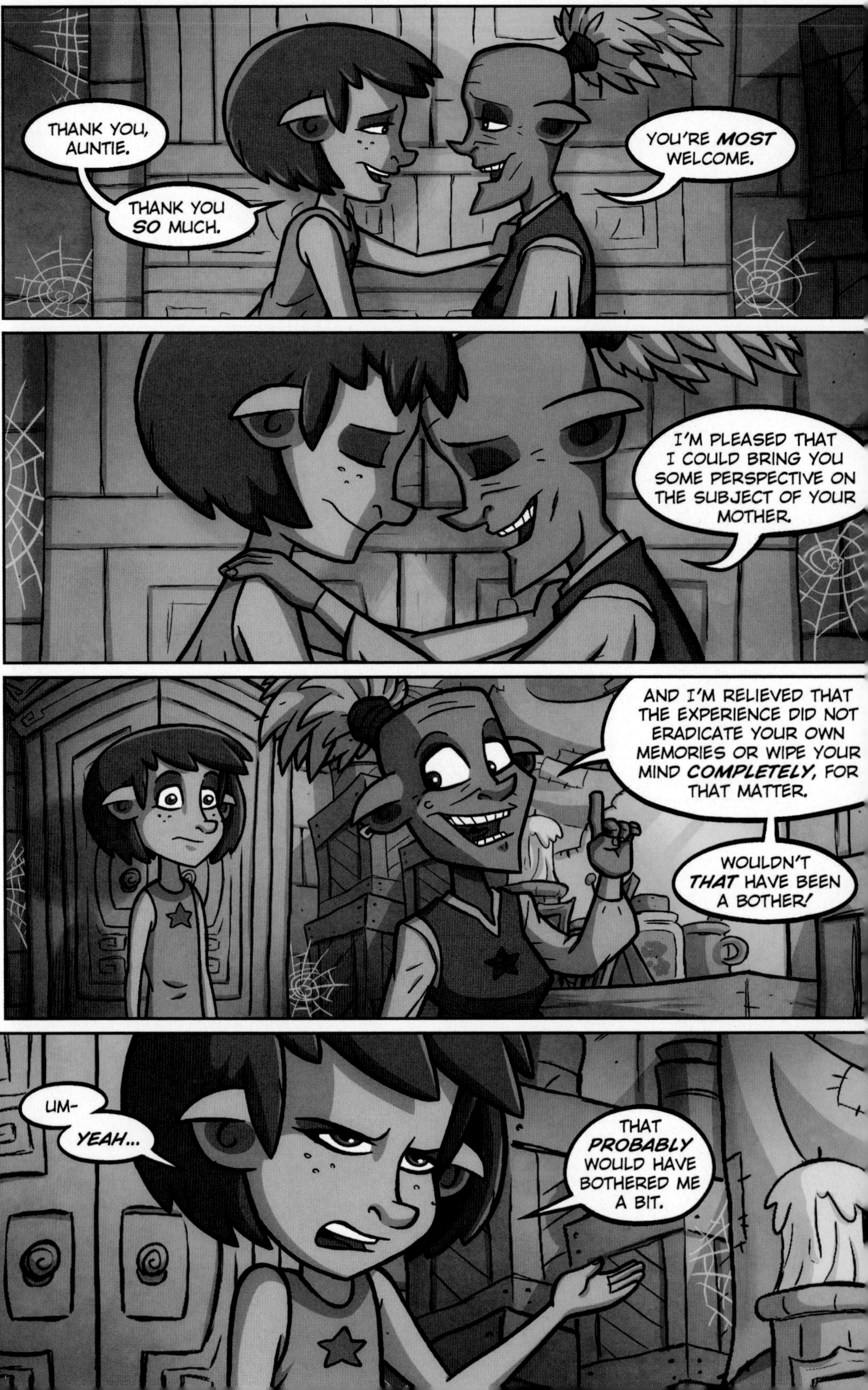
THANK YOU, AUNTIE.
THANK YOU *SO* MUCH.
YOU'RE *MOST* WELCOME.
I'M PLEASED THAT I COULD BRING YOU SOME PERSPECTIVE ON THE SUBJECT OF YOUR MOTHER.
AND I'M RELIEVED THAT THE EXPERIENCE DID NOT ERADICATE YOUR OWN MEMORIES OR WIPE YOUR MIND *COMPLETELY*, FOR THAT MATTER.
WOULDN'T *THAT* HAVE BEEN A BOTHER!
UM- *YEAH...*
THAT *PROBABLY* WOULD HAVE BOTHERED ME A BIT.

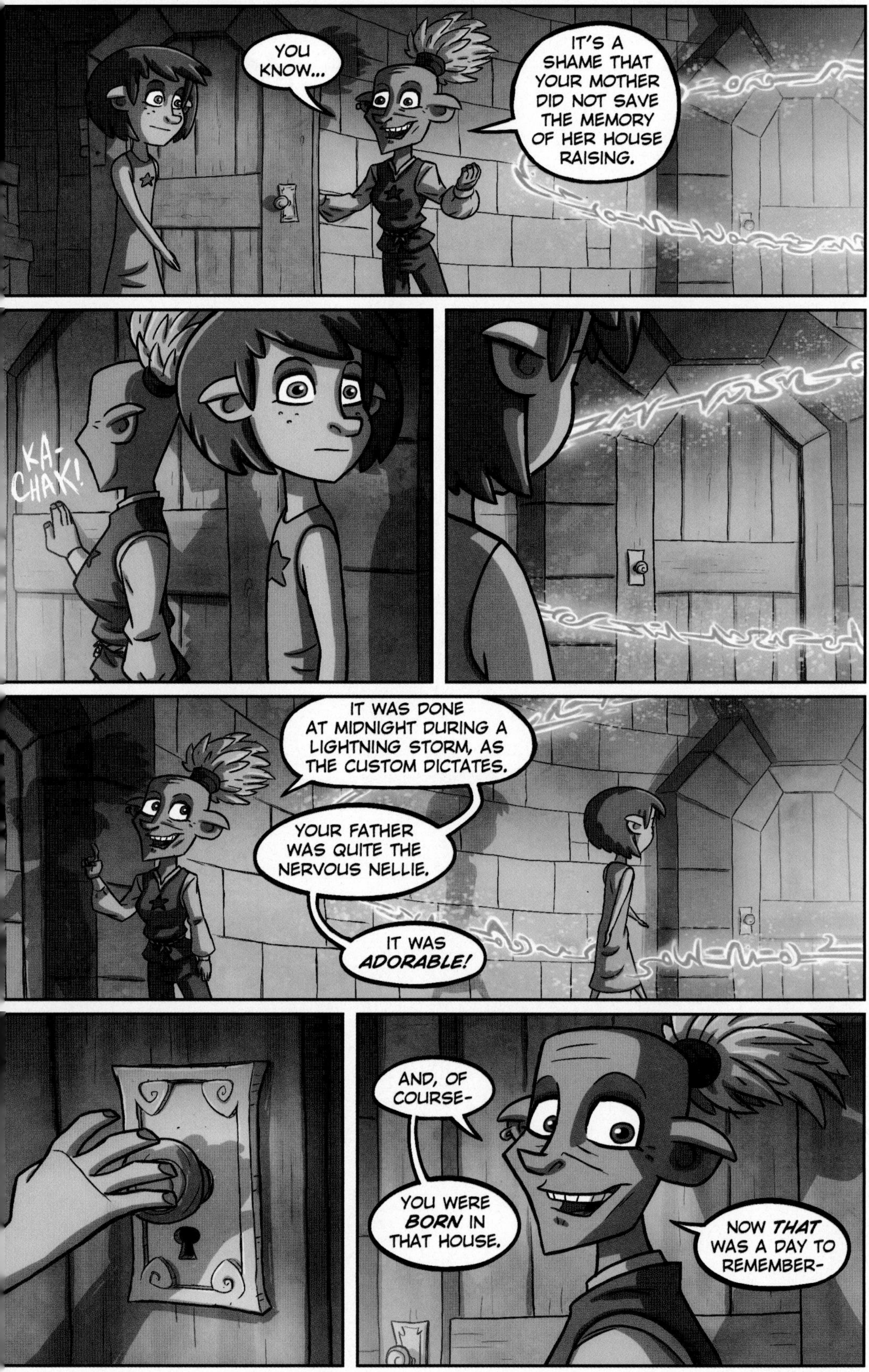
YOU KNOW...
IT'S A SHAME THAT YOUR MOTHER DID NOT SAVE THE MEMORY OF HER HOUSE RAISING.
KA-CHAK!
IT WAS DONE AT MIDNIGHT DURING A LIGHTNING STORM, AS THE CUSTOM DICTATES.
YOUR FATHER WAS QUITE THE NERVOUS NELLIE.
IT WAS *ADORABLE!*
AND, OF COURSE-
YOU WERE *BORN* IN THAT HOUSE.
NOW *THAT* WAS A DAY TO REMEMBER-

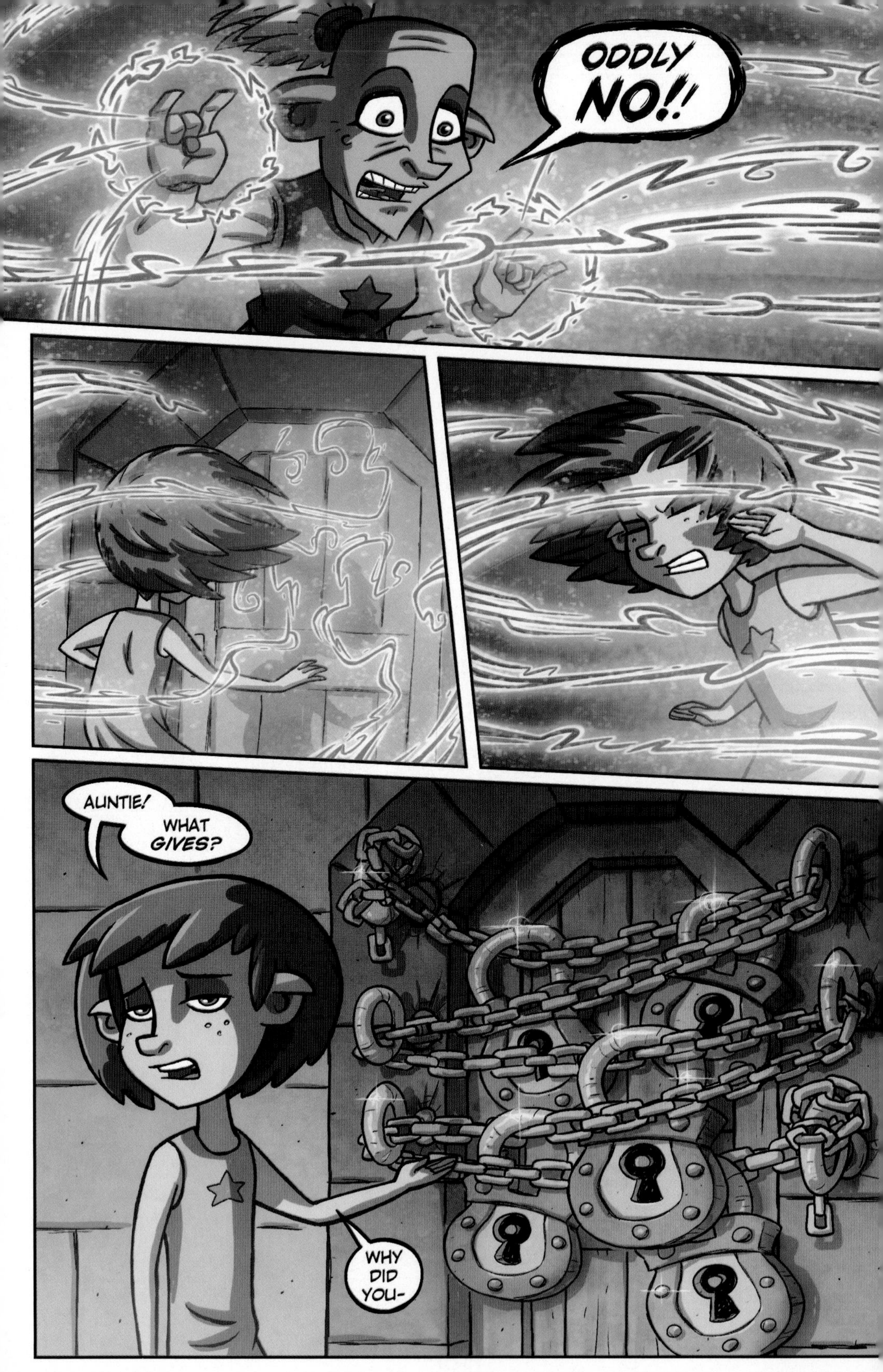
ODDLY NO!!
AUNTIE!
WHAT GIVES?
WHY DID YOU-

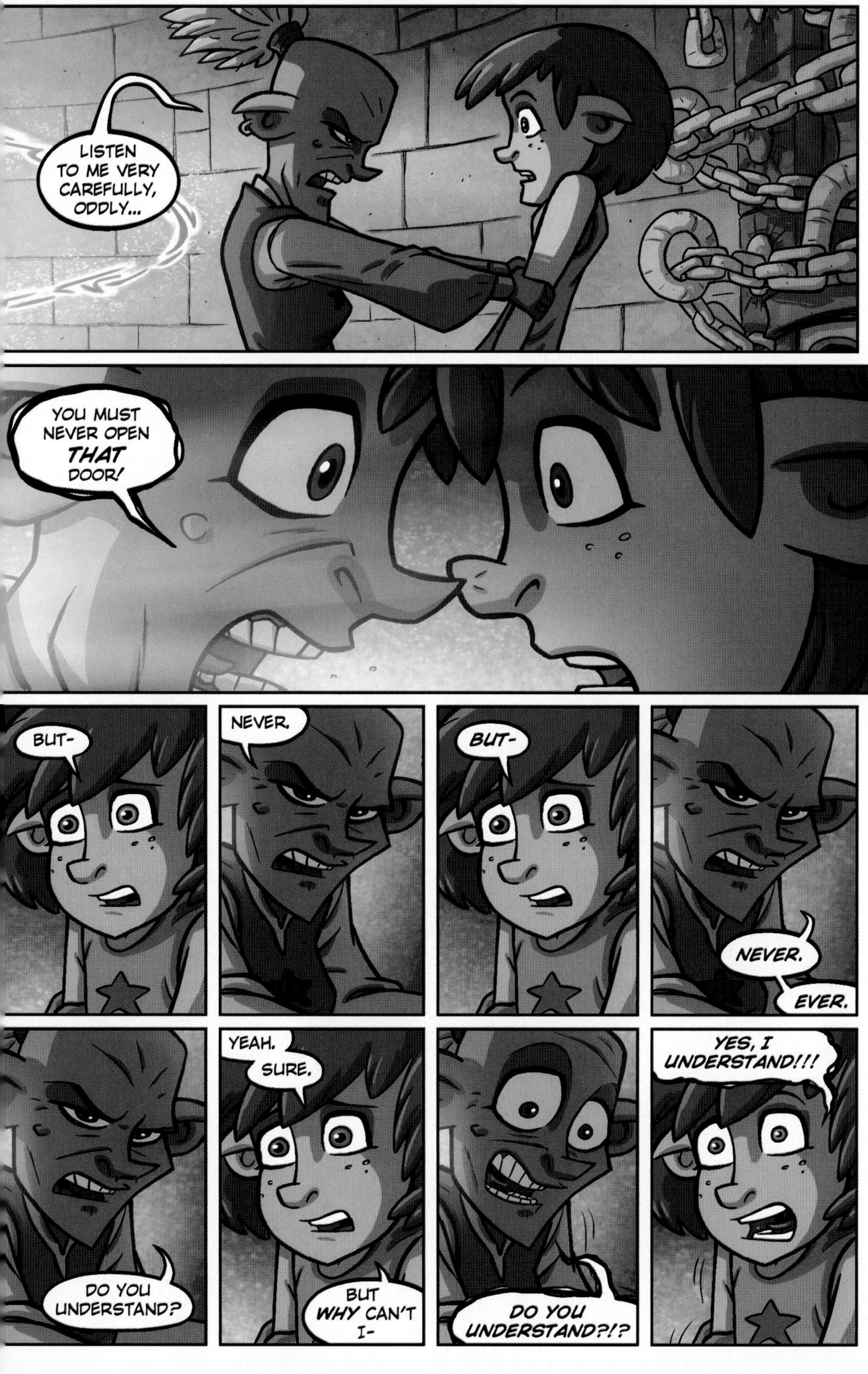
LISTEN TO ME VERY CAREFULLY, ODDLY...
YOU MUST NEVER OPEN THAT DOOR!
BUT-
NEVER.
BUT-
NEVER.
EVER.
DO YOU UNDERSTAND?
YEAH.
SURE.
BUT WHY CAN'T I-
DO YOU UNDERSTAND?!?
YES, I UNDERSTAND!!!

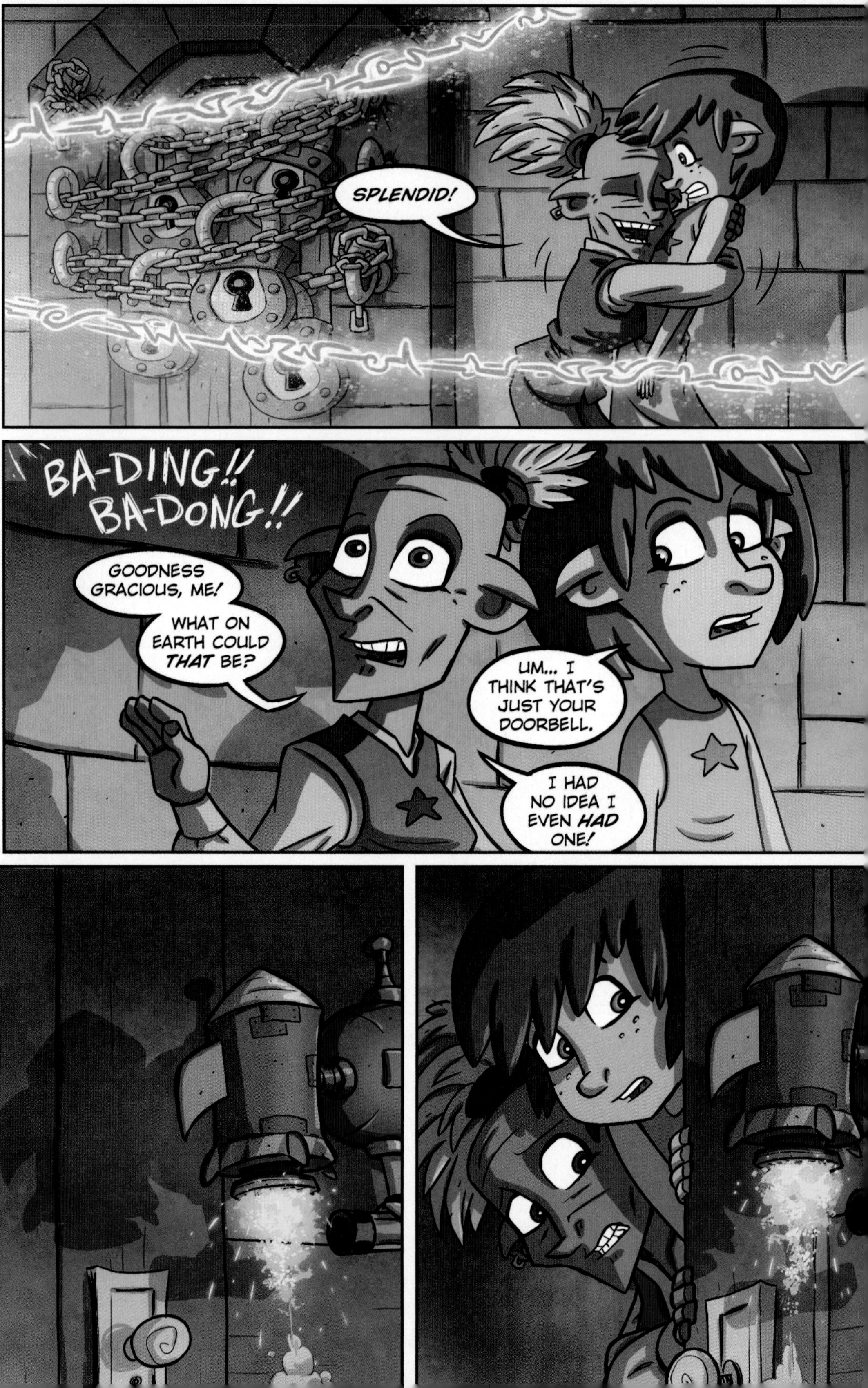
SPLENDID!
BA-DING!! BA-DONG!!
GOODNESS GRACIOUS, ME!
WHAT ON EARTH COULD *THAT* BE?
UM... I THINK THAT'S JUST YOUR DOORBELL.
I HAD NO IDEA I EVEN *HAD* ONE!

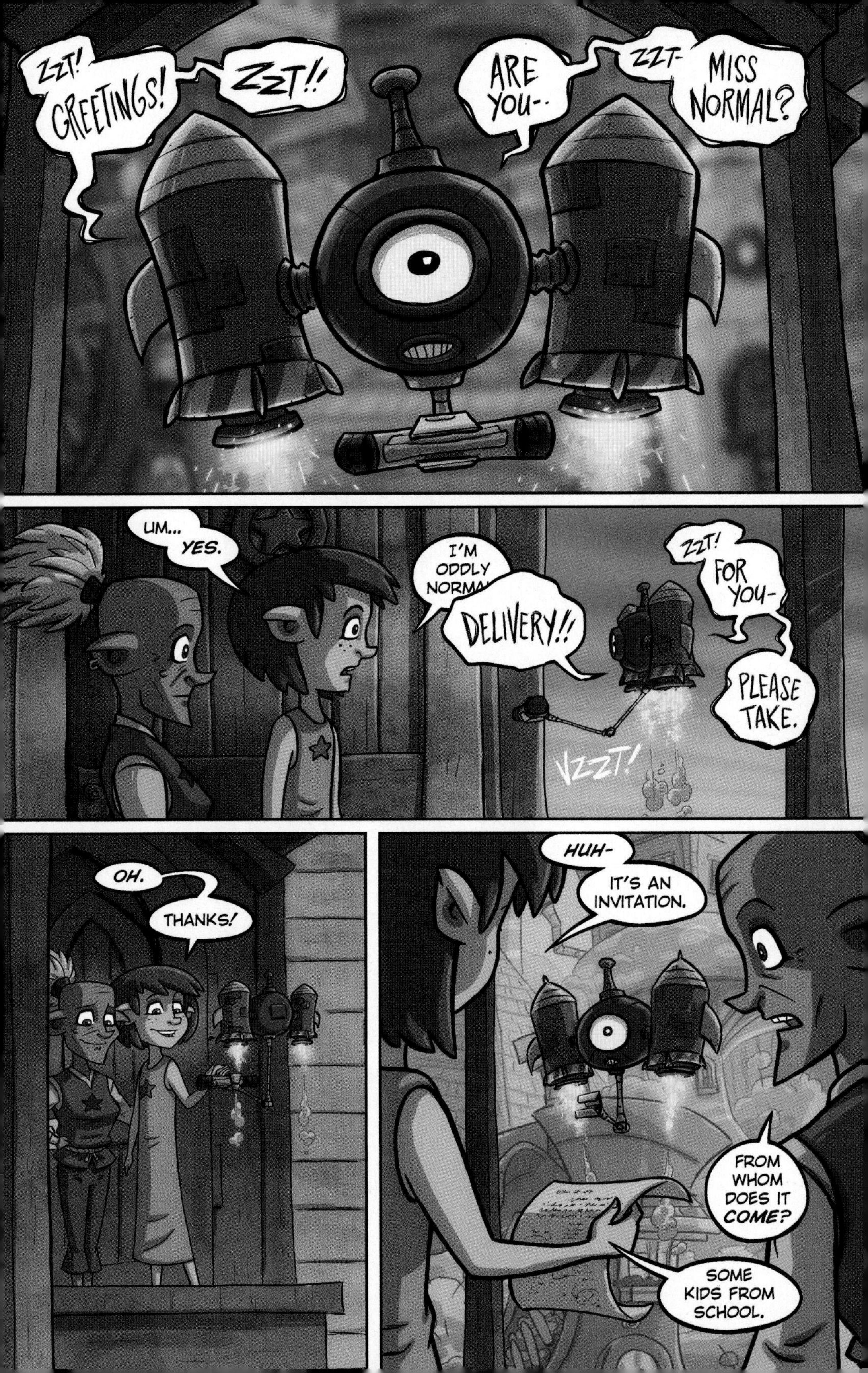
ZZT! GREETINGS!
ZZZT!!
ARE YOU-.
ZZT- MISS NORMAL?
UM... YES.
I'M ODDLY NORMAL
DELIVERY!!
ZZT! FOR YOU-
PLEASE TAKE.
VZZT!
OH.
THANKS!
HUH-
IT'S AN INVITATION.
FROM WHOM DOES IT COME?
SOME KIDS FROM SCHOOL.

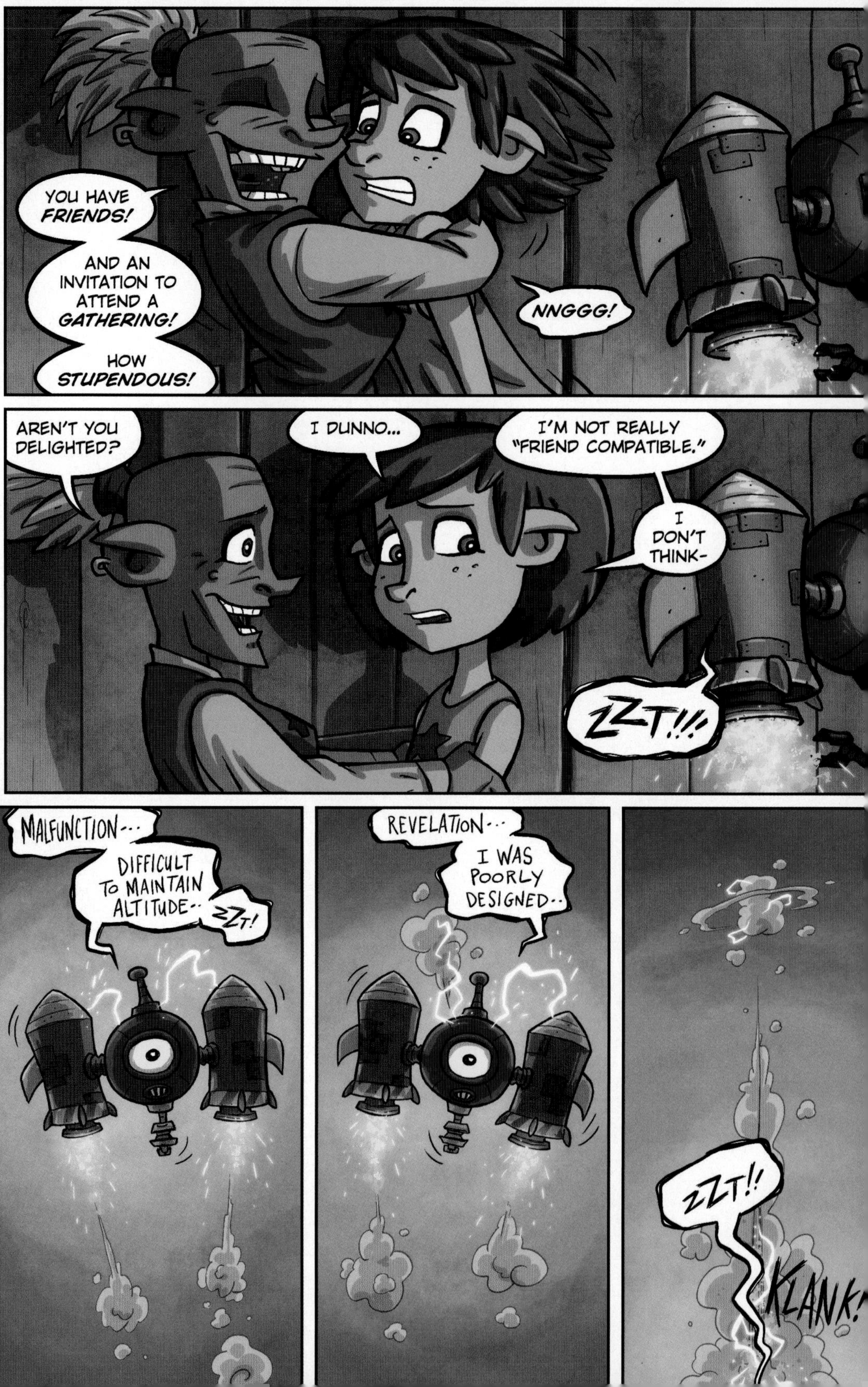
YOU HAVE FRIENDS!
AND AN INVITATION TO ATTEND A GATHERING!
HOW STUPENDOUS!
NNGGG!
AREN'T YOU DELIGHTED?
I DUNNO...
I'M NOT REALLY "FRIEND COMPATIBLE."
I DON'T THINK-
ZZT!!!
MALFUNCTION...
DIFFICULT TO MAINTAIN ALTITUDE..
ZZT!
REVELATION...
I WAS POORLY DESIGNED..
ZZT!!
KLANK!

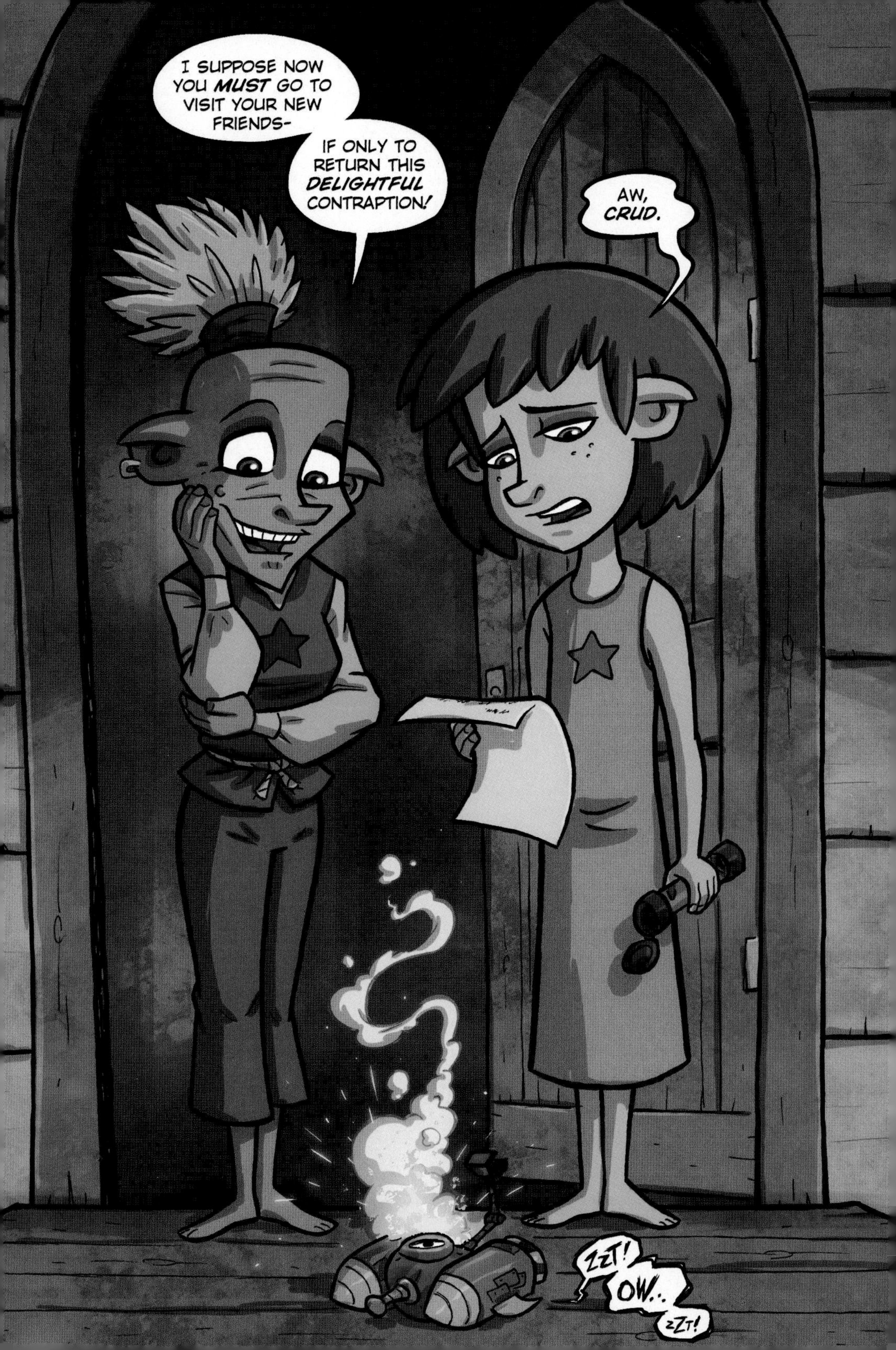
I SUPPOSE NOW YOU MUST GO TO VISIT YOUR NEW FRIENDS-
IF ONLY TO RETURN THIS DELIGHTFUL CONTRAPTION!
AW, CRUD.
ZZT!
OW..
ZZT!

Chapter 8
Kindred Spirits

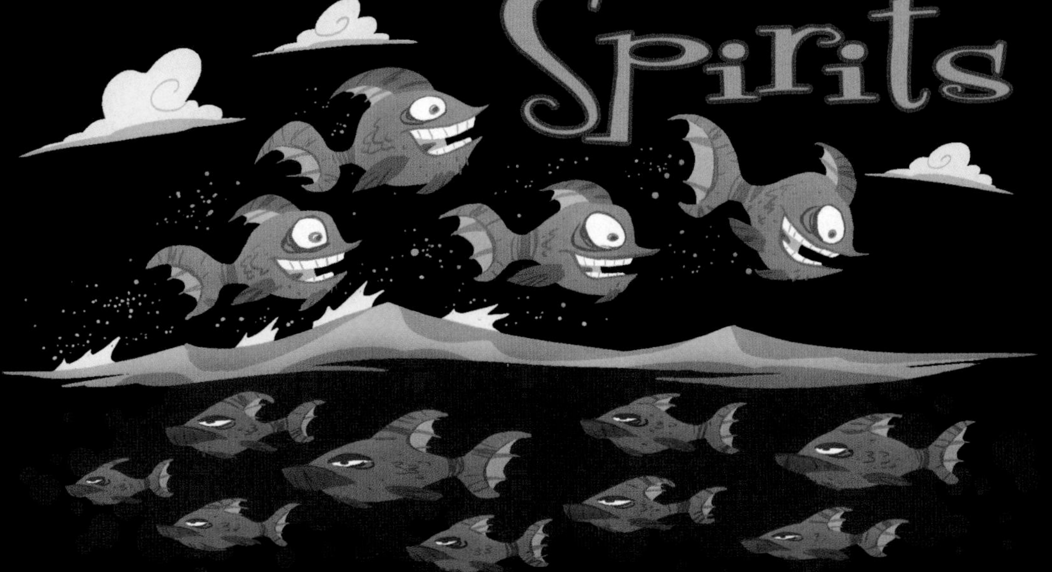

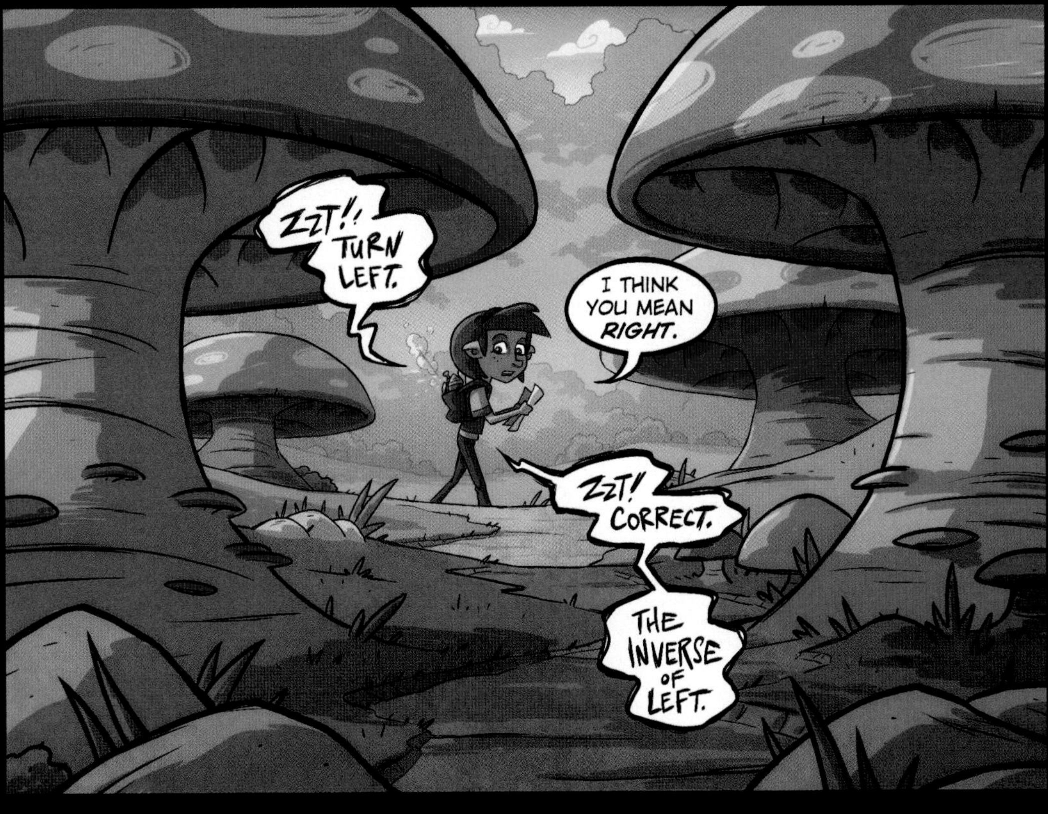
ZZT!! TURN LEFT.
I THINK YOU MEAN *RIGHT*.
ZZT! CORRECT.
THE INVERSE OF LEFT.

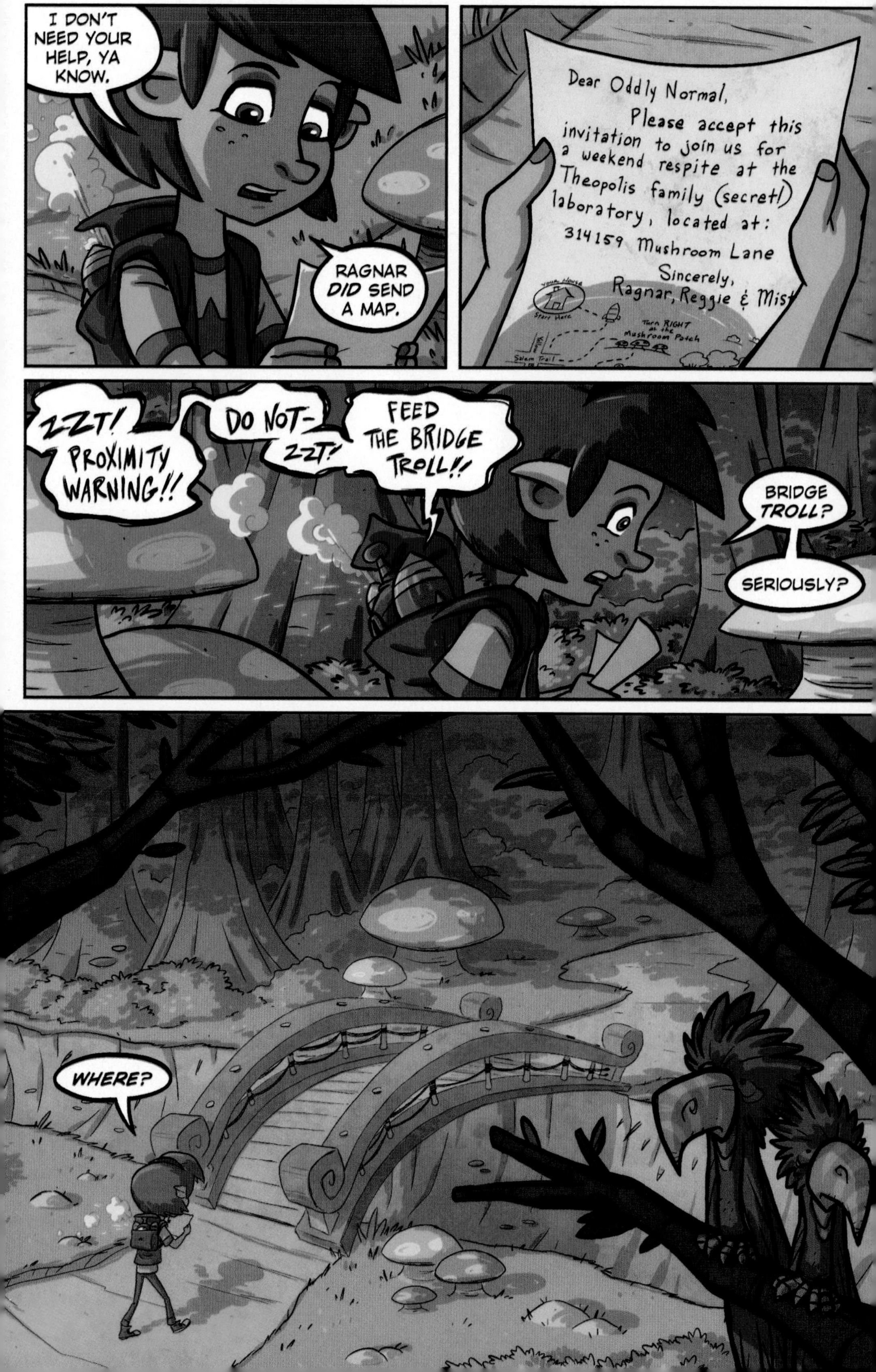
I DON'T NEED YOUR HELP, YA KNOW.
RAGNAR *DID* SEND A MAP.
Dear Oddly Normal,
Please accept this invitation to join us for a weekend respite at the Theopolis family (secret!) laboratory, located at:
314159 Mushroom Lane
Sincerely,
Ragnar, Reggie & Mist
Your House
Start Here
Turn RIGHT at the Mushroom Patch
Yellow
Salem Trail
ZZT! PROXIMITY WARNING!!
DO NOT-
ZZT!
FEED THE BRIDGE TROLL!!
BRIDGE *TROLL?*
SERIOUSLY?
WHERE?

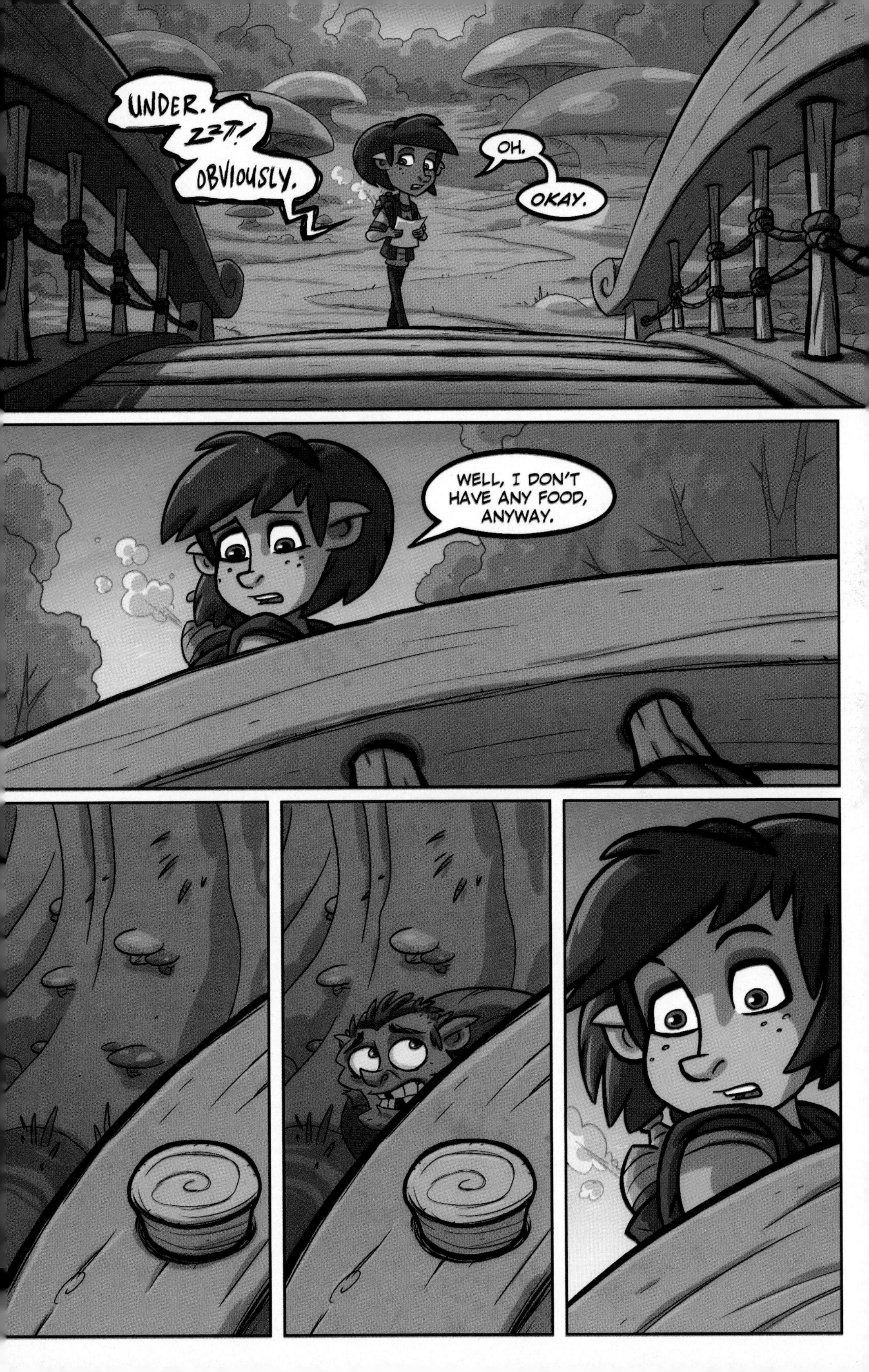
UNDER.
ZZT!
OBVIOUSLY.
OH.
OKAY.
WELL, I DON'T HAVE ANY FOOD, ANYWAY.

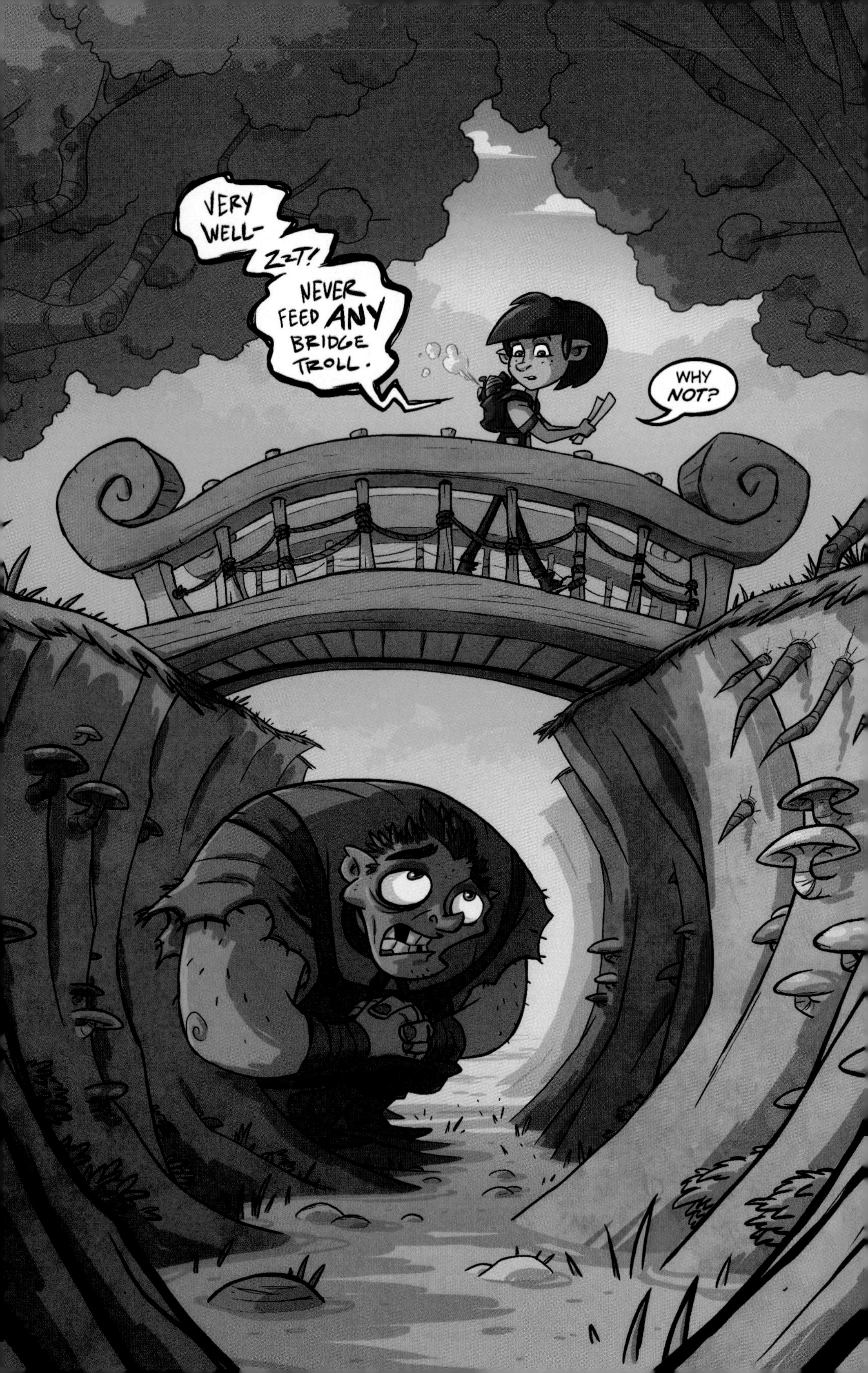
VERY WELL-
ZzT!
NEVER FEED ANY BRIDGE TROLL.
WHY NOT?

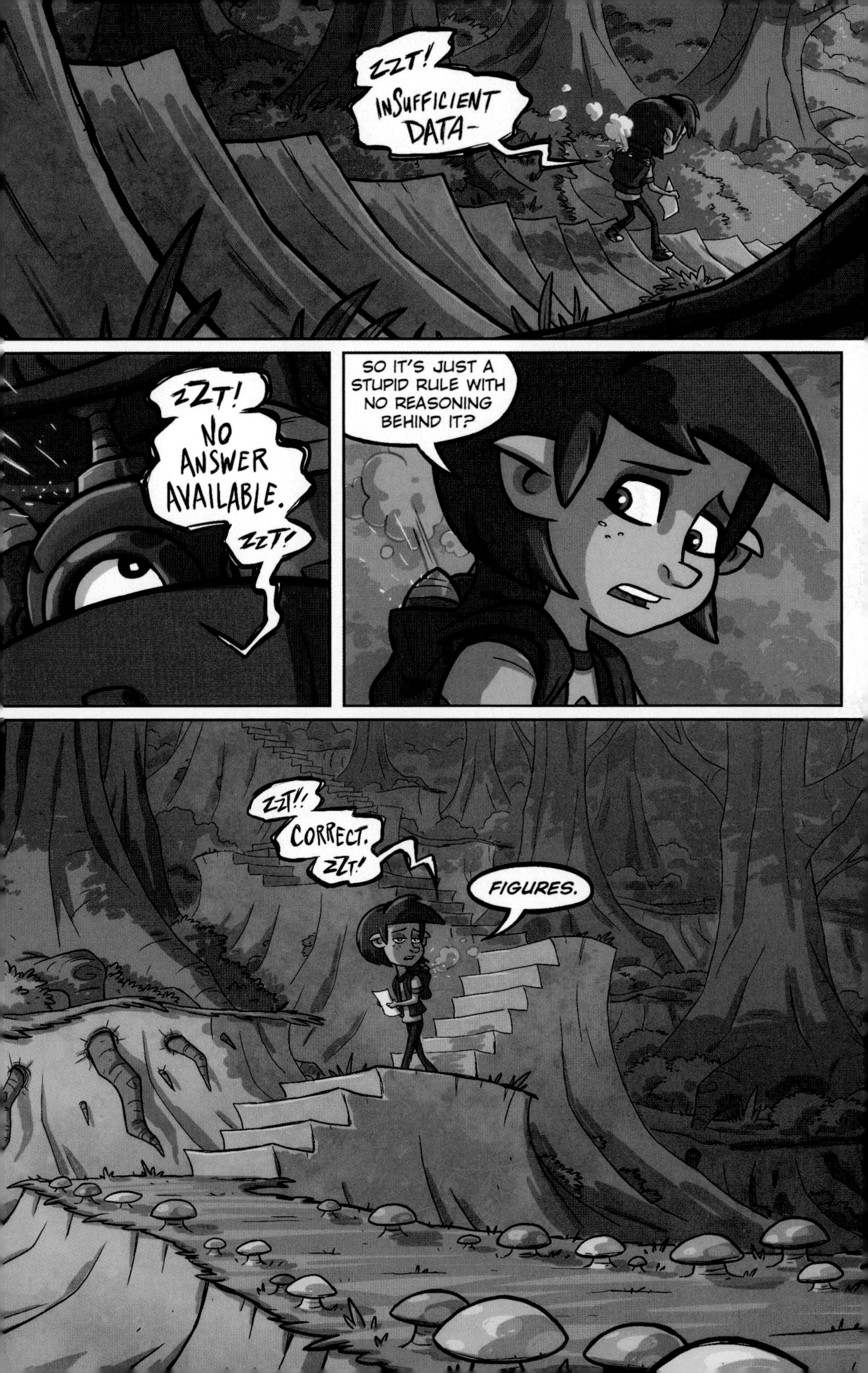

ZZT! INSUFFICIENT DATA-
ZZT! NO ANSWER AVAILABLE. ZZT!
SO IT'S JUST A STUPID RULE WITH NO REASONING BEHIND IT?
ZZT!! CORRECT. ZZT!
FIGURES.

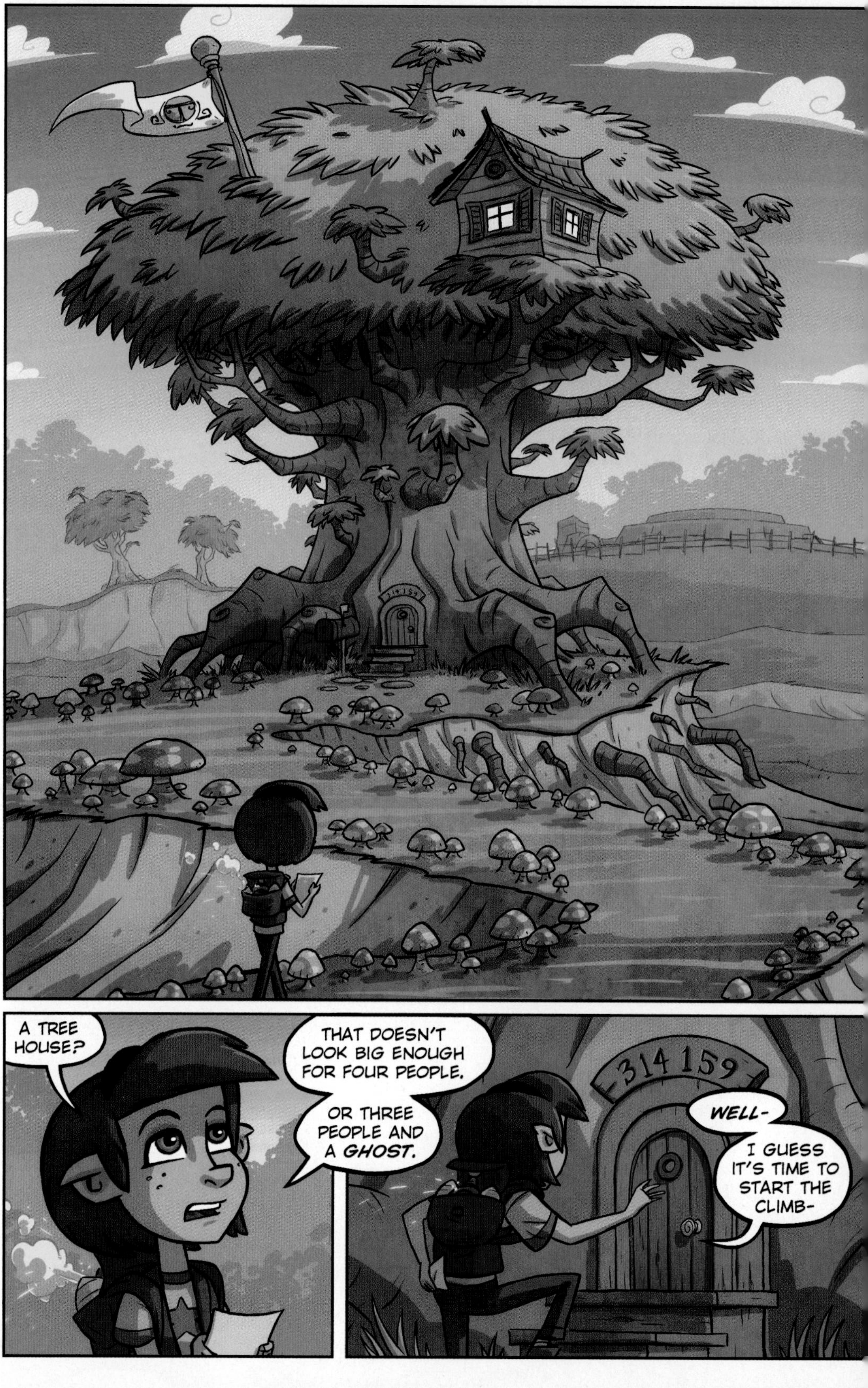
A TREE HOUSE?
THAT DOESN'T LOOK BIG ENOUGH FOR FOUR PEOPLE.
OR THREE PEOPLE AND A *GHOST*.
314 159
WELL-
I GUESS IT'S TIME TO START THE CLIMB-

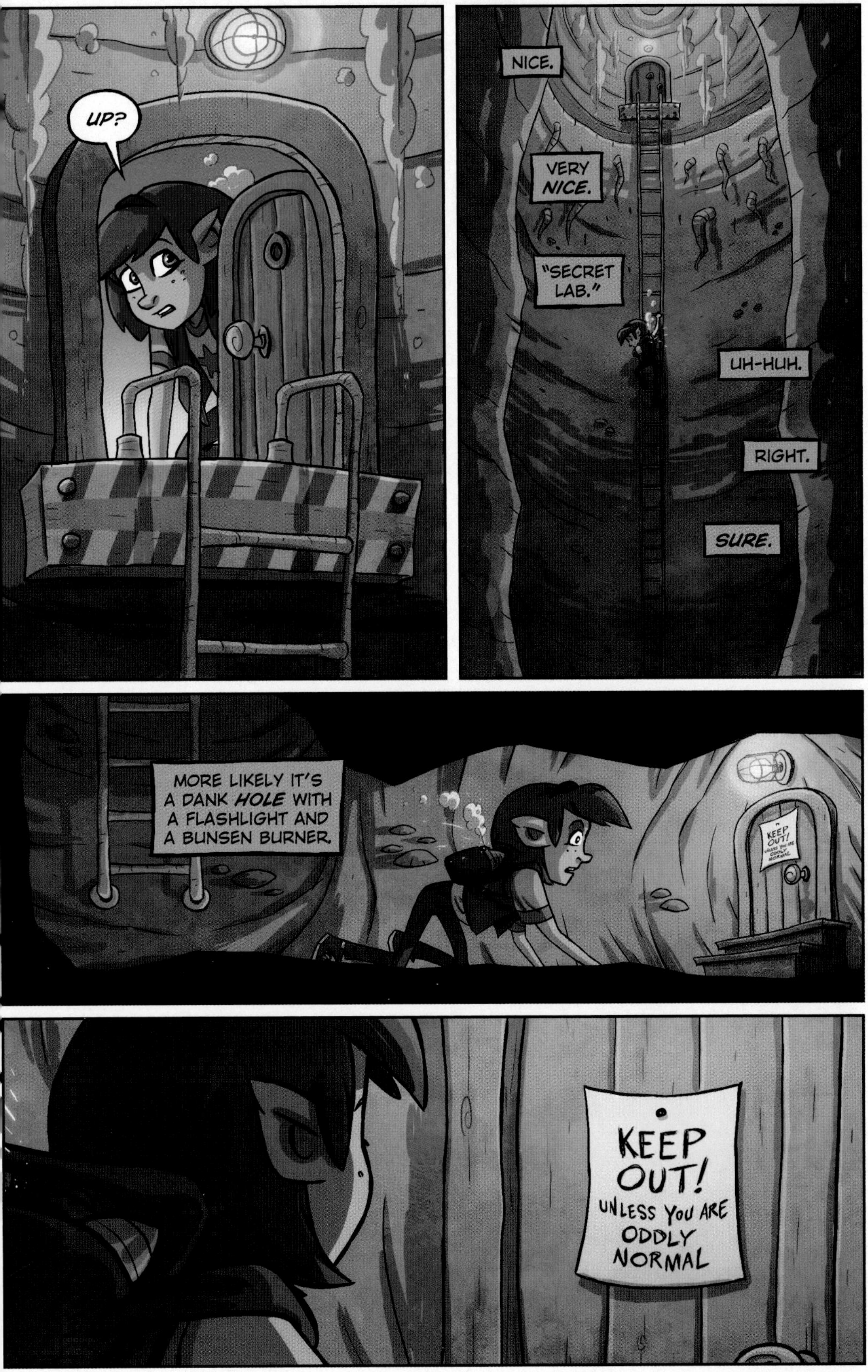
UP?
NICE.
VERY NICE.
"SECRET LAB."
UH-HUH.
RIGHT.
SURE.
MORE LIKELY IT'S A DANK HOLE WITH A FLASHLIGHT AND A BUNSEN BURNER.
KEEP OUT! UNLESS YOU ARE ODDLY NORMAL

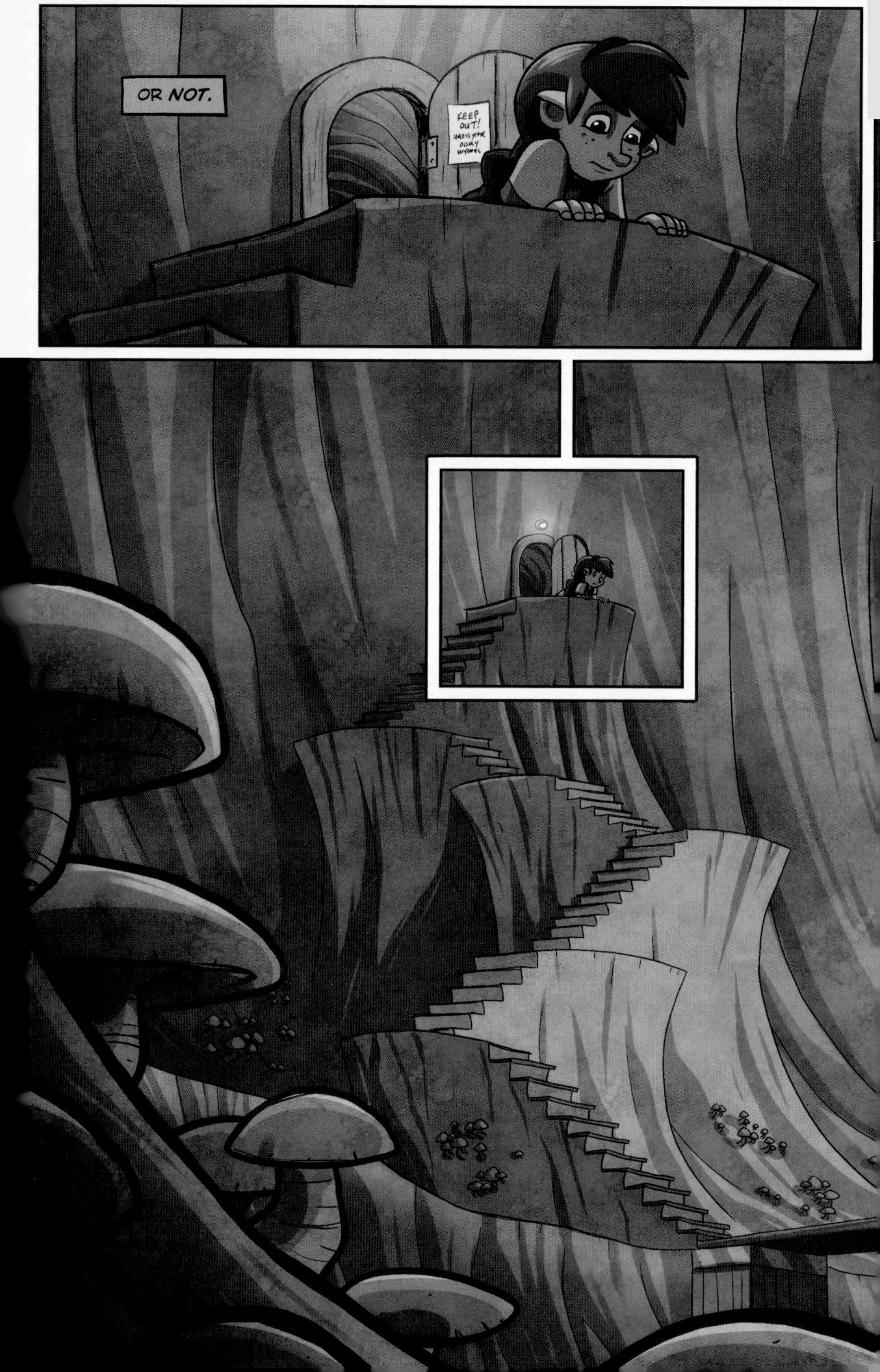
OR NOT.
KEEP OUT!

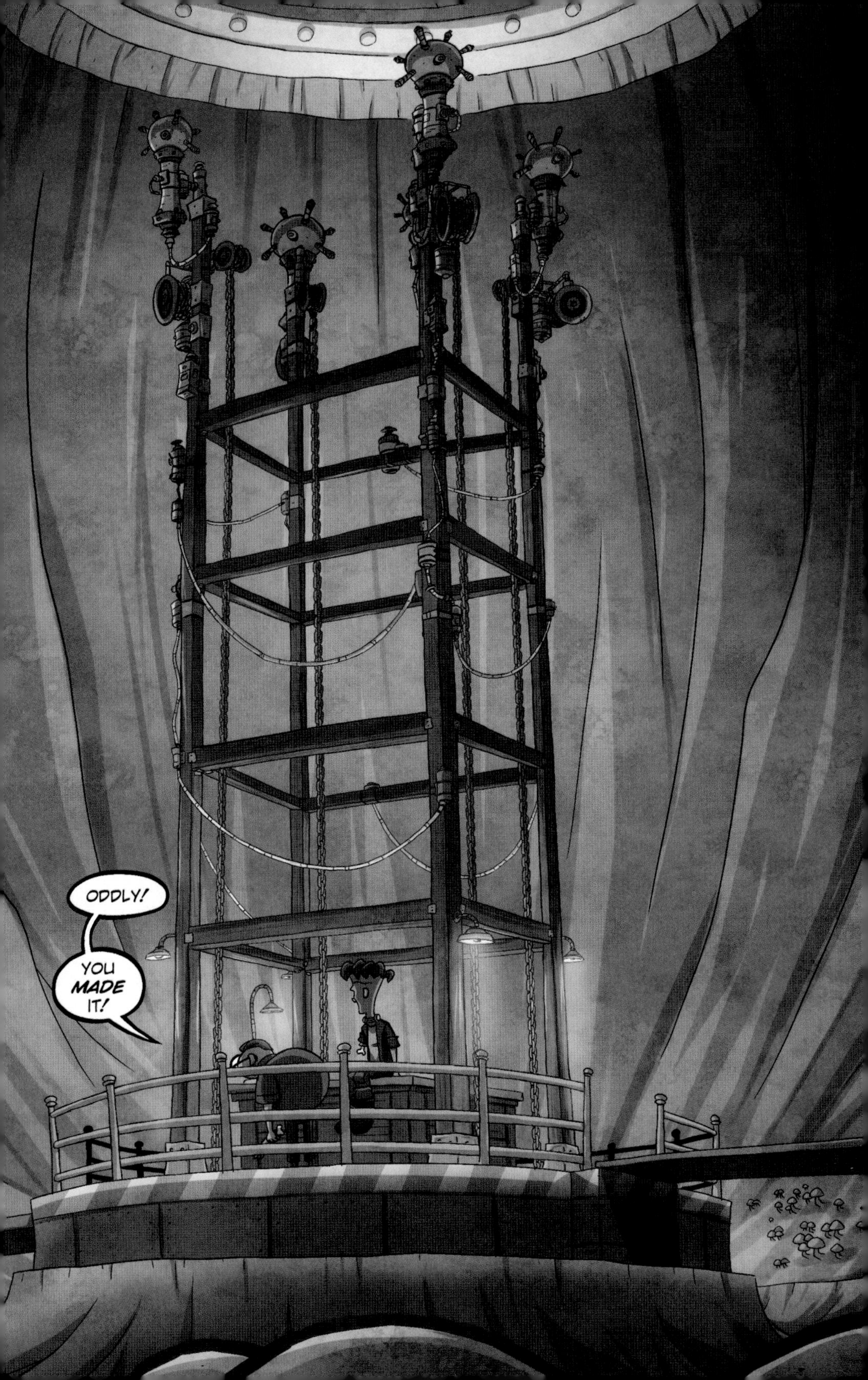
ODDLY!
YOU MADE IT!

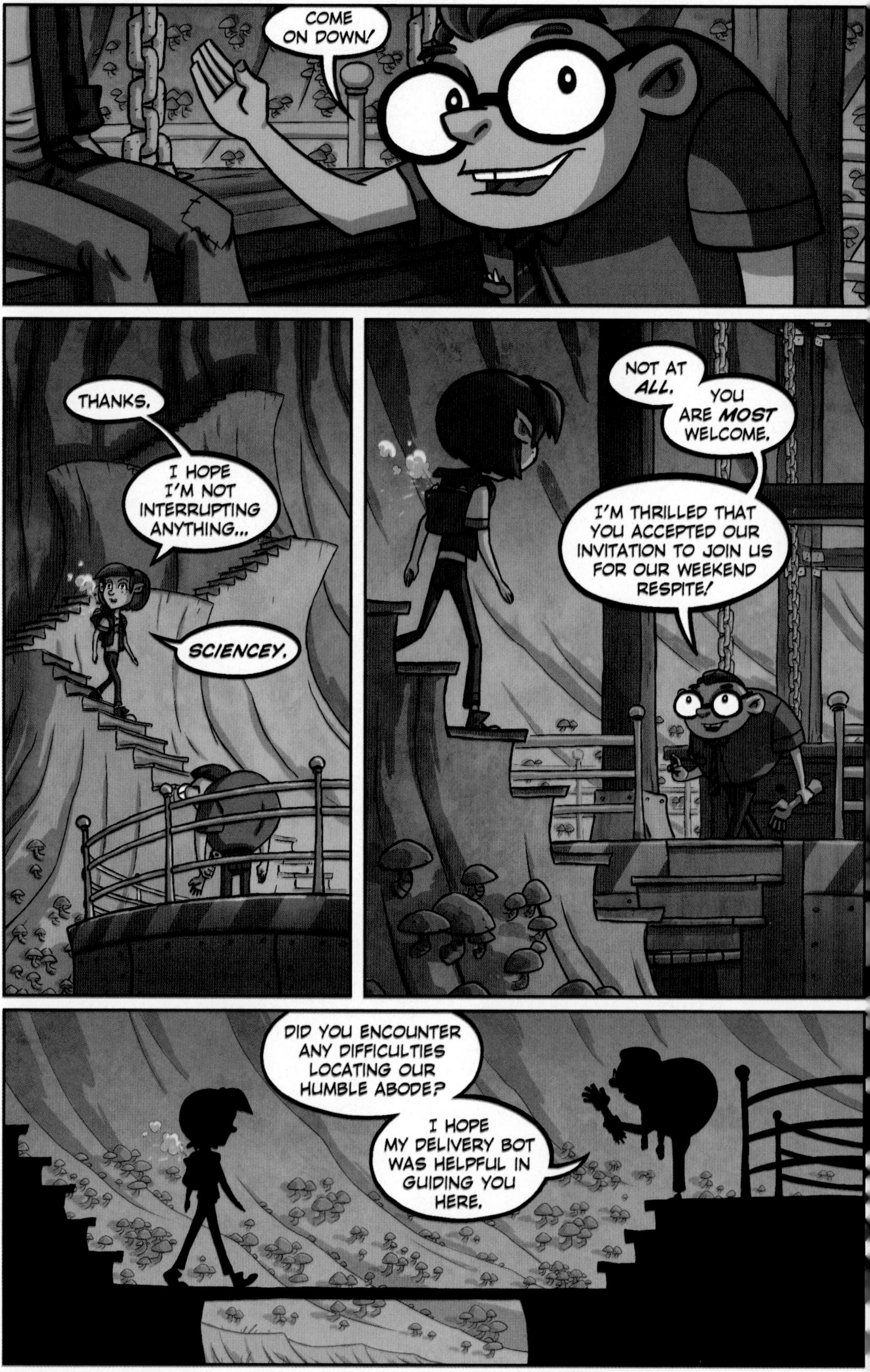
COME ON DOWN!
THANKS.
I HOPE I'M NOT INTERRUPTING ANYTHING...
SCIENCEY.
NOT AT ALL.
YOU ARE MOST WELCOME.
I'M THRILLED THAT YOU ACCEPTED OUR INVITATION TO JOIN US FOR OUR WEEKEND RESPITE!
DID YOU ENCOUNTER ANY DIFFICULTIES LOCATING OUR HUMBLE ABODE?
I HOPE MY DELIVERY BOT WAS HELPFUL IN GUIDING YOU HERE.

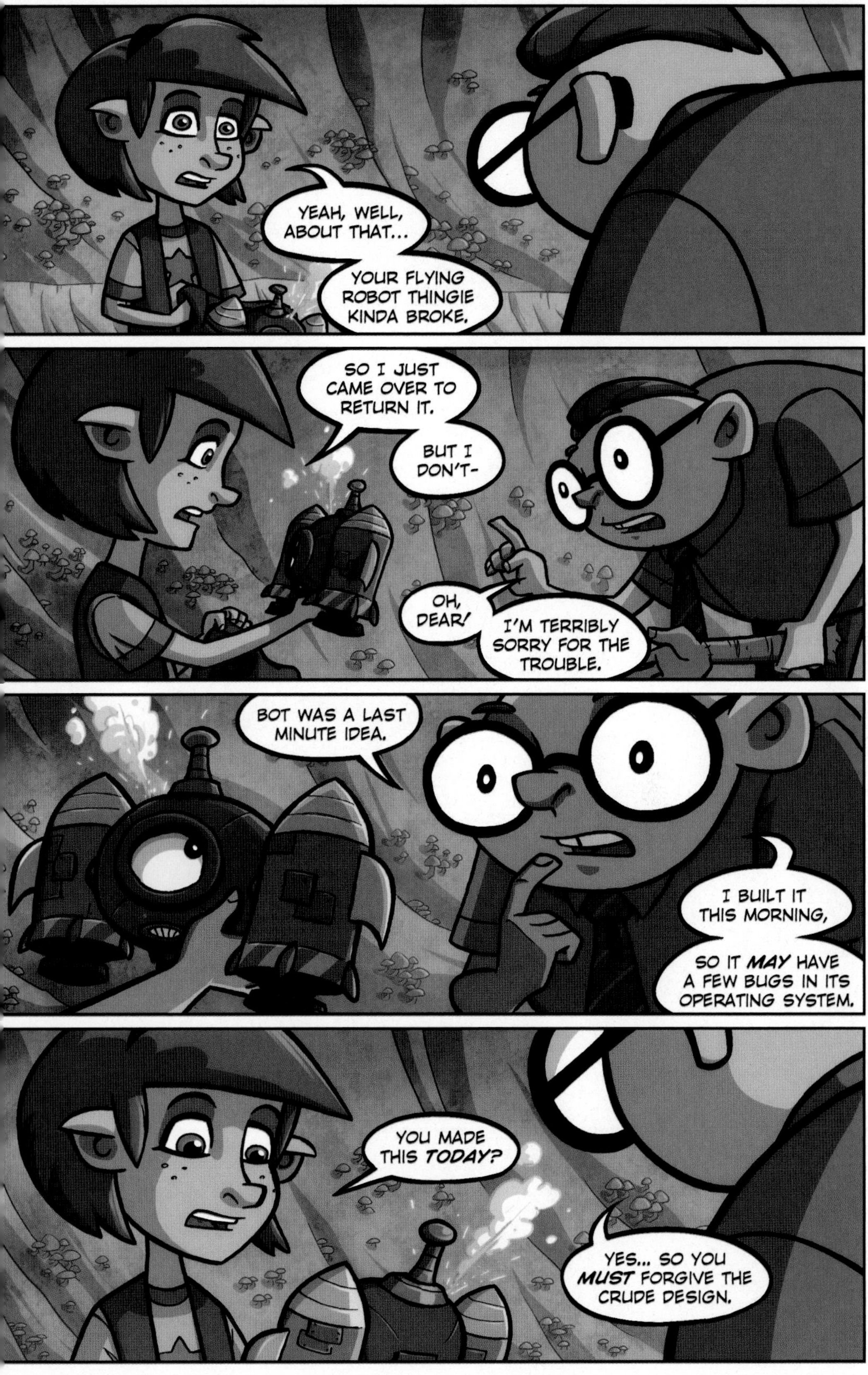
YEAH, WELL, ABOUT THAT...
YOUR FLYING ROBOT THINGIE KINDA BROKE.
SO I JUST CAME OVER TO RETURN IT.
BUT I DON'T-
OH, DEAR!
I'M TERRIBLY SORRY FOR THE TROUBLE.
BOT WAS A LAST MINUTE IDEA.
I BUILT IT THIS MORNING,
SO IT MAY HAVE A FEW BUGS IN ITS OPERATING SYSTEM.
YOU MADE THIS TODAY?
YES... SO YOU MUST FORGIVE THE CRUDE DESIGN.

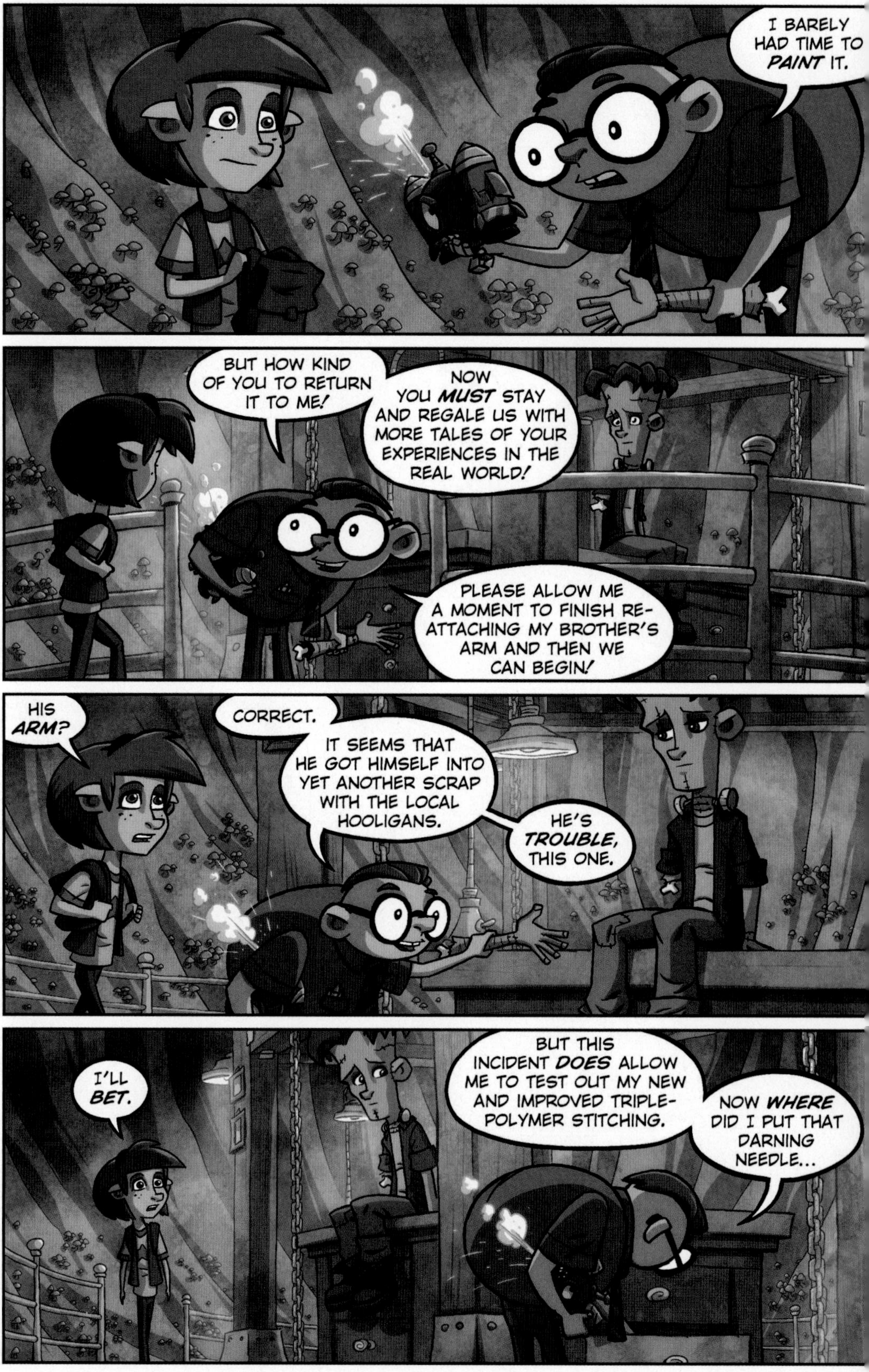
I BARELY HAD TIME TO *PAINT* IT.
BUT HOW KIND OF YOU TO RETURN IT TO ME!
NOW YOU *MUST* STAY AND REGALE US WITH MORE TALES OF YOUR EXPERIENCES IN THE REAL WORLD!
PLEASE ALLOW ME A MOMENT TO FINISH RE-ATTACHING MY BROTHER'S ARM AND THEN WE CAN BEGIN!
HIS *ARM?*
CORRECT.
IT SEEMS THAT HE GOT HIMSELF INTO YET ANOTHER SCRAP WITH THE LOCAL HOOLIGANS.
HE'S *TROUBLE,* THIS ONE.
I'LL *BET.*
BUT THIS INCIDENT *DOES* ALLOW ME TO TEST OUT MY NEW AND IMPROVED TRIPLE-POLYMER STITCHING.
NOW *WHERE* DID I PUT THAT DARNING NEEDLE...

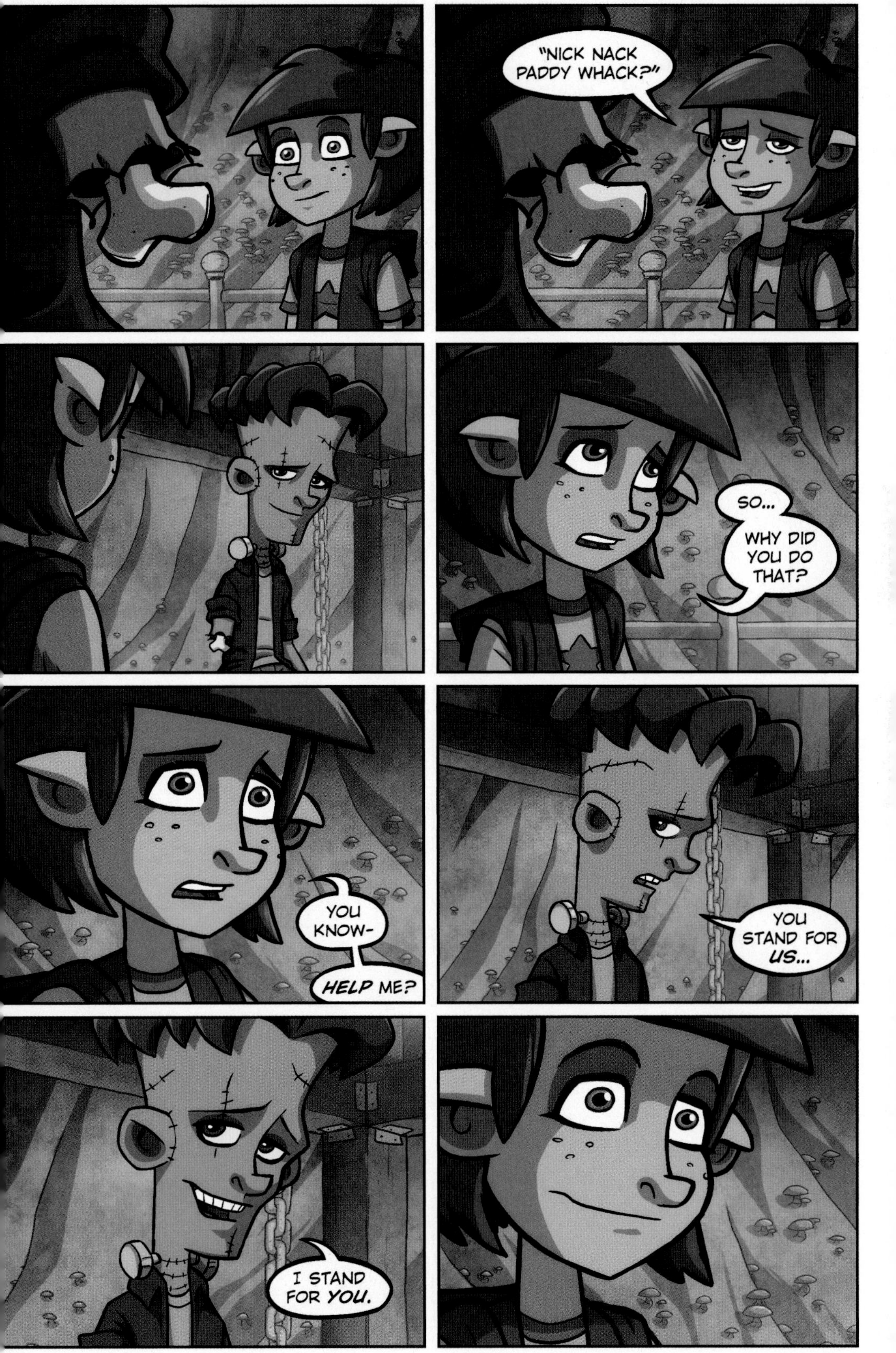
"NICK NACK PADDY WHACK?"
SO...
WHY DID YOU DO THAT?
YOU KNOW-
HELP ME?
YOU STAND FOR US...
I STAND FOR YOU.

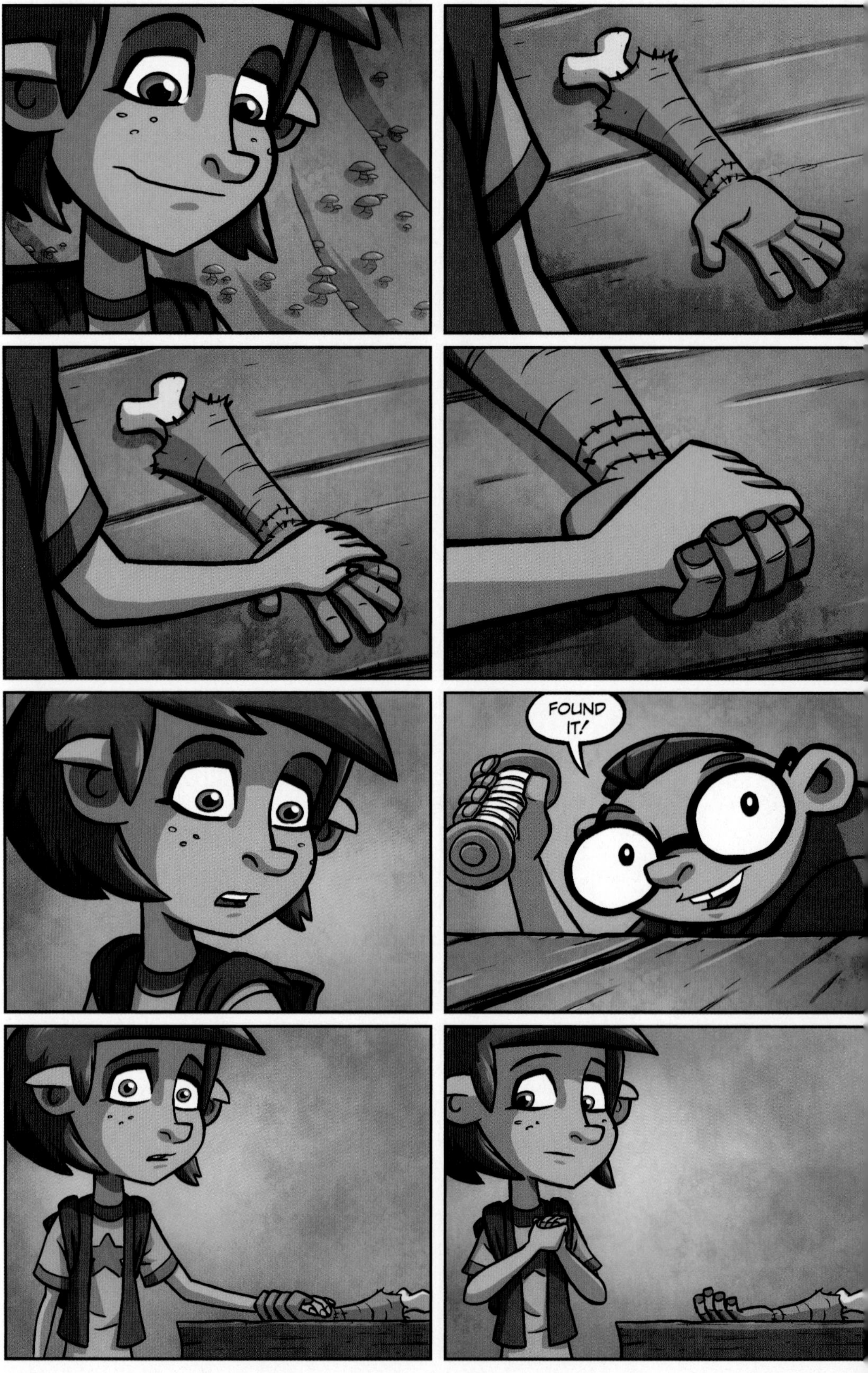
FOUND IT!

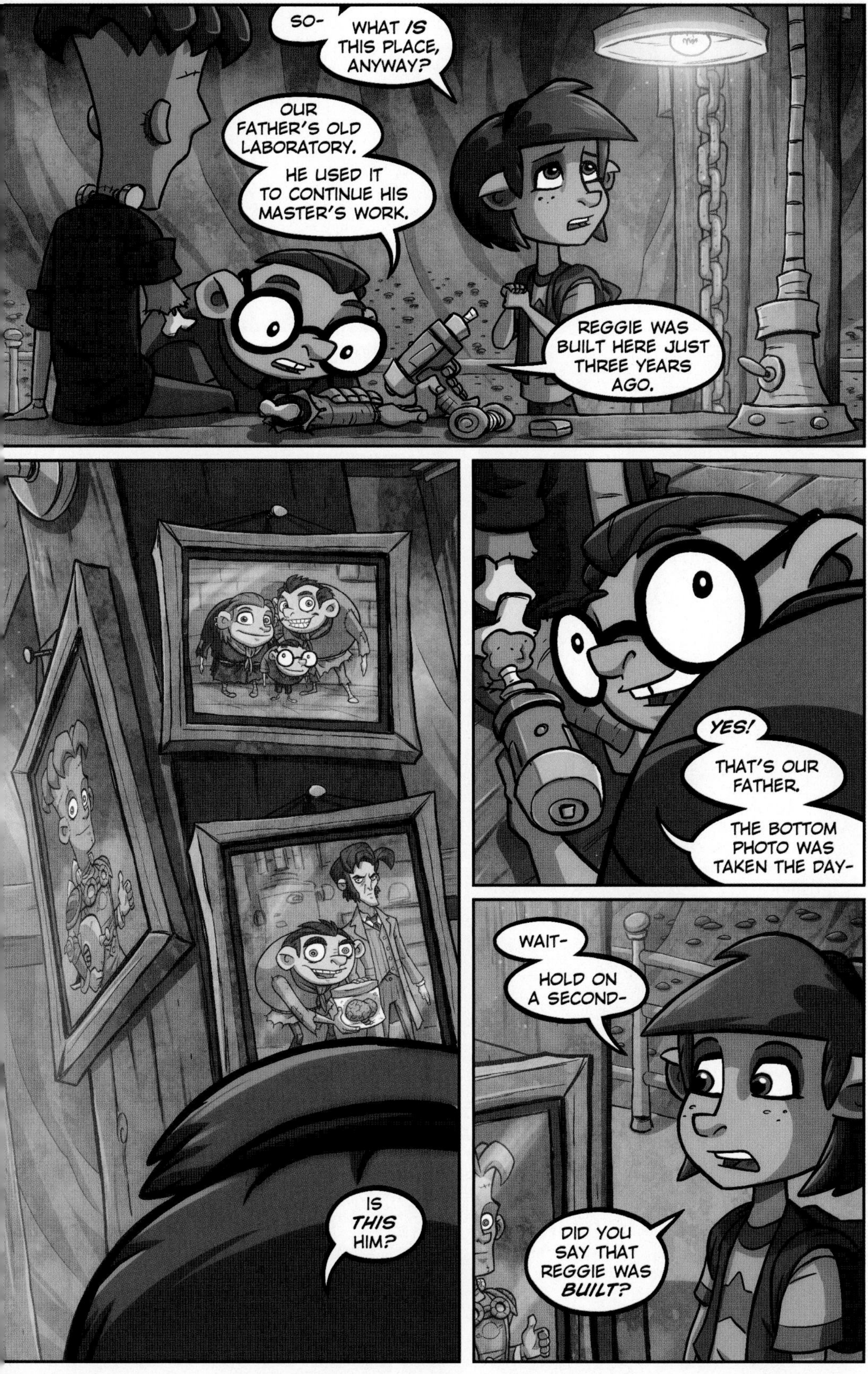
SO-
WHAT *IS* THIS PLACE, ANYWAY?
OUR FATHER'S OLD LABORATORY.
HE USED IT TO CONTINUE HIS MASTER'S WORK.
REGGIE WAS BUILT HERE JUST THREE YEARS AGO.
IS *THIS* HIM?
YES!
THAT'S OUR FATHER.
THE BOTTOM PHOTO WAS TAKEN THE DAY-
WAIT-
HOLD ON A SECOND-
DID YOU SAY THAT REGGIE WAS *BUILT?*

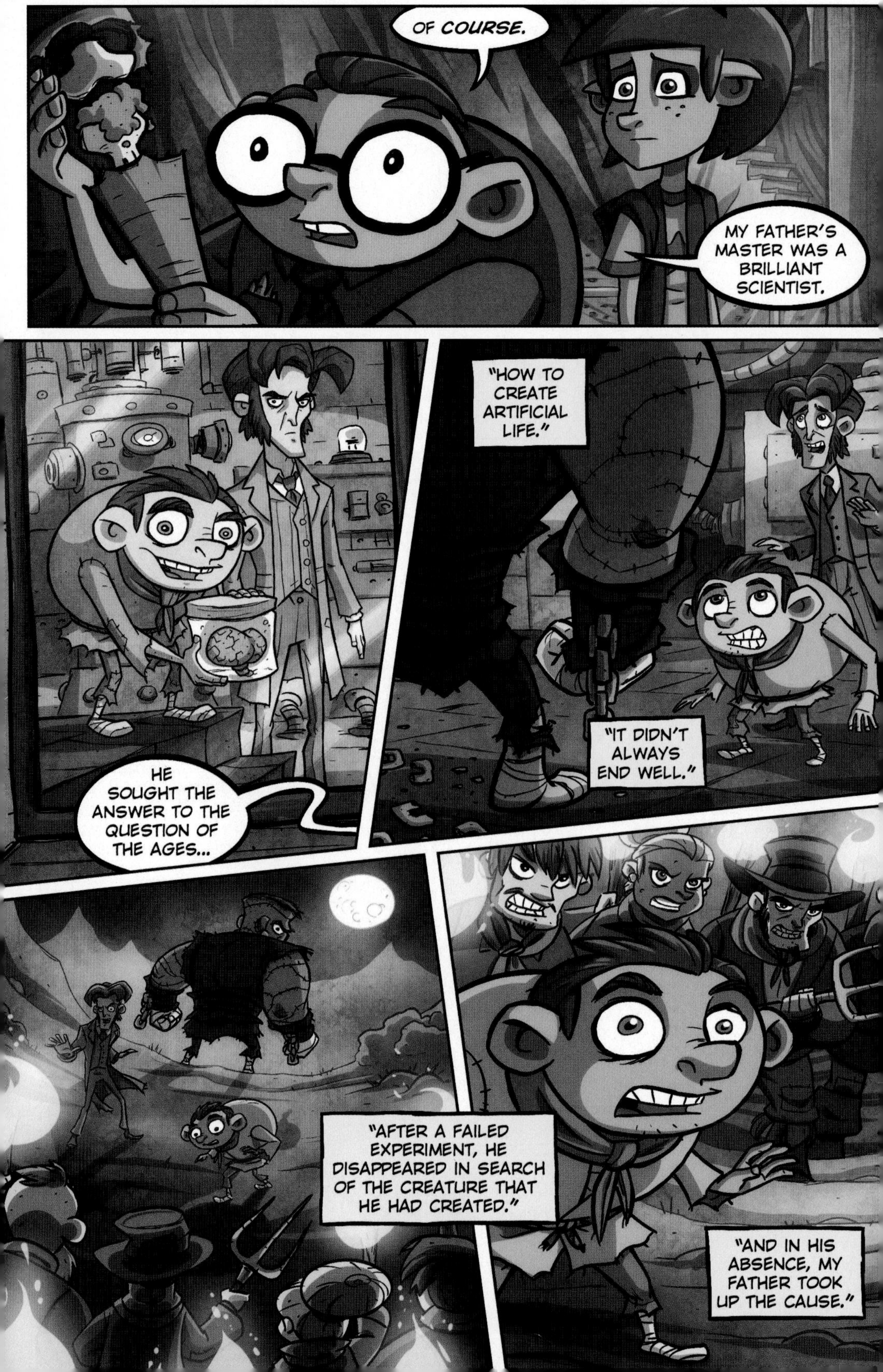
OF COURSE.
MY FATHER'S MASTER WAS A BRILLIANT SCIENTIST.
HE SOUGHT THE ANSWER TO THE QUESTION OF THE AGES...
"HOW TO CREATE ARTIFICIAL LIFE."
"IT DIDN'T ALWAYS END WELL."
"AFTER A FAILED EXPERIMENT, HE DISAPPEARED IN SEARCH OF THE CREATURE THAT HE HAD CREATED."
"AND IN HIS ABSENCE, MY FATHER TOOK UP THE CAUSE."

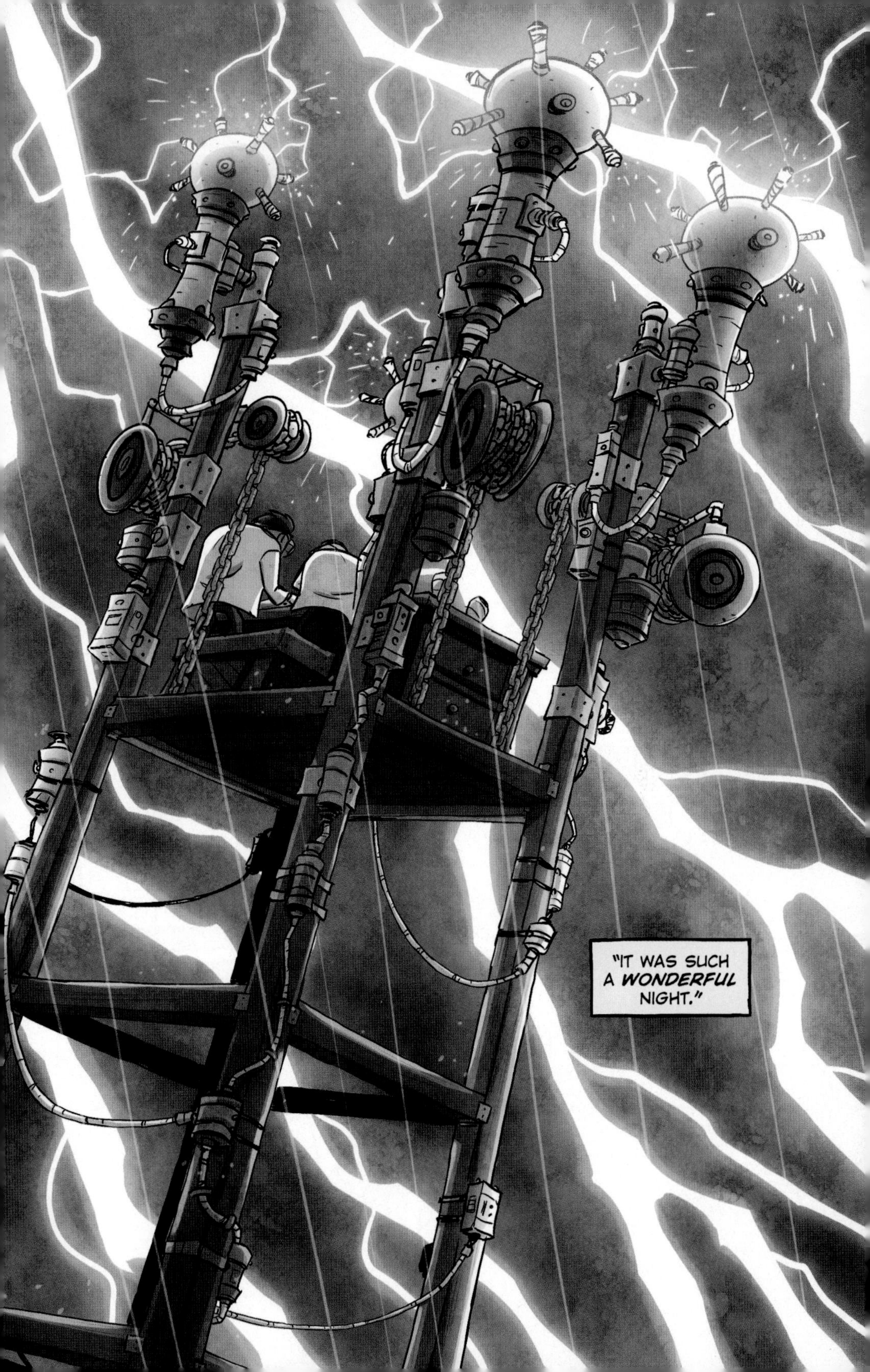
"IT WAS SUCH A *WONDERFUL* NIGHT."

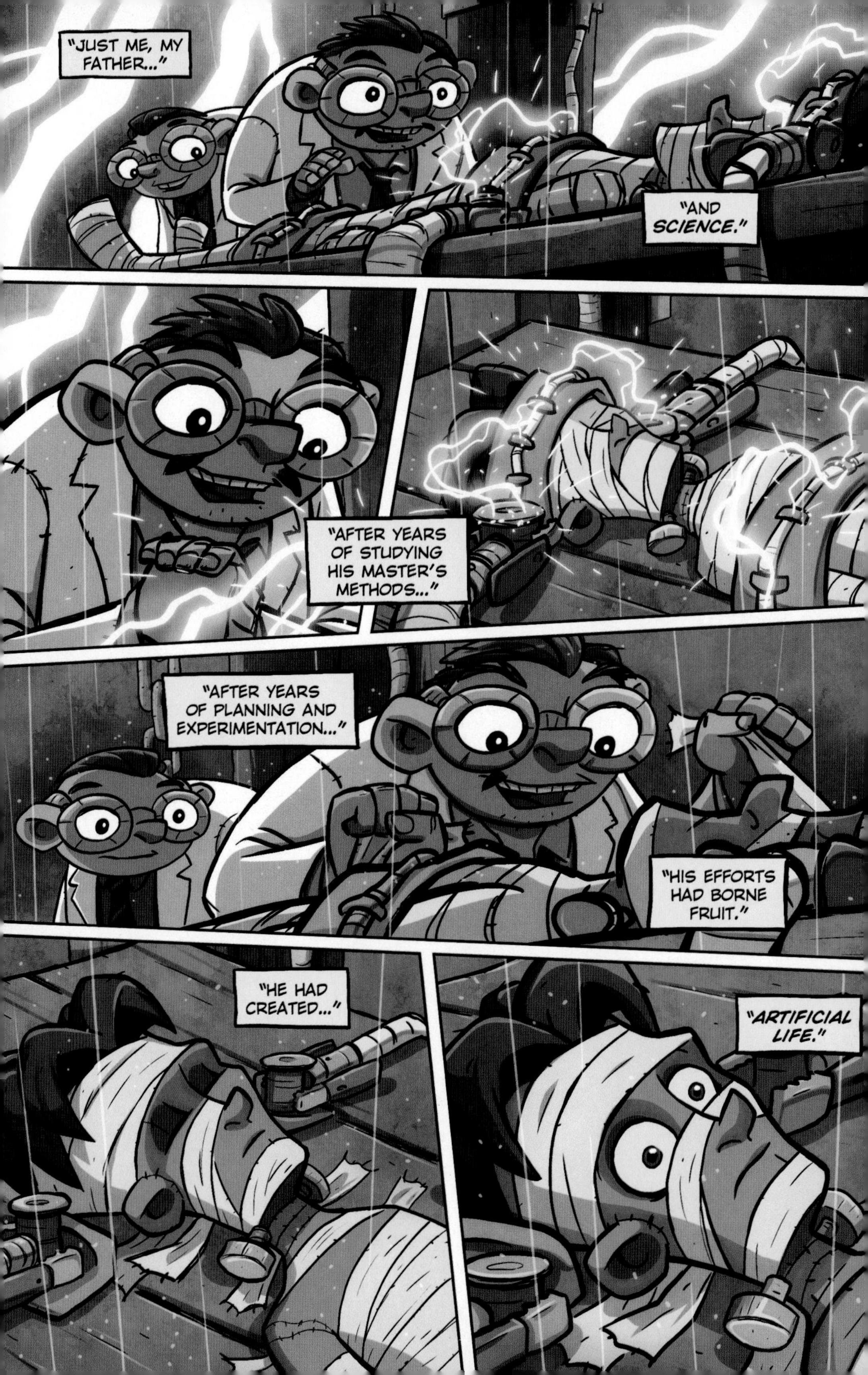
"JUST ME, MY FATHER..."
"AND SCIENCE."
"AFTER YEARS OF STUDYING HIS MASTER'S METHODS..."
"AFTER YEARS OF PLANNING AND EXPERIMENTATION..."
"HIS EFFORTS HAD BORNE FRUIT."
"HE HAD CREATED..."
"ARTIFICIAL LIFE."

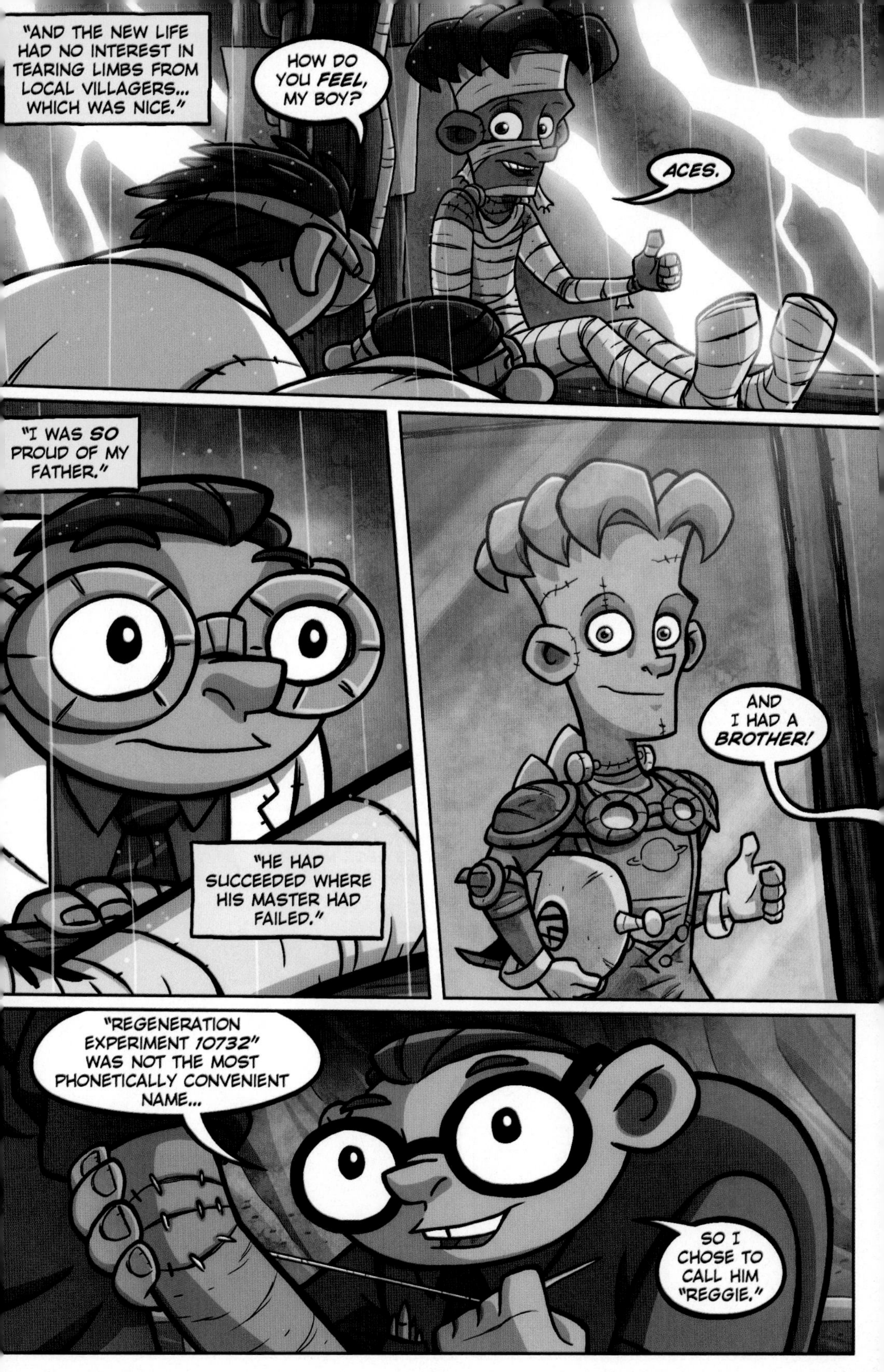
"AND THE NEW LIFE HAD NO INTEREST IN TEARING LIMBS FROM LOCAL VILLAGERS... WHICH WAS NICE."
HOW DO YOU *FEEL*, MY BOY?
ACES.
"I WAS *SO* PROUD OF MY FATHER."
"HE HAD SUCCEEDED WHERE HIS MASTER HAD FAILED."
AND I HAD A *BROTHER!*
"REGENERATION EXPERIMENT *10732*" WAS NOT THE MOST PHONETICALLY CONVENIENT NAME...
SO I CHOSE TO CALL HIM "REGGIE."

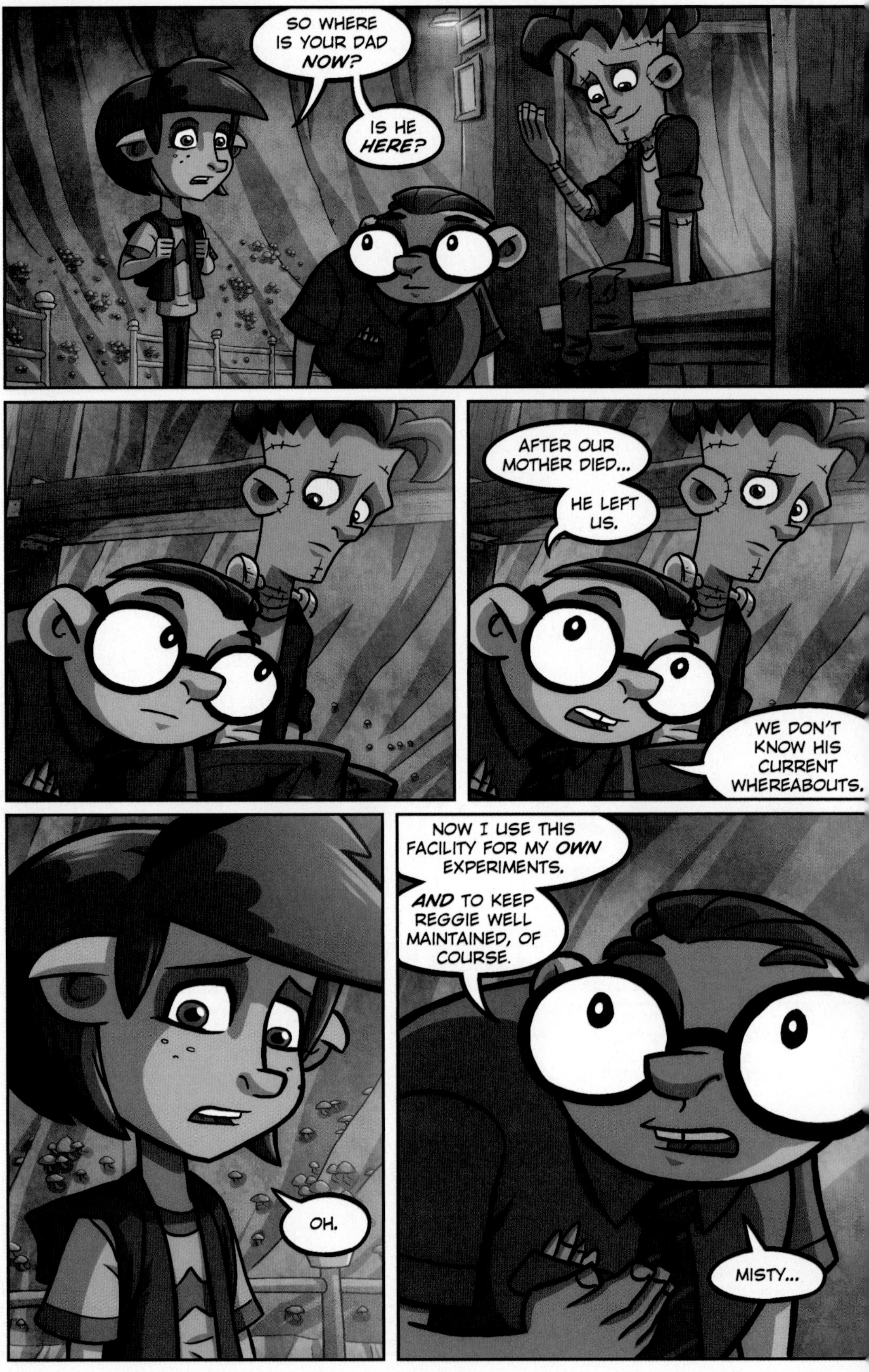
SO WHERE IS YOUR DAD *NOW?*
IS HE *HERE?*
AFTER OUR MOTHER DIED...
HE LEFT US.
WE DON'T KNOW HIS CURRENT WHEREABOUTS.
OH.
NOW I USE THIS FACILITY FOR MY *OWN* EXPERIMENTS.
AND TO KEEP REGGIE WELL MAINTAINED, OF COURSE.
MISTY...

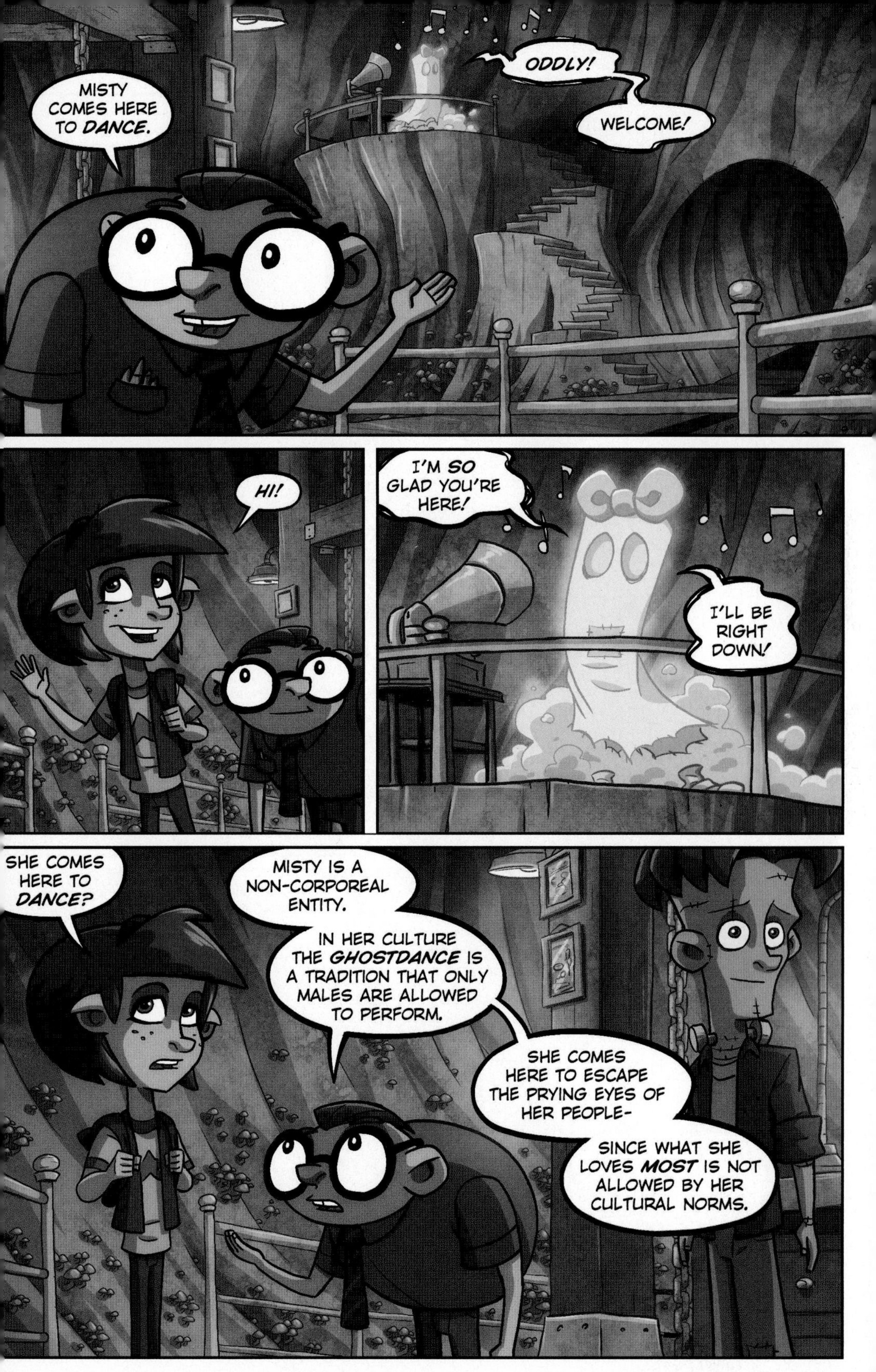

MISTY COMES HERE TO DANCE.
ODDLY!
WELCOME!
HI!
I'M SO GLAD YOU'RE HERE!
I'LL BE RIGHT DOWN!
SHE COMES HERE TO DANCE?
MISTY IS A NON-CORPOREAL ENTITY.
IN HER CULTURE THE GHOSTDANCE IS A TRADITION THAT ONLY MALES ARE ALLOWED TO PERFORM.
SHE COMES HERE TO ESCAPE THE PRYING EYES OF HER PEOPLE-
SINCE WHAT SHE LOVES MOST IS NOT ALLOWED BY HER CULTURAL NORMS.

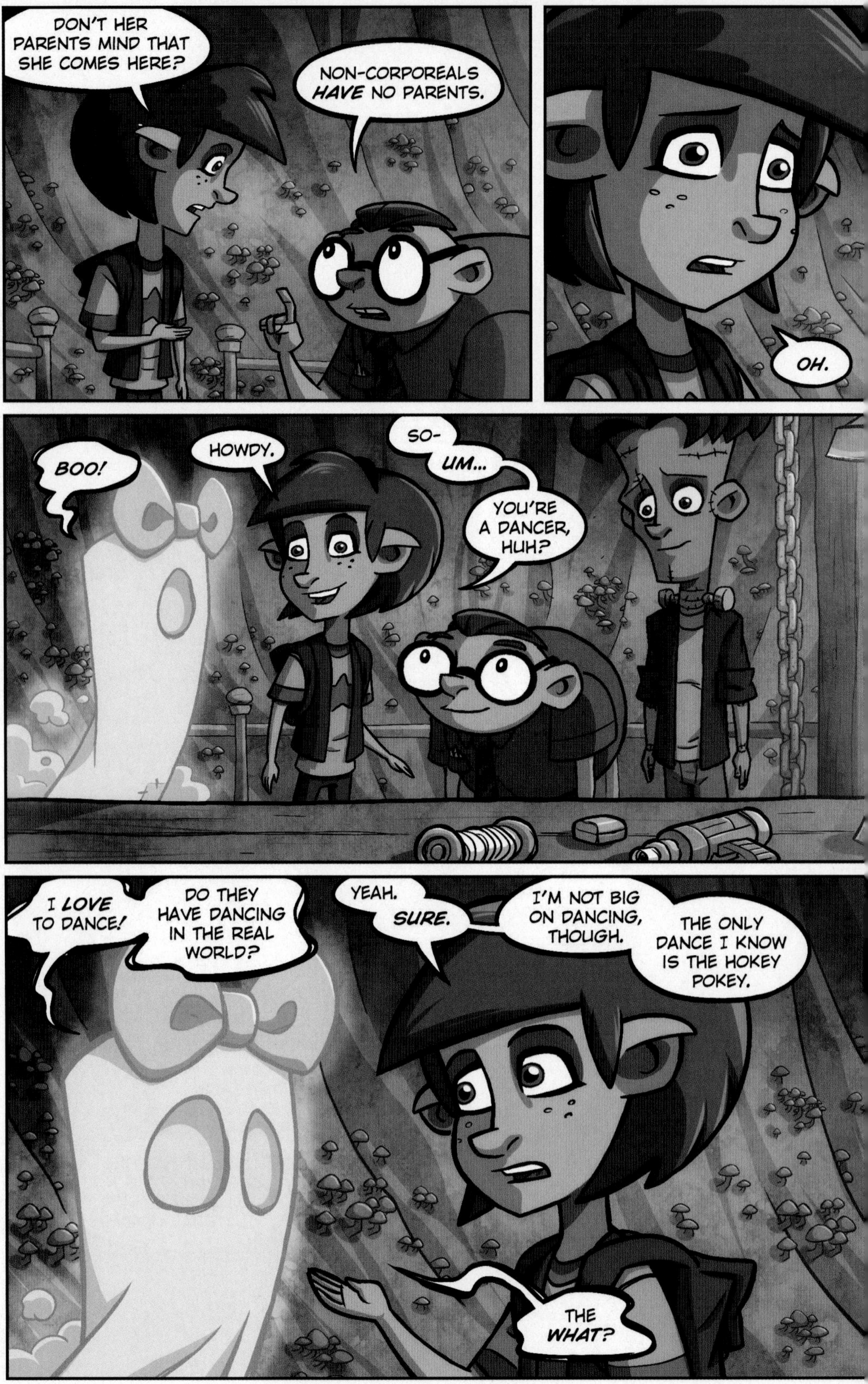
DON'T HER PARENTS MIND THAT SHE COMES HERE?
NON-CORPOREALS HAVE NO PARENTS.
OH.
BOO!
HOWDY.
SO- UM...
YOU'RE A DANCER, HUH?
I LOVE TO DANCE!
DO THEY HAVE DANCING IN THE REAL WORLD?
YEAH. SURE.
I'M NOT BIG ON DANCING, THOUGH.
THE ONLY DANCE I KNOW IS THE HOKEY POKEY.
THE WHAT?

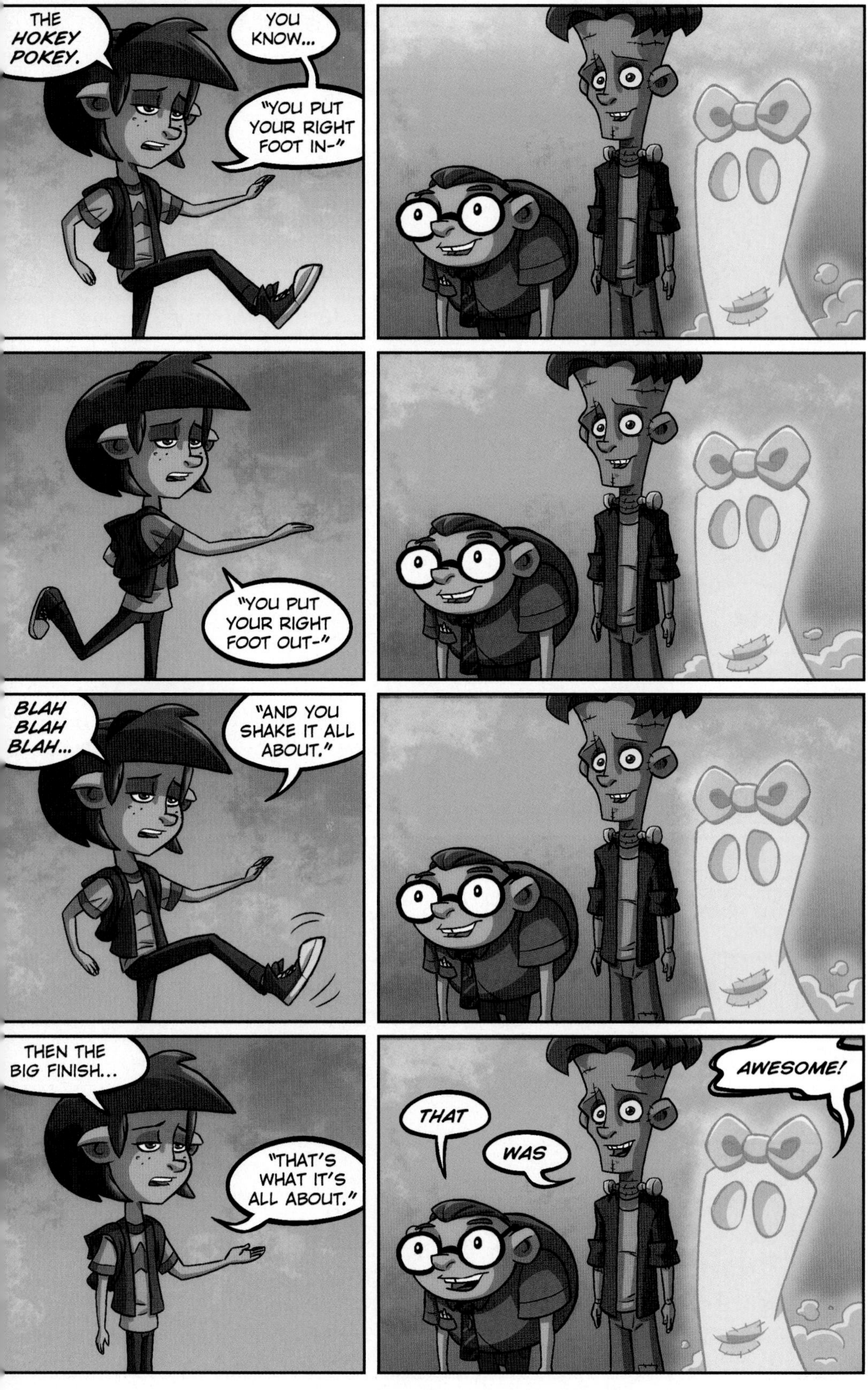
THE HOKEY POKEY.
YOU KNOW...
"YOU PUT YOUR RIGHT FOOT IN-"
"YOU PUT YOUR RIGHT FOOT OUT-"
BLAH BLAH BLAH...
"AND YOU SHAKE IT ALL ABOUT."
THEN THE BIG FINISH...
"THAT'S WHAT IT'S ALL ABOUT."
THAT
WAS
AWESOME!

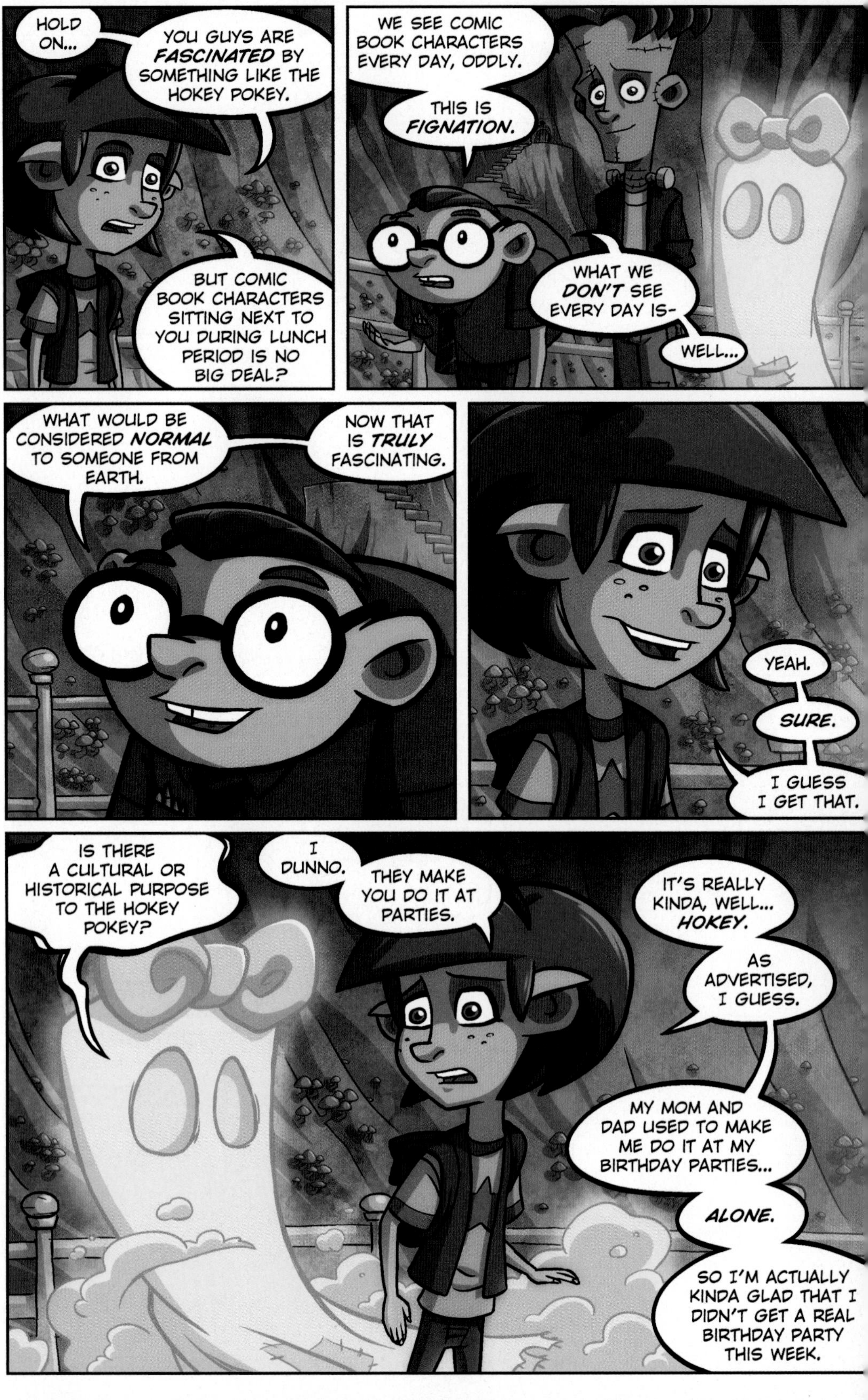

HOLD ON...
YOU GUYS ARE FASCINATED BY SOMETHING LIKE THE HOKEY POKEY.
BUT COMIC BOOK CHARACTERS SITTING NEXT TO YOU DURING LUNCH PERIOD IS NO BIG DEAL?
WE SEE COMIC BOOK CHARACTERS EVERY DAY, ODDLY.
THIS IS FIGNATION.
WHAT WE DON'T SEE EVERY DAY IS-
WELL...
WHAT WOULD BE CONSIDERED NORMAL TO SOMEONE FROM EARTH.
NOW THAT IS TRULY FASCINATING.
YEAH.
SURE.
I GUESS I GET THAT.
IS THERE A CULTURAL OR HISTORICAL PURPOSE TO THE HOKEY POKEY?
I DUNNO.
THEY MAKE YOU DO IT AT PARTIES.
IT'S REALLY KINDA, WELL... HOKEY.
AS ADVERTISED, I GUESS.
MY MOM AND DAD USED TO MAKE ME DO IT AT MY BIRTHDAY PARTIES...
ALONE.
SO I'M ACTUALLY KINDA GLAD THAT I DIDN'T GET A REAL BIRTHDAY PARTY THIS WEEK.

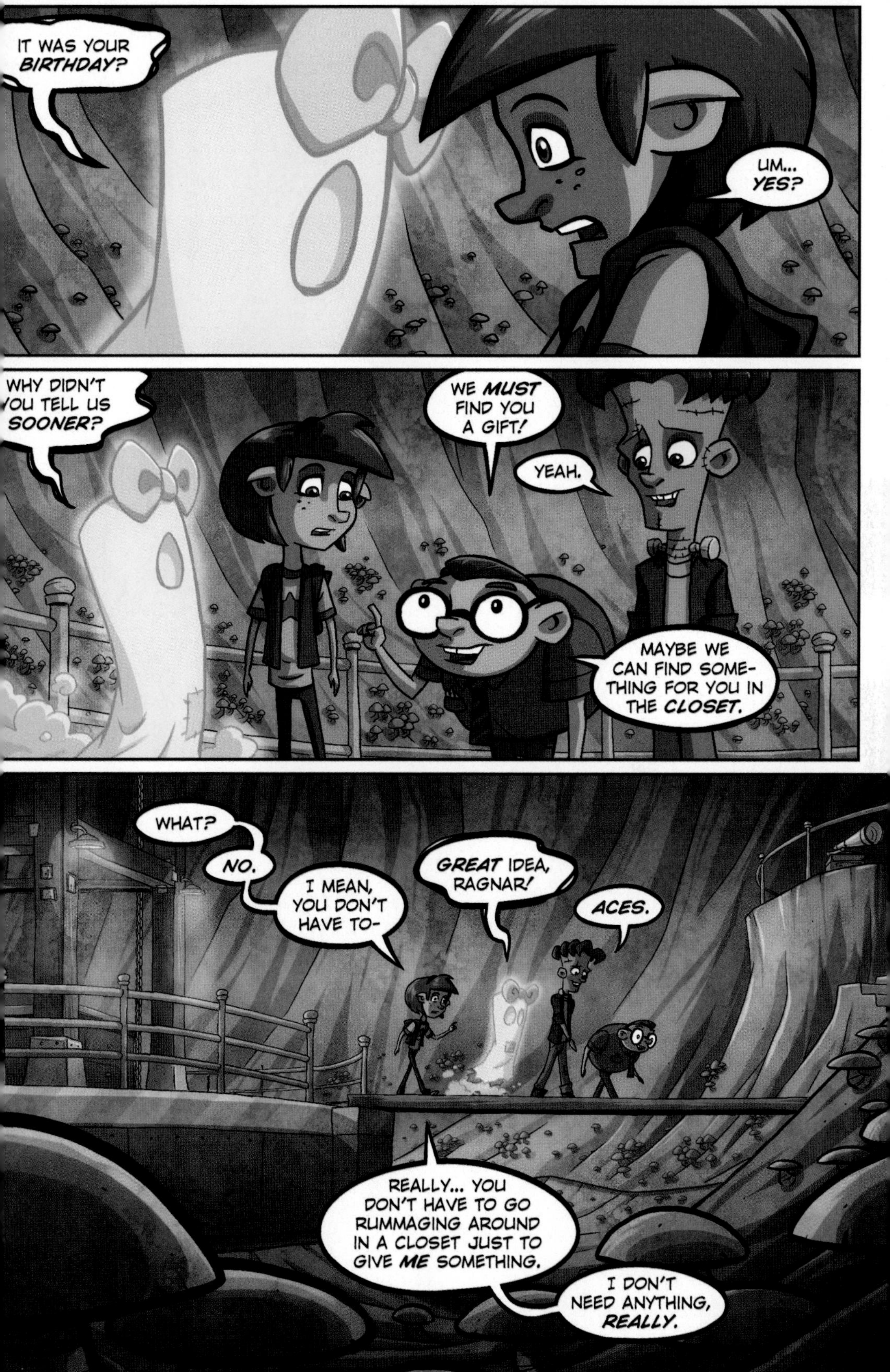
IT WAS YOUR BIRTHDAY?
UM... YES?
WHY DIDN'T YOU TELL US SOONER?
WE MUST FIND YOU A GIFT!
YEAH.
MAYBE WE CAN FIND SOMETHING FOR YOU IN THE CLOSET.
WHAT?
NO.
I MEAN, YOU DON'T HAVE TO-
GREAT IDEA, RAGNAR!
ACES.
REALLY... YOU DON'T HAVE TO GO RUMMAGING AROUND IN A CLOSET JUST TO GIVE ME SOMETHING.
I DON'T NEED ANYTHING, REALLY.

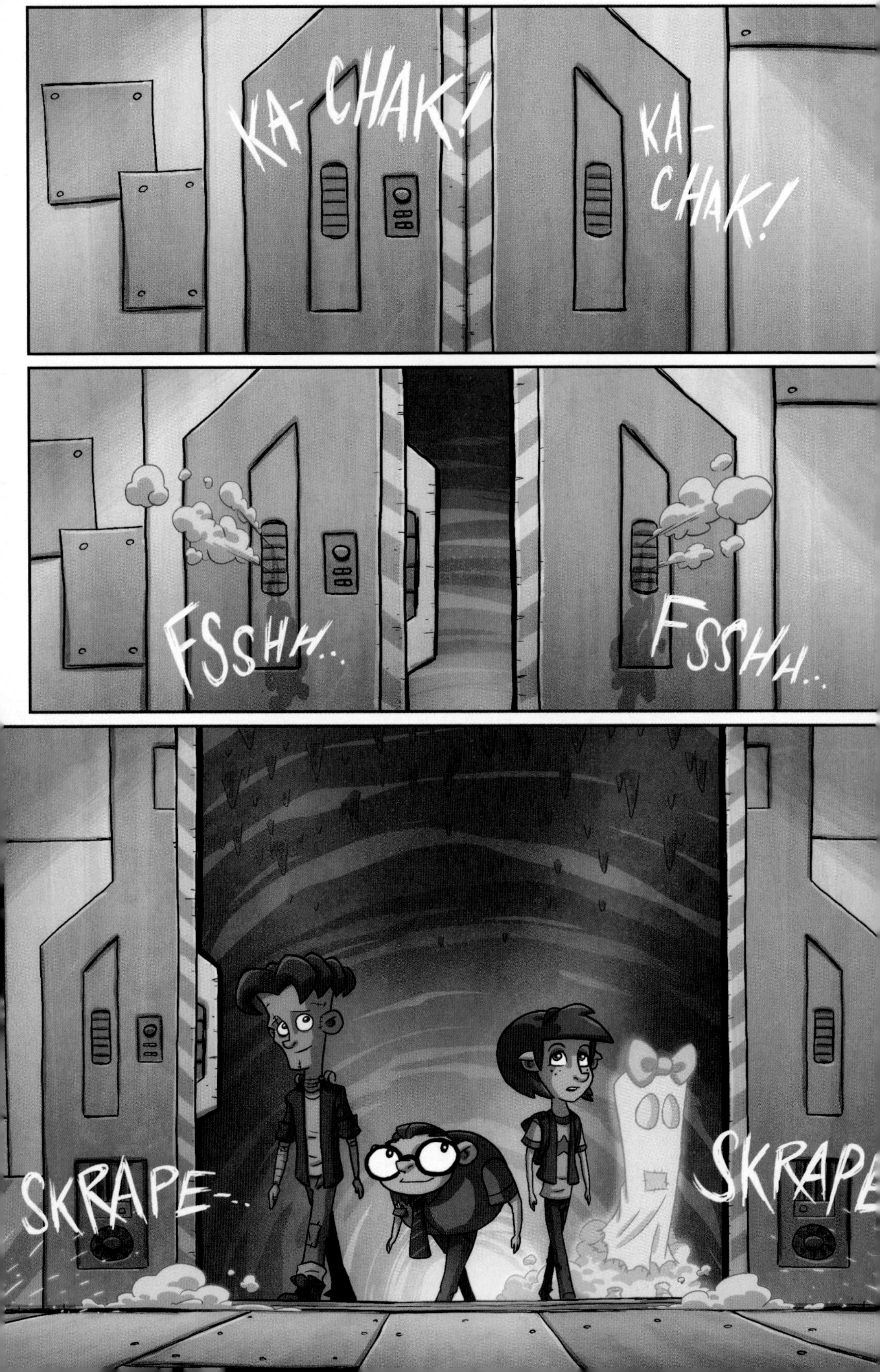
KA-CHAK!
KA-CHAK!
FSSHH..
FSSHH..
SKRAPE...
SKRAPE

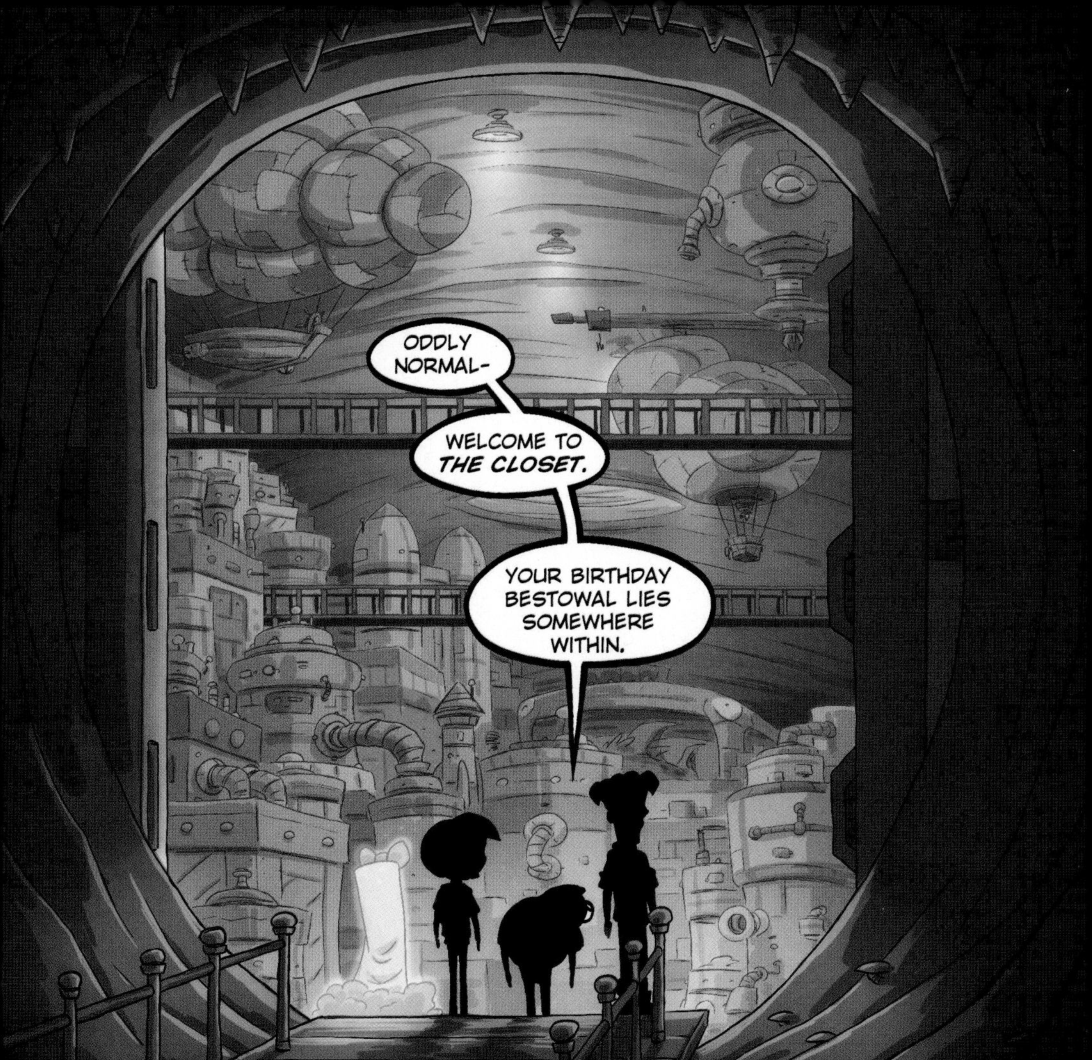
ODDLY NORMAL-
WELCOME TO THE CLOSET.
YOUR BIRTHDAY BESTOWAL LIES SOMEWHERE WITHIN.

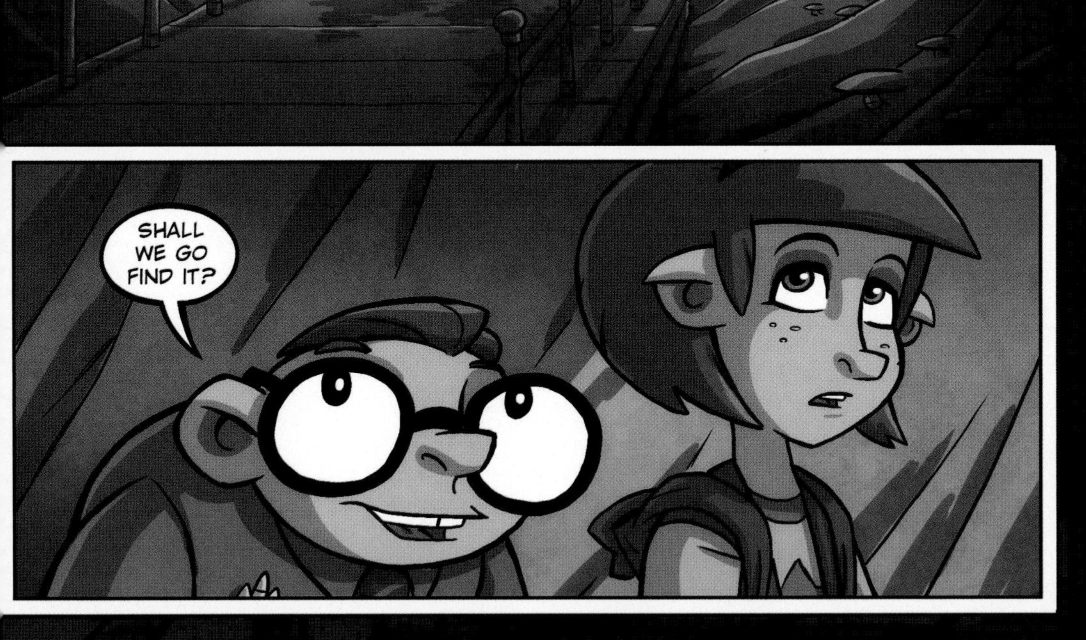
SHALL WE GO FIND IT?

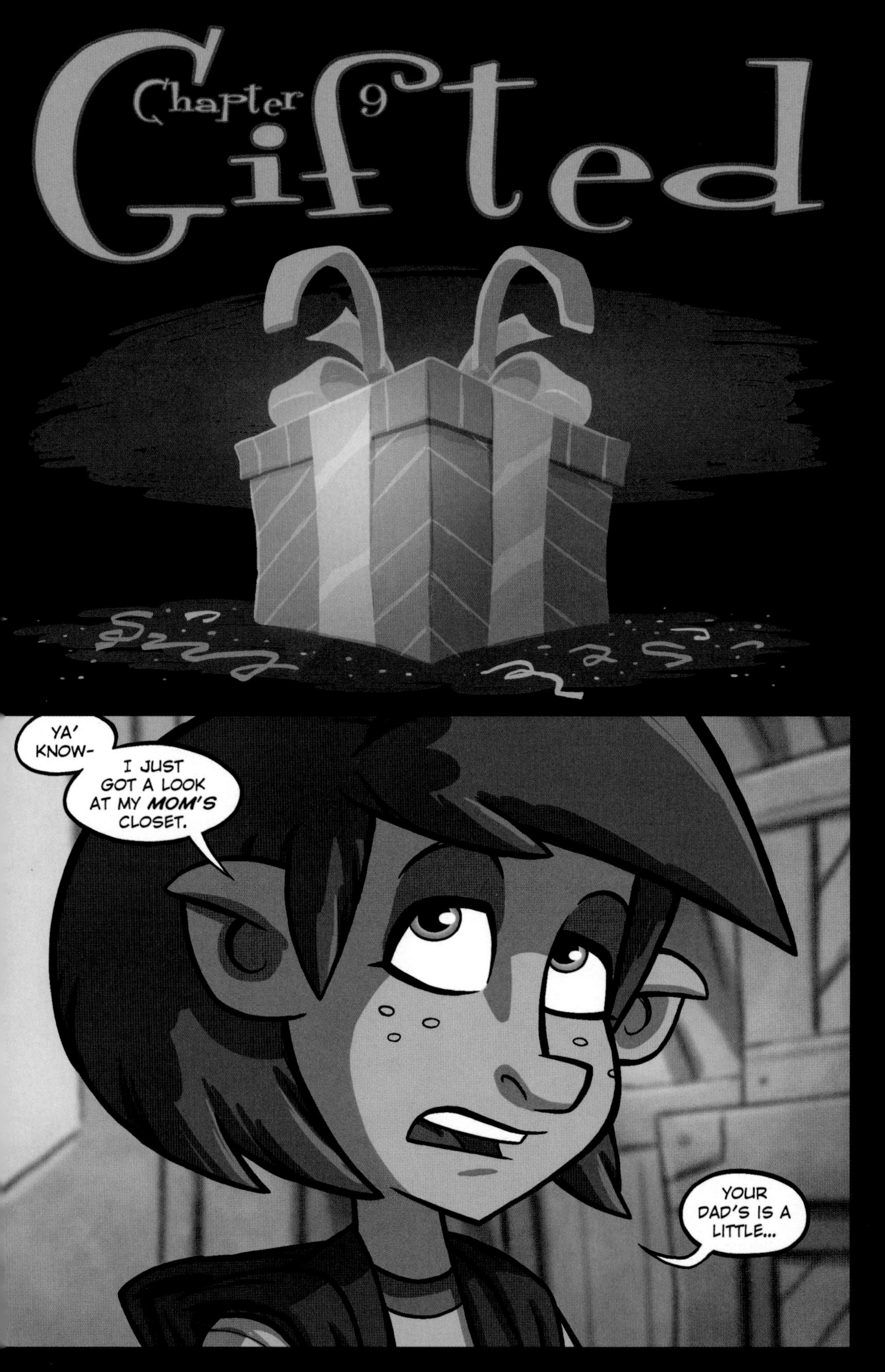

Chapter 9
Gifted
YA' KNOW-
I JUST GOT A LOOK AT MY **MOM'S** CLOSET.
YOUR DAD'S IS A LITTLE...

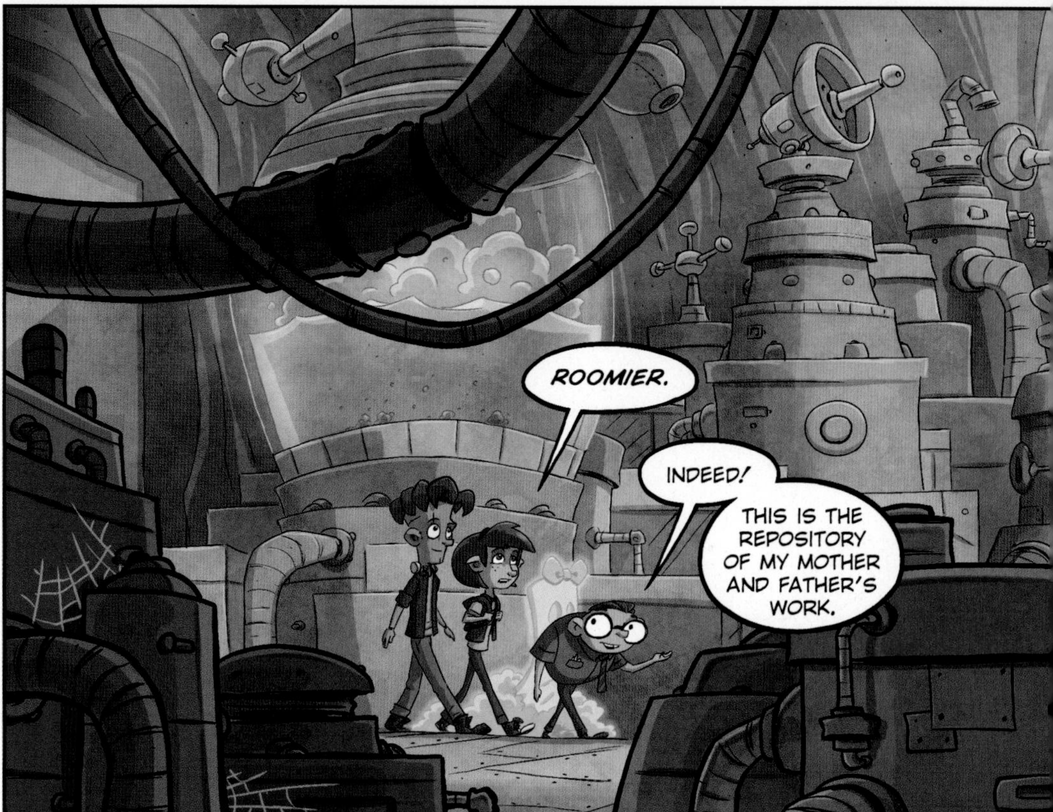
ROOMIER.
INDEED!
THIS IS THE REPOSITORY OF MY MOTHER AND FATHER'S WORK.

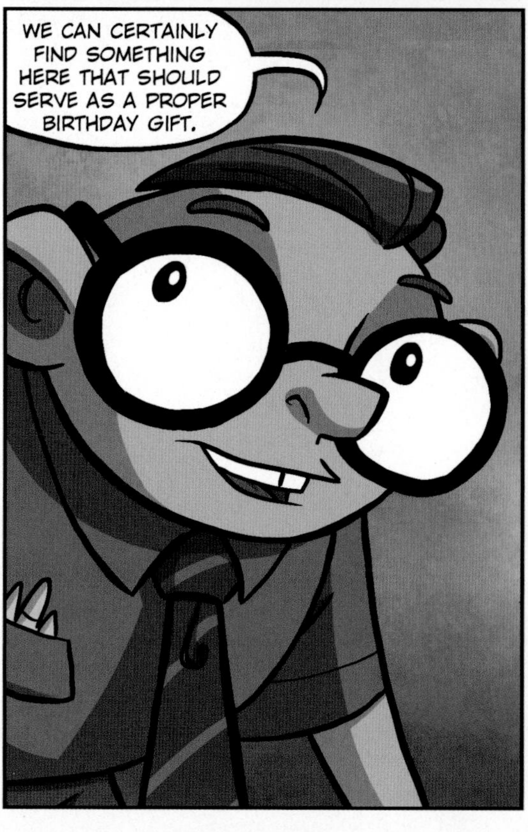
WE CAN CERTAINLY FIND SOMETHING HERE THAT SHOULD SERVE AS A PROPER BIRTHDAY GIFT.

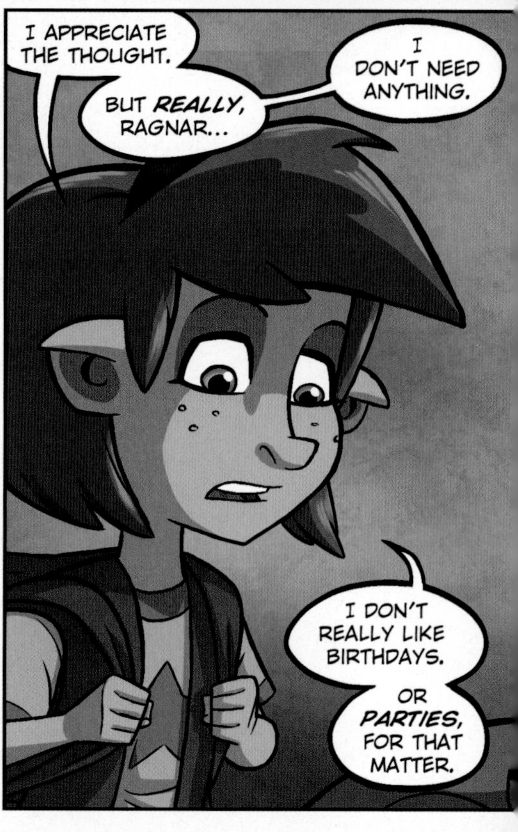
I APPRECIATE THE THOUGHT.
BUT REALLY, RAGNAR...
I DON'T NEED ANYTHING.
I DON'T REALLY LIKE BIRTHDAYS.
OR PARTIES, FOR THAT MATTER.

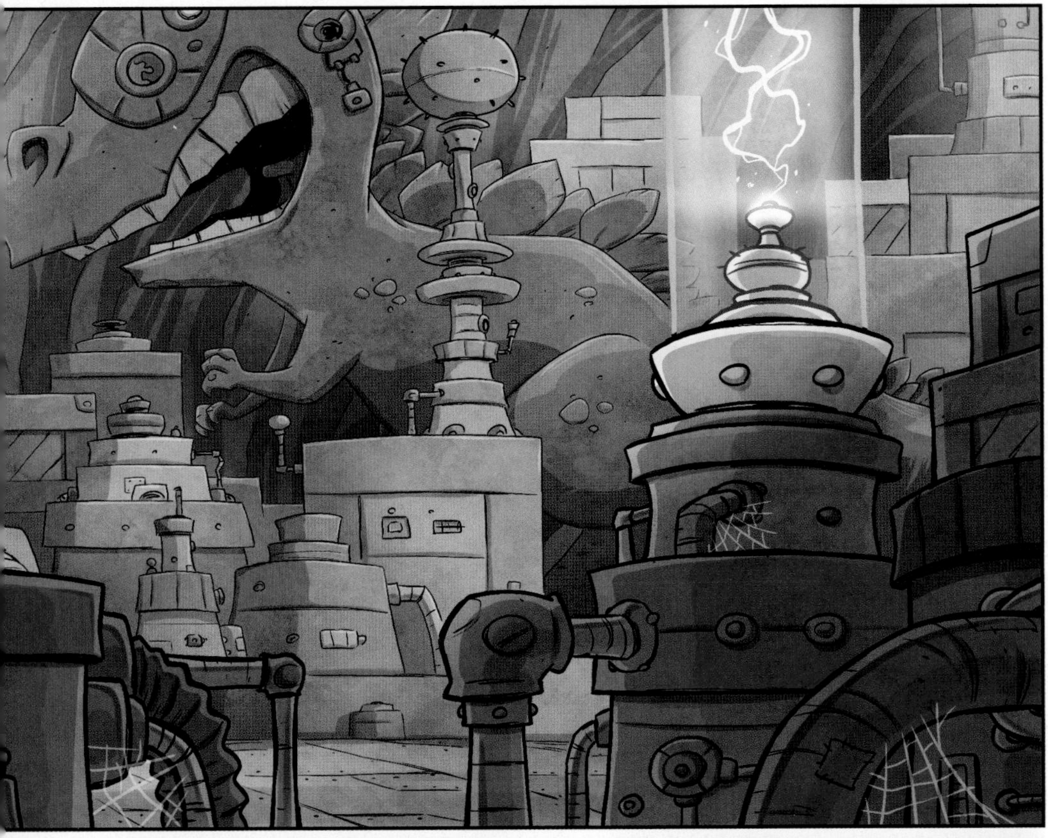

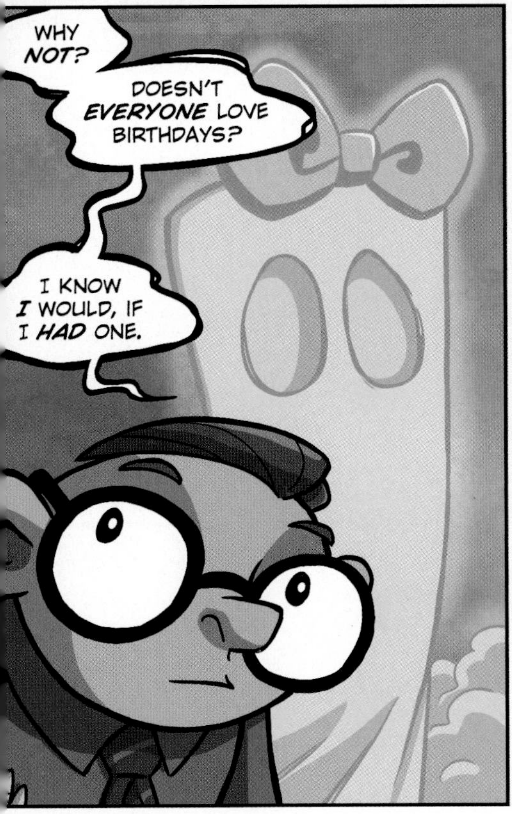
WHY *NOT?*
DOESN'T *EVERYONE* LOVE BIRTHDAYS?
I KNOW *I* WOULD, IF I *HAD* ONE.

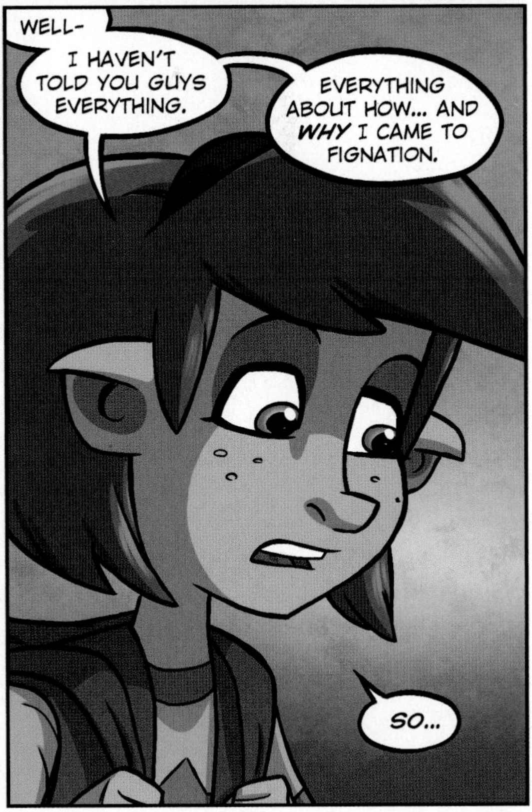
WELL-
I HAVEN'T TOLD YOU GUYS EVERYTHING.
EVERYTHING ABOUT HOW... AND *WHY* I CAME TO FIGNATION.
SO...

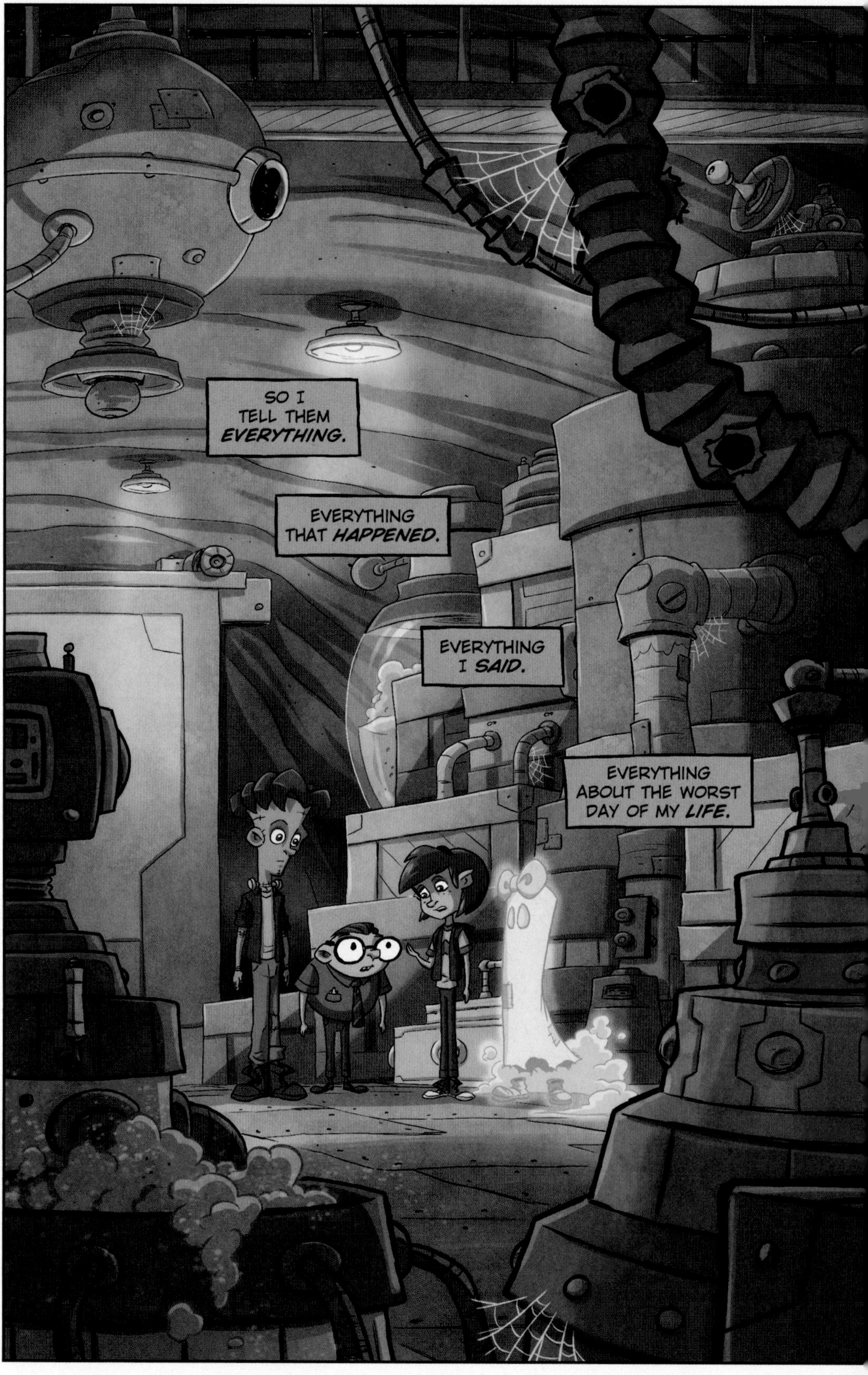
SO I TELL THEM EVERYTHING.
EVERYTHING THAT HAPPENED.
EVERYTHING I SAID.
EVERYTHING ABOUT THE WORST DAY OF MY LIFE.

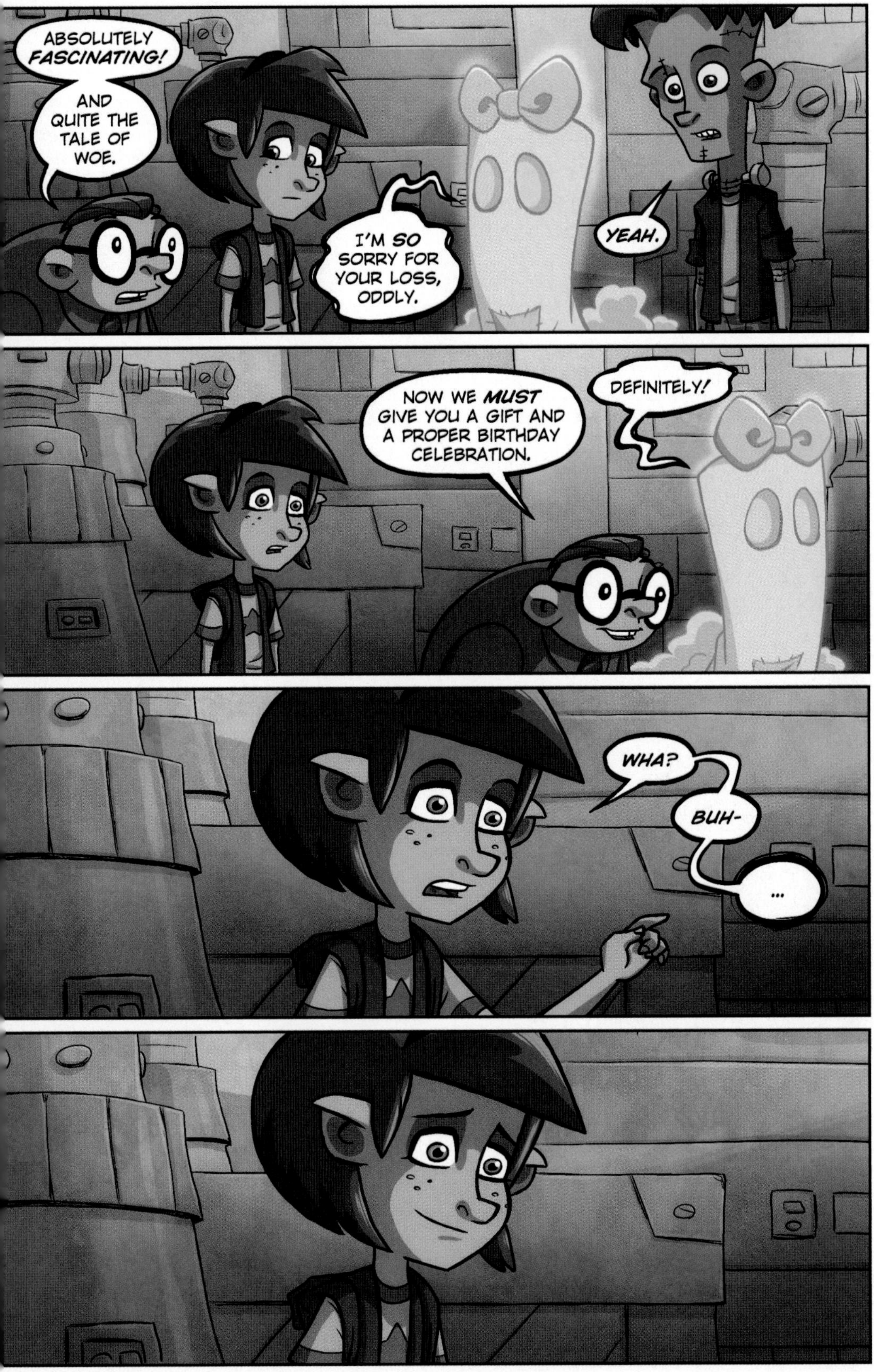
ABSOLUTELY *FASCINATING!*
AND QUITE THE TALE OF WOE.
I'M *SO* SORRY FOR YOUR LOSS, ODDLY.
YEAH.
NOW WE *MUST* GIVE YOU A GIFT AND A PROPER BIRTHDAY CELEBRATION.
DEFINITELY!
WHA?
BUH-
...

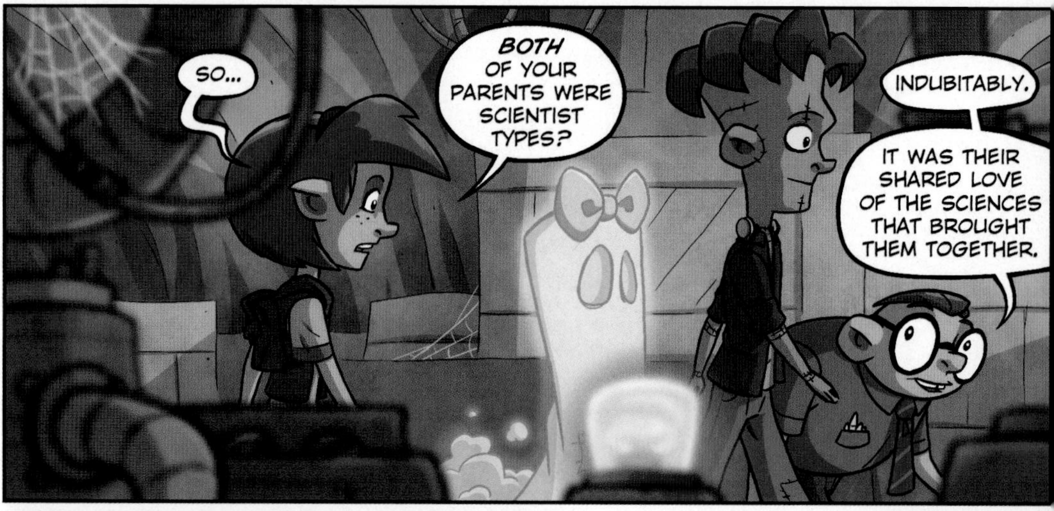
SO...
BOTH OF YOUR PARENTS WERE SCIENTIST TYPES?
INDUBITABLY.
IT WAS THEIR SHARED LOVE OF THE SCIENCES THAT BROUGHT THEM TOGETHER.

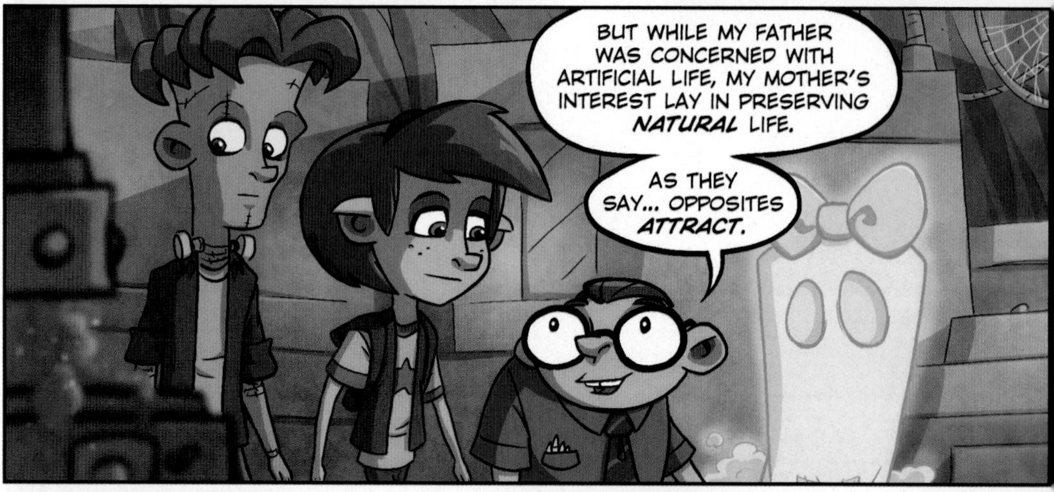
BUT WHILE MY FATHER WAS CONCERNED WITH ARTIFICIAL LIFE, MY MOTHER'S INTEREST LAY IN PRESERVING NATURAL LIFE.
AS THEY SAY... OPPOSITES ATTRACT.

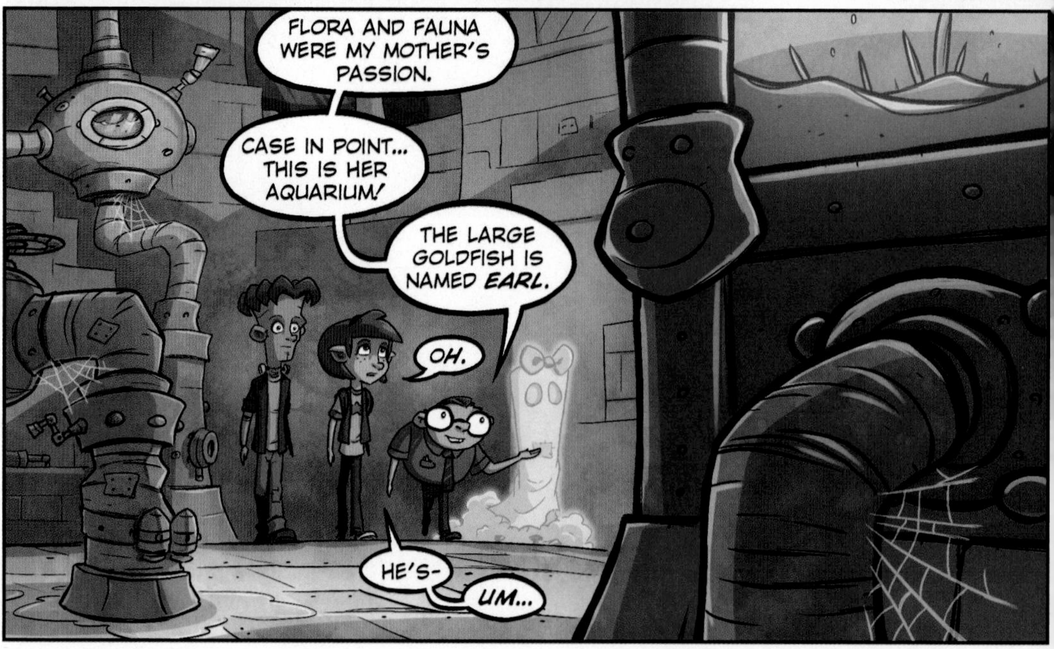
FLORA AND FAUNA WERE MY MOTHER'S PASSION.
CASE IN POINT... THIS IS HER AQUARIUM!
THE LARGE GOLDFISH IS NAMED EARL.
OH.
HE'S-
UM...

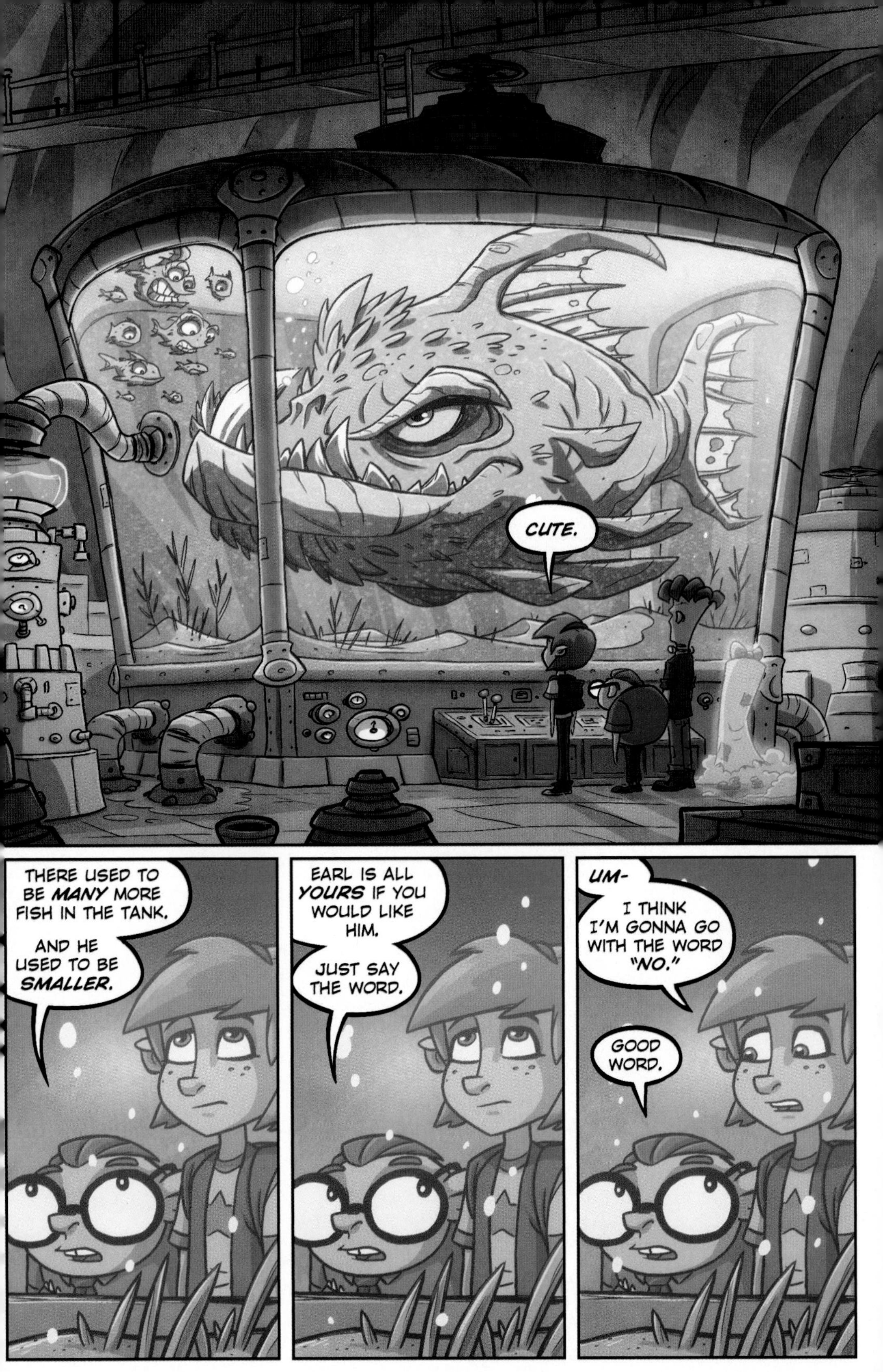
CUTE.
THERE USED TO BE MANY MORE FISH IN THE TANK.
AND HE USED TO BE SMALLER.
EARL IS ALL YOURS IF YOU WOULD LIKE HIM.
JUST SAY THE WORD.
UM-
I THINK I'M GONNA GO WITH THE WORD "NO."
GOOD WORD.

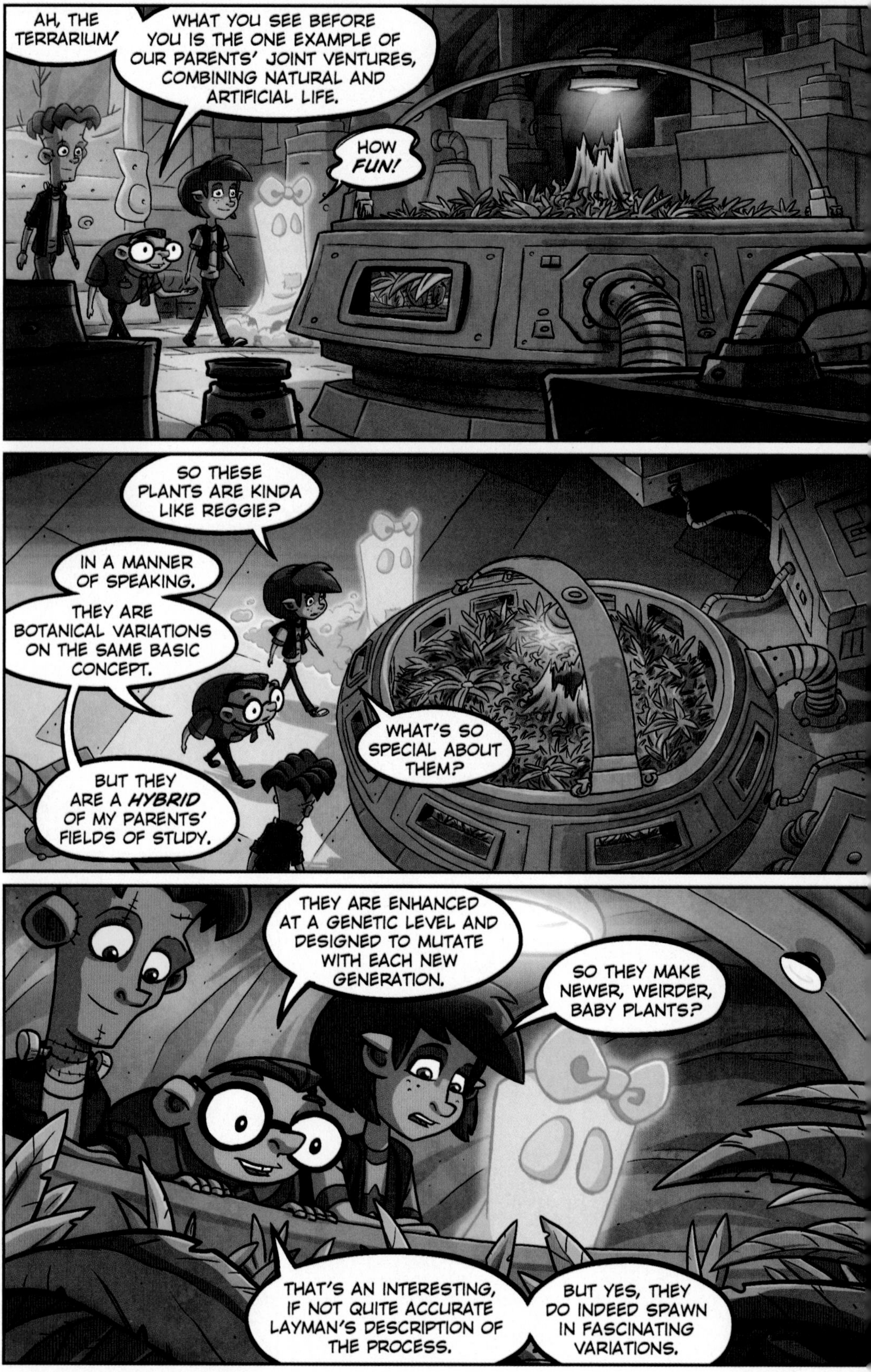

AH, THE TERRARIUM!
WHAT YOU SEE BEFORE YOU IS THE ONE EXAMPLE OF OUR PARENTS' JOINT VENTURES, COMBINING NATURAL AND ARTIFICIAL LIFE.
HOW *FUN!*
SO THESE PLANTS ARE KINDA LIKE REGGIE?
IN A MANNER OF SPEAKING.
THEY ARE BOTANICAL VARIATIONS ON THE SAME BASIC CONCEPT.
BUT THEY ARE A *HYBRID* OF MY PARENTS' FIELDS OF STUDY.
WHAT'S SO SPECIAL ABOUT THEM?
THEY ARE ENHANCED AT A GENETIC LEVEL AND DESIGNED TO MUTATE WITH EACH NEW GENERATION.
SO THEY MAKE NEWER, WEIRDER, BABY PLANTS?
THAT'S AN INTERESTING, IF NOT QUITE ACCURATE LAYMAN'S DESCRIPTION OF THE PROCESS.
BUT YES, THEY DO INDEED SPAWN IN FASCINATING VARIATIONS.

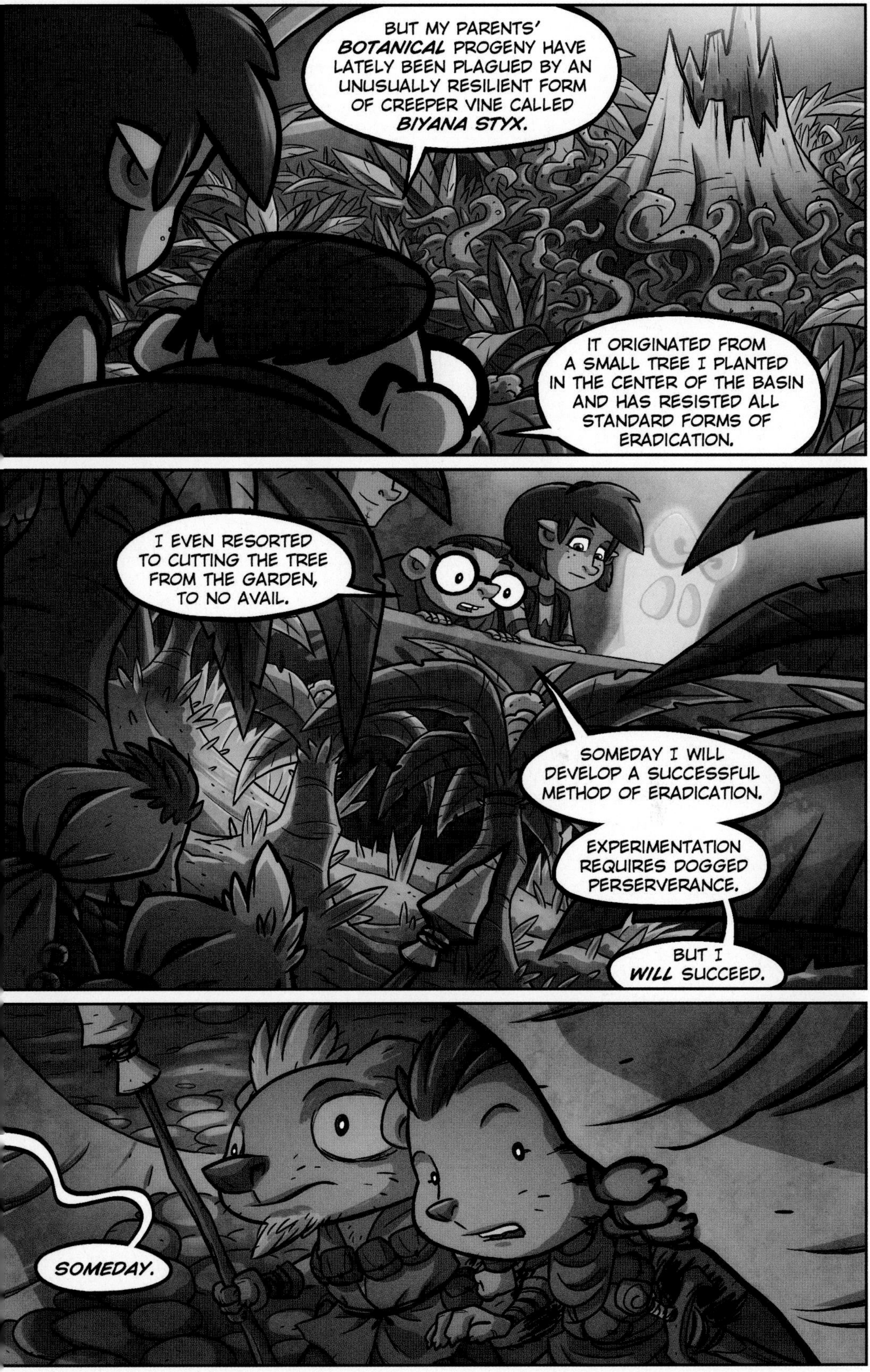
BUT MY PARENTS' BOTANICAL PROGENY HAVE LATELY BEEN PLAGUED BY AN UNUSUALLY RESILIENT FORM OF CREEPER VINE CALLED BIYANA STYX.
IT ORIGINATED FROM A SMALL TREE I PLANTED IN THE CENTER OF THE BASIN AND HAS RESISTED ALL STANDARD FORMS OF ERADICATION.
I EVEN RESORTED TO CUTTING THE TREE FROM THE GARDEN, TO NO AVAIL.
SOMEDAY I WILL DEVELOP A SUCCESSFUL METHOD OF ERADICATION.
EXPERIMENTATION REQUIRES DOGGED PERSERVERANCE.
BUT I WILL SUCCEED.
SOMEDAY.

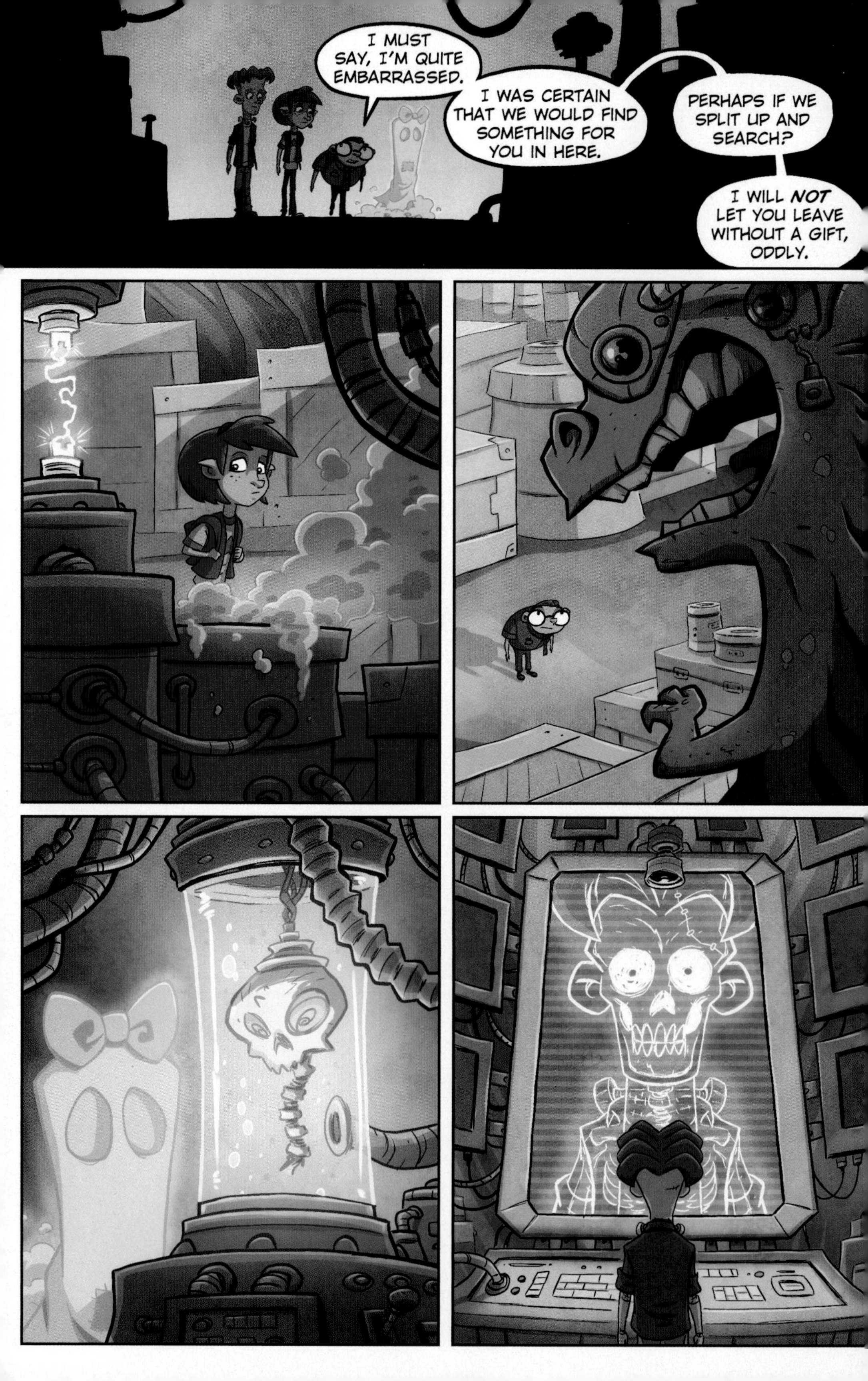
I MUST SAY, I'M QUITE EMBARRASSED.
I WAS CERTAIN THAT WE WOULD FIND SOMETHING FOR YOU IN HERE.
PERHAPS IF WE SPLIT UP AND SEARCH?
I WILL *NOT* LET YOU LEAVE WITHOUT A GIFT, ODDLY.

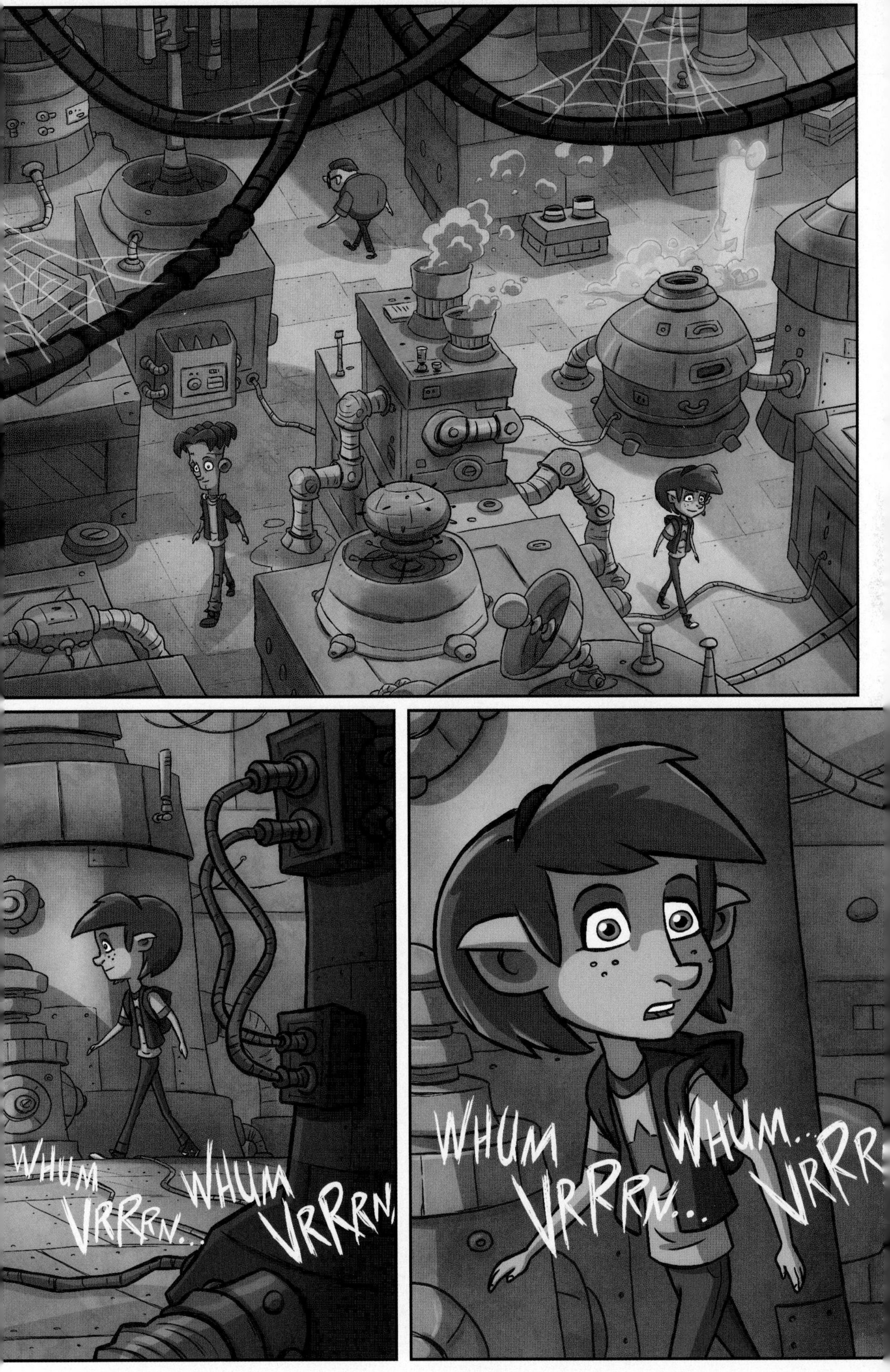
WHUM
VRRRN...
WHUM
VRRRN,
WHUM
VRRRN...
WHUM...
VRRR

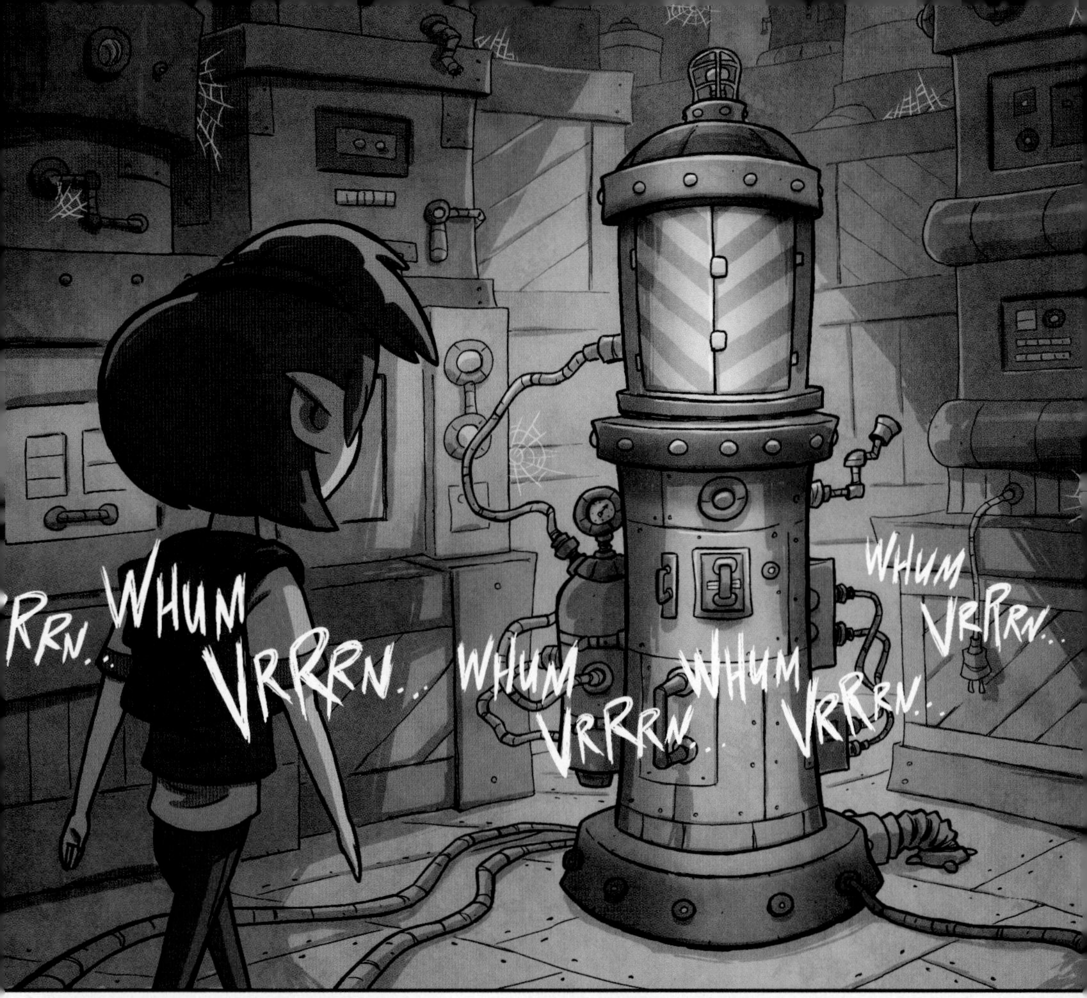
RRN...
WHUM
VRRRRN...
WHUM
VRRRN...
WHUM
VRRRN...
WHUM
VRRRN...

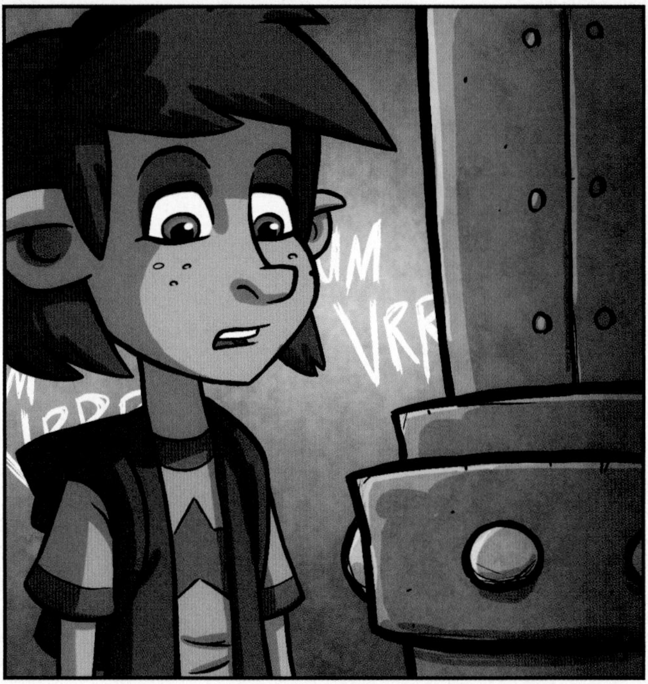

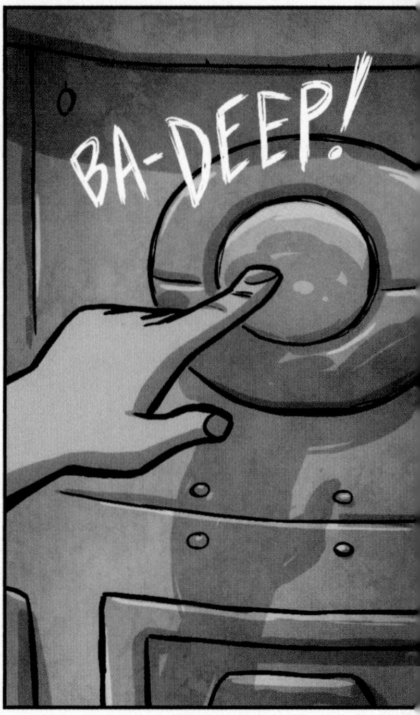
BA-DEEP!

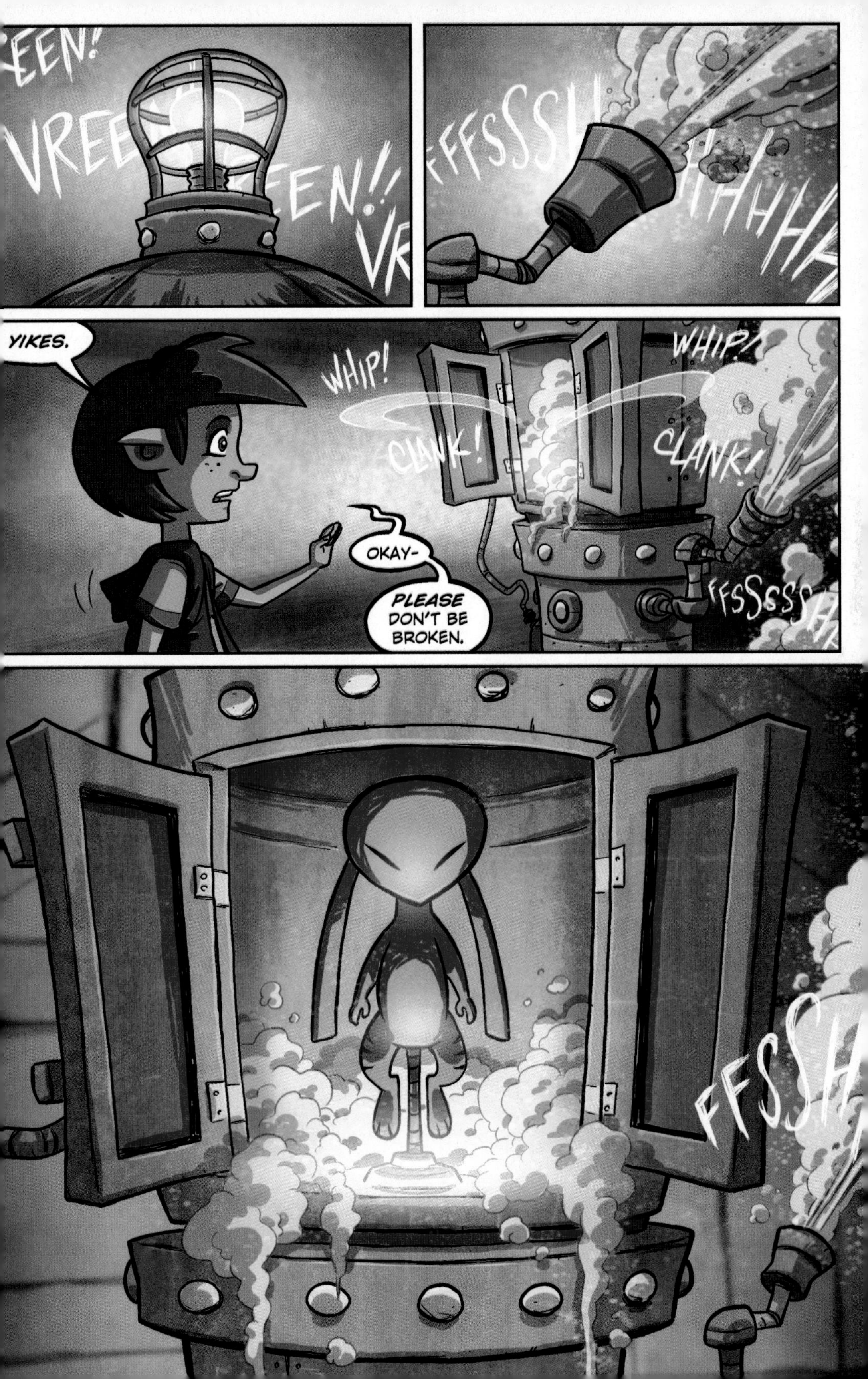
EEN!
VREEEEEEN!!
VR
FFFSSSSHHHHHH
YIKES.
WHIP!
CLANK!
WHIP!
CLANK!
OKAY-
PLEASE DON'T BE BROKEN.
FFSSSSSH
FFSSH

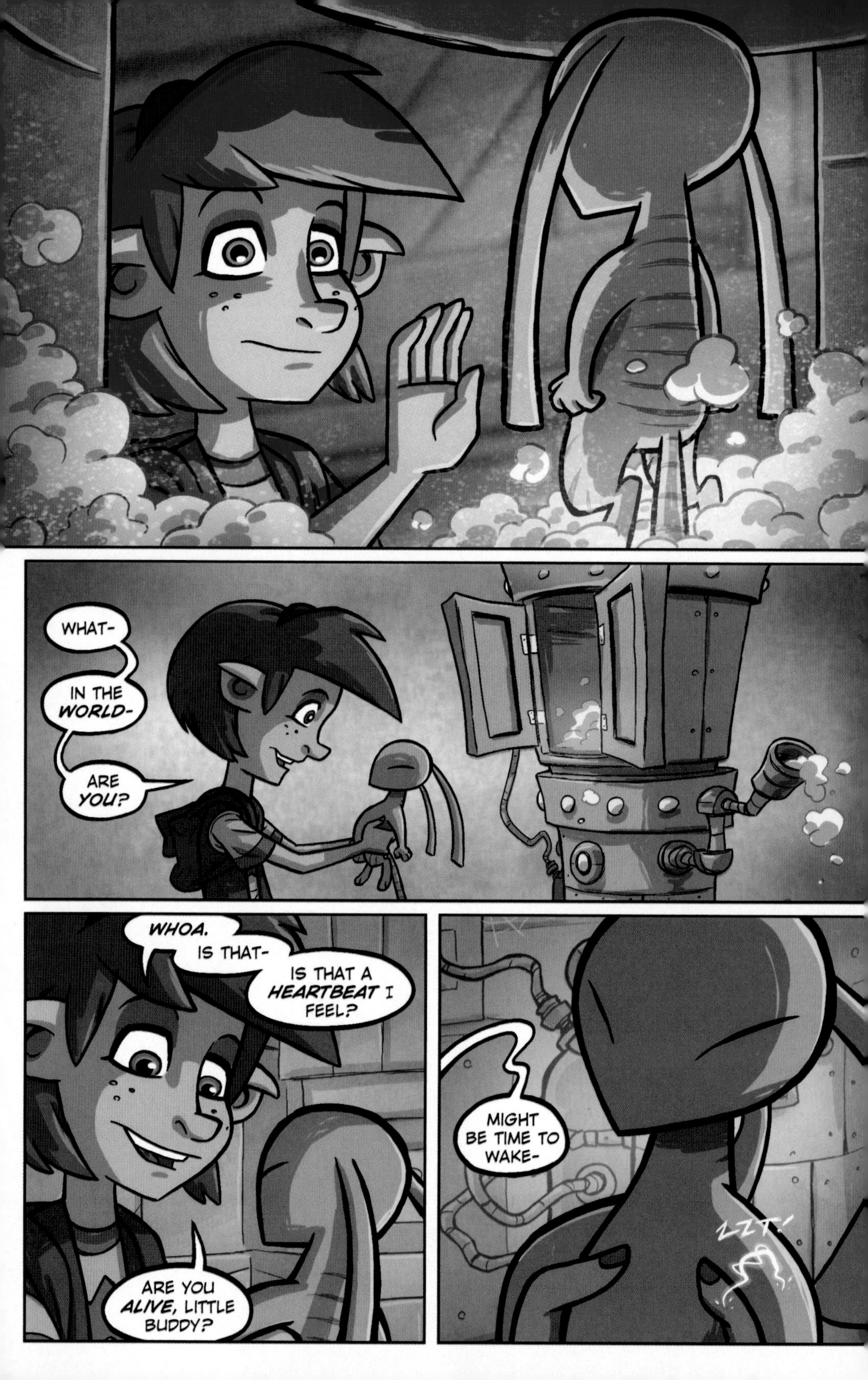
WHAT-
IN THE WORLD-
ARE YOU?
WHOA.
IS THAT-
IS THAT A HEARTBEAT I FEEL?
ARE YOU ALIVE, LITTLE BUDDY?
MIGHT BE TIME TO WAKE-
ZZT!

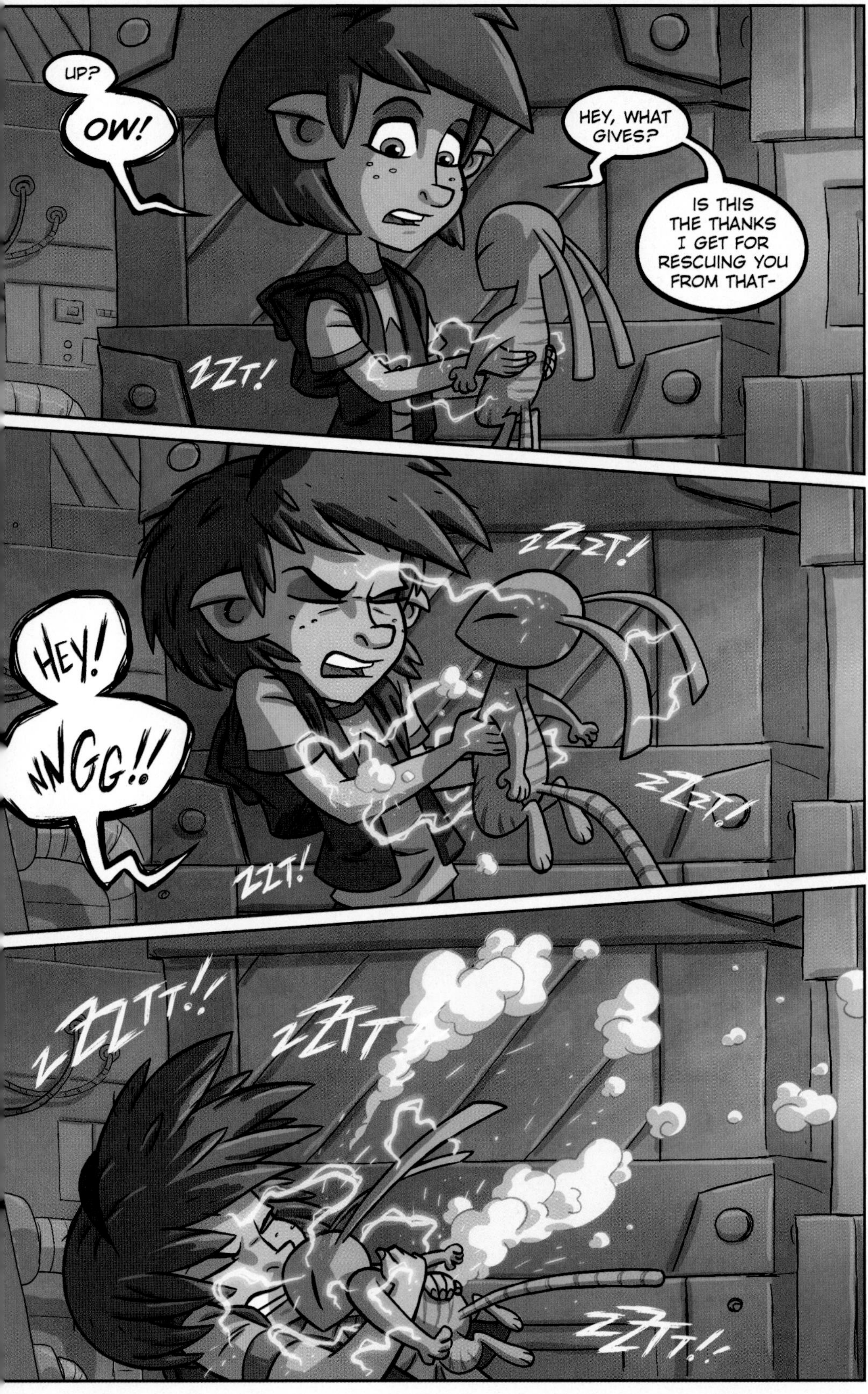
UP?
OW!
HEY, WHAT GIVES?
IS THIS THE THANKS I GET FOR RESCUING YOU FROM THAT-
ZZT!
HEY!
NNGG!!
zZzzT!
zZzT!
ZZT!
zZZTTT!!
zZTTT
ZZTTT!!

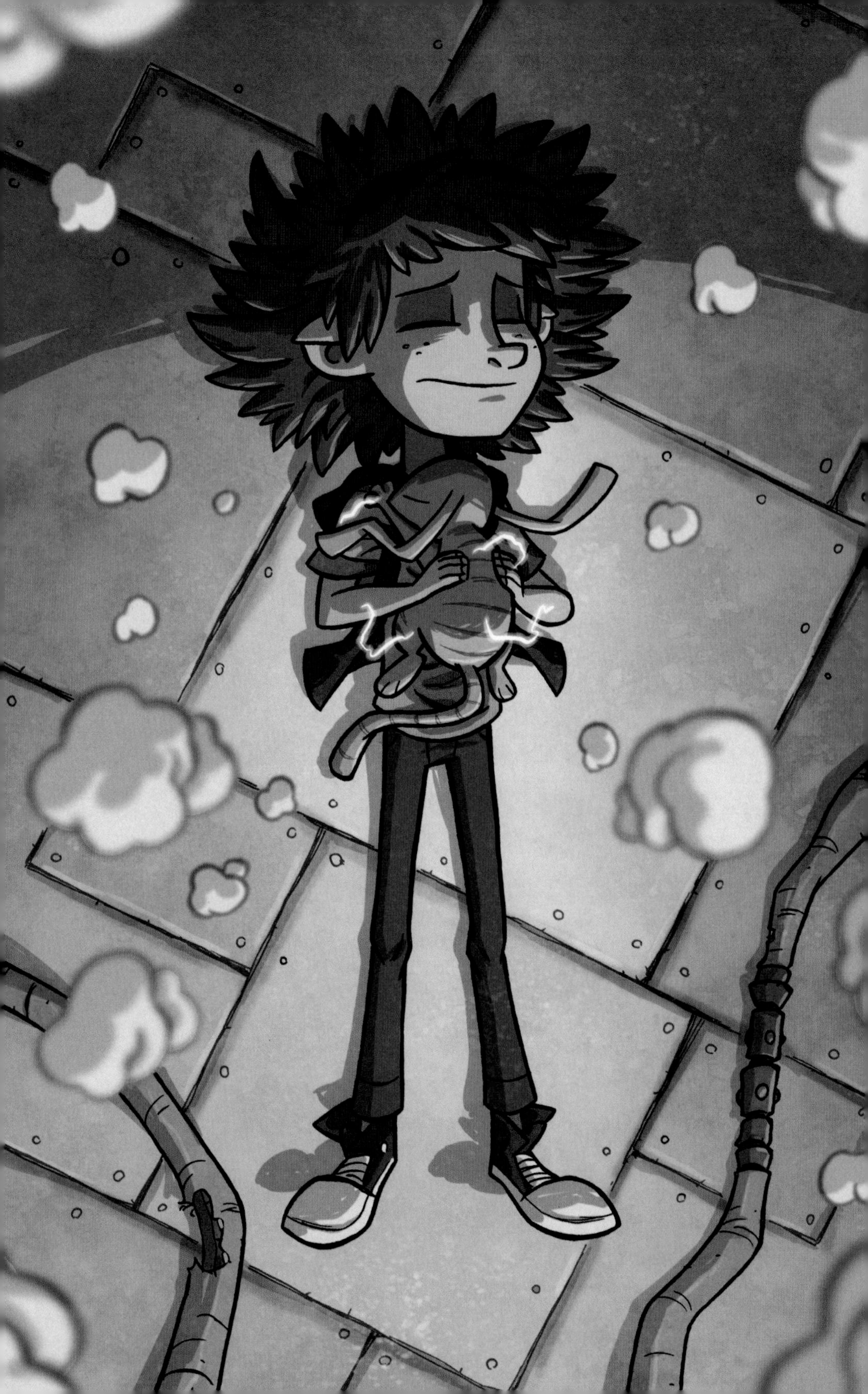

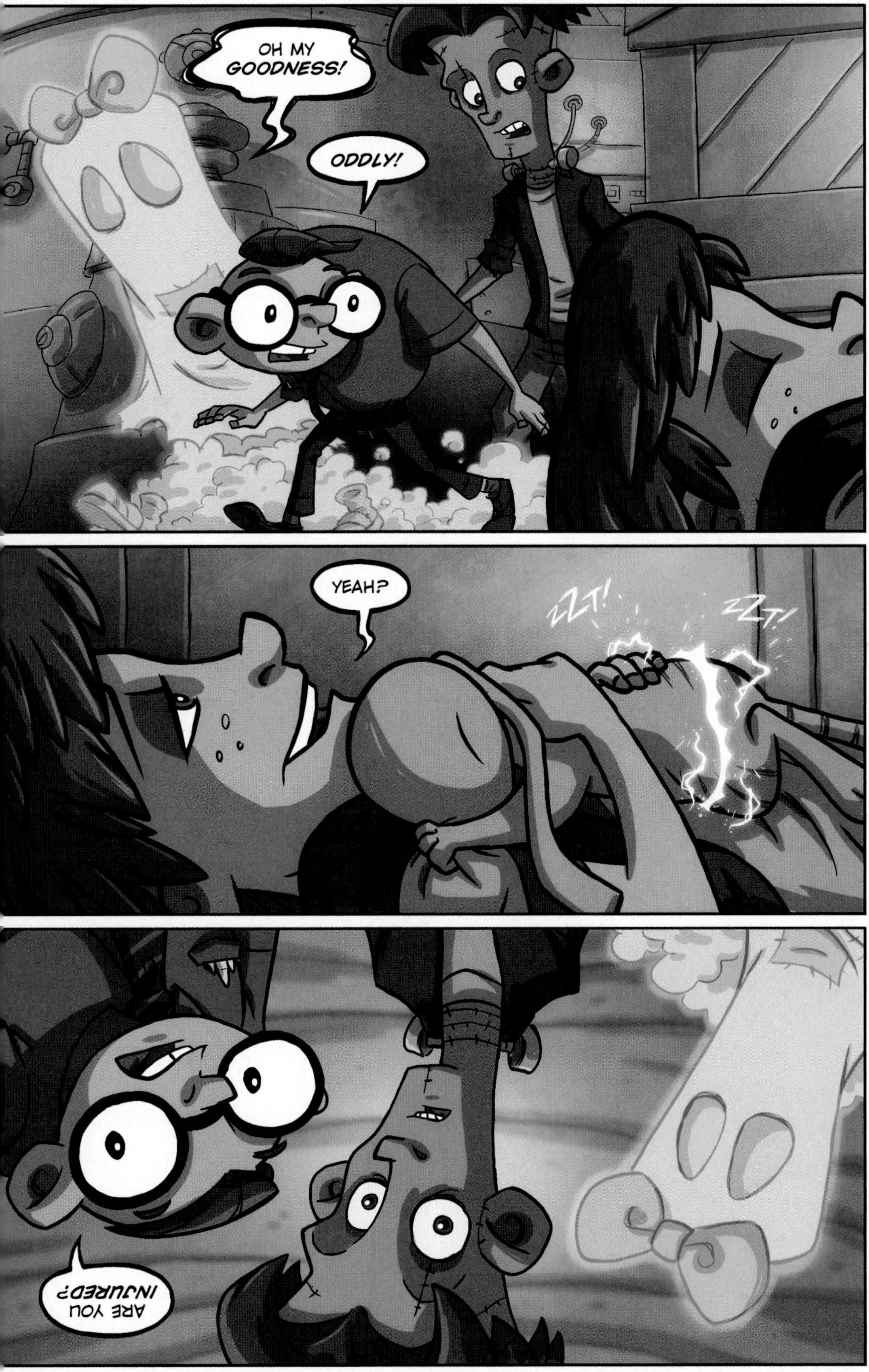
OH MY GOODNESS!
ODDLY!
YEAH?
ZZT!
ZZT!
ARE YOU INJURED?

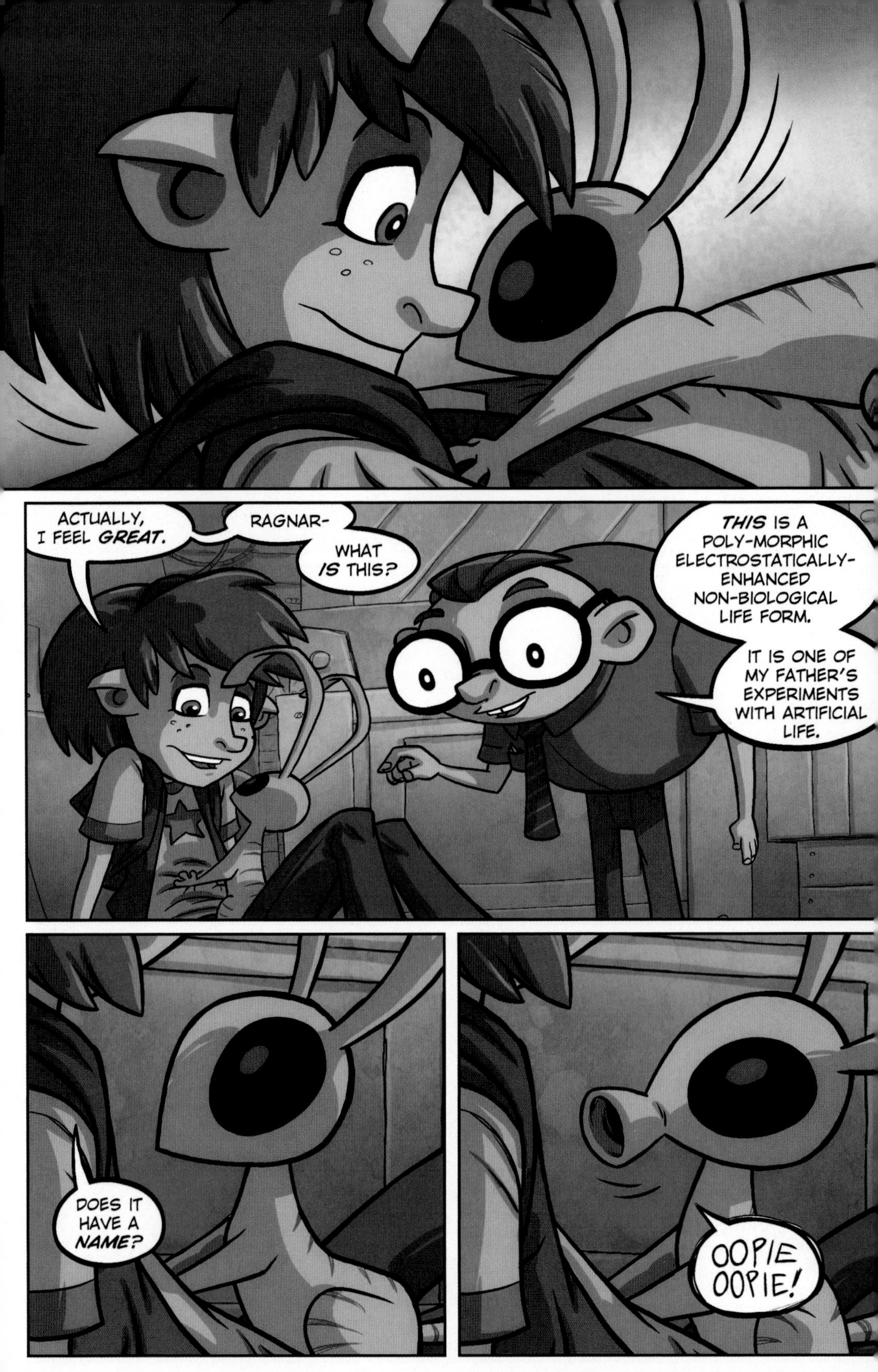
ACTUALLY, I FEEL *GREAT*.
RAGNAR-
WHAT *IS* THIS?
THIS IS A POLY-MORPHIC ELECTROSTATICALLY-ENHANCED NON-BIOLOGICAL LIFE FORM.
IT IS ONE OF MY FATHER'S EXPERIMENTS WITH ARTIFICIAL LIFE.
DOES IT HAVE A *NAME*?
OOPIE OOPIE!

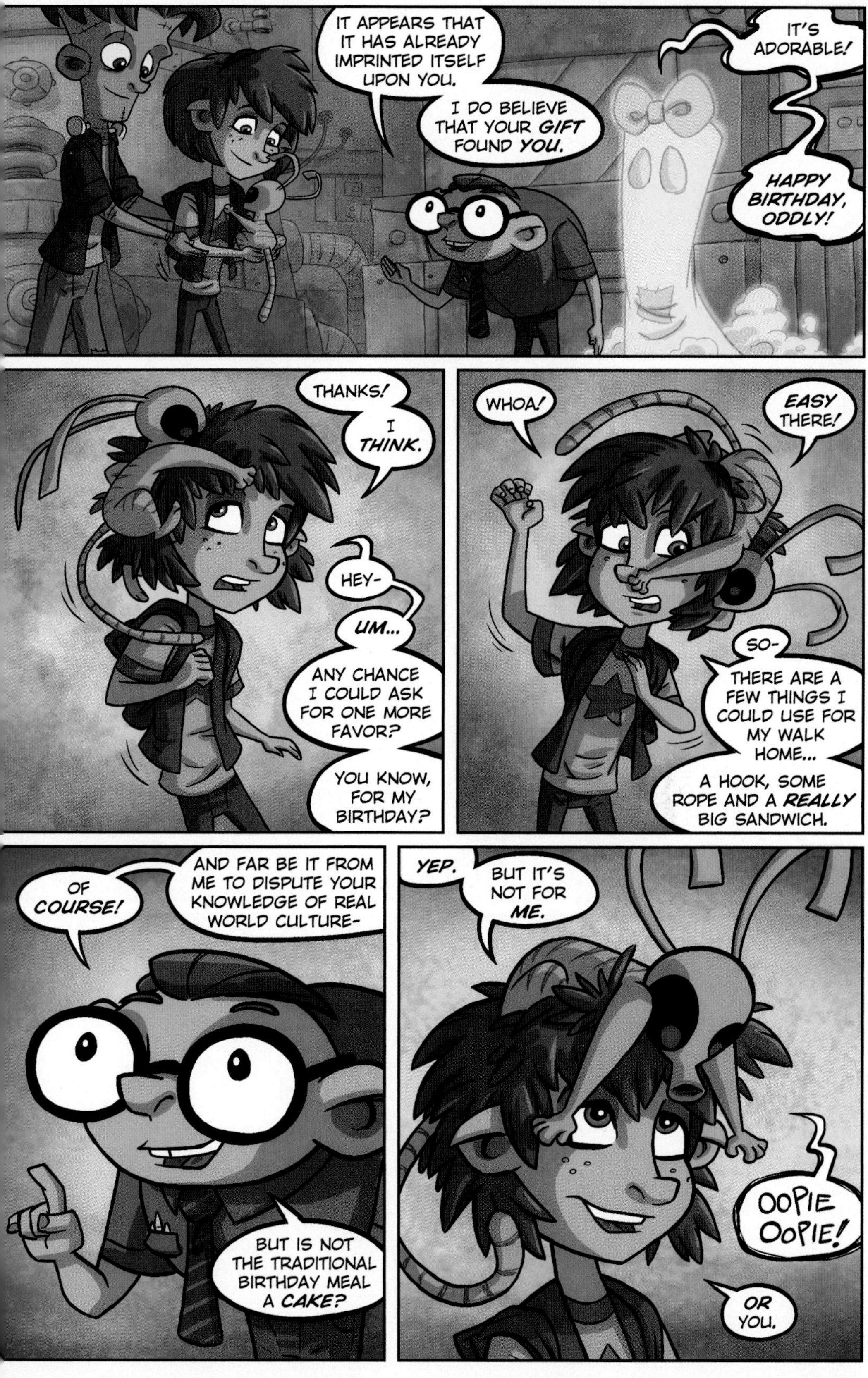
IT APPEARS THAT IT HAS ALREADY IMPRINTED ITSELF UPON YOU.
I DO BELIEVE THAT YOUR *GIFT* FOUND *YOU*.
IT'S ADORABLE!
HAPPY BIRTHDAY, ODDLY!
THANKS!
I *THINK*.
HEY-
UM...
ANY CHANCE I COULD ASK FOR ONE MORE FAVOR?
YOU KNOW, FOR MY BIRTHDAY?
WHOA!
EASY THERE!
SO-
THERE ARE A FEW THINGS I COULD USE FOR MY WALK HOME...
A HOOK, SOME ROPE AND A *REALLY* BIG SANDWICH.
OF *COURSE!*
AND FAR BE IT FROM ME TO DISPUTE YOUR KNOWLEDGE OF REAL WORLD CULTURE-
BUT IS NOT THE TRADITIONAL BIRTHDAY MEAL A *CAKE?*
YEP.
BUT IT'S NOT FOR *ME*.
OOPIE OOPIE!
OR YOU.

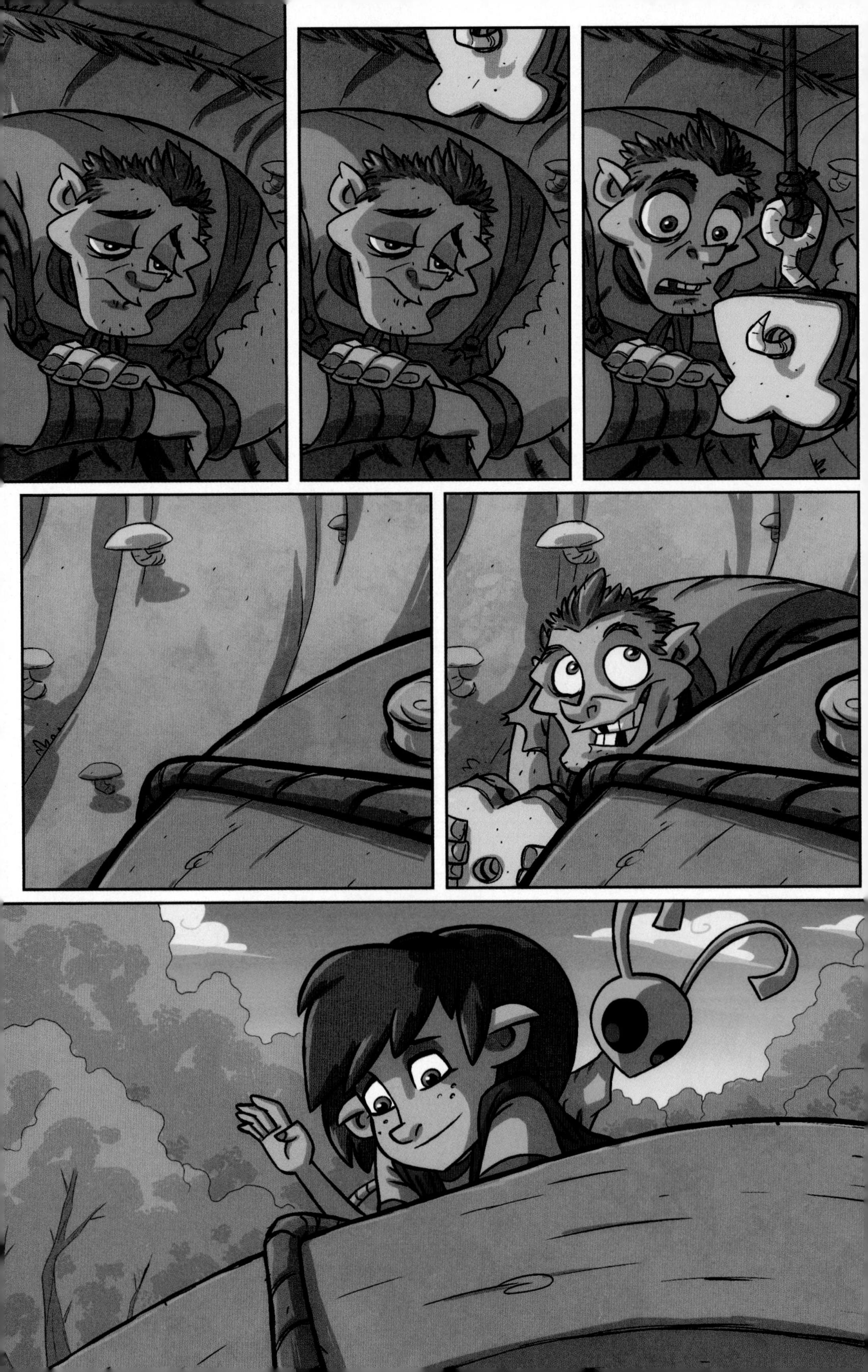

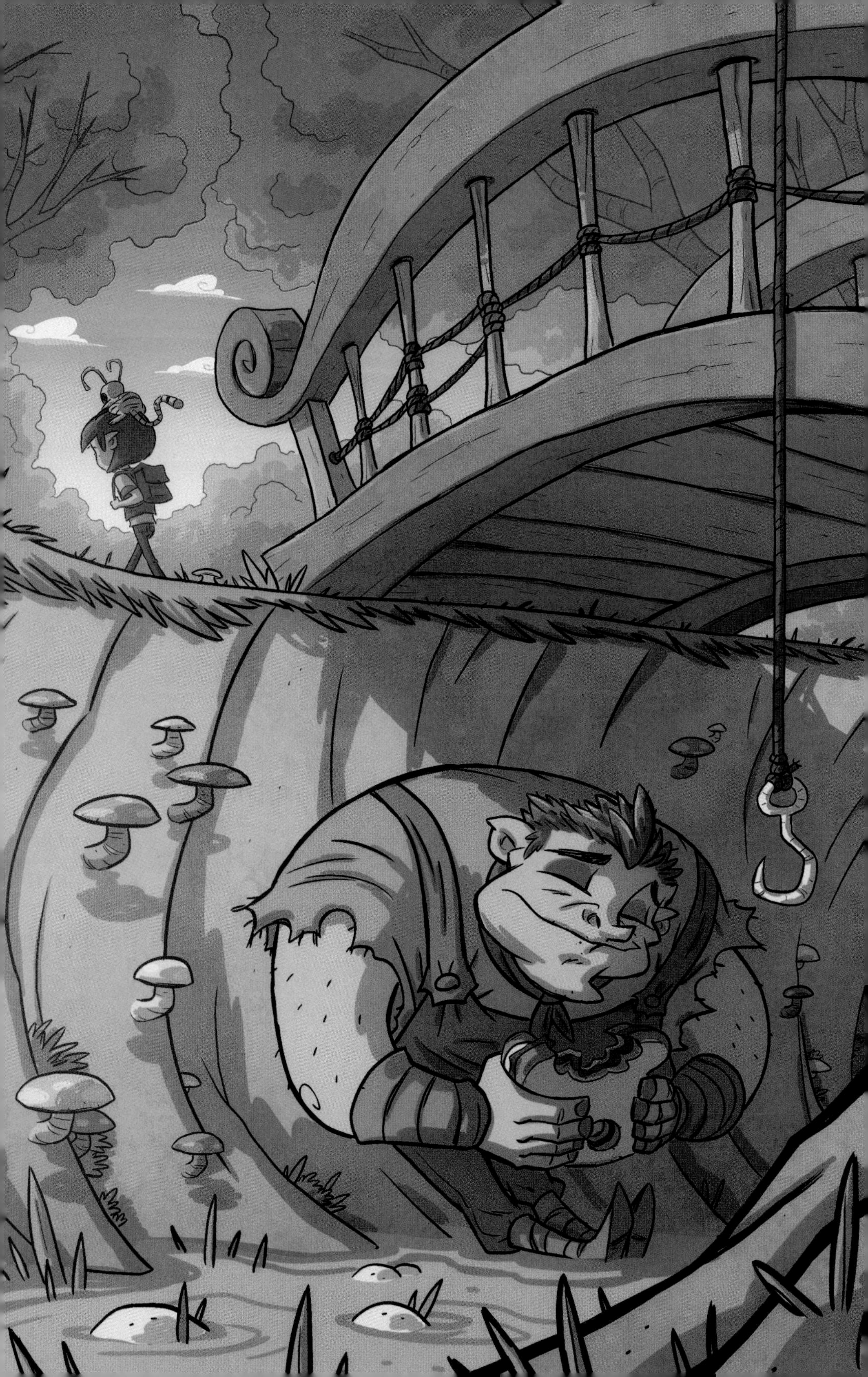

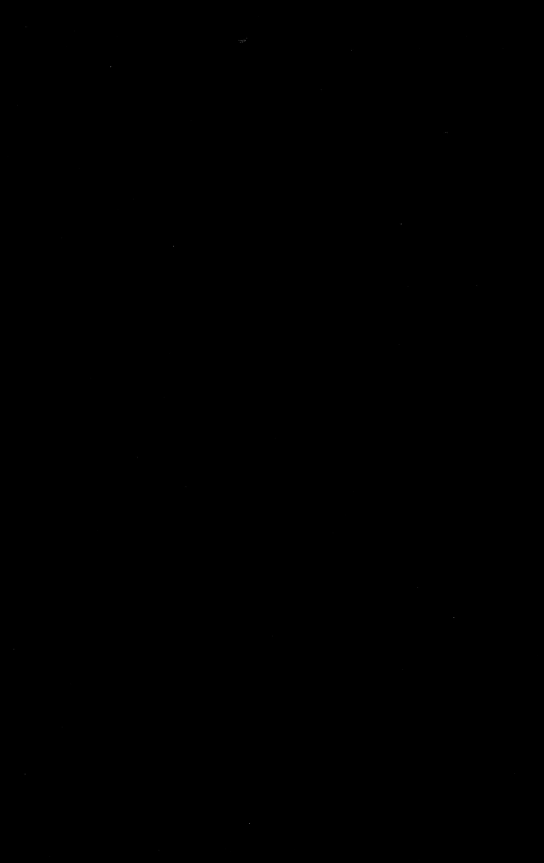

Chapter 10

Hero Worship

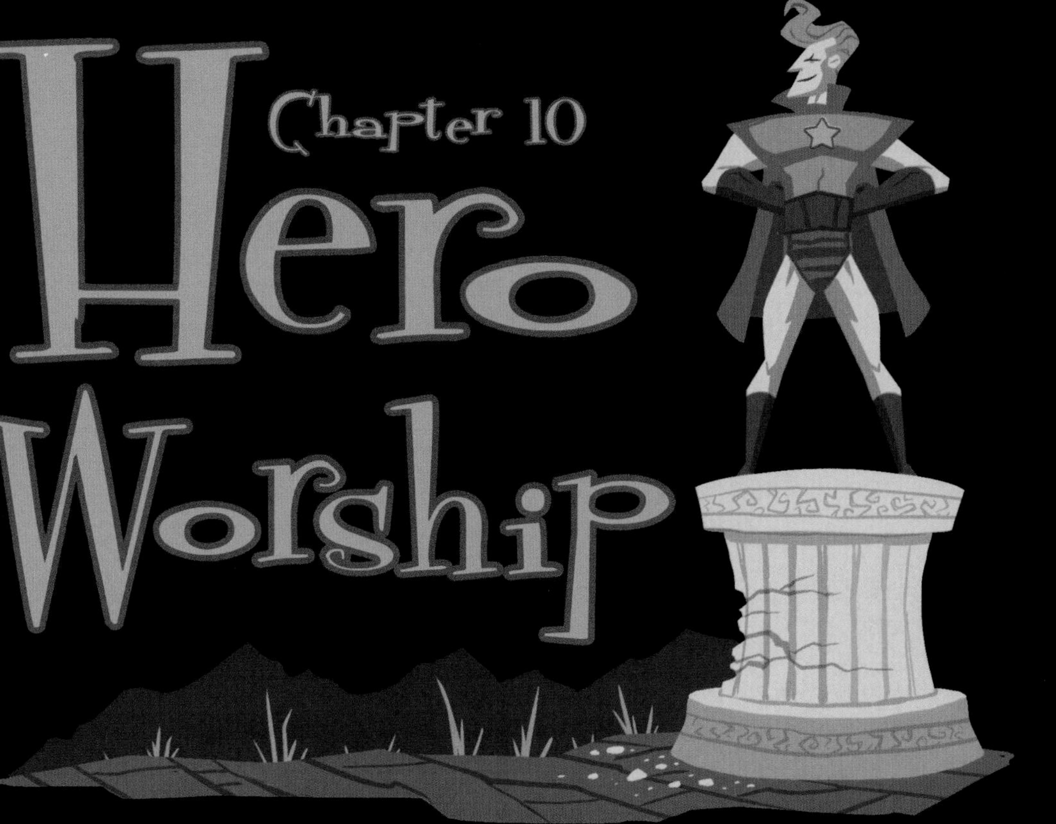

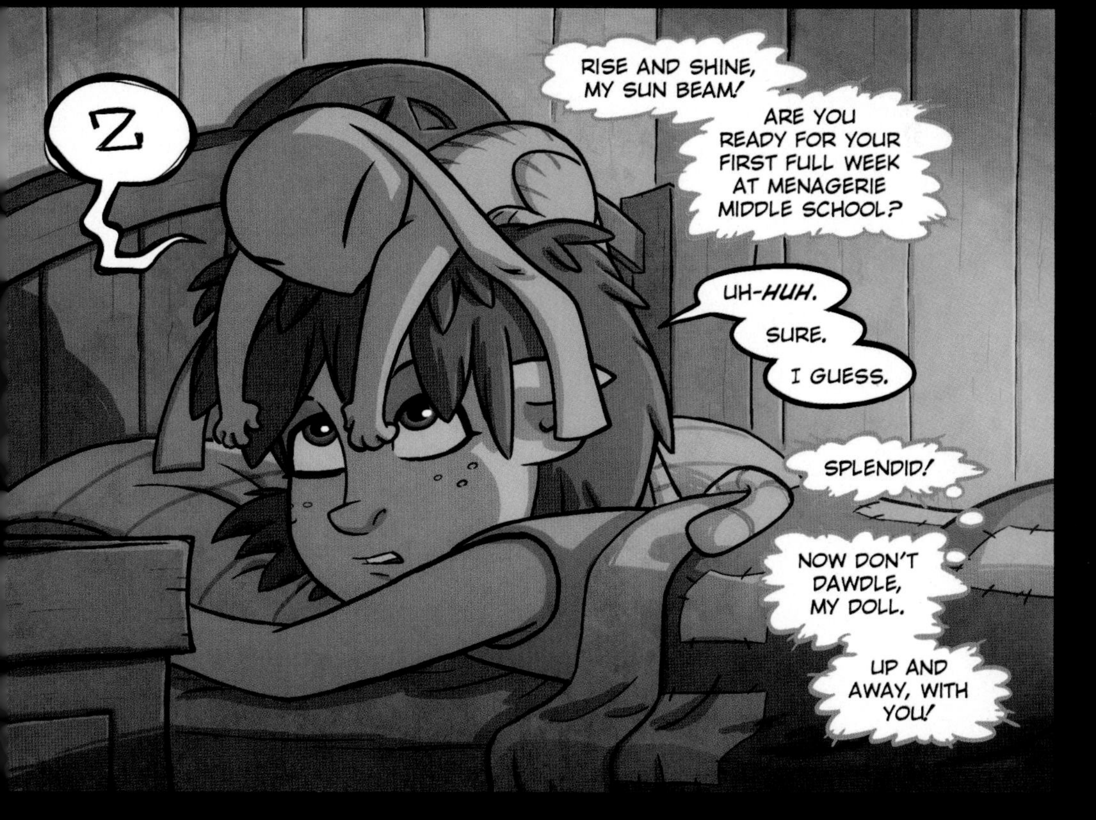
Z
RISE AND SHINE, MY SUN BEAM!
ARE YOU READY FOR YOUR FIRST FULL WEEK AT MENAGERIE MIDDLE SCHOOL?
UH-HUH.
SURE.
I GUESS.
SPLENDID!
NOW DON'T DAWDLE, MY DOLL.
UP AND AWAY, WITH YOU!

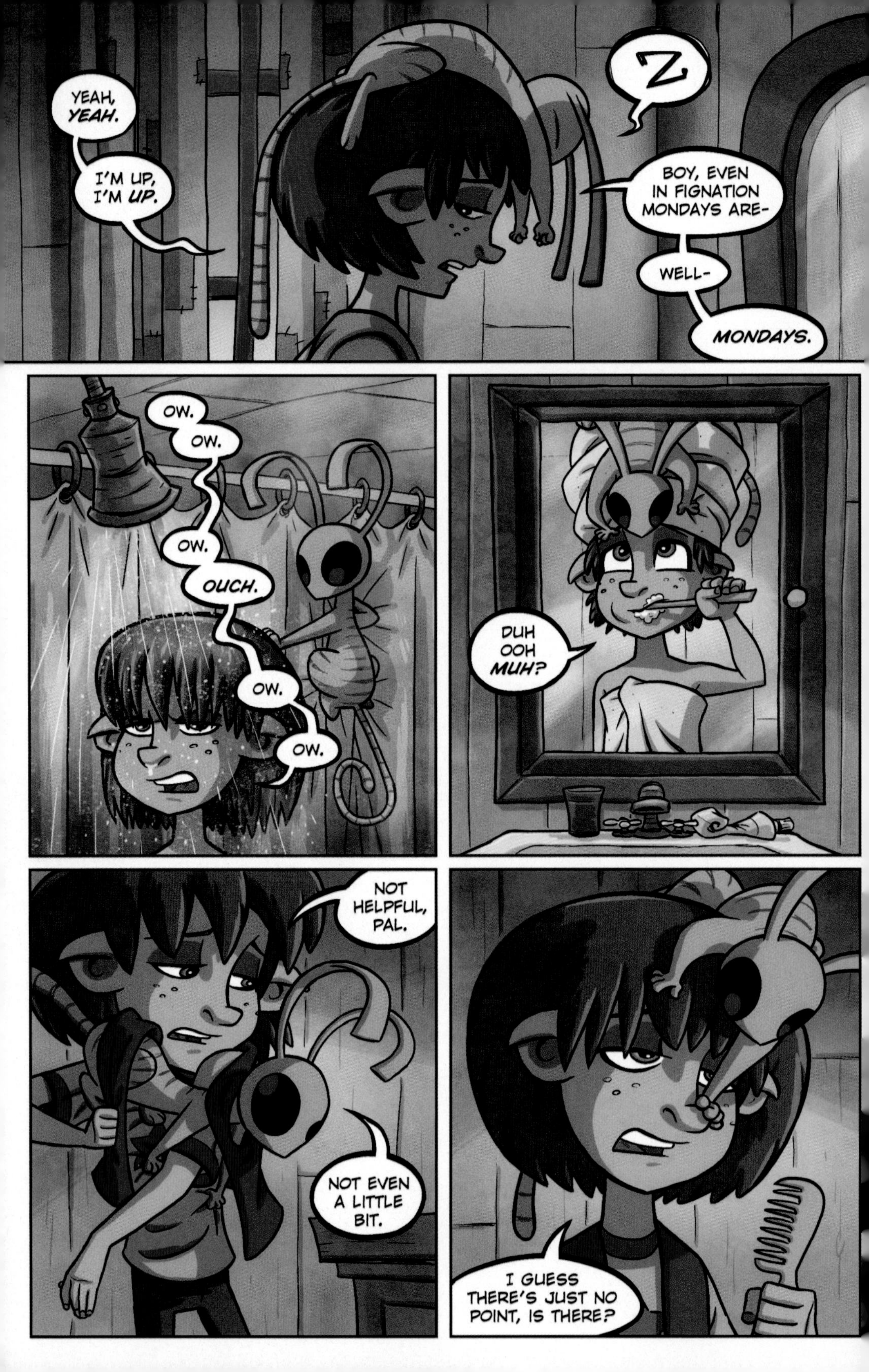
YEAH, YEAH.
I'M UP, I'M UP.
Z
BOY, EVEN IN FIGNATION MONDAYS ARE-
WELL-
MONDAYS.
OW.
OW.
OW.
OUCH.
OW.
OW.
DUH OOH MUH?
NOT HELPFUL, PAL.
NOT EVEN A LITTLE BIT.
I GUESS THERE'S JUST NO POINT, IS THERE?

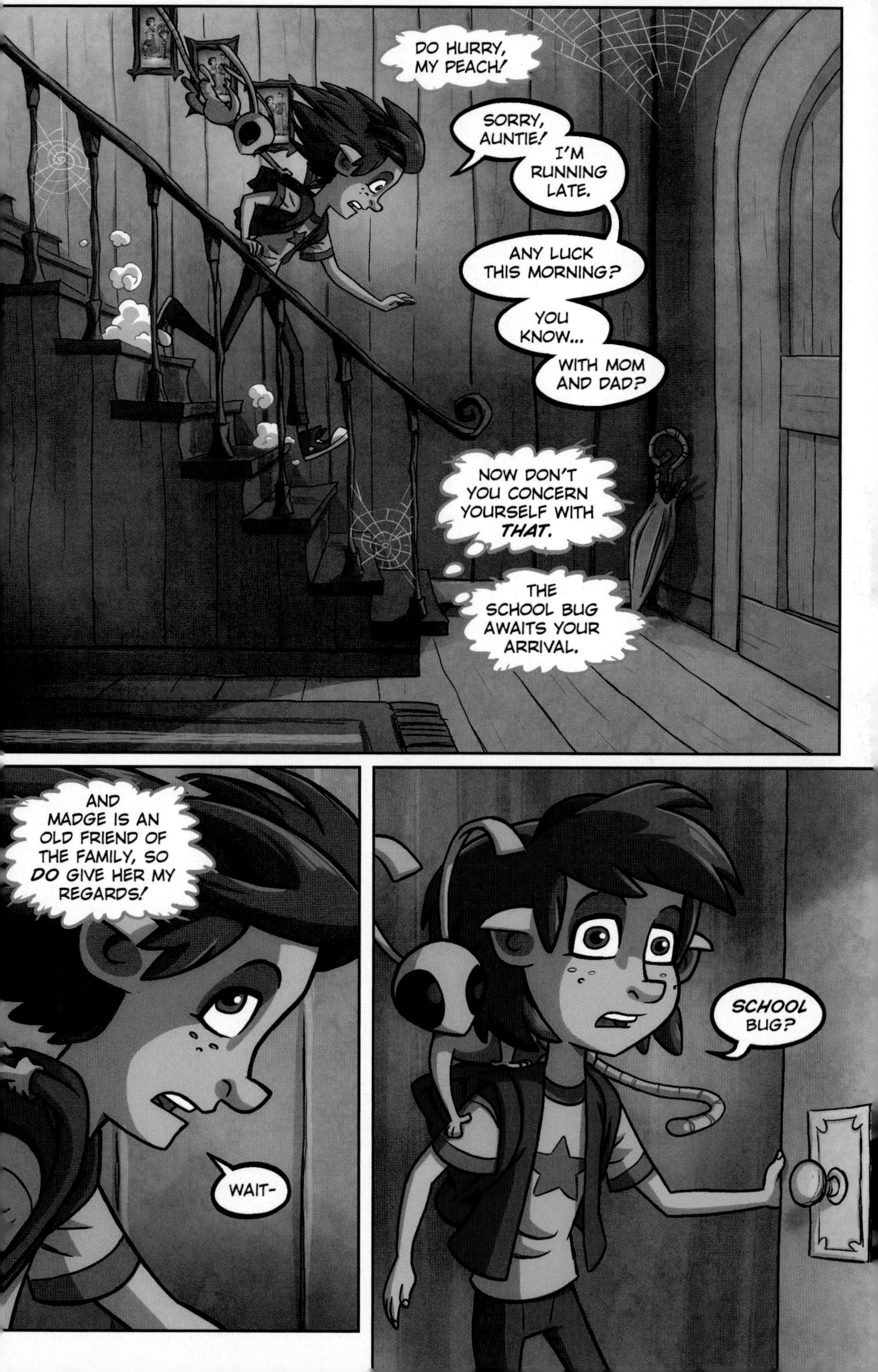
DO HURRY, MY PEACH!
SORRY, AUNTIE!
I'M RUNNING LATE.
ANY LUCK THIS MORNING?
YOU KNOW...
WITH MOM AND DAD?
NOW DON'T YOU CONCERN YOURSELF WITH THAT.
THE SCHOOL BUG AWAITS YOUR ARRIVAL.
AND MADGE IS AN OLD FRIEND OF THE FAMILY, SO DO GIVE HER MY REGARDS!
WAIT-
SCHOOL BUG?

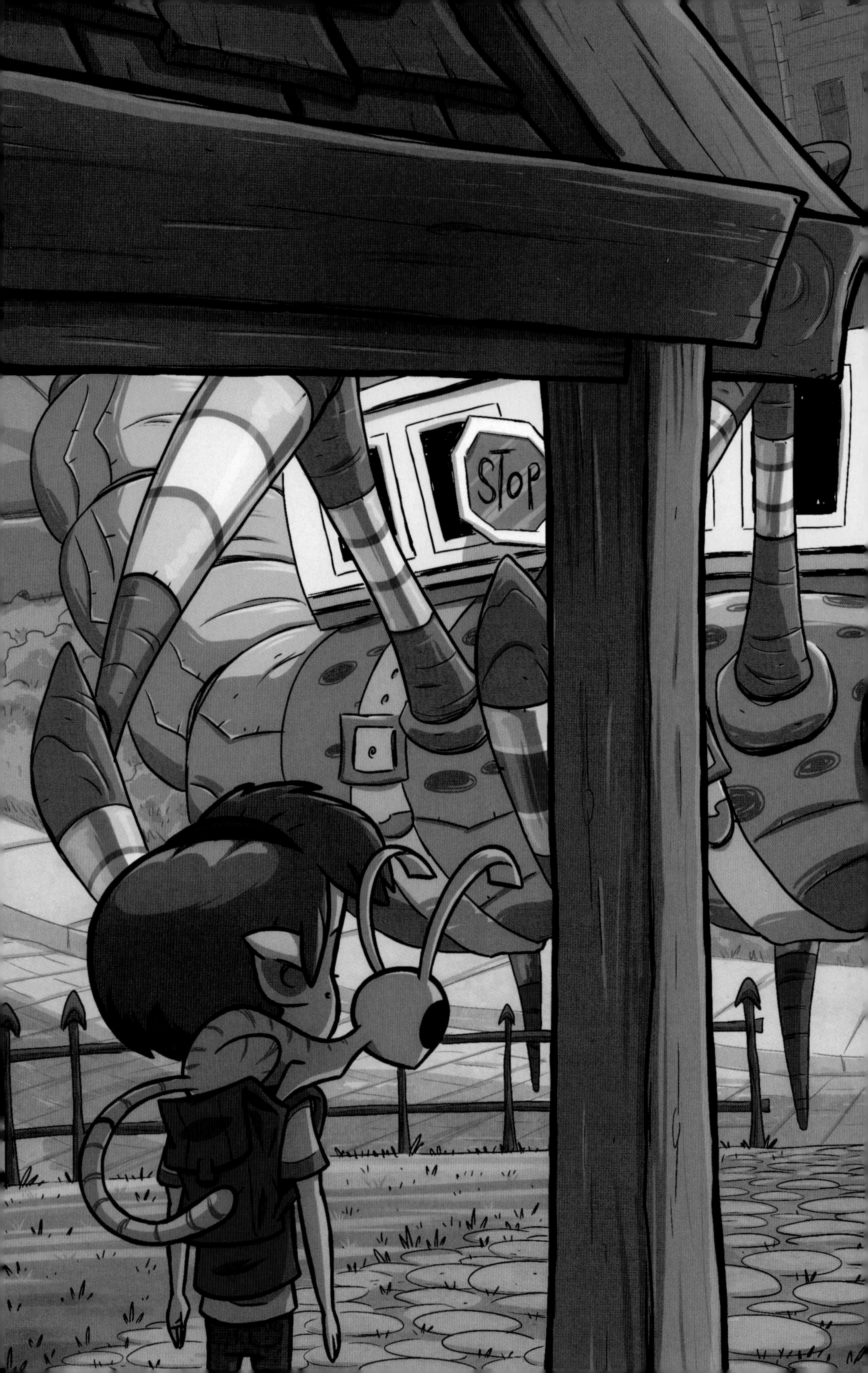
STOP

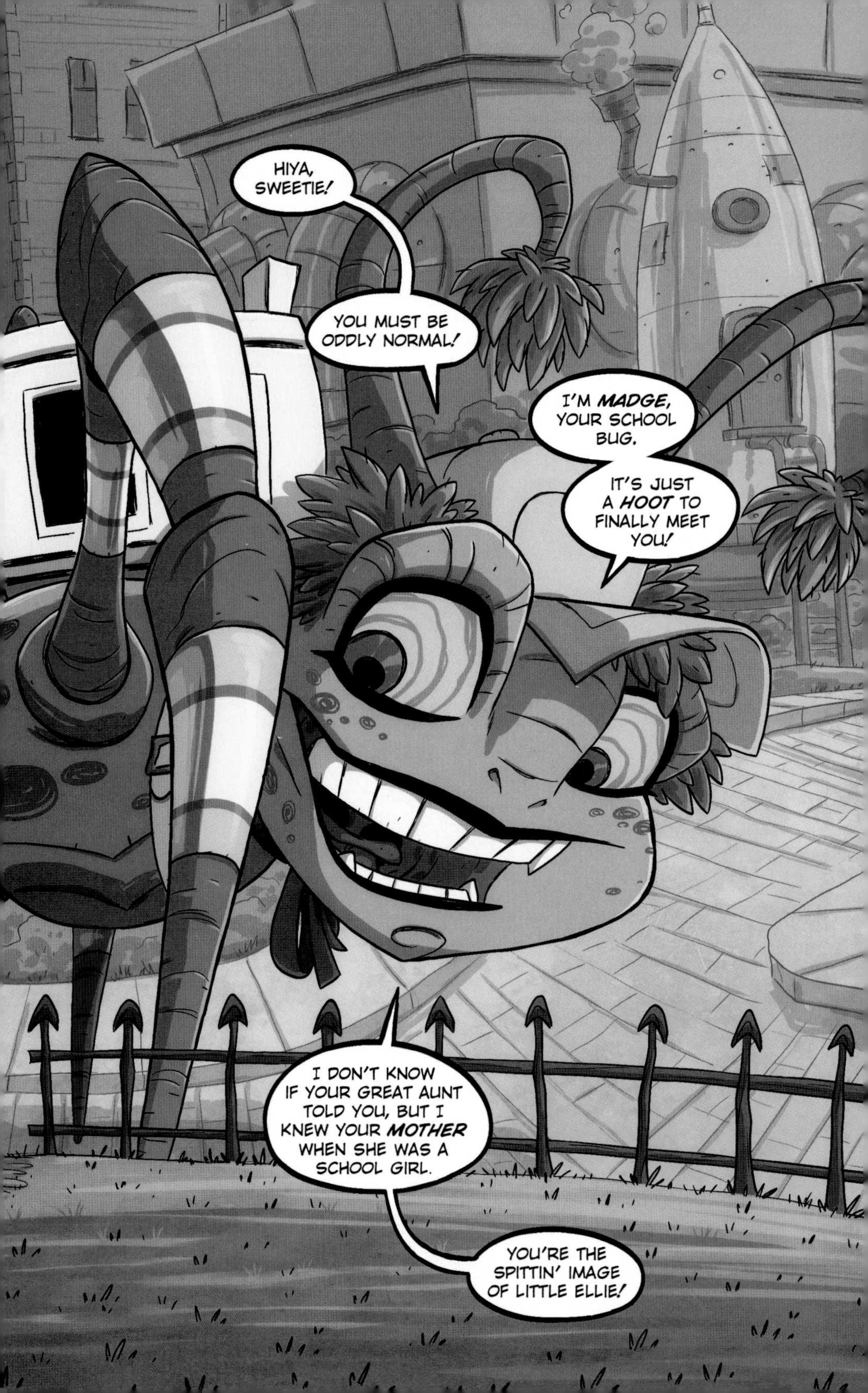
HIYA, SWEETIE!
YOU MUST BE ODDLY NORMAL!
I'M *MADGE*, YOUR SCHOOL BUG.
IT'S JUST A *HOOT* TO FINALLY MEET YOU!
I DON'T KNOW IF YOUR GREAT AUNT TOLD YOU, BUT I KNEW YOUR *MOTHER* WHEN SHE WAS A SCHOOL GIRL.
YOU'RE THE SPITTIN' IMAGE OF LITTLE ELLIE!

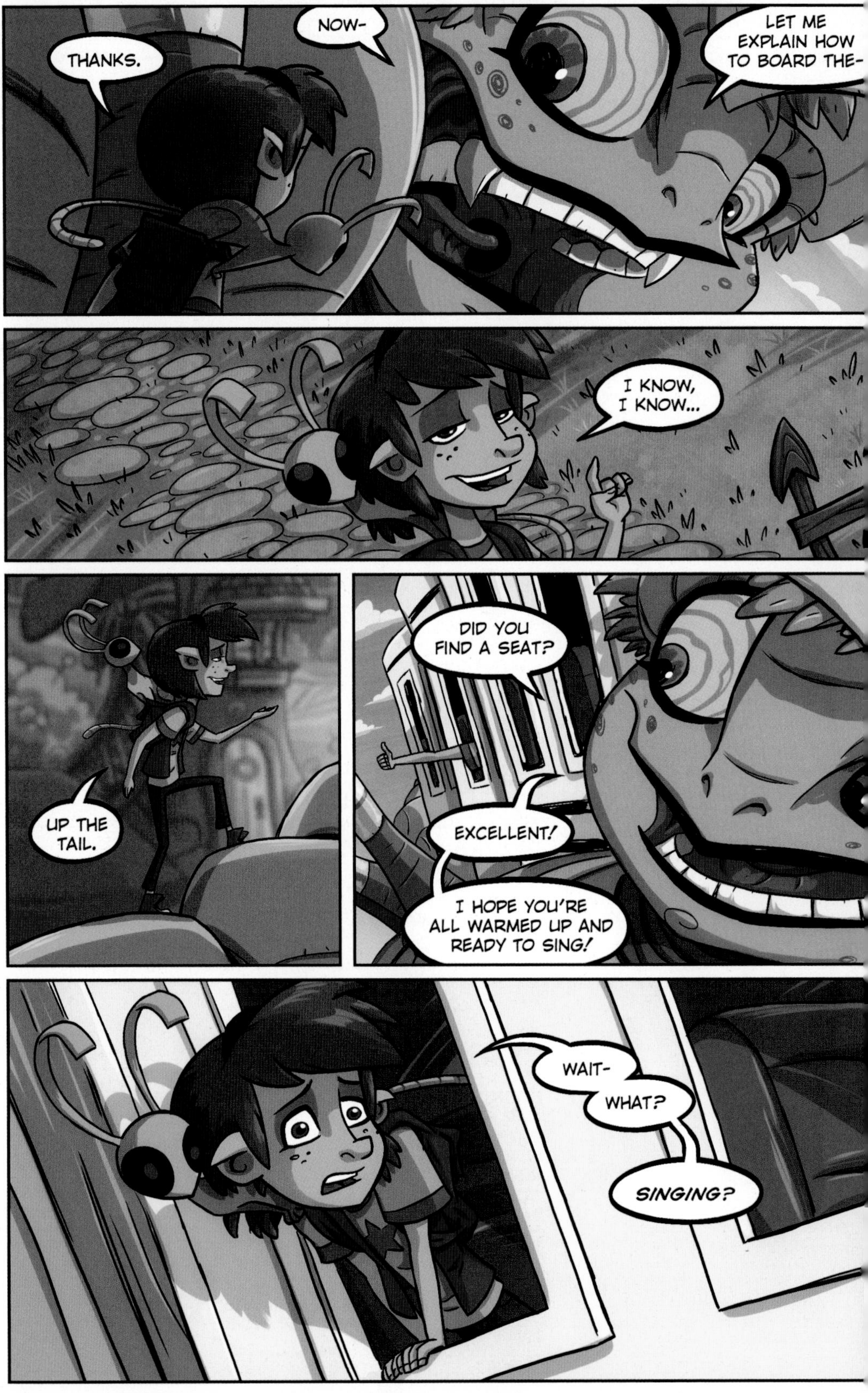
THANKS.
NOW-
LET ME EXPLAIN HOW TO BOARD THE-
I KNOW, I KNOW...
UP THE TAIL.
DID YOU FIND A SEAT?
EXCELLENT!
I HOPE YOU'RE ALL WARMED UP AND READY TO SING!
WAIT-
WHAT?
SINGING?

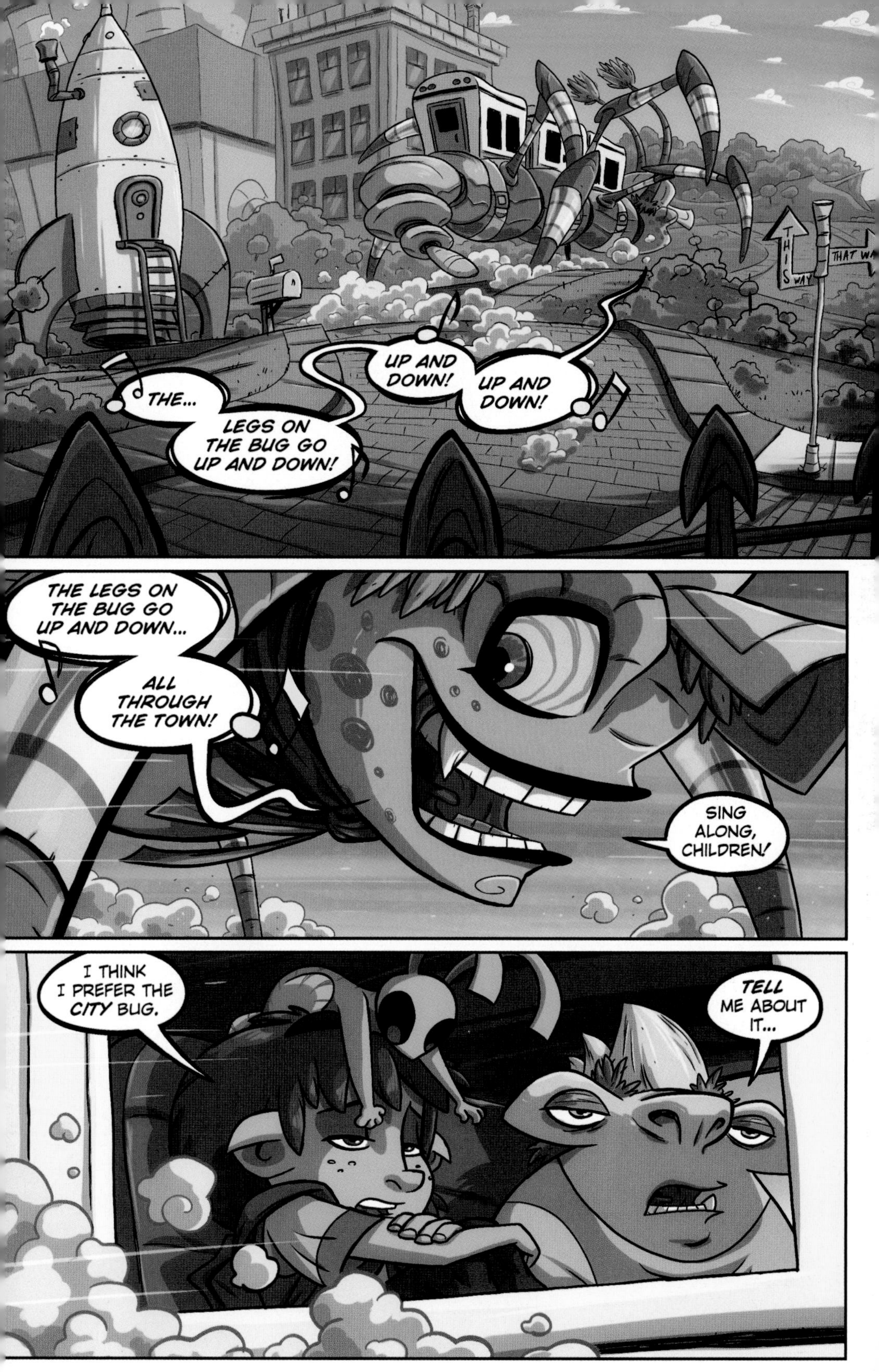
THIS WAY
THAT WA
THE...
LEGS ON THE BUG GO UP AND DOWN!
UP AND DOWN!
UP AND DOWN!
THE LEGS ON THE BUG GO UP AND DOWN...
ALL THROUGH THE TOWN!
SING ALONG, CHILDREN!
I THINK I PREFER THE *CITY* BUG.
TELL ME ABOUT IT...

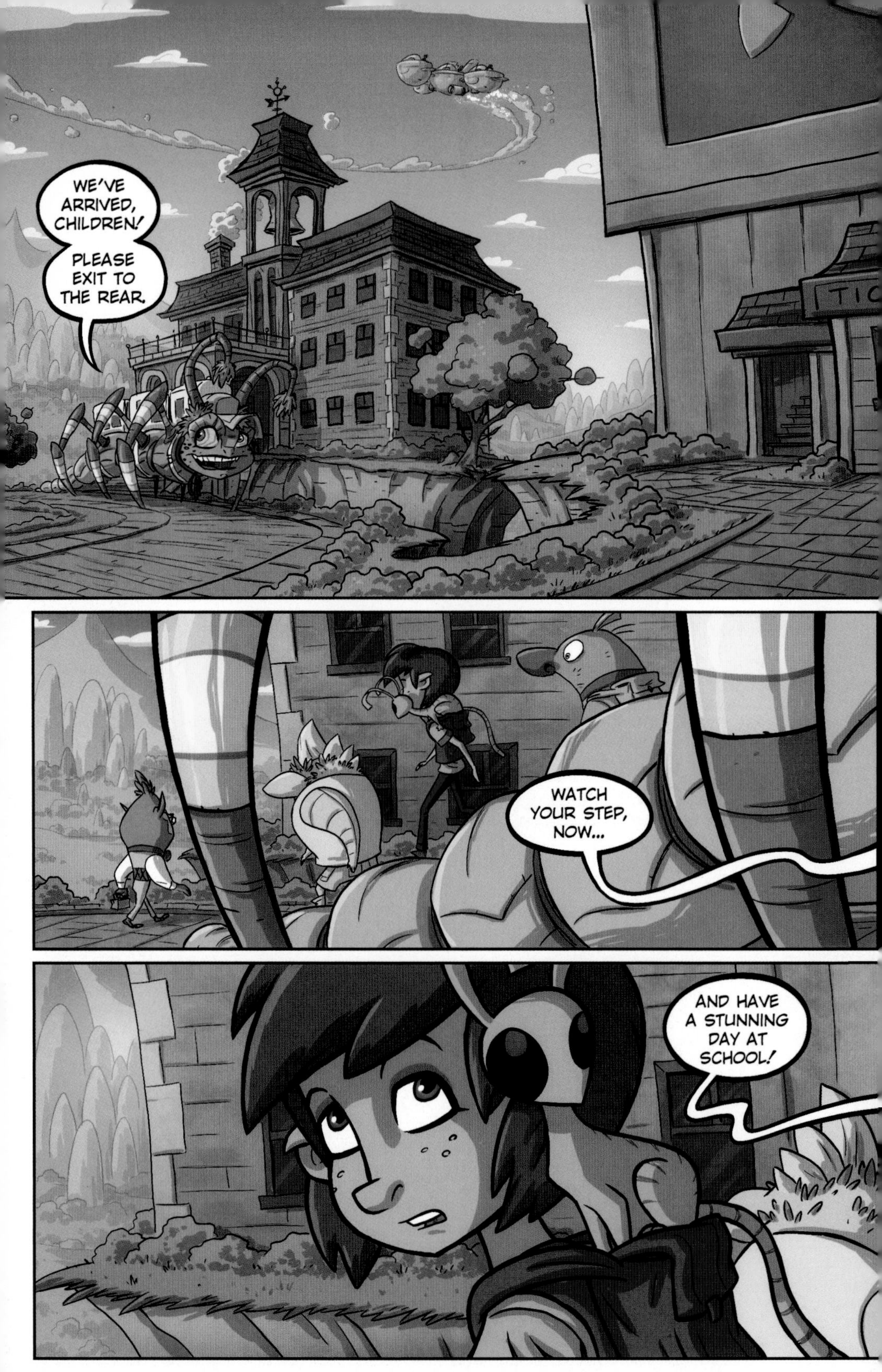
WE'VE ARRIVED, CHILDREN!
PLEASE EXIT TO THE REAR.
WATCH YOUR STEP, NOW...
AND HAVE A STUNNING DAY AT SCHOOL!

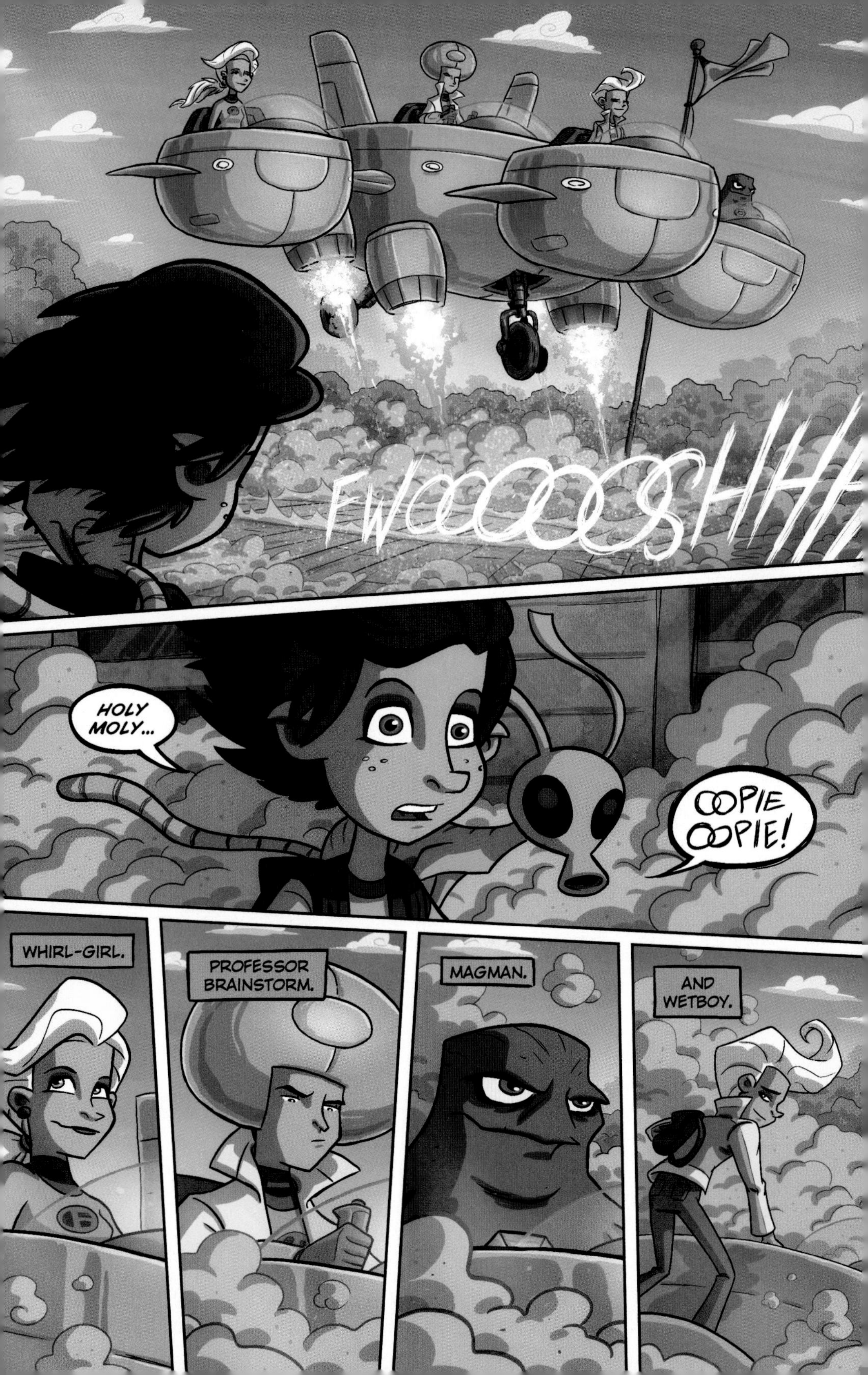
FWOOOOOOSHHH
HOLY MOLY...
OOPIE OOPIE!
WHIRL-GIRL.
PROFESSOR BRAINSTORM.
MAGMAN.
AND WETBOY.

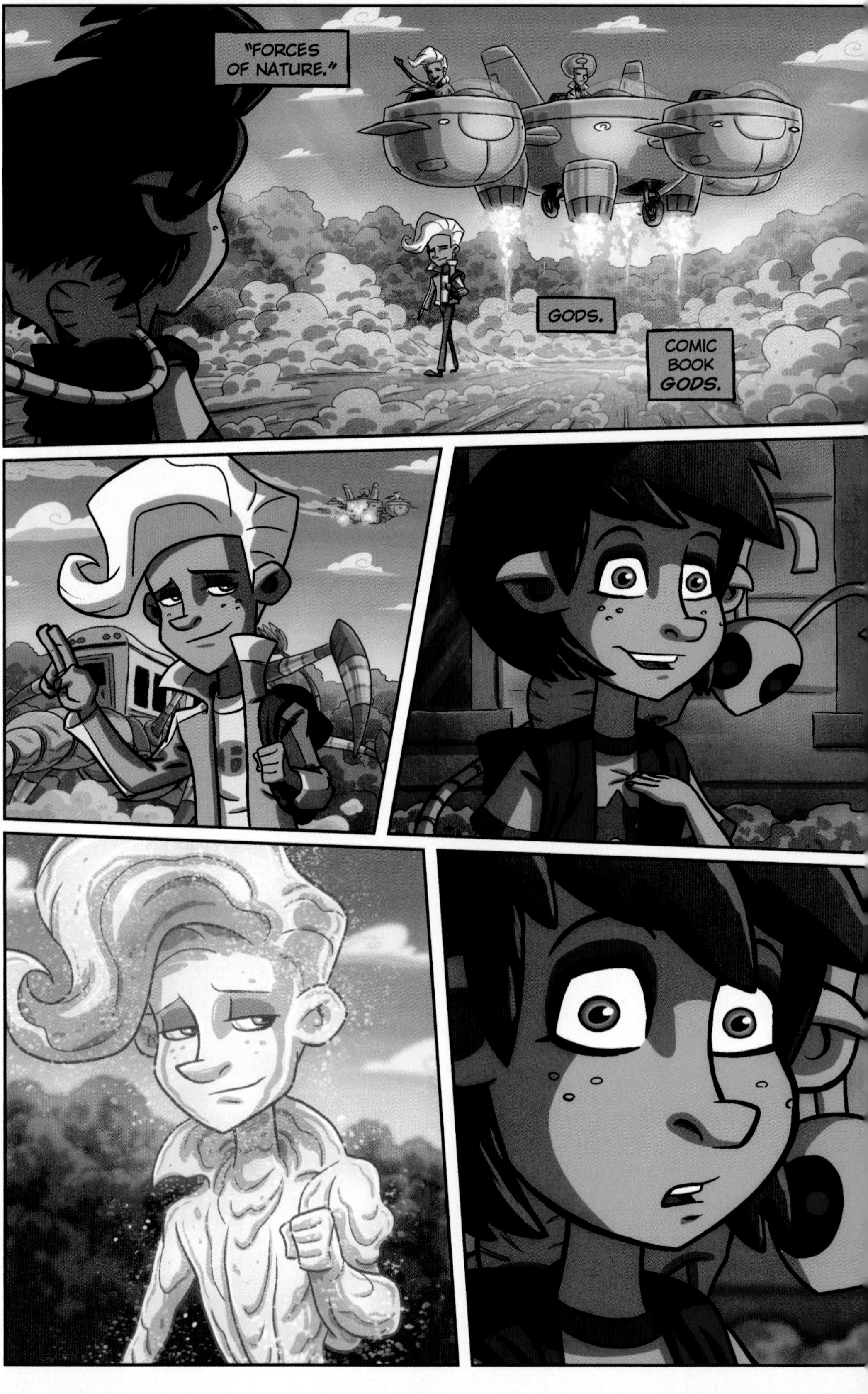
"FORCES OF NATURE."
GODS.
COMIC BOOK GODS.

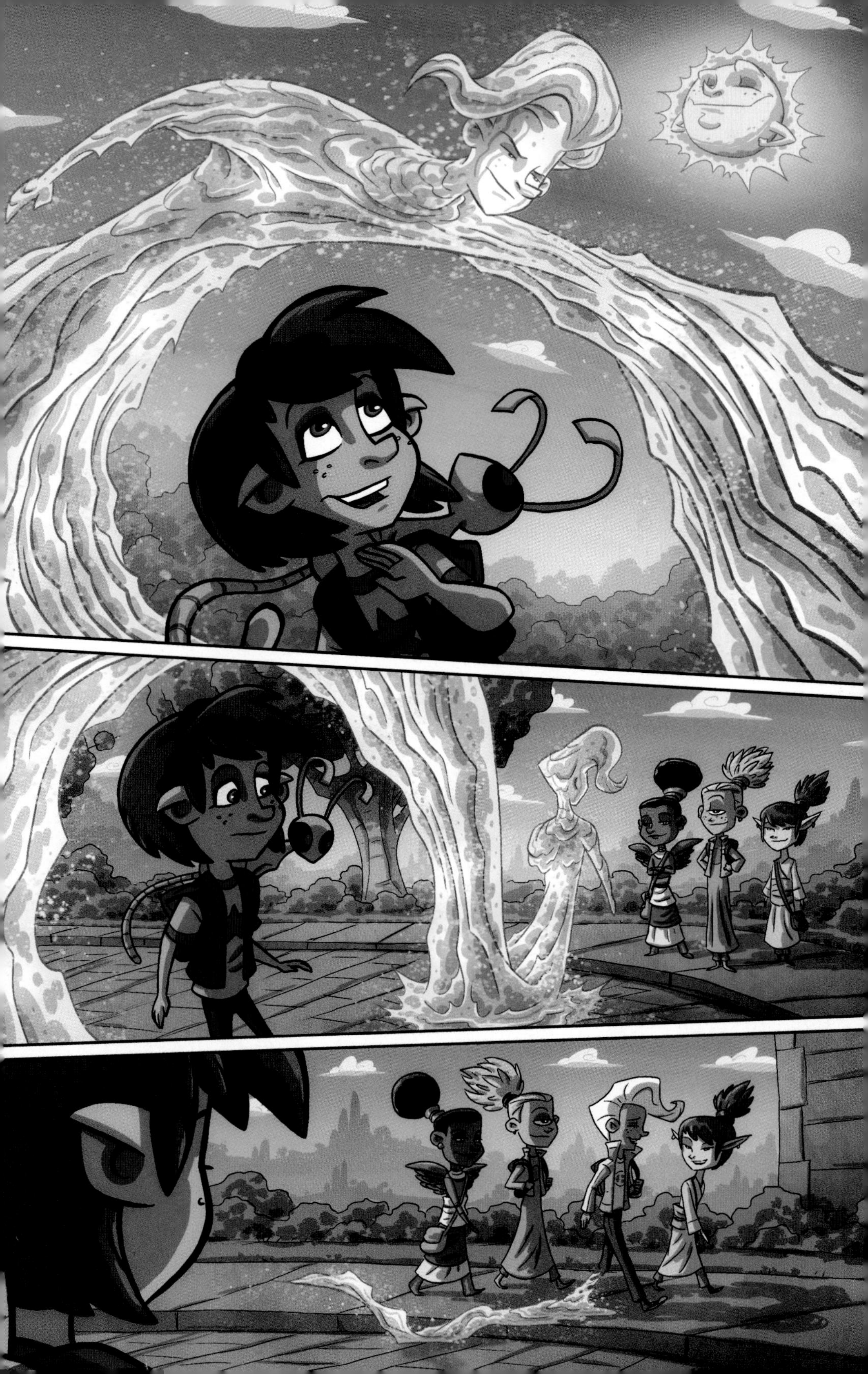

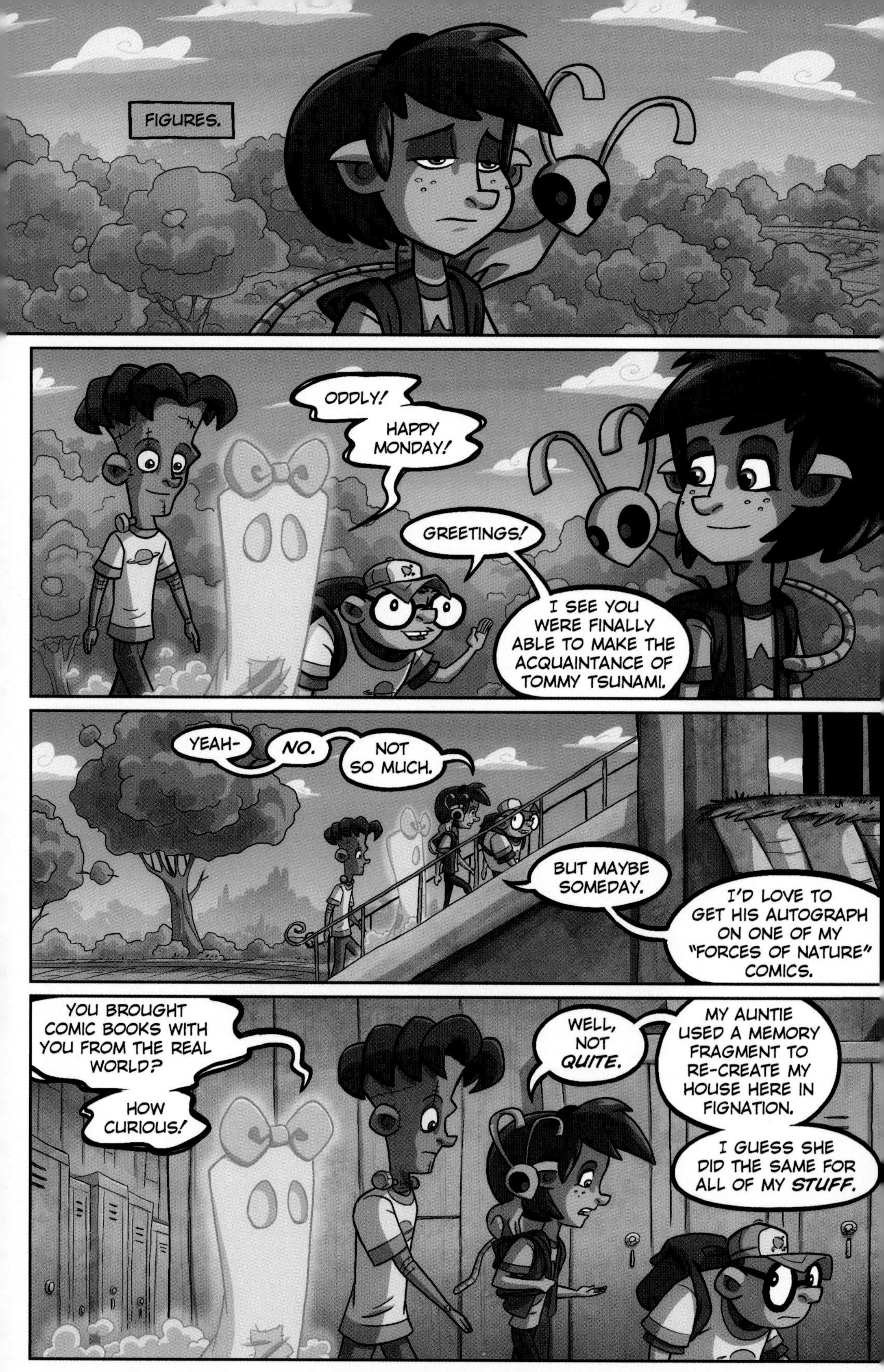
FIGURES.
ODDLY!
HAPPY MONDAY!
GREETINGS!
I SEE YOU WERE FINALLY ABLE TO MAKE THE ACQUAINTANCE OF TOMMY TSUNAMI.
YEAH-
NO.
NOT SO MUCH.
BUT MAYBE SOMEDAY.
I'D LOVE TO GET HIS AUTOGRAPH ON ONE OF MY "FORCES OF NATURE" COMICS.
YOU BROUGHT COMIC BOOKS WITH YOU FROM THE REAL WORLD?
HOW CURIOUS!
WELL, NOT QUITE.
MY AUNTIE USED A MEMORY FRAGMENT TO RE-CREATE MY HOUSE HERE IN FIGNATION.
I GUESS SHE DID THE SAME FOR ALL OF MY STUFF.

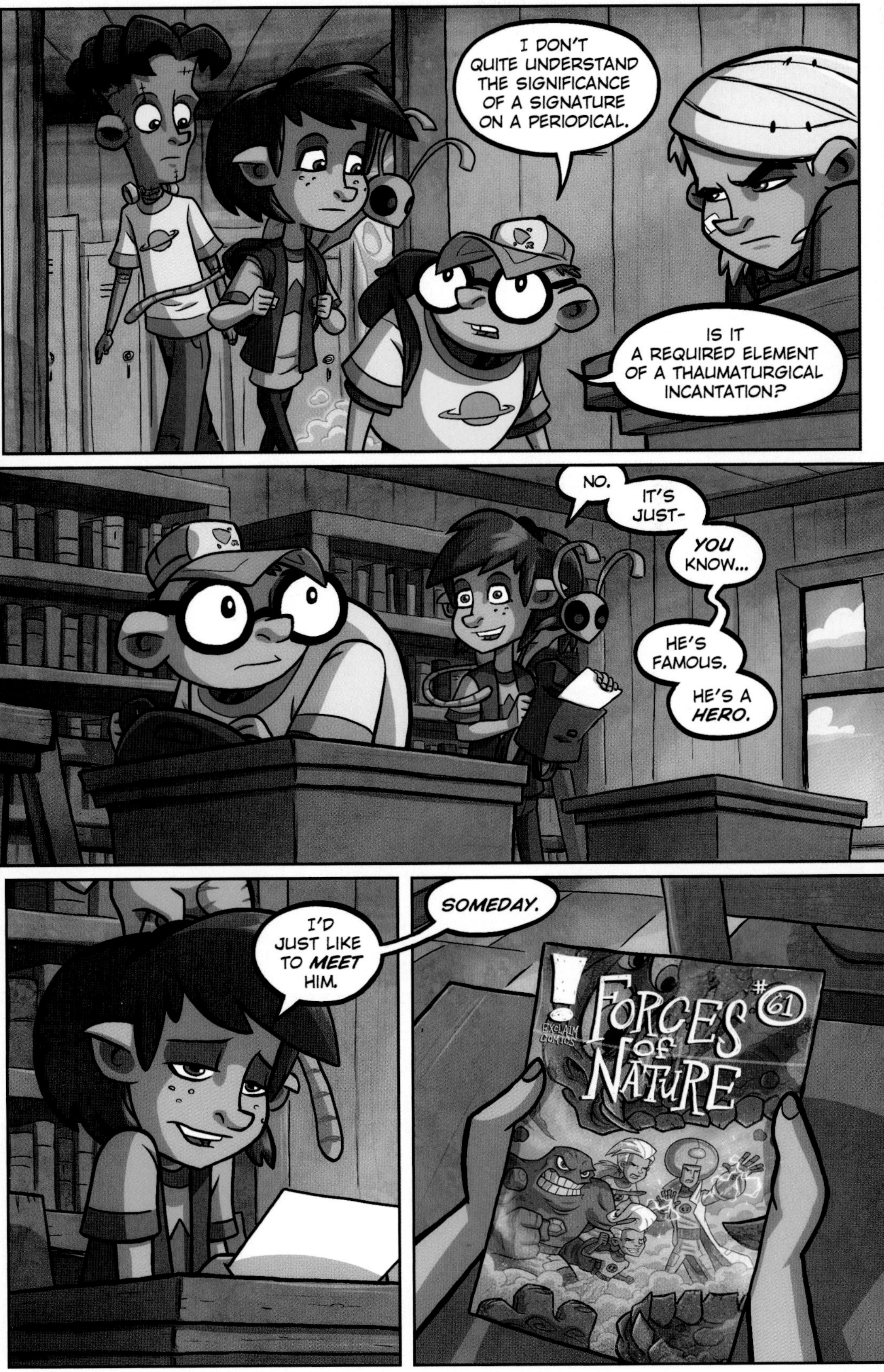
I DON'T QUITE UNDERSTAND THE SIGNIFICANCE OF A SIGNATURE ON A PERIODICAL.
IS IT A REQUIRED ELEMENT OF A THAUMATURGICAL INCANTATION?
NO.
IT'S JUST-
YOU KNOW...
HE'S FAMOUS.
HE'S A *HERO*.
I'D JUST LIKE TO *MEET* HIM.
SOMEDAY.
EXCLAIM COMICS
FORCES OF NATURE
#61

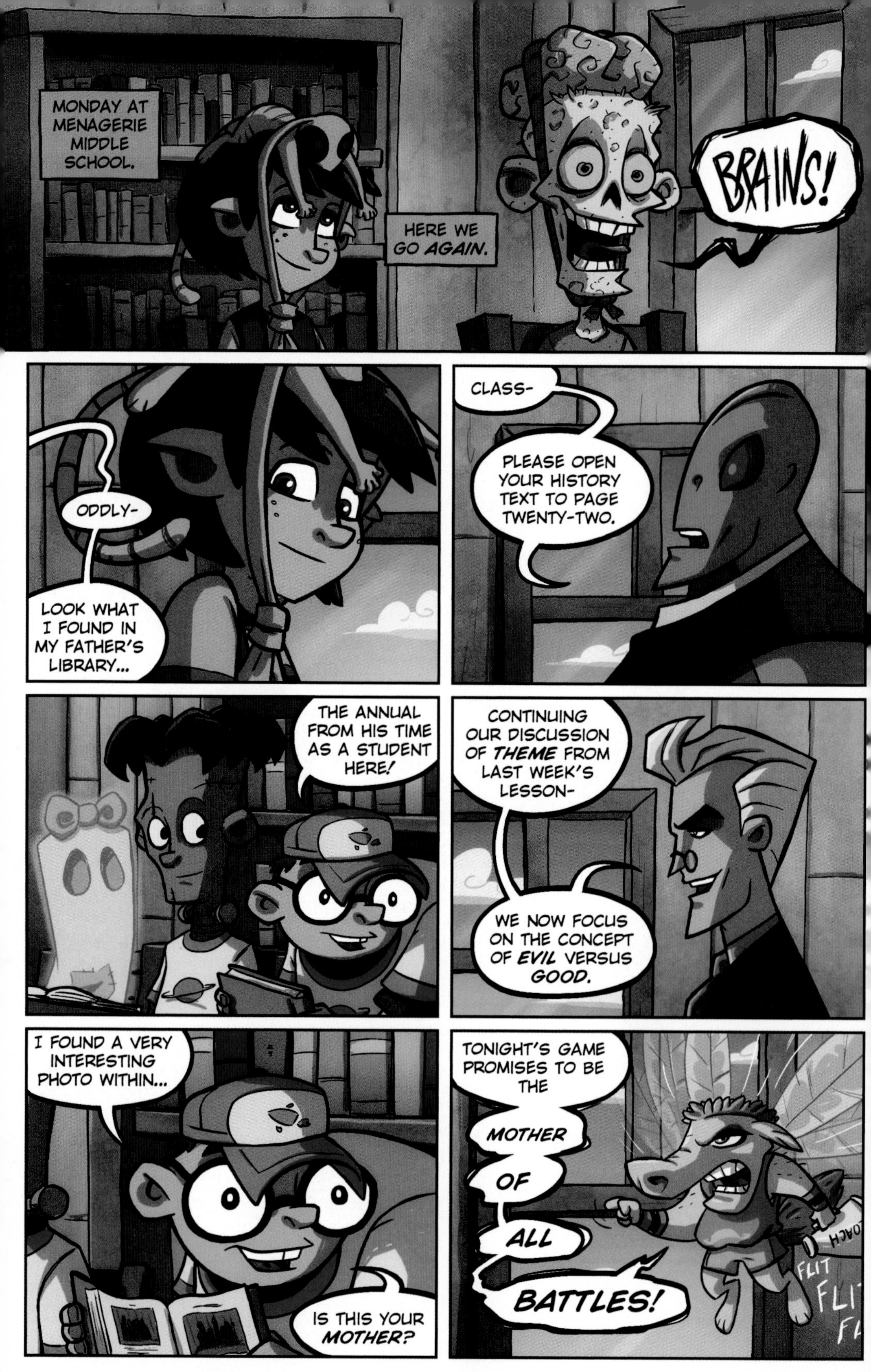
MONDAY AT MENAGERIE MIDDLE SCHOOL.
HERE WE GO *AGAIN*.
BRAINS!
ODDLY-
LOOK WHAT I FOUND IN MY FATHER'S LIBRARY...
CLASS-
PLEASE OPEN YOUR HISTORY TEXT TO PAGE TWENTY-TWO.
THE ANNUAL FROM HIS TIME AS A STUDENT HERE!
CONTINUING OUR DISCUSSION OF *THEME* FROM LAST WEEK'S LESSON-
WE NOW FOCUS ON THE CONCEPT OF *EVIL* VERSUS *GOOD*.
I FOUND A VERY INTERESTING PHOTO WITHIN...
IS THIS YOUR *MOTHER?*
TONIGHT'S GAME PROMISES TO BE THE
MOTHER
OF
ALL
BATTLES!
FLIT
FLIT

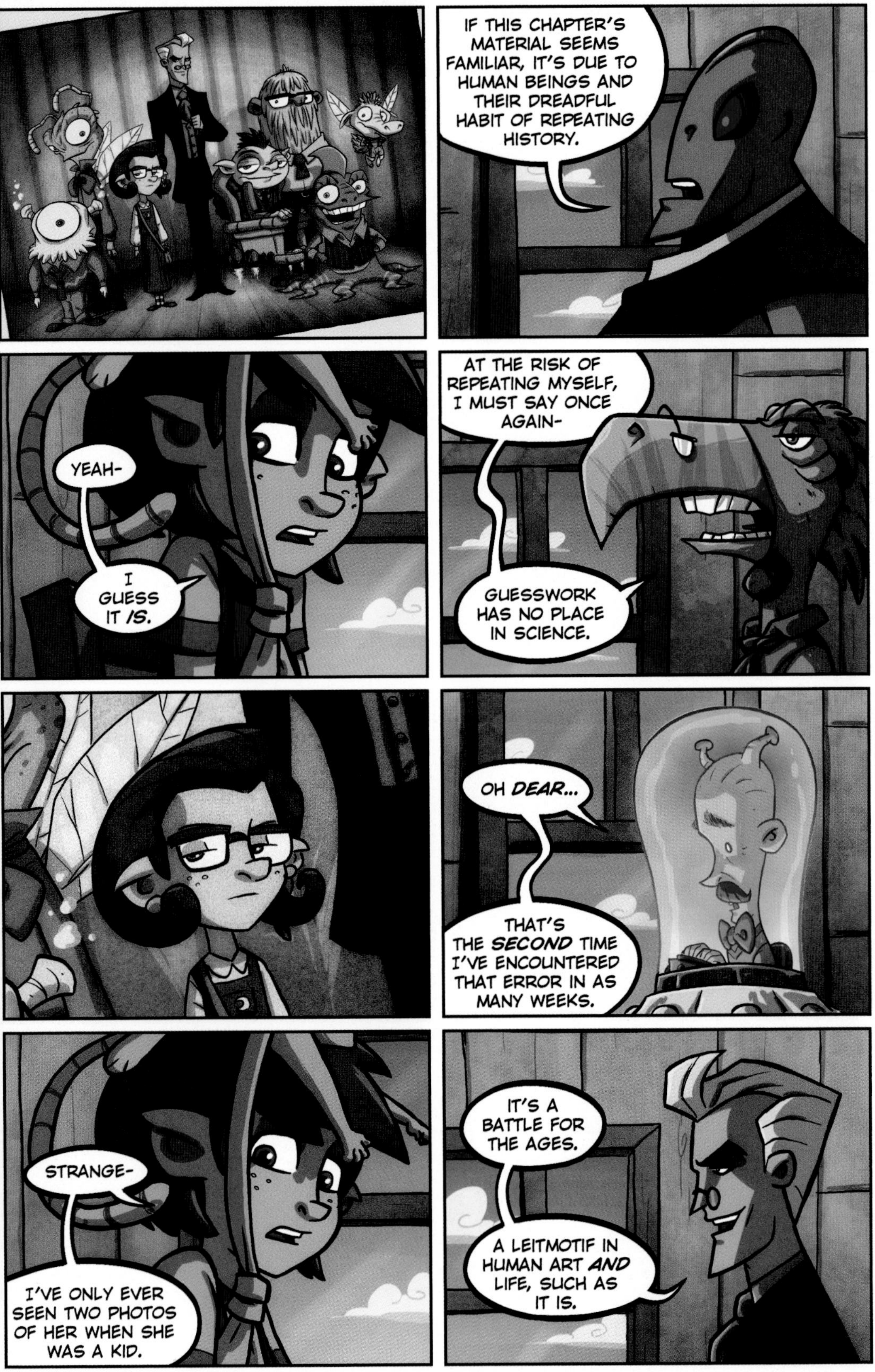
IF THIS CHAPTER'S MATERIAL SEEMS FAMILIAR, IT'S DUE TO HUMAN BEINGS AND THEIR DREADFUL HABIT OF REPEATING HISTORY.
YEAH-
I GUESS IT *IS*.
AT THE RISK OF REPEATING MYSELF, I MUST SAY ONCE AGAIN-
GUESSWORK HAS NO PLACE IN SCIENCE.
OH *DEAR*...
THAT'S THE ***SECOND*** TIME I'VE ENCOUNTERED THAT ERROR IN AS MANY WEEKS.
STRANGE-
I'VE ONLY EVER SEEN TWO PHOTOS OF HER WHEN SHE WAS A KID.
IT'S A BATTLE FOR THE AGES.
A LEITMOTIF IN HUMAN ART *AND* LIFE, SUCH AS IT IS.

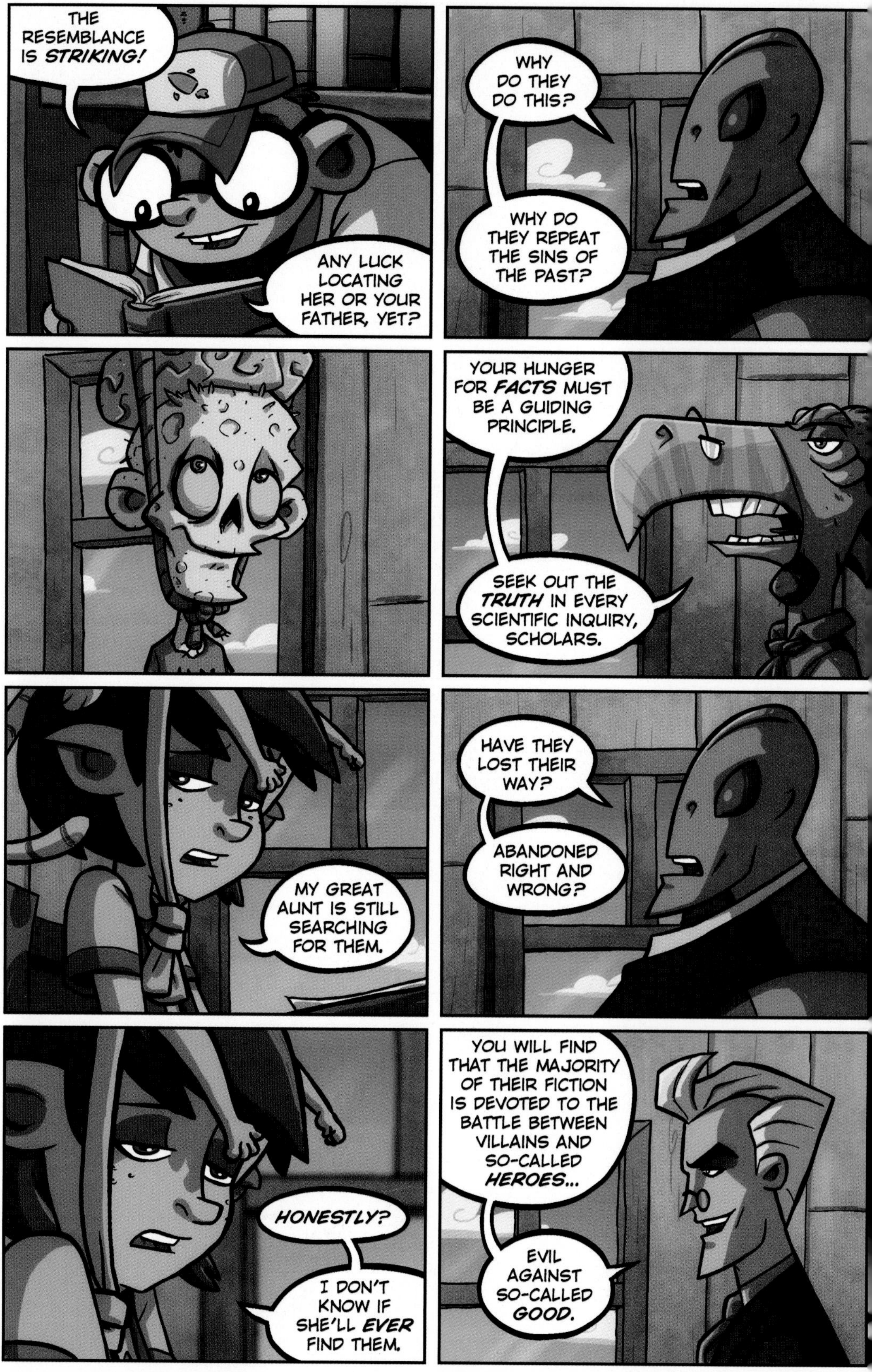
THE RESEMBLANCE IS STRIKING!
ANY LUCK LOCATING HER OR YOUR FATHER, YET?
WHY DO THEY DO THIS?
WHY DO THEY REPEAT THE SINS OF THE PAST?
YOUR HUNGER FOR FACTS MUST BE A GUIDING PRINCIPLE.
SEEK OUT THE TRUTH IN EVERY SCIENTIFIC INQUIRY, SCHOLARS.
MY GREAT AUNT IS STILL SEARCHING FOR THEM.
HAVE THEY LOST THEIR WAY?
ABANDONED RIGHT AND WRONG?
HONESTLY?
I DON'T KNOW IF SHE'LL EVER FIND THEM.
YOU WILL FIND THAT THE MAJORITY OF THEIR FICTION IS DEVOTED TO THE BATTLE BETWEEN VILLAINS AND SO-CALLED HEROES...
EVIL AGAINST SO-CALLED GOOD.

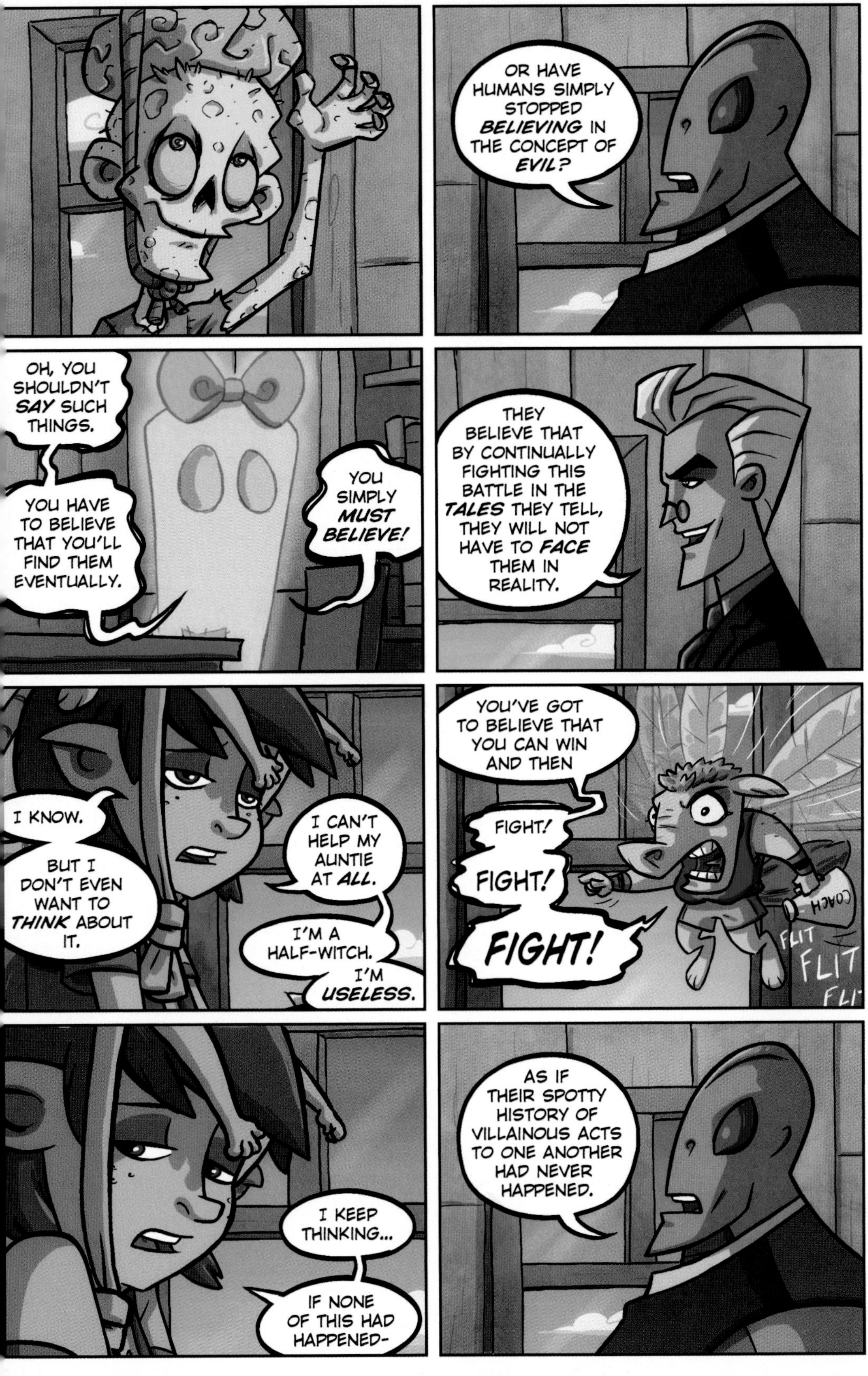
OR HAVE HUMANS SIMPLY STOPPED BELIEVING IN THE CONCEPT OF EVIL?
OH, YOU SHOULDN'T SAY SUCH THINGS.
YOU HAVE TO BELIEVE THAT YOU'LL FIND THEM EVENTUALLY.
YOU SIMPLY MUST BELIEVE!
THEY BELIEVE THAT BY CONTINUALLY FIGHTING THIS BATTLE IN THE TALES THEY TELL, THEY WILL NOT HAVE TO FACE THEM IN REALITY.
I KNOW.
BUT I DON'T EVEN WANT TO THINK ABOUT IT.
I CAN'T HELP MY AUNTIE AT ALL.
I'M A HALF-WITCH.
I'M USELESS.
YOU'VE GOT TO BELIEVE THAT YOU CAN WIN AND THEN
FIGHT!
FIGHT!
FIGHT!
COACH
FLIT
FLIT
FLI-
I KEEP THINKING...
IF NONE OF THIS HAD HAPPENED-
AS IF THEIR SPOTTY HISTORY OF VILLAINOUS ACTS TO ONE ANOTHER HAD NEVER HAPPENED.

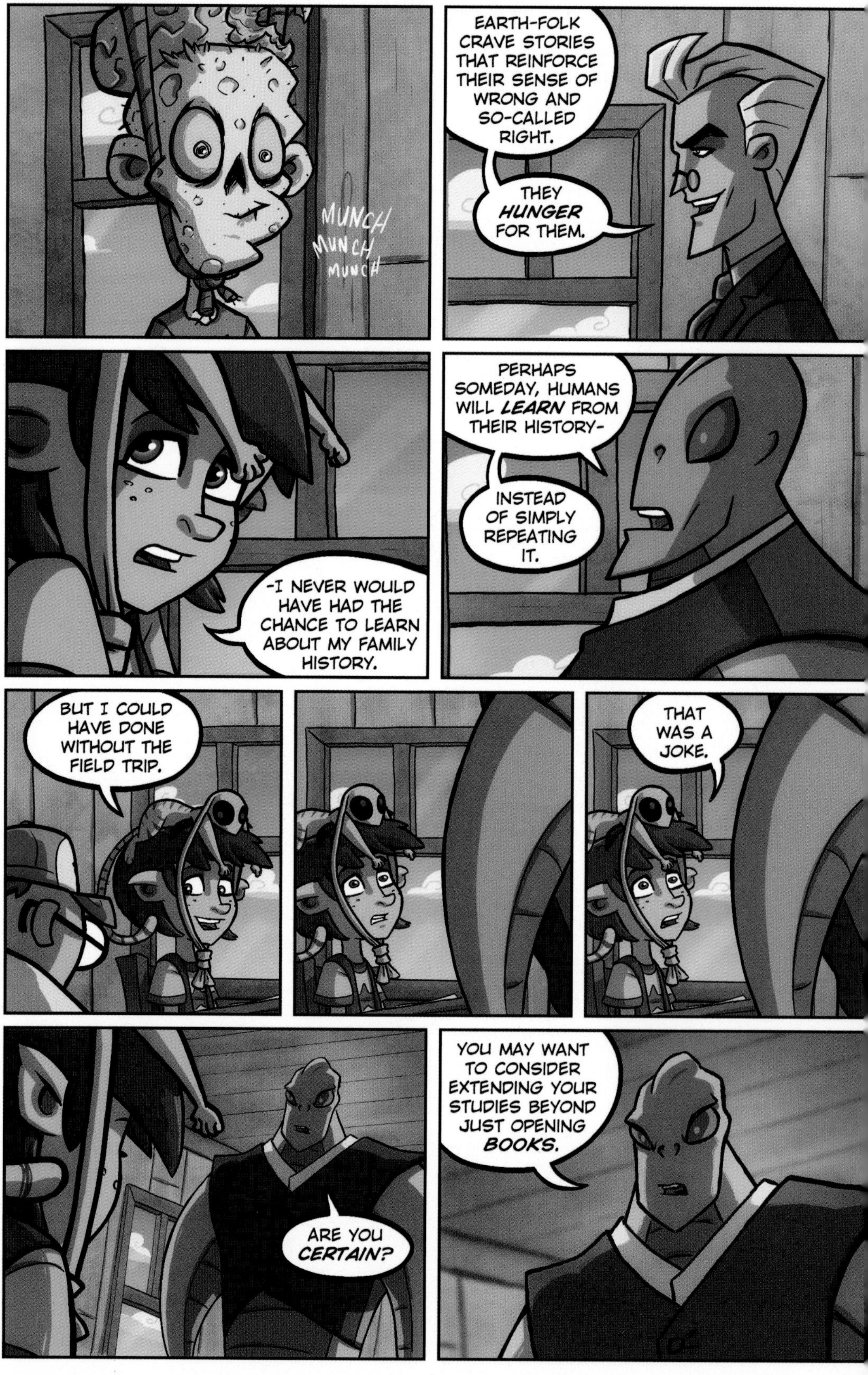
MUNCH
MUNCH
MUNCH
EARTH-FOLK CRAVE STORIES THAT REINFORCE THEIR SENSE OF WRONG AND SO-CALLED RIGHT.
THEY HUNGER FOR THEM.
-I NEVER WOULD HAVE HAD THE CHANCE TO LEARN ABOUT MY FAMILY HISTORY.
PERHAPS SOMEDAY, HUMANS WILL LEARN FROM THEIR HISTORY-
INSTEAD OF SIMPLY REPEATING IT.
BUT I COULD HAVE DONE WITHOUT THE FIELD TRIP.
THAT WAS A JOKE.
ARE YOU CERTAIN?
YOU MAY WANT TO CONSIDER EXTENDING YOUR STUDIES BEYOND JUST OPENING BOOKS.

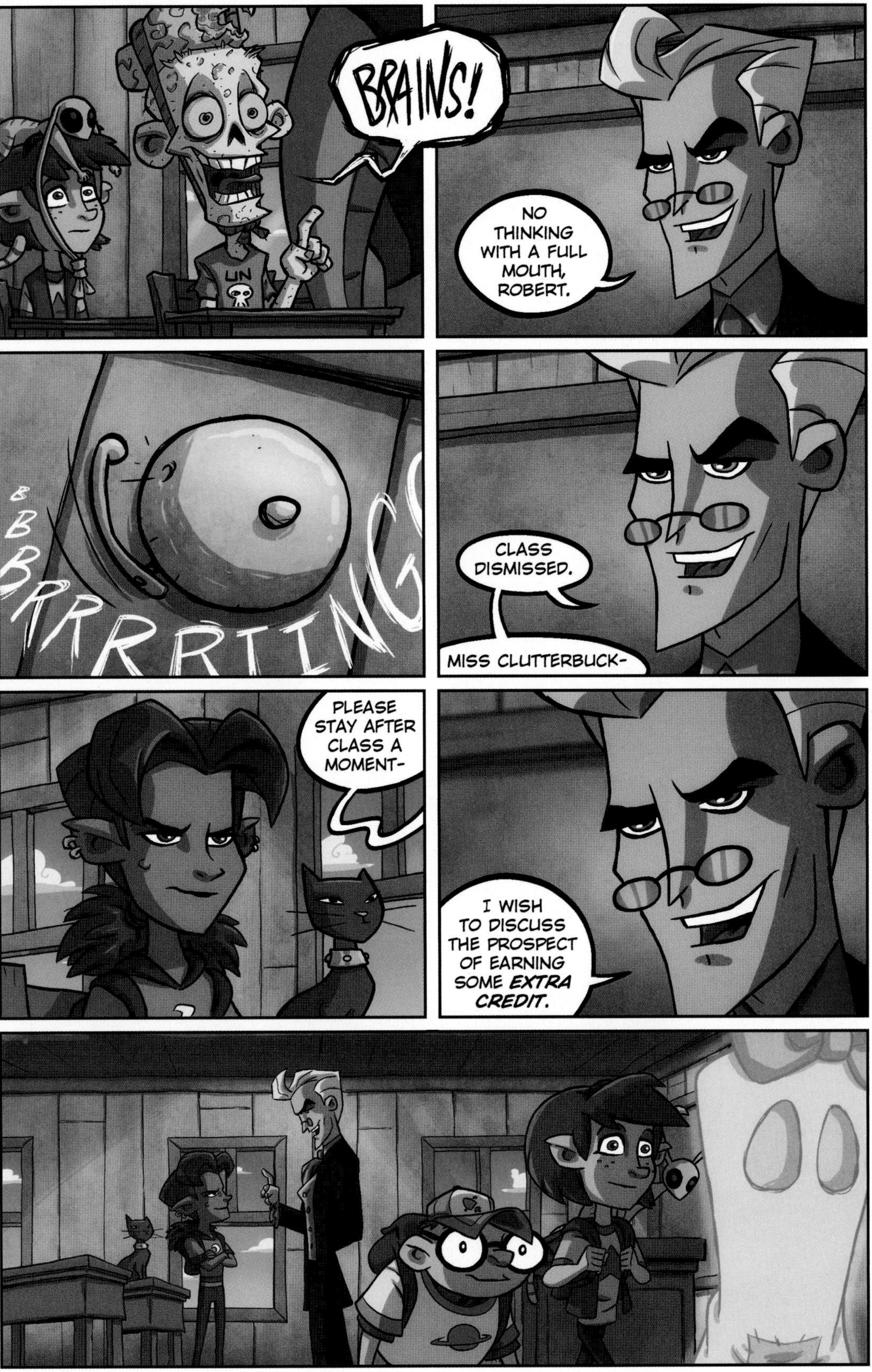
BRAINS!
NO THINKING WITH A FULL MOUTH, ROBERT.
BBBRRRRRING
CLASS DISMISSED.
MISS CLUTTERBUCK-
PLEASE STAY AFTER CLASS A MOMENT-
I WISH TO DISCUSS THE PROSPECT OF EARNING SOME *EXTRA CREDIT*.

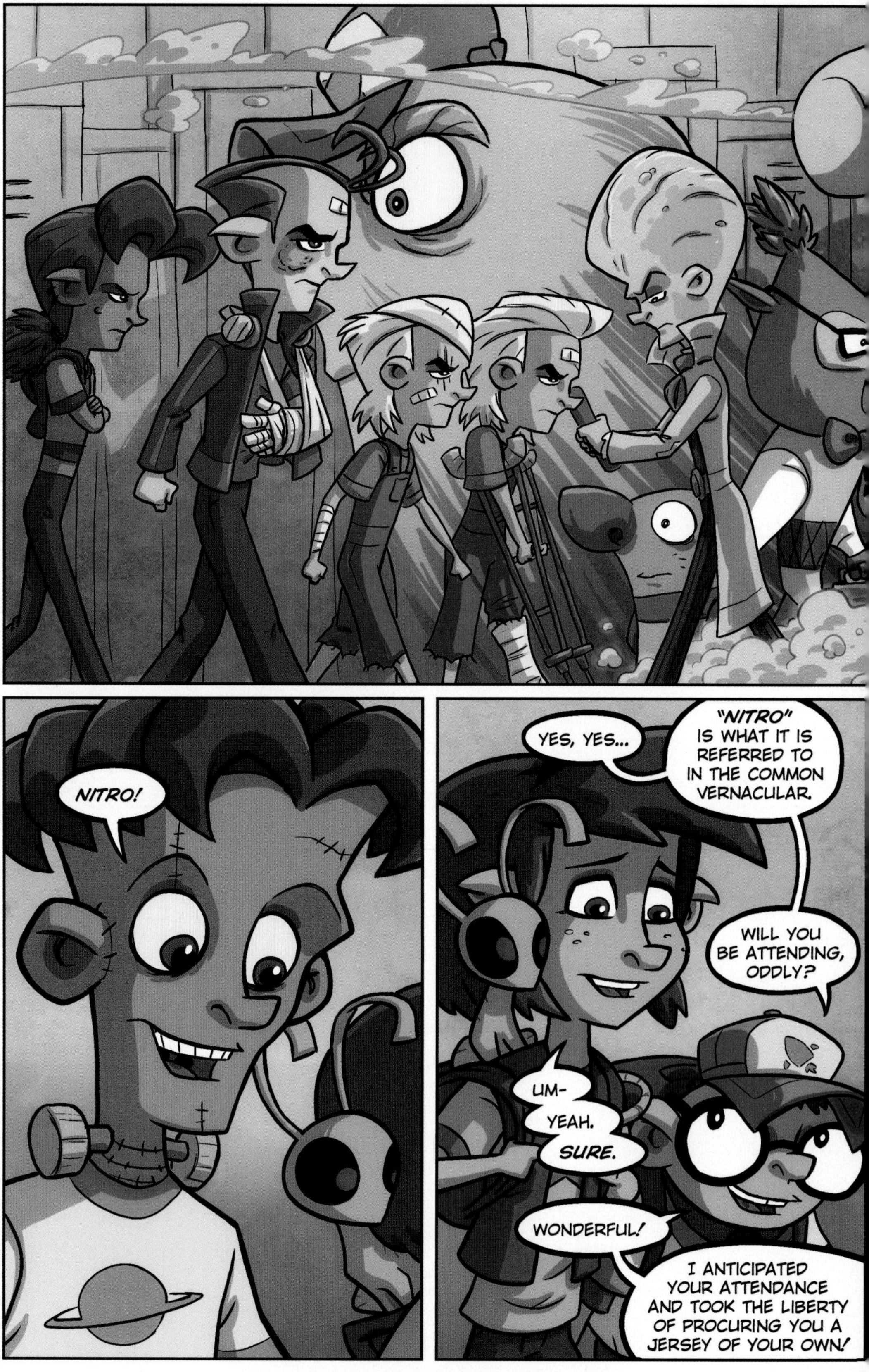
NITRO!
YES, YES...
"NITRO" IS WHAT IT IS REFERRED TO IN THE COMMON VERNACULAR.
WILL YOU BE ATTENDING, ODDLY?
UM-
YEAH.
SURE.
WONDERFUL!
I ANTICIPATED YOUR ATTENDANCE AND TOOK THE LIBERTY OF PROCURING YOU A JERSEY OF YOUR OWN!

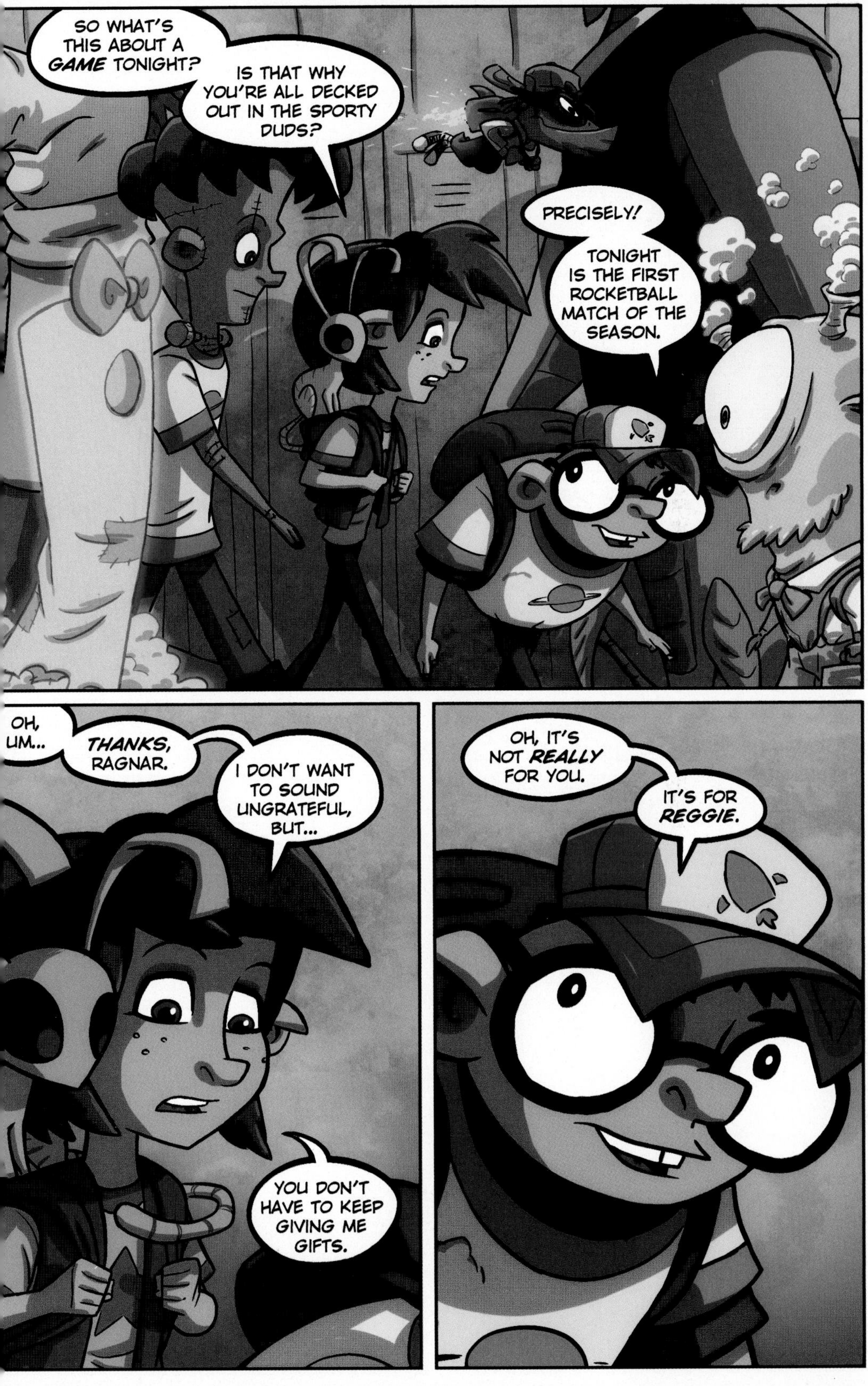
SO WHAT'S THIS ABOUT A *GAME* TONIGHT?
IS THAT WHY YOU'RE ALL DECKED OUT IN THE SPORTY DUDS?
PRECISELY!
TONIGHT IS THE FIRST ROCKETBALL MATCH OF THE SEASON.
OH, UM...
THANKS, RAGNAR.
I DON'T WANT TO SOUND UNGRATEFUL, BUT...
YOU DON'T HAVE TO KEEP GIVING ME GIFTS.
OH, IT'S NOT *REALLY* FOR YOU.
IT'S FOR *REGGIE*.

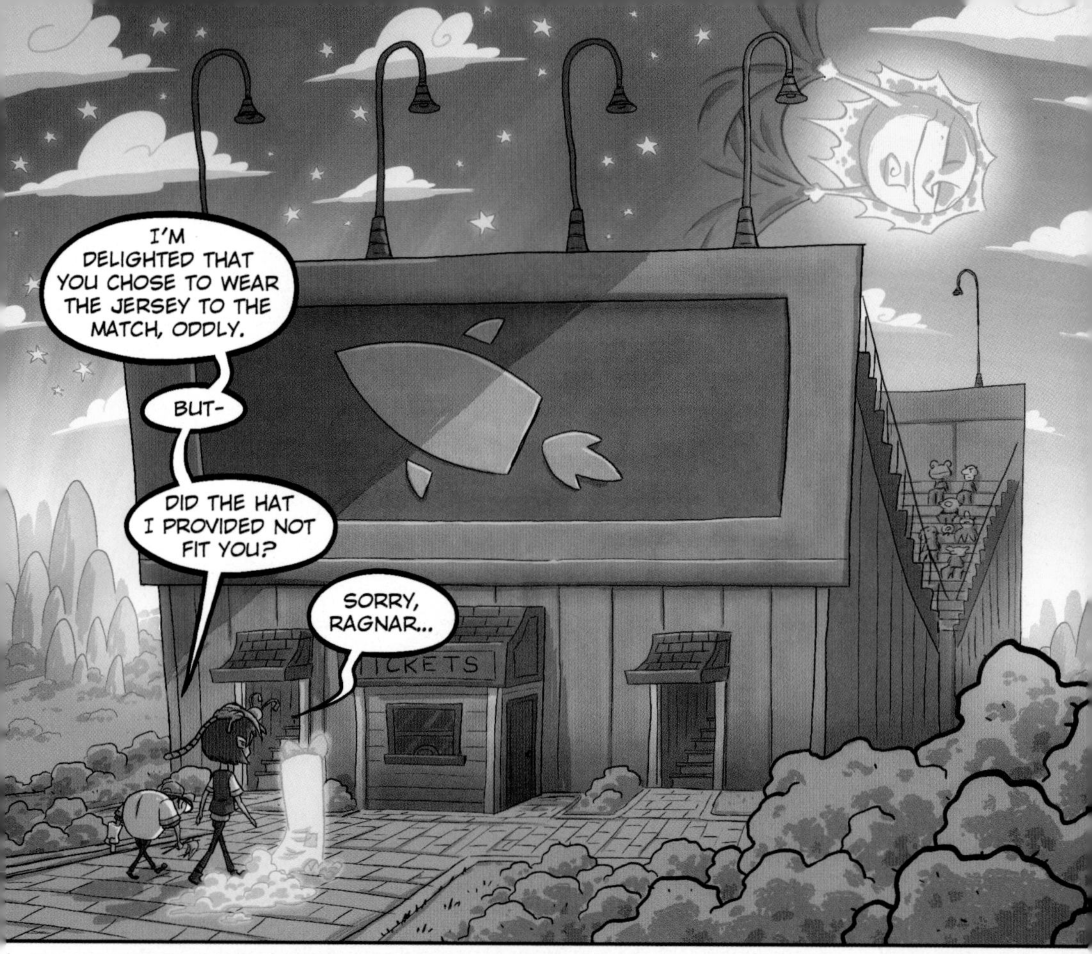
I'M DELIGHTED THAT YOU CHOSE TO WEAR THE JERSEY TO THE MATCH, ODDLY.
BUT-
DID THE HAT I PROVIDED NOT FIT YOU?
SORRY, RAGNAR...
ICKETS

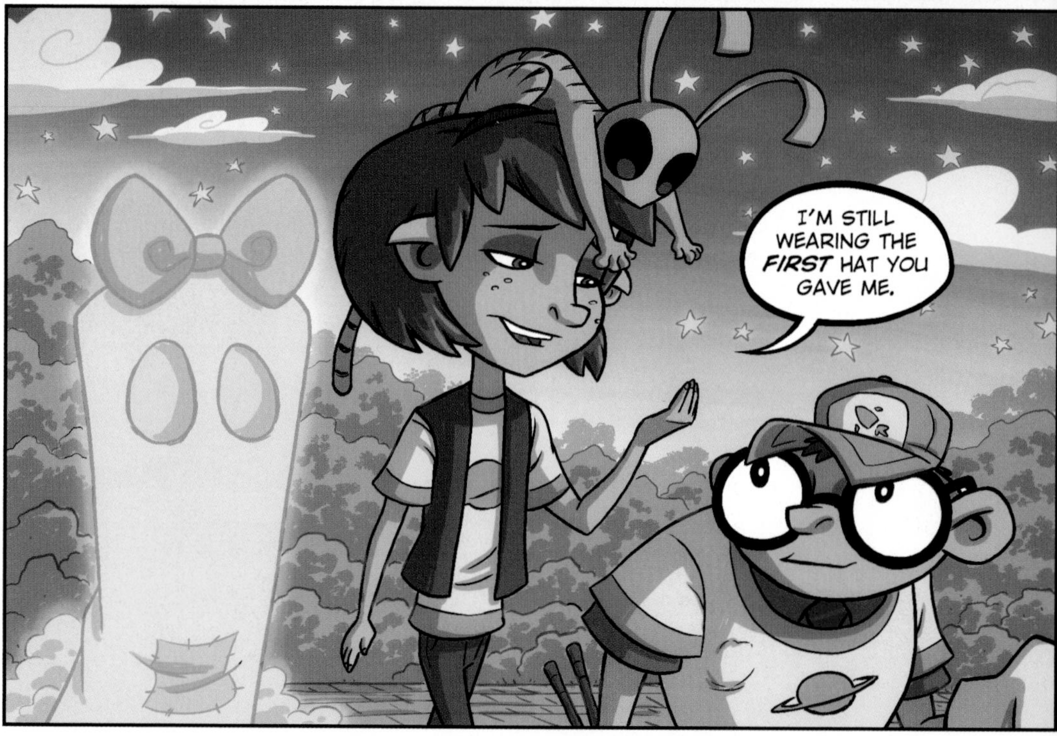
I'M STILL WEARING THE *FIRST* HAT YOU GAVE ME.

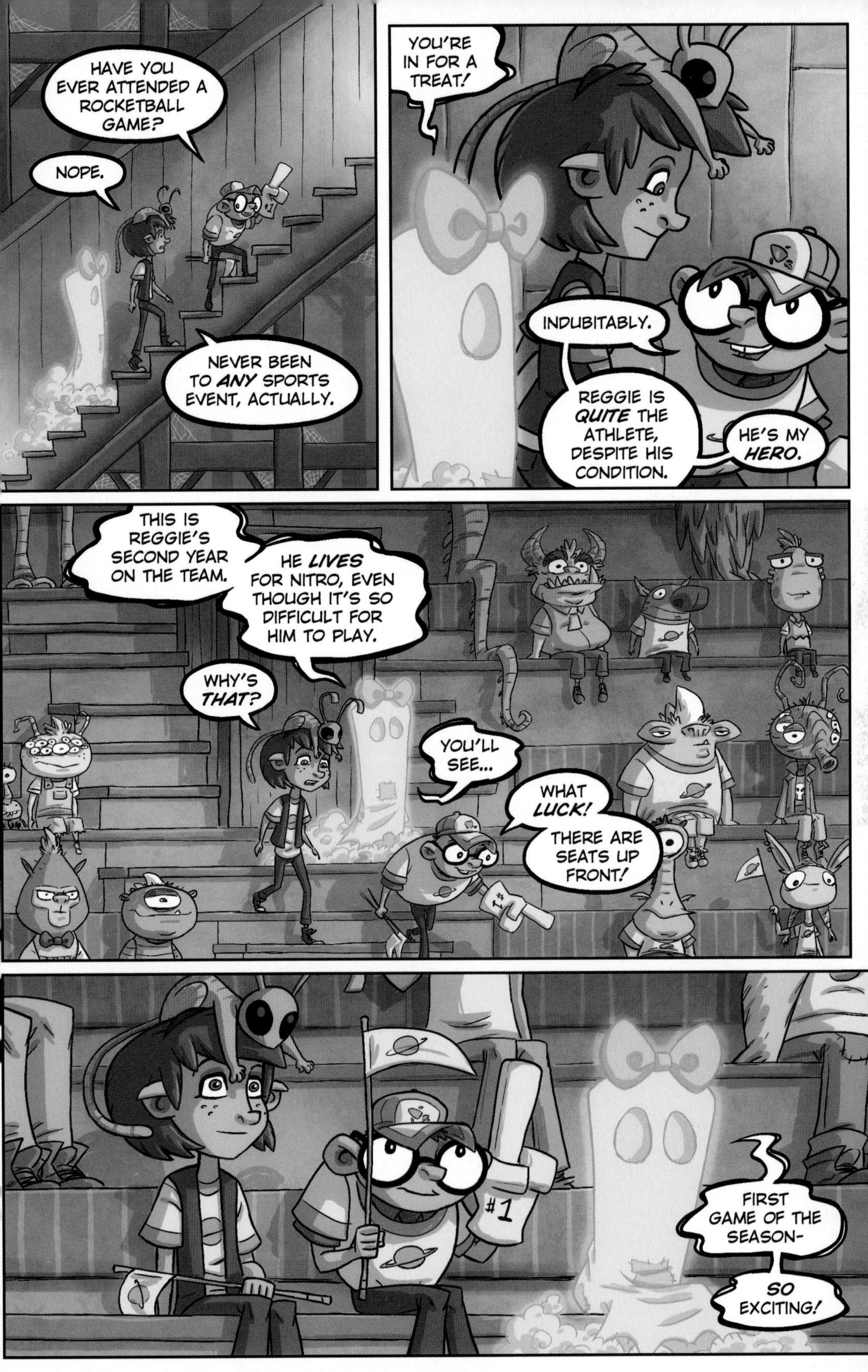
HAVE YOU EVER ATTENDED A ROCKETBALL GAME?
NOPE.
NEVER BEEN TO ANY SPORTS EVENT, ACTUALLY.
YOU'RE IN FOR A TREAT!
INDUBITABLY.
REGGIE IS QUITE THE ATHLETE, DESPITE HIS CONDITION.
HE'S MY HERO.
THIS IS REGGIE'S SECOND YEAR ON THE TEAM.
HE LIVES FOR NITRO, EVEN THOUGH IT'S SO DIFFICULT FOR HIM TO PLAY.
WHY'S THAT?
YOU'LL SEE...
WHAT LUCK!
THERE ARE SEATS UP FRONT!
#1
FIRST GAME OF THE SEASON-
SO EXCITING!

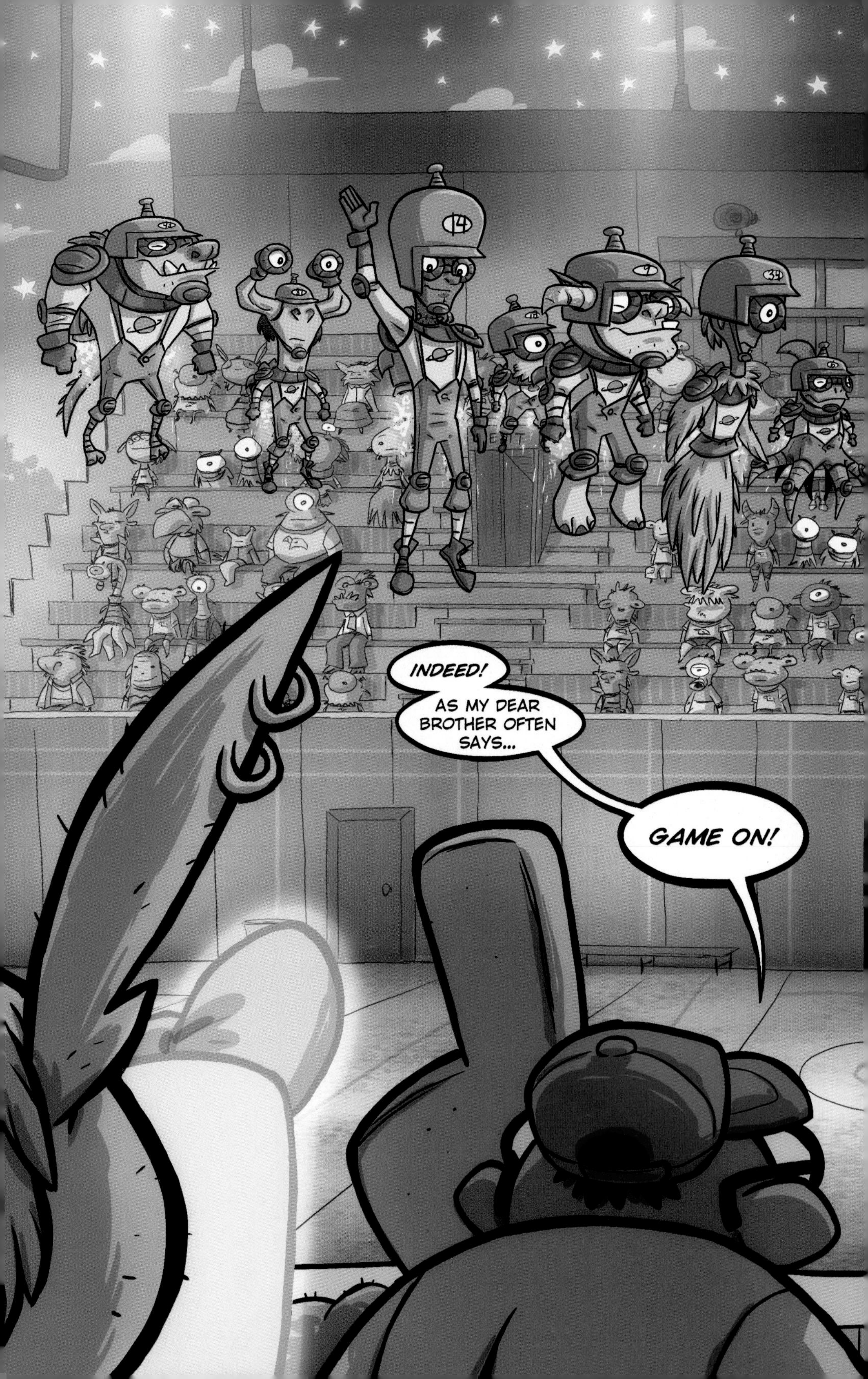
INDEED!
AS MY DEAR BROTHER OFTEN SAYS...
GAME ON!

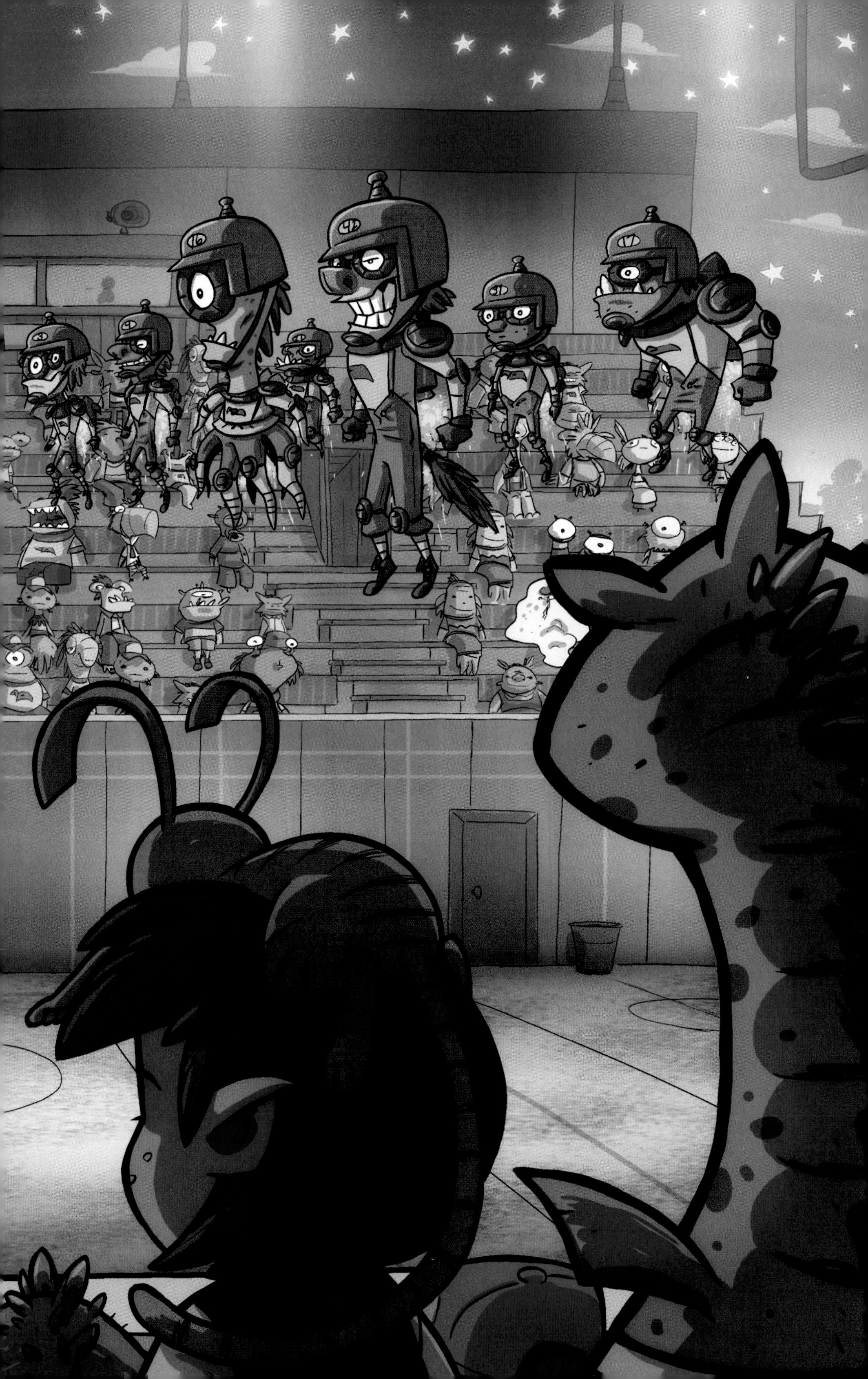

Oddly Normal

BOOK 2

WRITTEN, ILLUSTRATED & LETTERED BY

OTIS FRAMPTON

COLORED BY

OTIS FRAMPTON

&

TRACY BAILEY

COLOR FLATS BY
DANIEL MEAD, TRACY BAILEY,
OTIS FRAMPTON AND THOMAS BOATWRIGHT

ABOUT THE AUTHOR

Otis Frampton is a comic book writer/artist, freelance illustrator
and animator. He is the creator of the webcomic and animated
series "ABCDEFGeek." He is also one of the artists on the popular
animated web series "How It Should Have Ended."

You can visit Otis on the web at: www.otisframpton.com

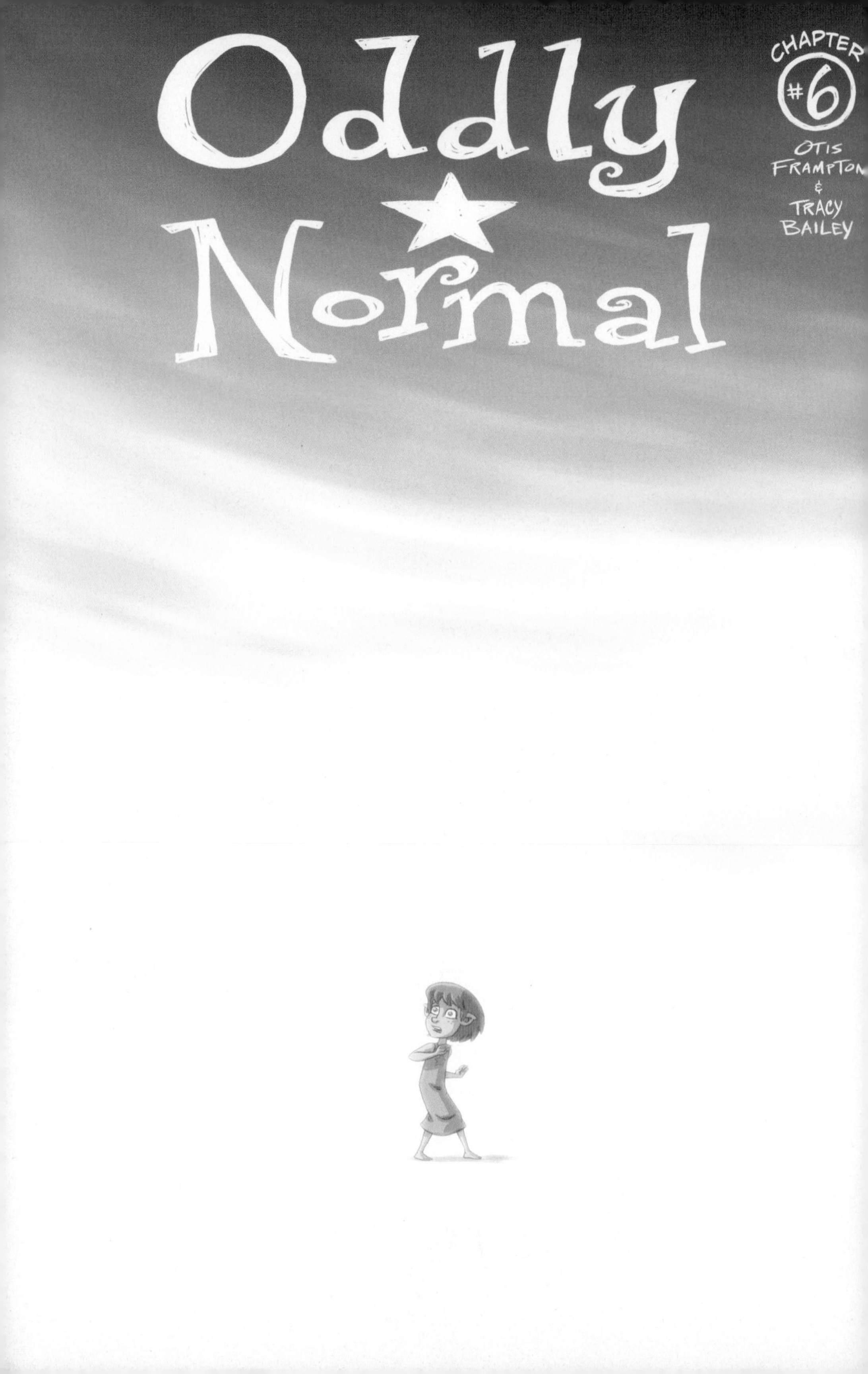
Oddly Normal
CHAPTER #6
OTIS FRAMPTON & TRACY BAILEY

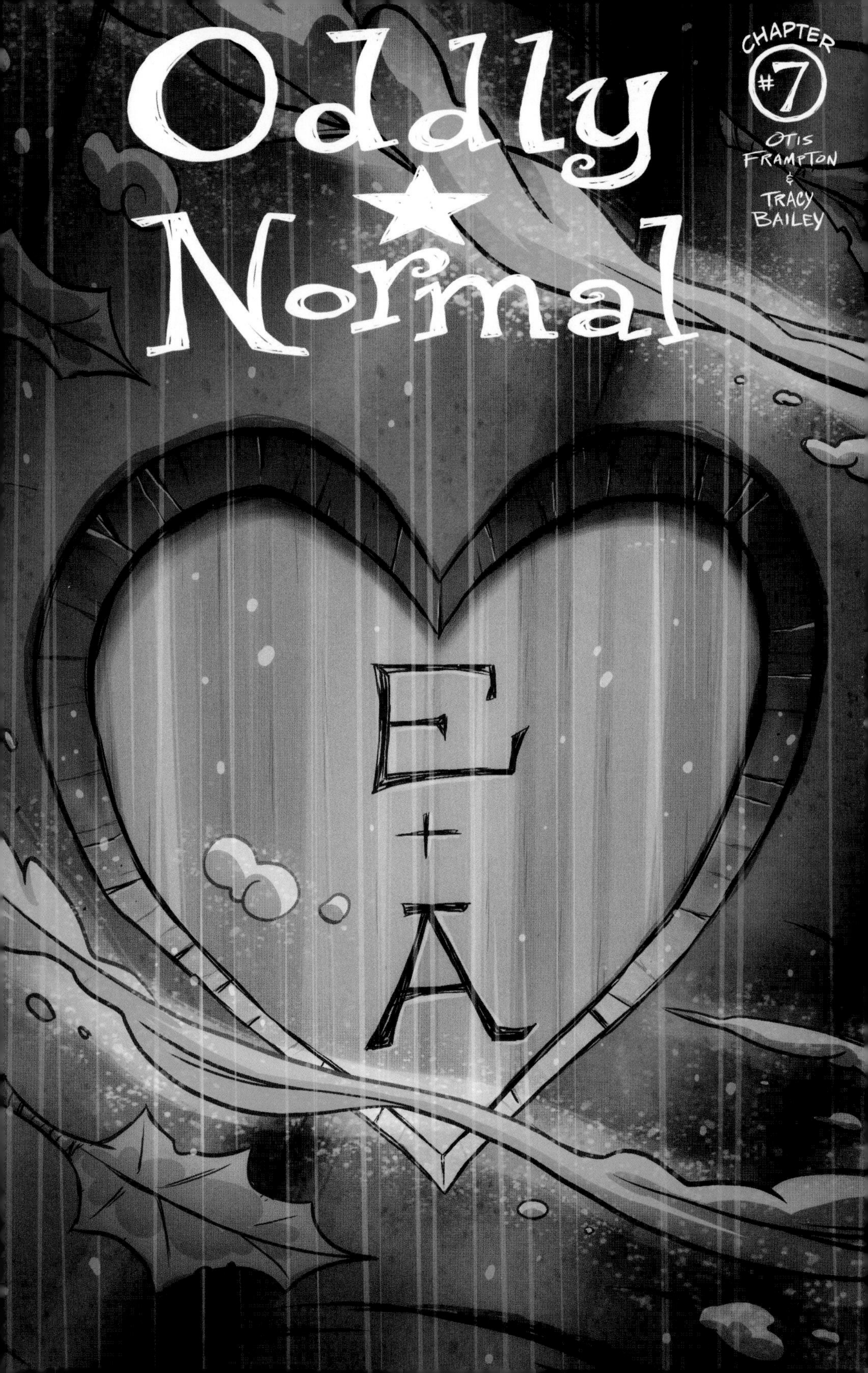
Oddly ★ Normal
CHAPTER #7
OTIS FRAMPTON & TRACY BAILEY
E + A

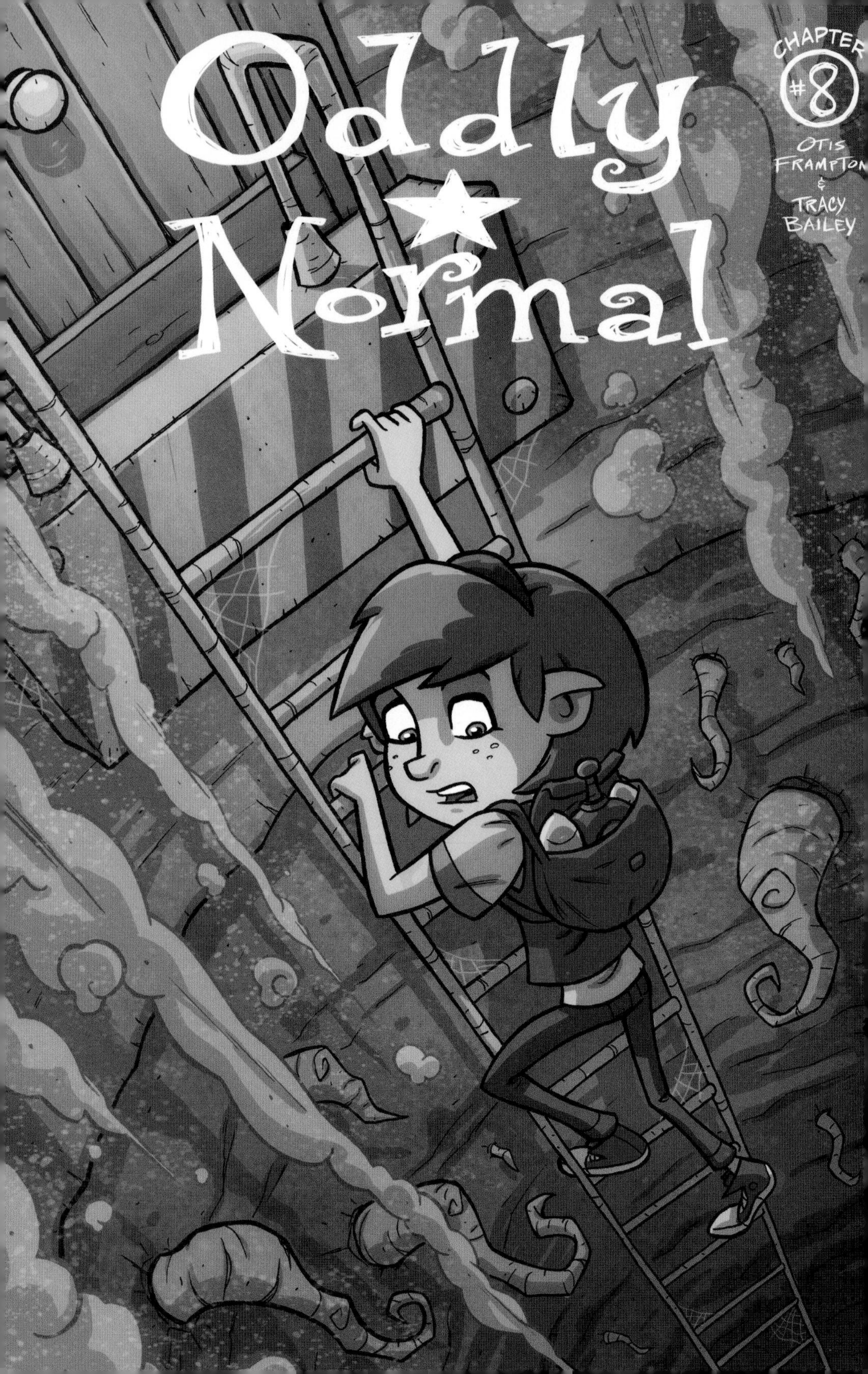
Oddly Normal
CHAPTER #8
OTIS FRAMPTON & TRACY BAILEY

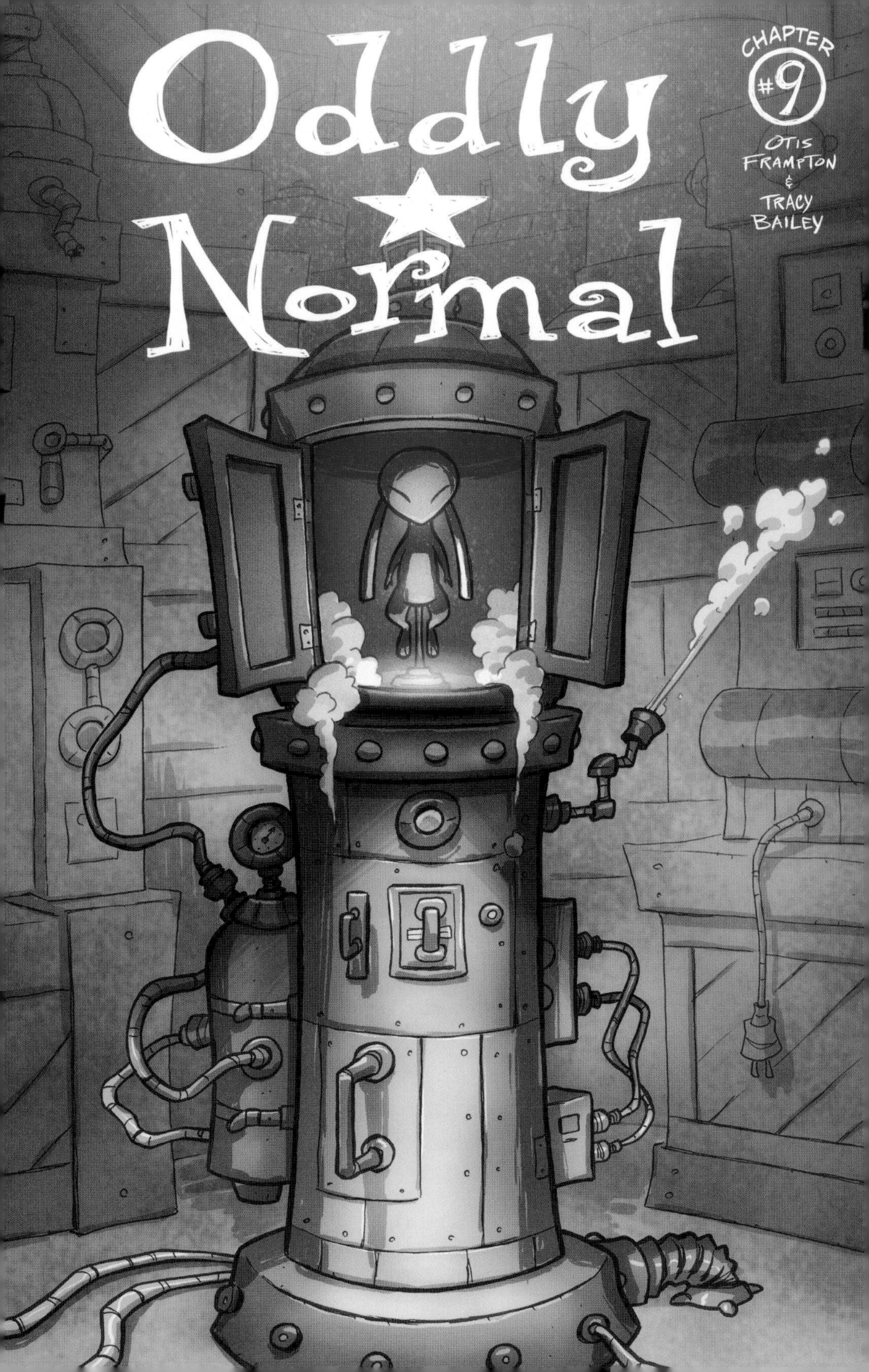
Oddly ★ Normal
CHAPTER #9
OTIS FRAMPTON & TRACY BAILEY

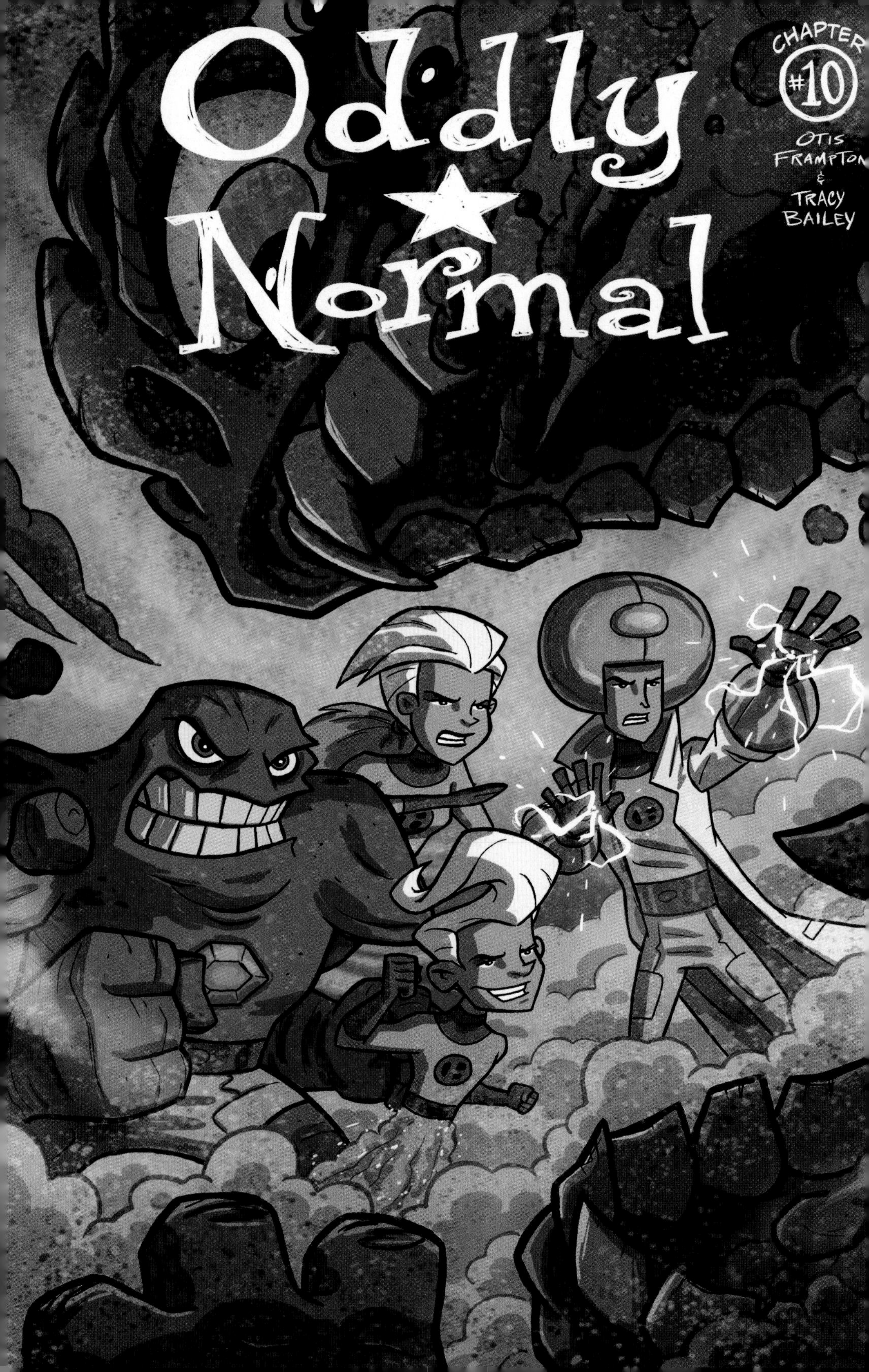
Oddly Normal
CHAPTER #10
OTIS FRAMPTON & TRACY BAILEY

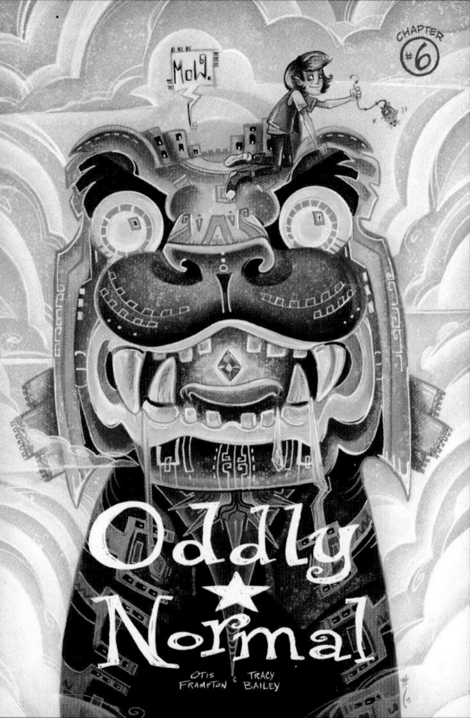
CHAPTER #6
MOW.
Oddly Normal
OTIS FRAMPTON & TRACY BAILEY

ISSUE #6 VARIANT COVER BY
SARA RICHARD

Oddly
Normal
CHAPTER #8
OTIS FRAMPTON & TRACY BAILEY
MENAGERIE
MIDDLE
SCHOOL

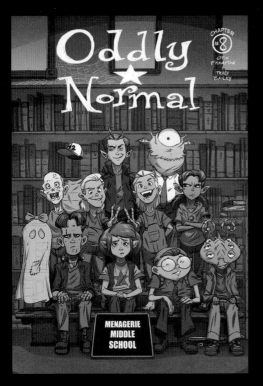

ISSUE #8 VARIANT COVER BY
DAN SCHOENING
AND
TRACY BAILEY

Oddly
Normal
CHAPTER #9
OTIS FRAMPTON & TRACY BAILEY

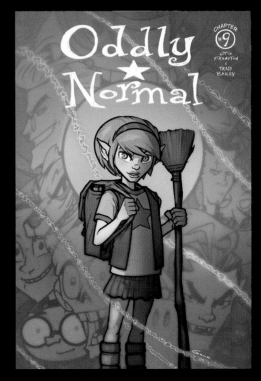

ISSUE #9 VARIANT COVER BY
GRANT GOULD